AN INTRODUCTION

I began reading Li'l Depressed Boy at a strange time in my life. Not so much strange, I suppose, but it was rather serendipitous because in all ways I saw my life playing out in the pages of this comic series. In a lot of ways, it was home when I felt I had none to return to.

Which makes it difficult to write about because I know that Li'l Depressed Boy is a slice of life dramedy but to me it's a stroke of horror. And I mean that as the highest compliment, because this is a series that has always had the most relatable protagonist in recent memory. All my insecurities and doubts are made real by a patchwork face that is more me than I would care to admit.

Li'l Depressed Boy is masterful and honest. It's made the journey of a sad doll man the story of us all in those times of loneliness, depression and doubt. But always with a glimmer of hope.

And that's why I always come back.

-Kurtis J. Wiebe

Kurtis Wiebe is a two time Joe Shuster Award-winning comic writer based in Vancouver, Canada. He currently pens the Eisner-nominated Rat Queens and the Image Comics horror series Pisces. Known as a curmudgeon with a heart of gold and a lover of grilled cheese. For more information about what he's up to visit http://kurtiswiebe.com

PREVIOUSLY IN...

THE LI'L DEPRESSED BOY

LDB IS A TWENTY-SOMETHING LIVING IN AMARILLO, TEXAS.

UNHAPPY WITH SELF-SECLUSION AND BEING LONELY, LDB DECIDED TO MAKE A CHANGE AND SEARCH FOR HAPPINESS OUTSIDE THE CONFINES OF HIS APARTMENT.

HE MET A GIRL NAMED JAZZ, WHO HE FELT A GOOD CONNECTION WITH.

LDB THOUGHT HE'D FOUND THE GIRL OF HIS DREAMS, AND THEY STARTED DATING.

ONLY WHEN HE MET HER ACTUAL BOYFRIEND, HE REALIZED THE RELATIONSHIP WAS ONLY IN HIS MIND.

HE WAS DEVASTATED.

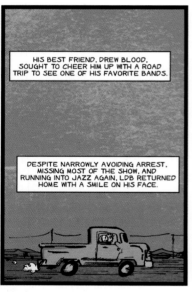

HIS BEST FRIEND, DREW BLOOD, SOUGHT TO CHEER HIM UP WITH A ROAD TRIP TO SEE ONE OF HIS FAVORITE BANDS.

DESPITE NARROWLY AVOIDING ARREST, MISSING MOST OF THE SHOW, AND RUNNING INTO JAZZ AGAIN, LDB RETURNED HOME WITH A SMILE ON HIS FACE.

HAPPY, BUT BROKE, LDB GOT A JOB AT A MOVIE THEATRE.

SURE, IT'S A TEENAGER'S JOB, BUT IT ALLOWED HIM TO KEEP THE LIGHTS ON.

ALSO, HE MET SPIKE THERE.

HI...

SHE RECIPROCATED HIS FEELINGS, BUT BEING HIS MANAGER THEY HAD TO DATE IN SECRET BECAUSE IT WAS AGAINST COMPANY RULES.

THEY GOT CAUGHT.

RATTED OUT BY ANOTHER MANAGER, TOBY, THEY WERE BOTH SUSPENDED FOR MISCONDUCT.

IN A CONFRONTATION THAT FOLLOWED, TOBY PUNCHED LDB.

KRAK!

NOW IT'S THE FIRST DAY OF THEIR SUSPENSION.

SPIKE AND LDB HAVE TO FIGURE OUT HOW TO SPEND THIS UNEXPECTED TIME OFF...

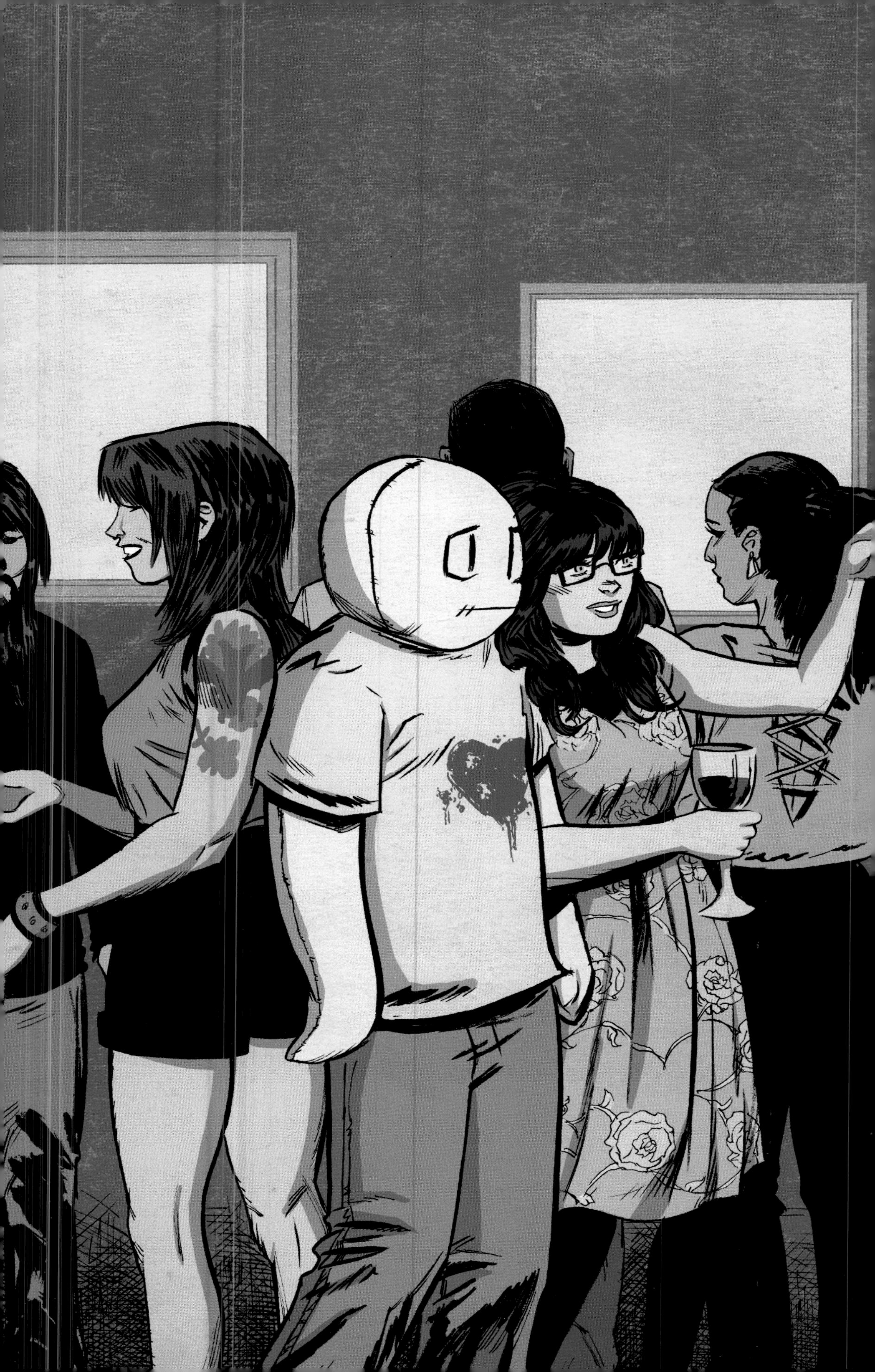

CHAPTER SEVENTEEN:
"ALWAYS SOMETHING IN MY BLINDSPOT"

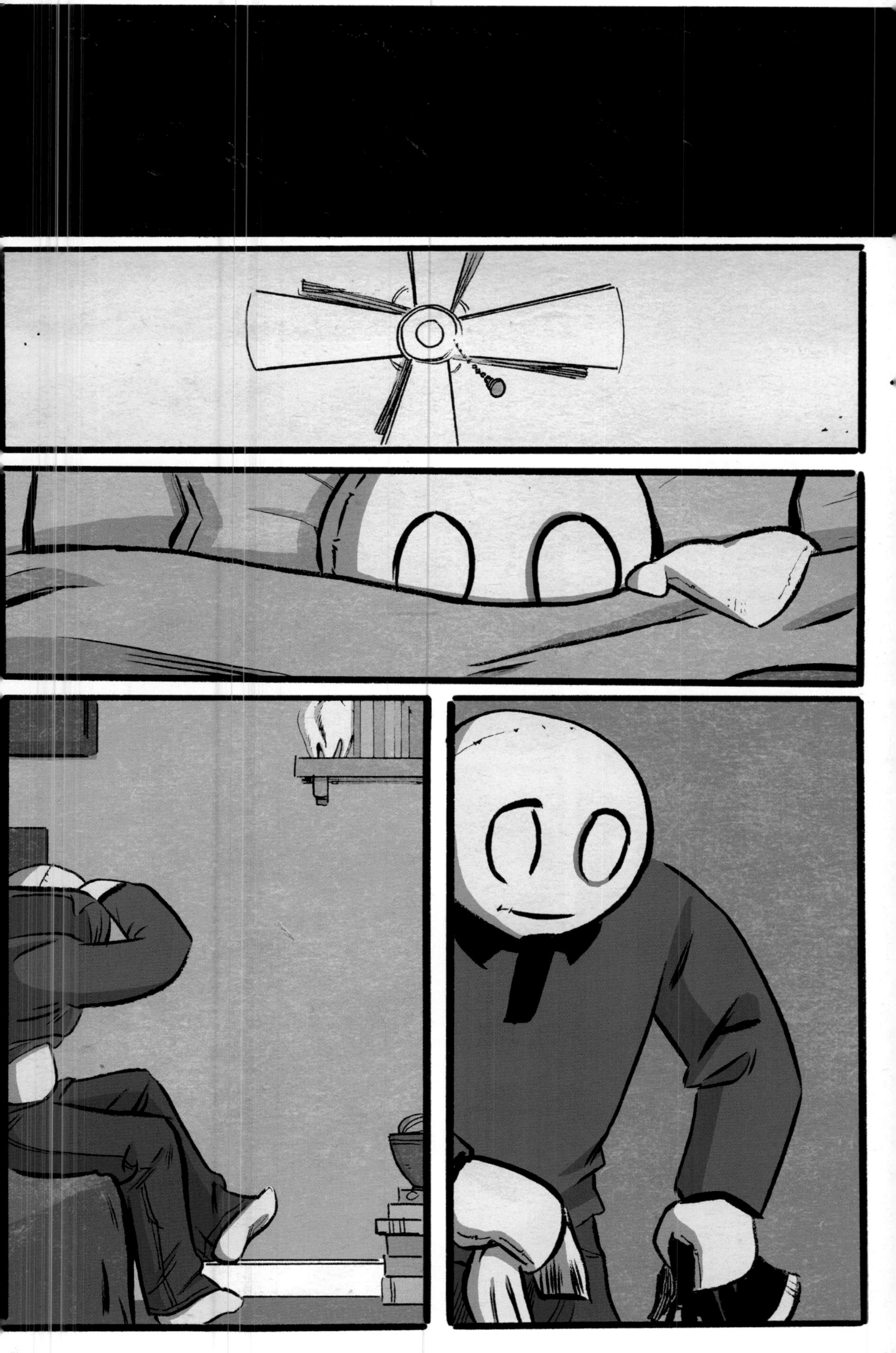

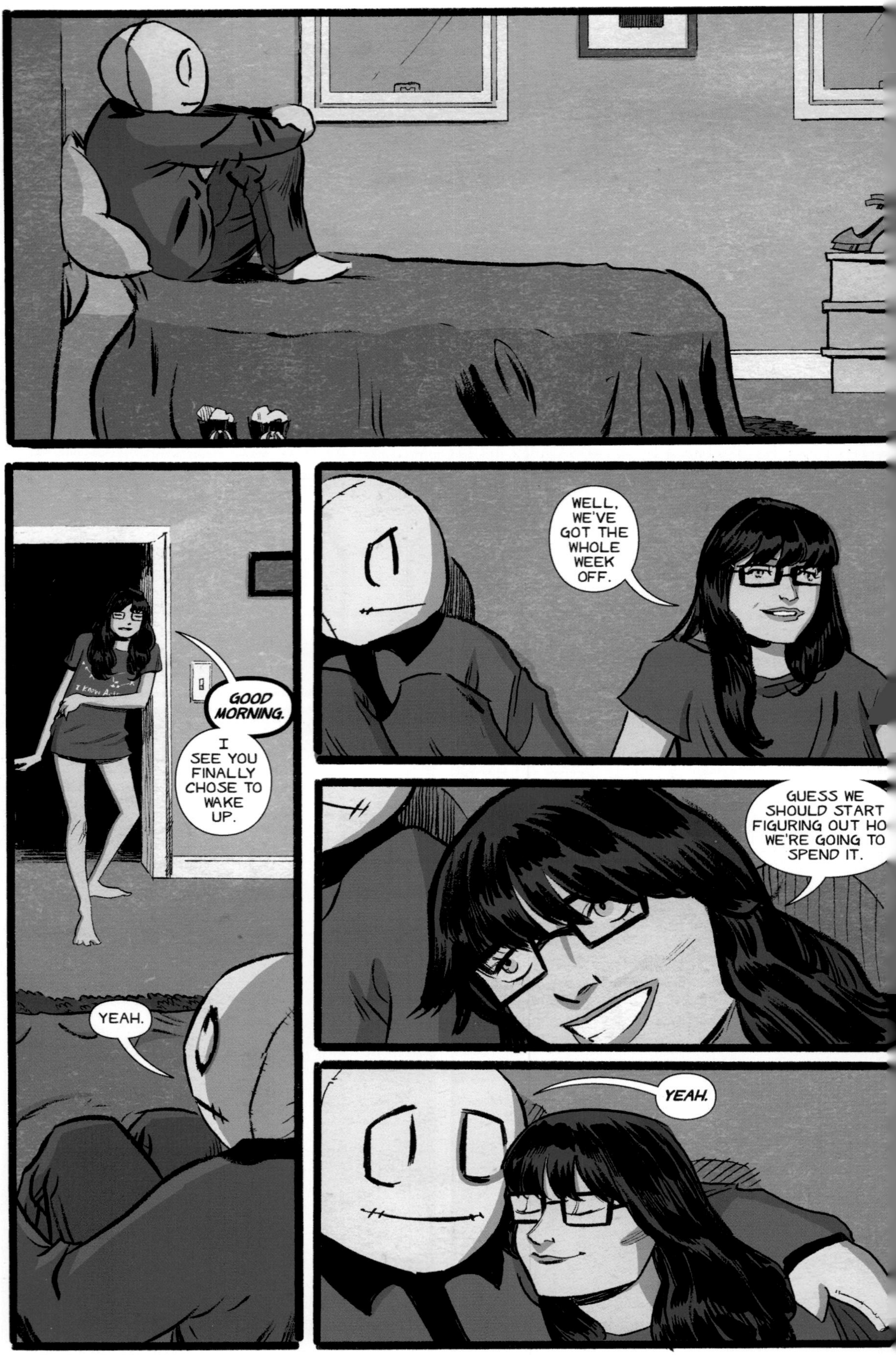

GOOD MORNING.
I SEE YOU FINALLY CHOSE TO WAKE UP.
YEAH.
WELL, WE'VE GOT THE WHOLE WEEK OFF.
GUESS WE SHOULD START FIGURING OUT HO
WE'RE GOING TO SPEND IT.
YEAH.

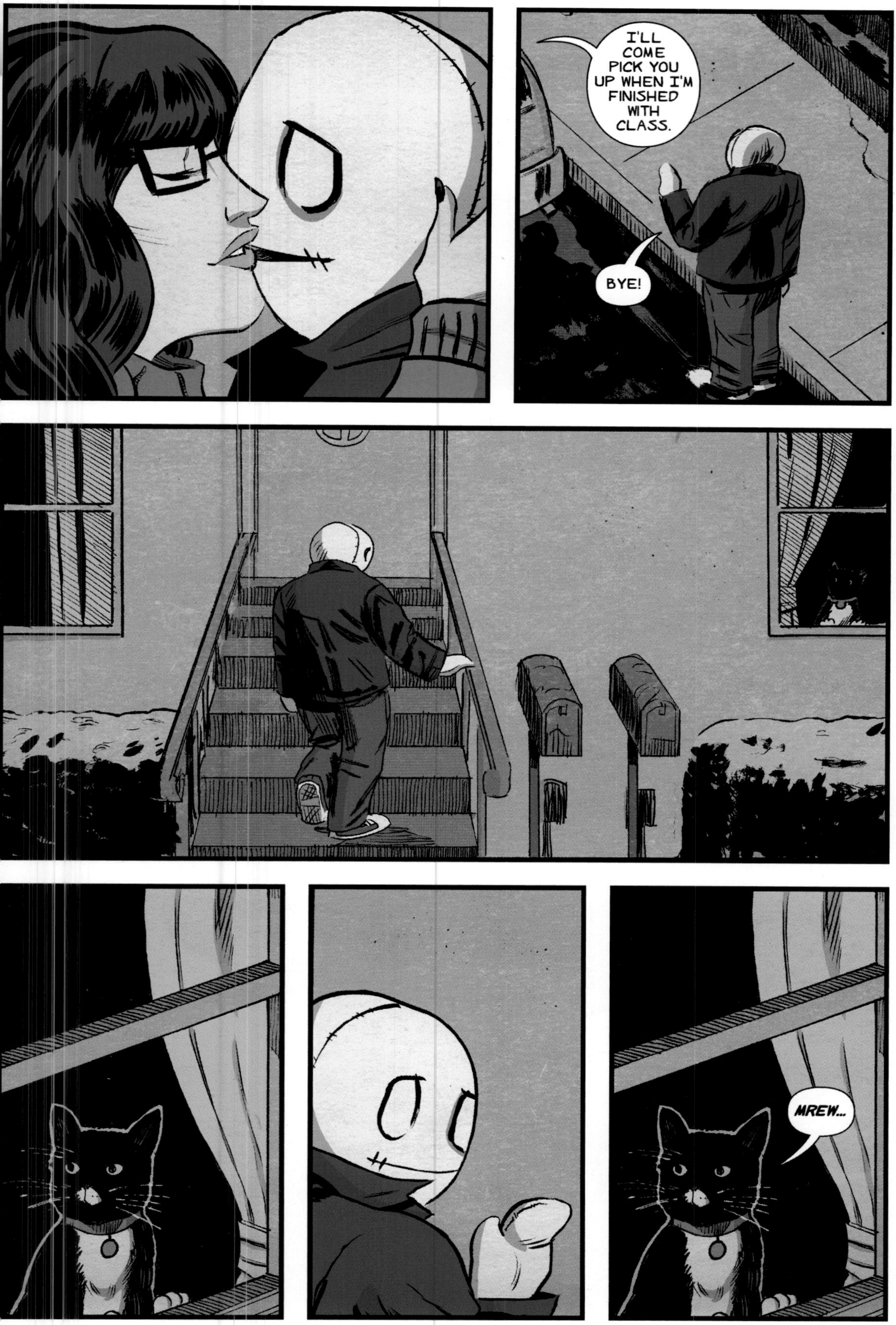
I'LL COME PICK YOU UP WHEN I'M FINISHED WITH CLASS.
BYE!
MREW...

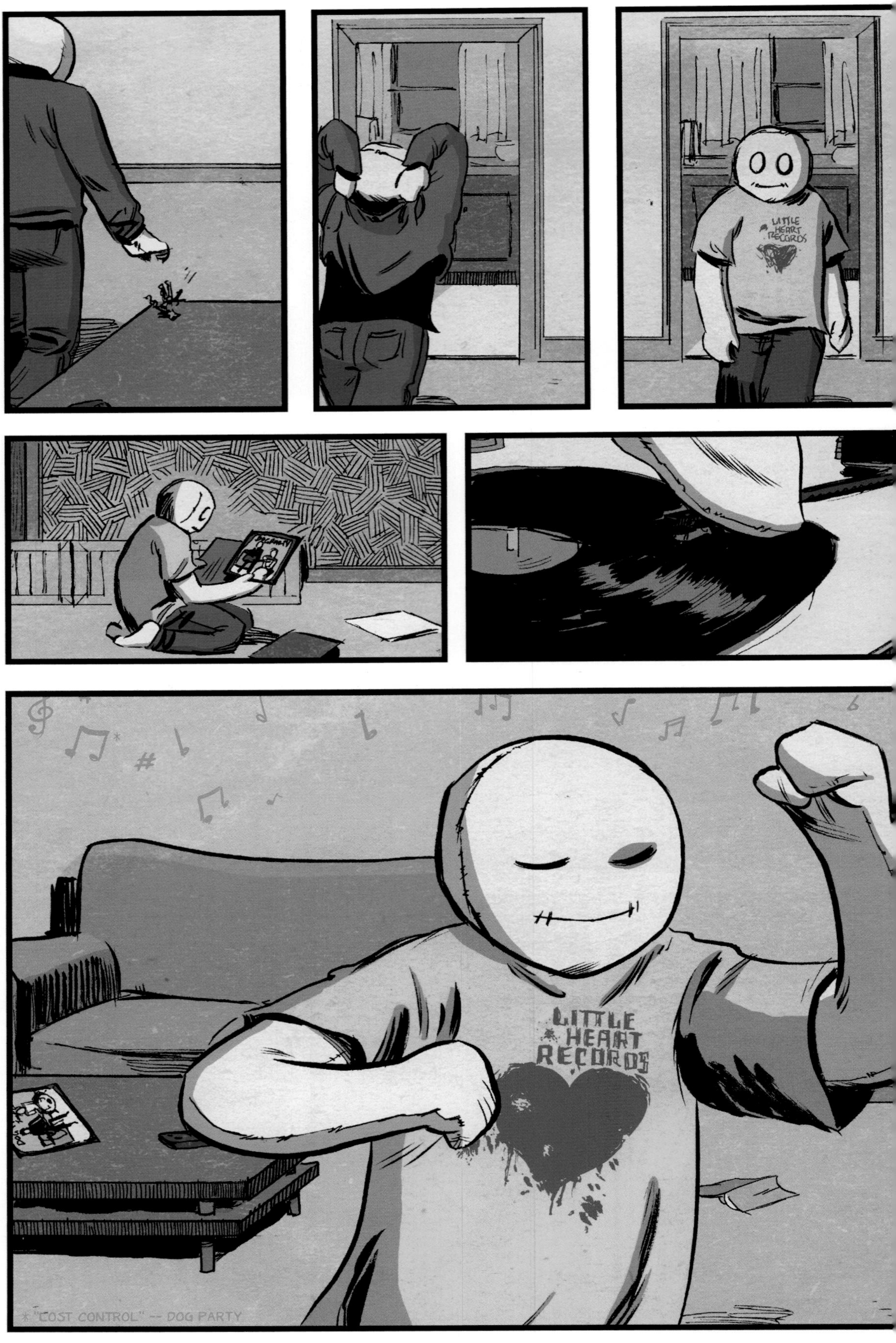
LITTLE HEART RECORDS
LITTLE HEART RECORDS
* "LOST CONTROL" -- DOG PARTY

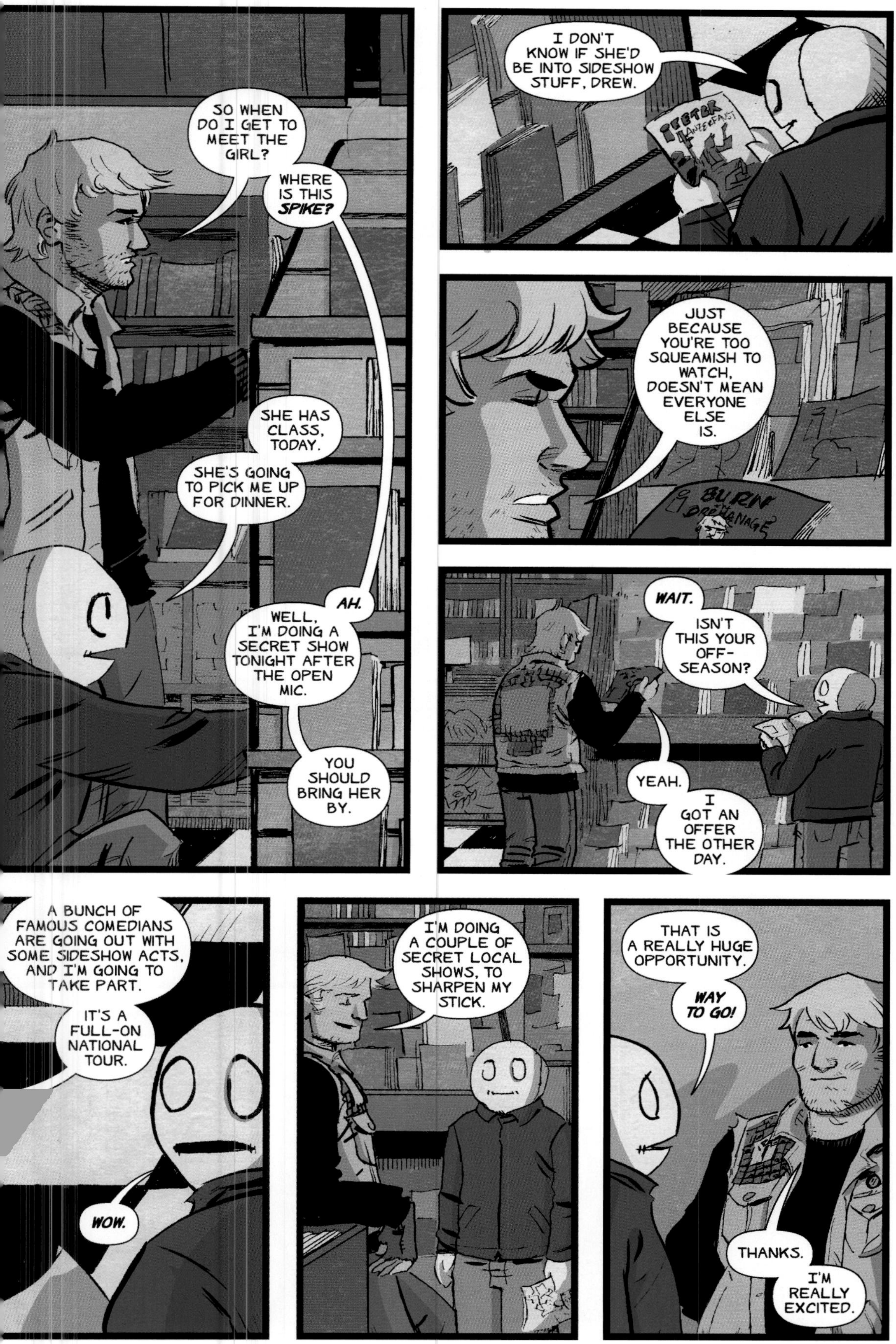
SO WHEN DO I GET TO MEET THE GIRL?
WHERE IS THIS *SPIKE?*
SHE HAS CLASS, TODAY.
SHE'S GOING TO PICK ME UP FOR DINNER.
AH.
WELL, I'M DOING A SECRET SHOW TONIGHT AFTER THE OPEN MIC.
YOU SHOULD BRING HER BY.
I DON'T KNOW IF SHE'D BE INTO SIDESHOW STUFF, DREW.
JUST BECAUSE YOU'RE TOO SQUEAMISH TO WATCH, DOESN'T MEAN EVERYONE ELSE IS.
WAIT.
ISN'T THIS YOUR OFF-SEASON?
YEAH.
I GOT AN OFFER THE OTHER DAY.
A BUNCH OF FAMOUS COMEDIANS ARE GOING OUT WITH SOME SIDESHOW ACTS, AND I'M GOING TO TAKE PART.
IT'S A FULL-ON NATIONAL TOUR.
WOW.
I'M DOING A COUPLE OF SECRET LOCAL SHOWS, TO SHARPEN MY STICK.
THAT IS A REALLY HUGE OPPORTUNITY.
WAY TO GO!
THANKS.
I'M REALLY EXCITED.

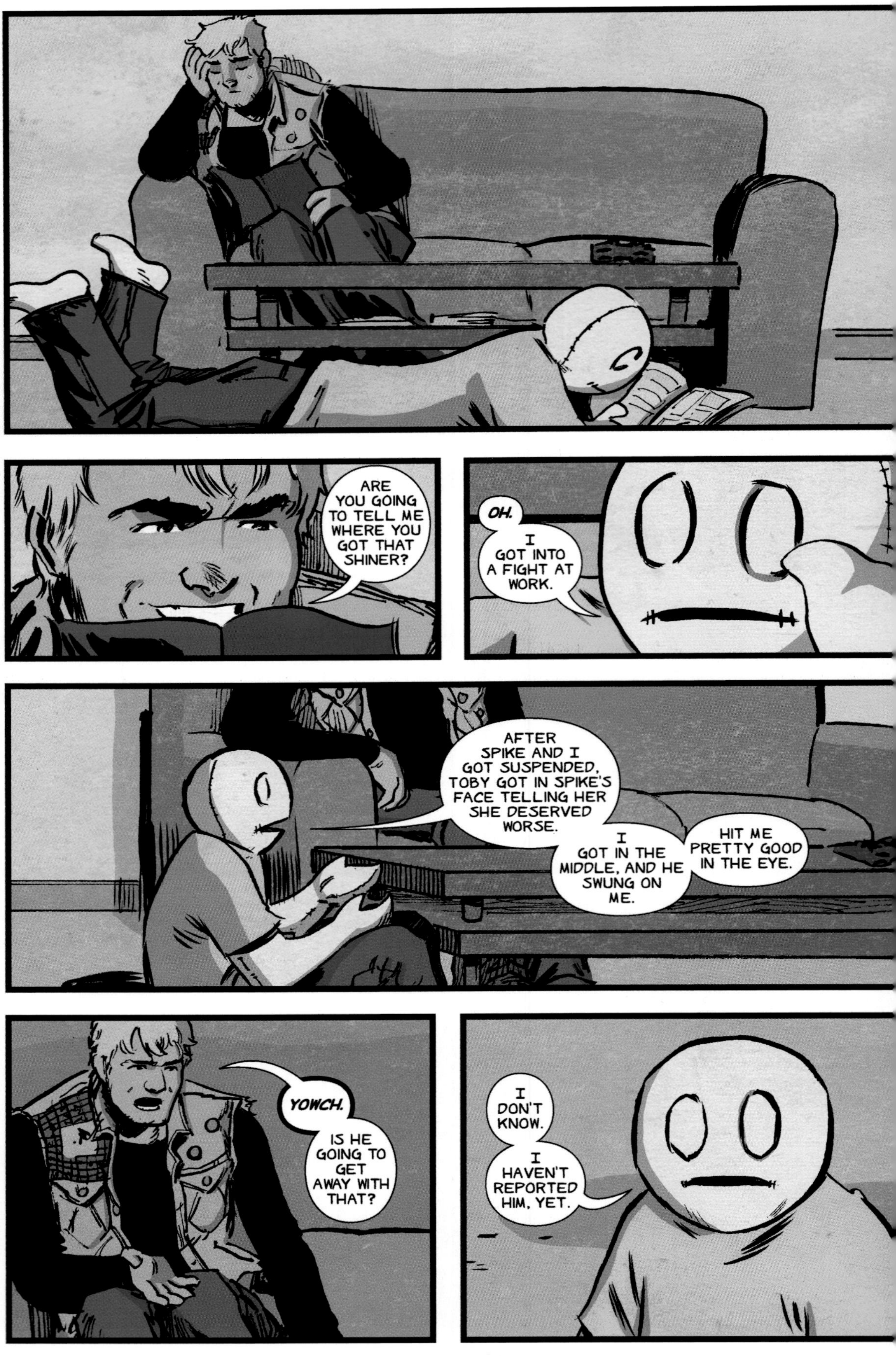
ARE YOU GOING TO TELL ME WHERE YOU GOT THAT SHINER?
OH.
I GOT INTO A FIGHT AT WORK.
AFTER SPIKE AND I GOT SUSPENDED, TOBY GOT IN SPIKE'S FACE TELLING HER SHE DESERVED WORSE.
I GOT IN THE MIDDLE, AND HE SWUNG ON ME.
HIT ME PRETTY GOOD IN THE EYE.
YOWCH.
IS HE GOING TO GET AWAY WITH THAT?
I DON'T KNOW.
I HAVEN'T REPORTED HIM, YET.

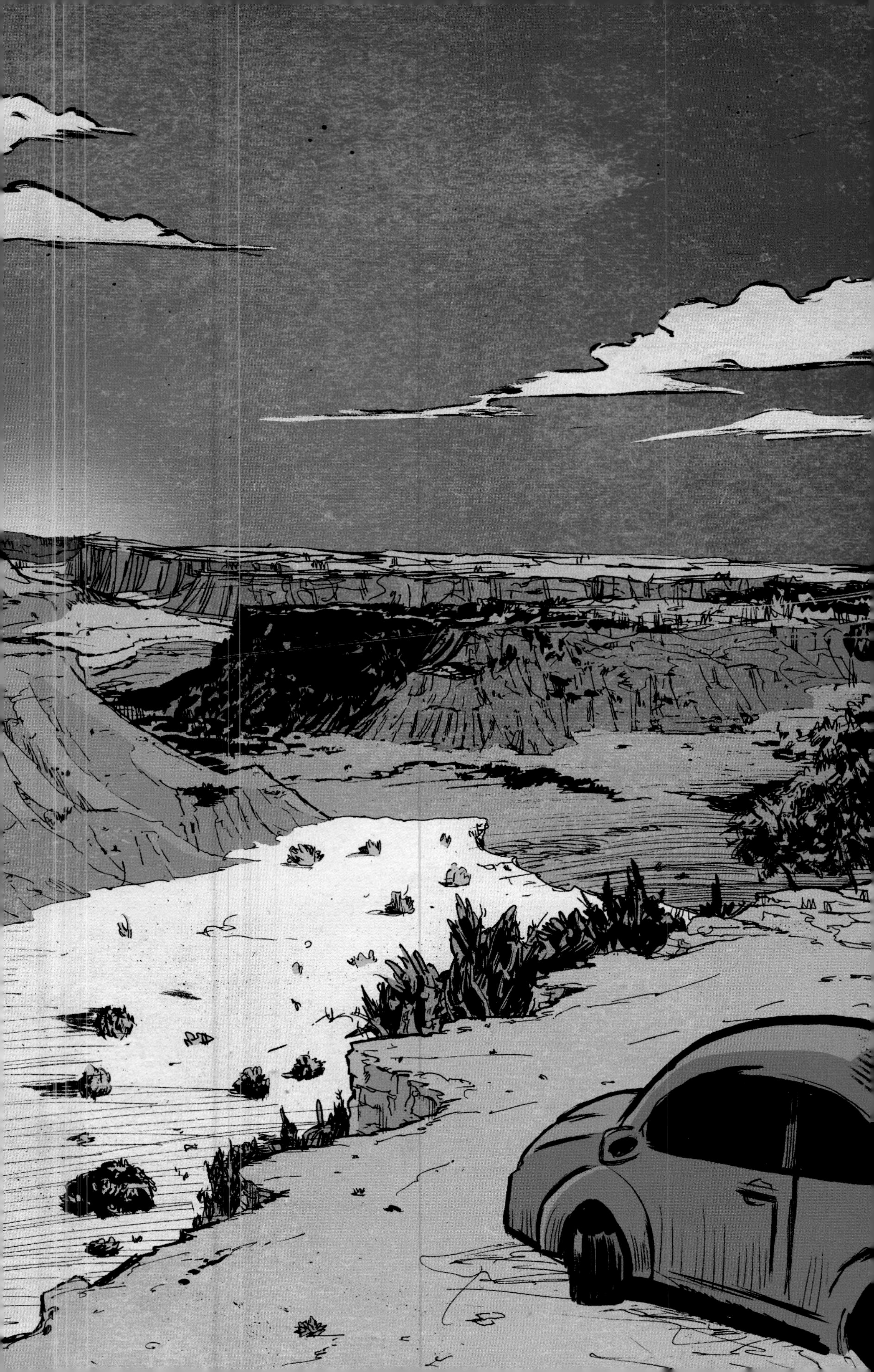

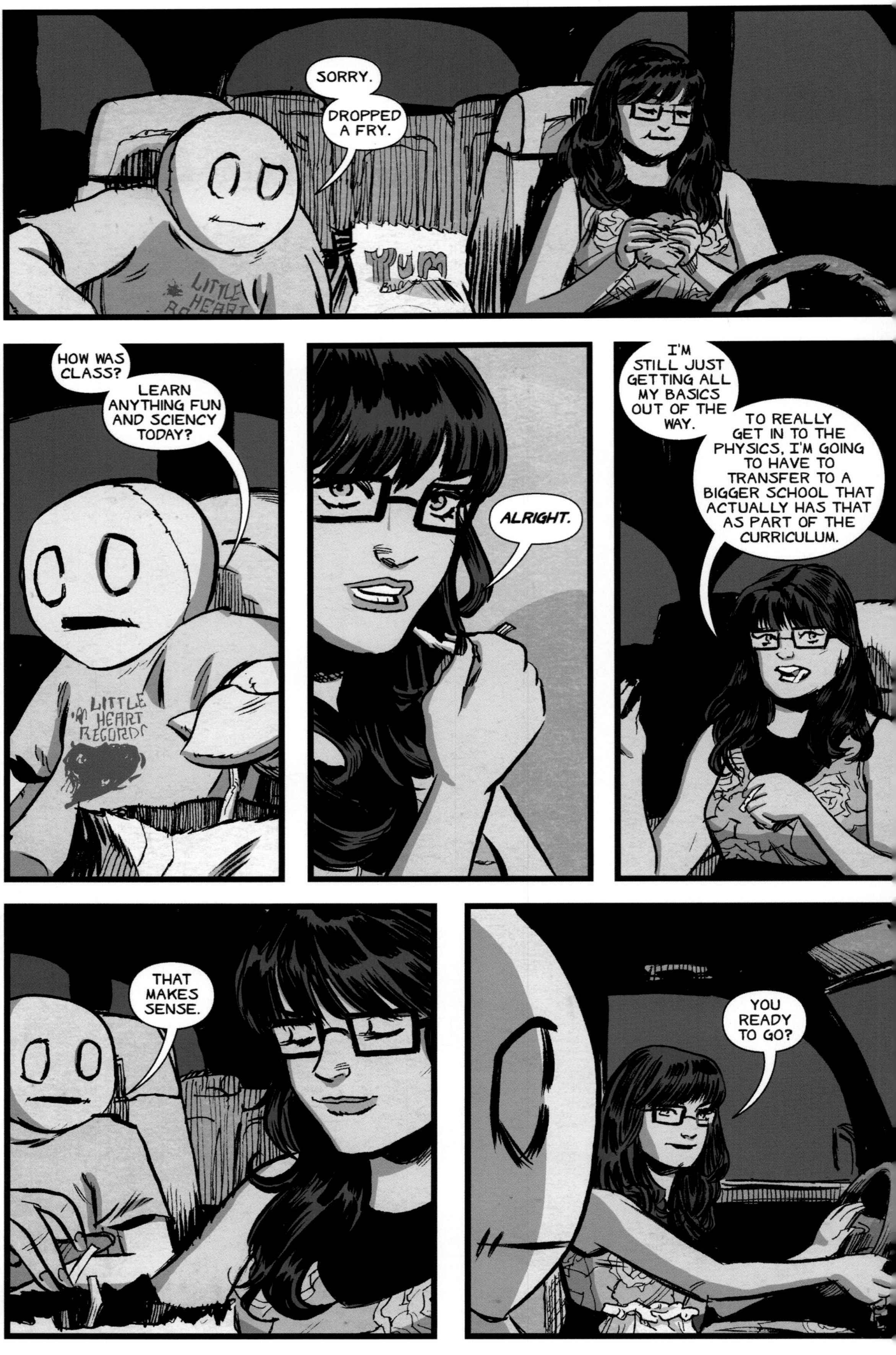

SORRY.
DROPPED A FRY.
YUM
LITTLE HEART
HOW WAS CLASS?
LEARN ANYTHING FUN AND SCIENCY TODAY?
LITTLE HEART RECORDS
ALRIGHT.
I'M STILL JUST GETTING ALL MY BASICS OUT OF THE WAY.
TO REALLY GET IN TO THE PHYSICS, I'M GOING TO HAVE TO TRANSFER TO A BIGGER SCHOOL THAT ACTUALLY HAS THAT AS PART OF THE CURRICULUM.
THAT MAKES SENSE.
YOU READY TO GO?

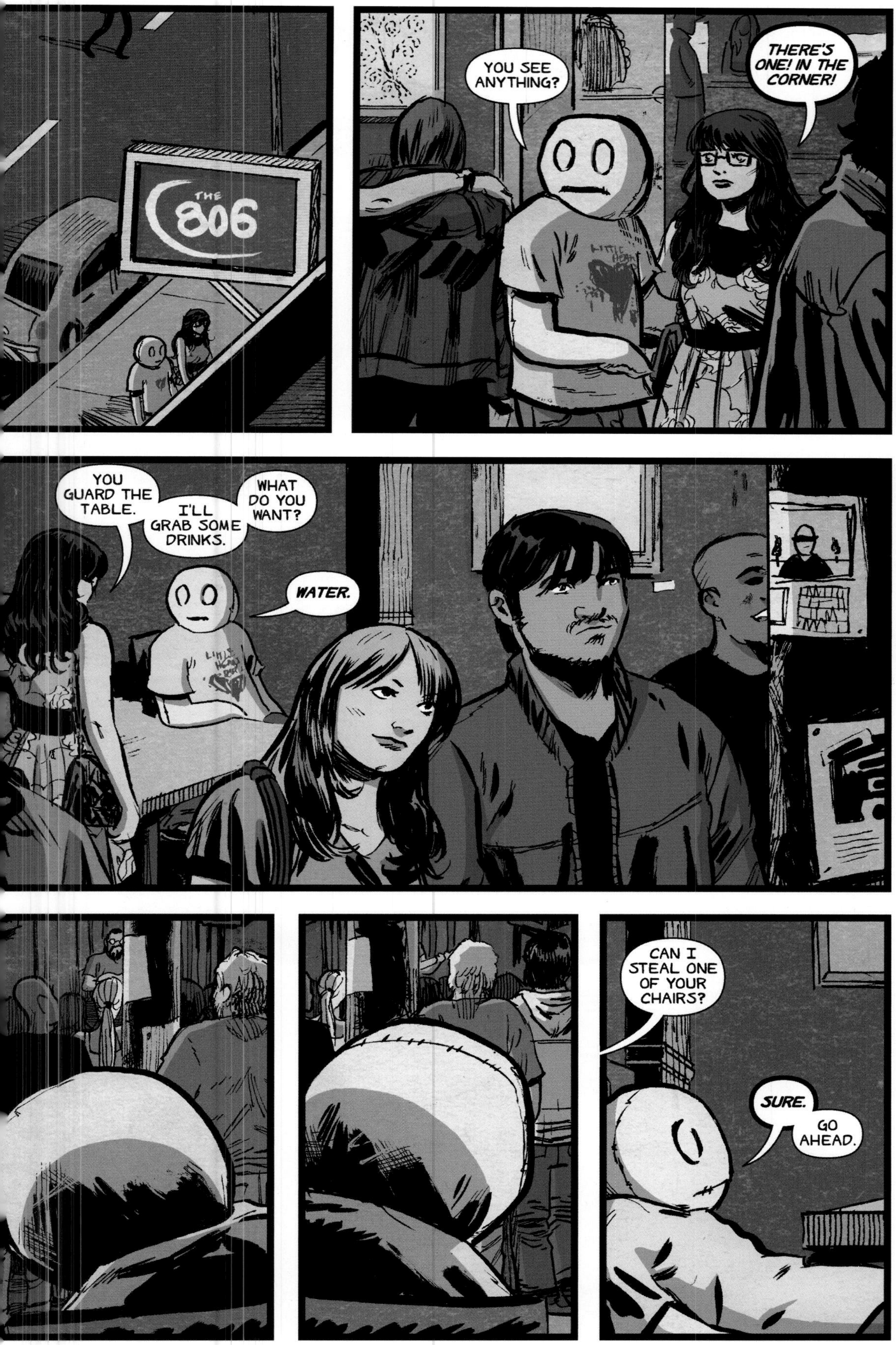
THE 806
YOU SEE ANYTHING?
THERE'S ONE! IN THE CORNER!
YOU GUARD THE TABLE.
I'LL GRAB SOME DRINKS.
WHAT DO YOU WANT?
WATER.
CAN I STEAL ONE OF YOUR CHAIRS?
SURE.
GO AHEAD.

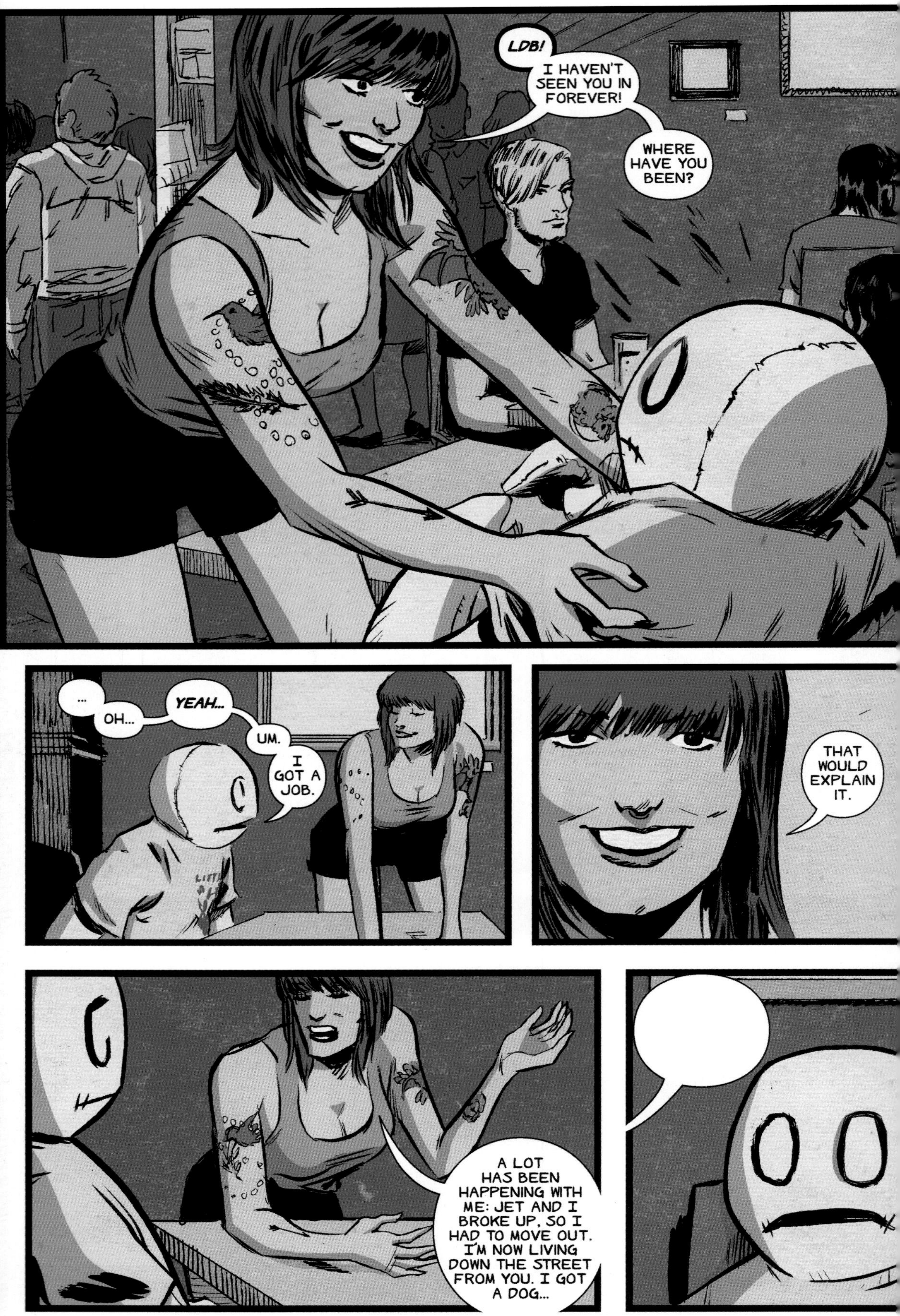
LDB!
I HAVEN'T SEEN YOU IN FOREVER!
WHERE HAVE YOU BEEN?
...
OH...
YEAH...
UM.
I GOT A JOB.
THAT WOULD EXPLAIN IT.
A LOT HAS BEEN HAPPENING WITH ME: JET AND I BROKE UP, SO I HAD TO MOVE OUT. I'M NOW LIVING DOWN THE STREET FROM YOU. I GOT A DOG...

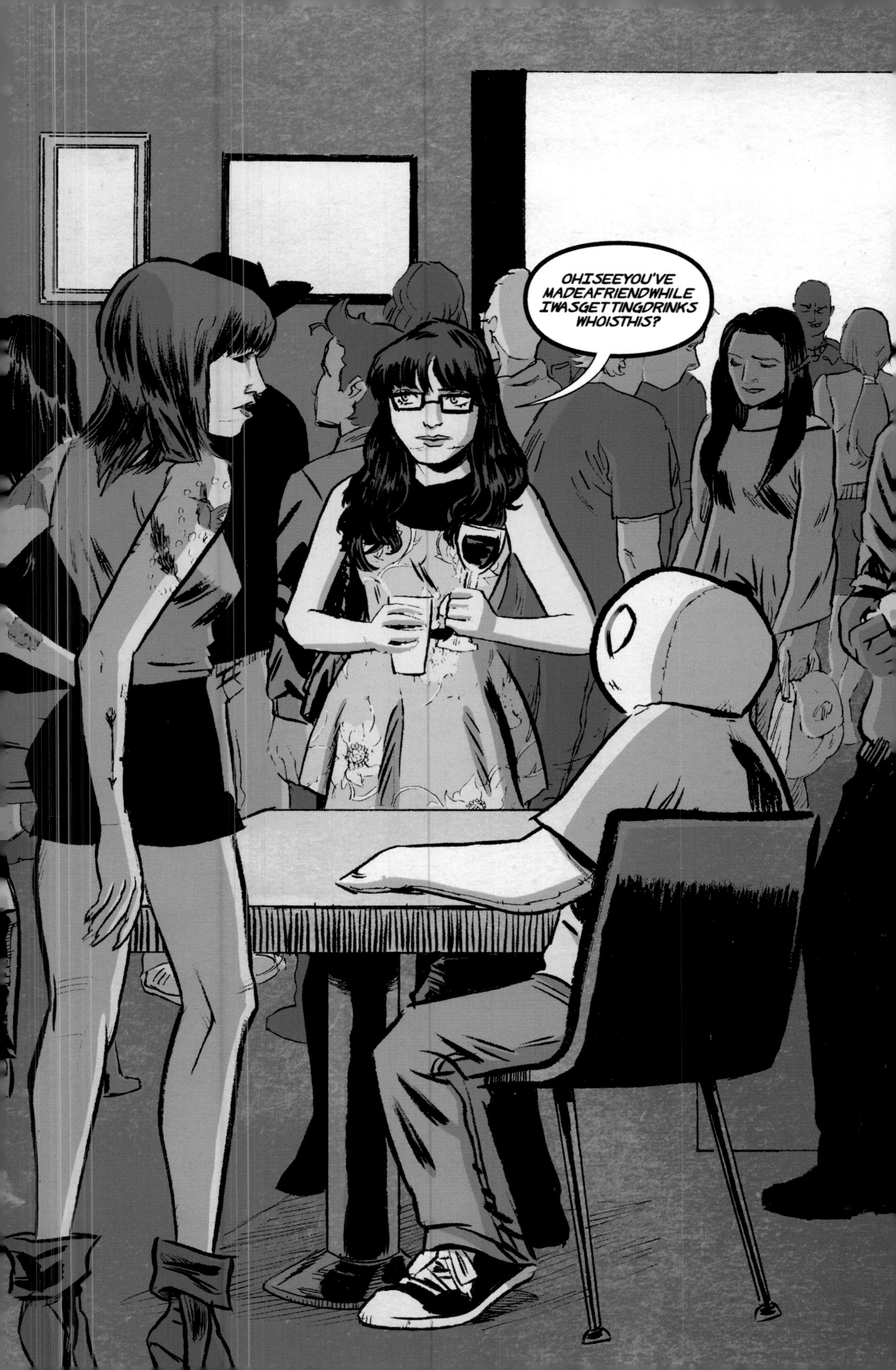
OHISEEYOU'VE MADEAFRIENDWHILE IWASGETTINGDRINKS WHOISTHIS?

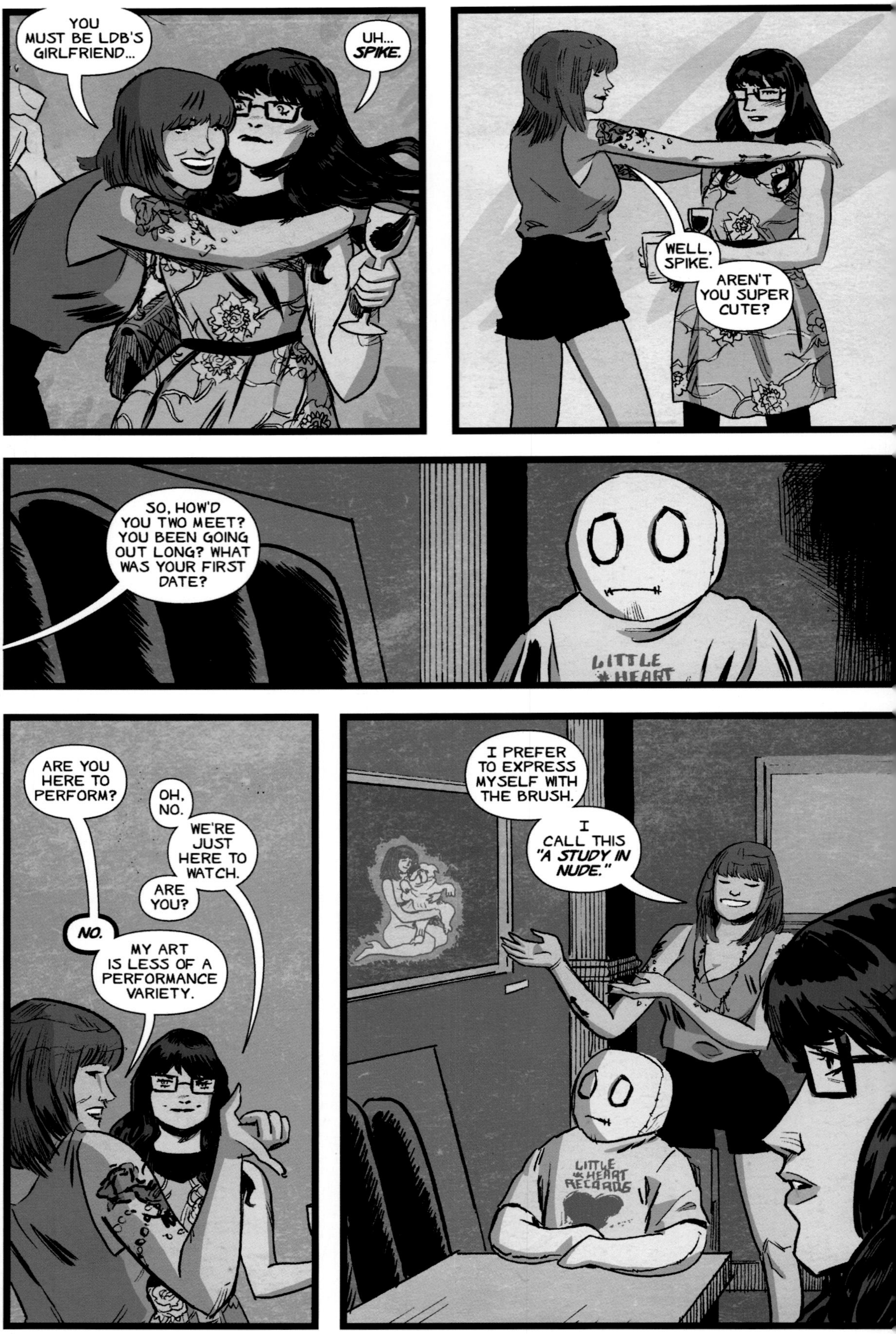
YOU MUST BE LDB'S GIRLFRIEND...
UH... *SPIKE.*
WELL, SPIKE.
AREN'T YOU SUPER CUTE?
SO, HOW'D YOU TWO MEET? YOU BEEN GOING OUT LONG? WHAT WAS YOUR FIRST DATE?
LITTLE HEART
ARE YOU HERE TO PERFORM?
OH, NO.
WE'RE JUST HERE TO WATCH.
ARE YOU?
NO.
MY ART IS LESS OF A PERFORMANCE VARIETY.
I PREFER TO EXPRESS MYSELF WITH THE BRUSH.
I CALL THIS *"A STUDY IN NUDE."*
LITTLE HEART RECORDS

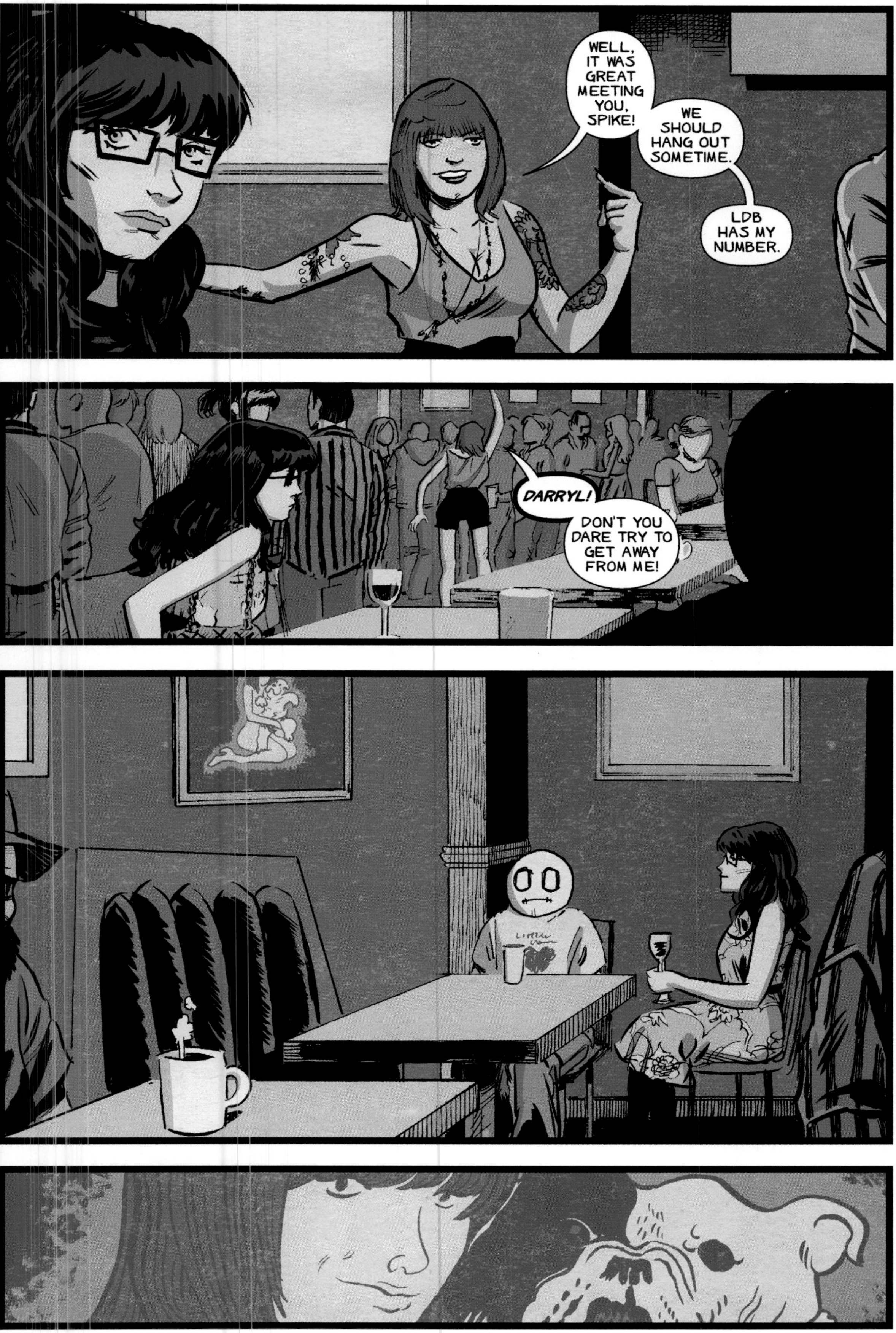
WELL, IT WAS GREAT MEETING YOU, SPIKE!
WE SHOULD HANG OUT SOMETIME.
LDB HAS MY NUMBER.
DARRYL!
DON'T YOU DARE TRY TO GET AWAY FROM ME!

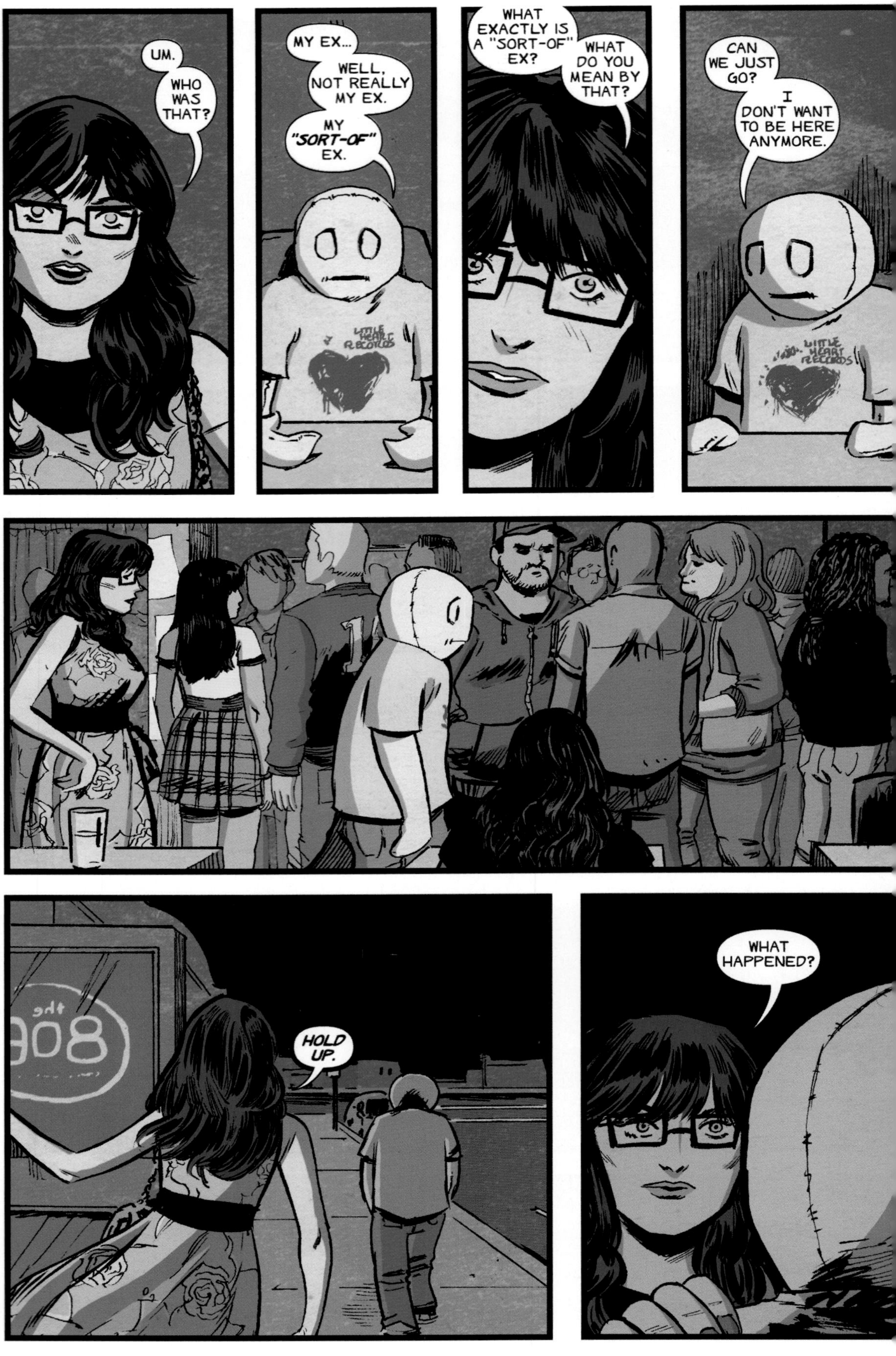
UM.
WHO WAS THAT?
MY EX...
WELL, NOT REALLY MY EX.
MY "SORT-OF" EX.
LITTLE HEART RECORDS
WHAT EXACTLY IS A "SORT-OF" EX?
WHAT DO YOU MEAN BY THAT?
CAN WE JUST GO?
I DON'T WANT TO BE HERE ANYMORE.
LITTLE HEART RECORDS
the 808
HOLD UP.
WHAT HAPPENED?

JAZZ AND I'S RELATIONSHIP IS *AWKWARD*.

WE MET EARLY LAST YEAR.

WE HUNG OUT FOR AWHILE, AND IN MY MIND WE WERE DATING...

...BUT, TO HER, WE WERE *NOT*.

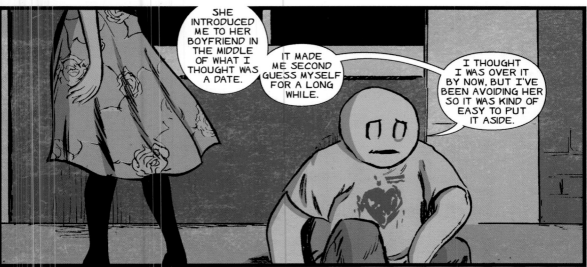

SHE INTRODUCED ME TO HER BOYFRIEND IN THE MIDDLE OF WHAT I THOUGHT WAS A DATE.

IT MADE ME SECOND GUESS MYSELF FOR A LONG WHILE.

I THOUGHT I WAS OVER IT BY NOW, BUT I'VE BEEN AVOIDING HER SO IT WAS KIND OF EASY TO PUT IT ASIDE.

IT STILL HURTS.

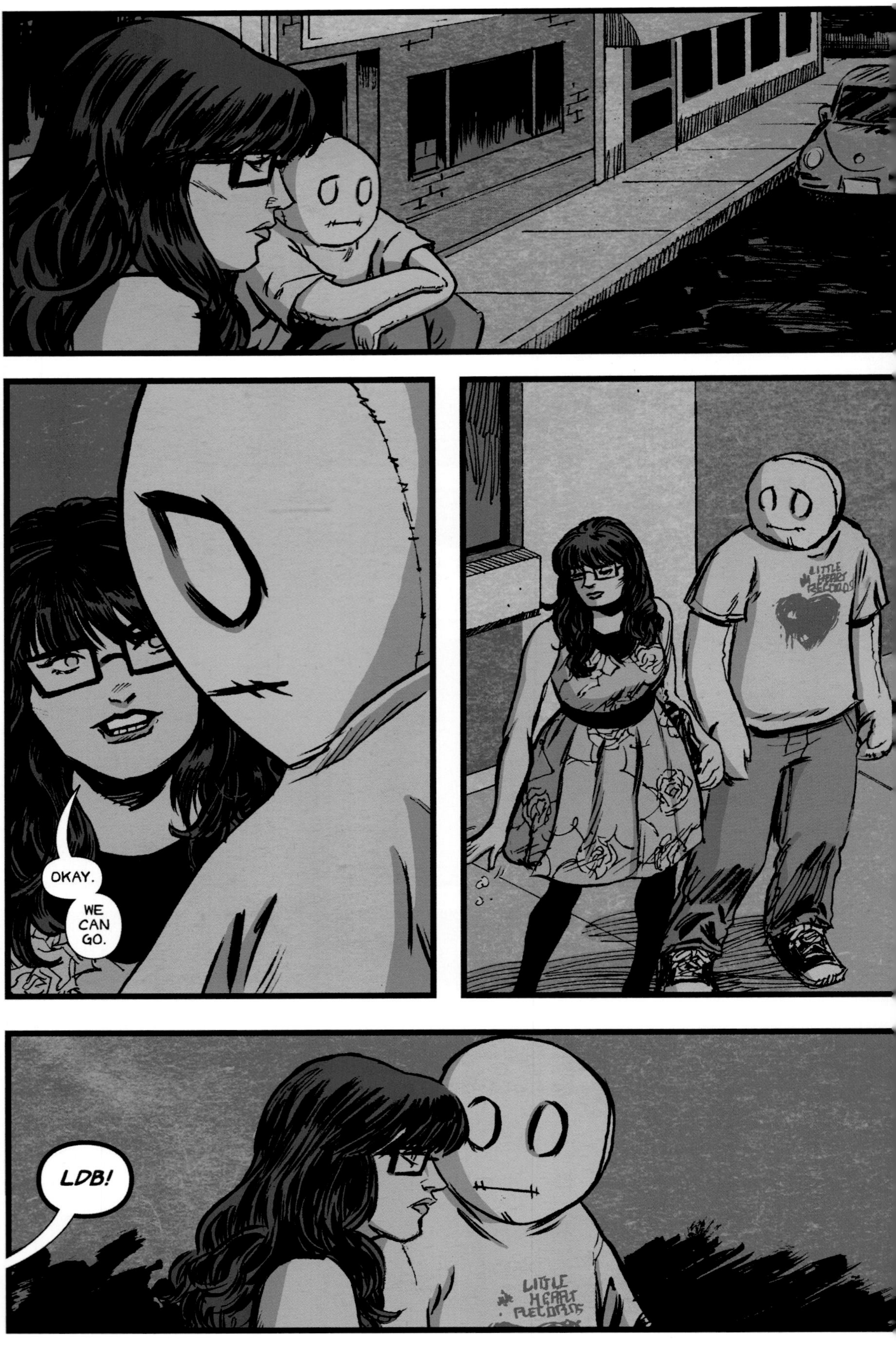
OKAY.
WE CAN GO.
LITTLE HEART RECORDS
LDB!
LITTLE HEART RECORDS

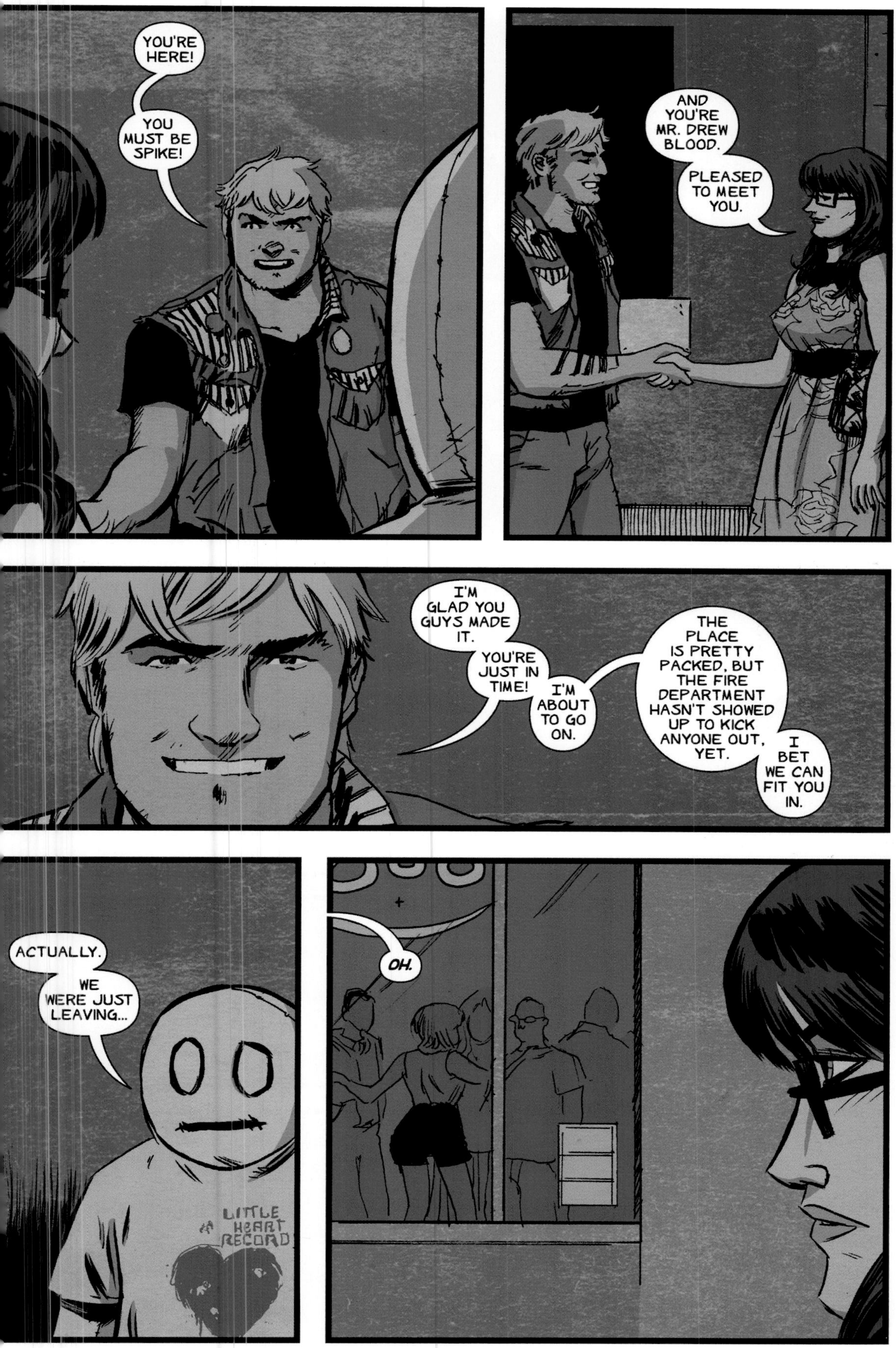
YOU'RE HERE!
YOU MUST BE SPIKE!
AND YOU'RE MR. DREW BLOOD.
PLEASED TO MEET YOU.
I'M GLAD YOU GUYS MADE IT.
YOU'RE JUST IN TIME!
I'M ABOUT TO GO ON.
THE PLACE IS PRETTY PACKED, BUT THE FIRE DEPARTMENT HASN'T SHOWED UP TO KICK ANYONE OUT, YET.
I BET WE CAN FIT YOU IN.
ACTUALLY.
WE WERE JUST LEAVING...
LITTLE HEART RECORD
OH.

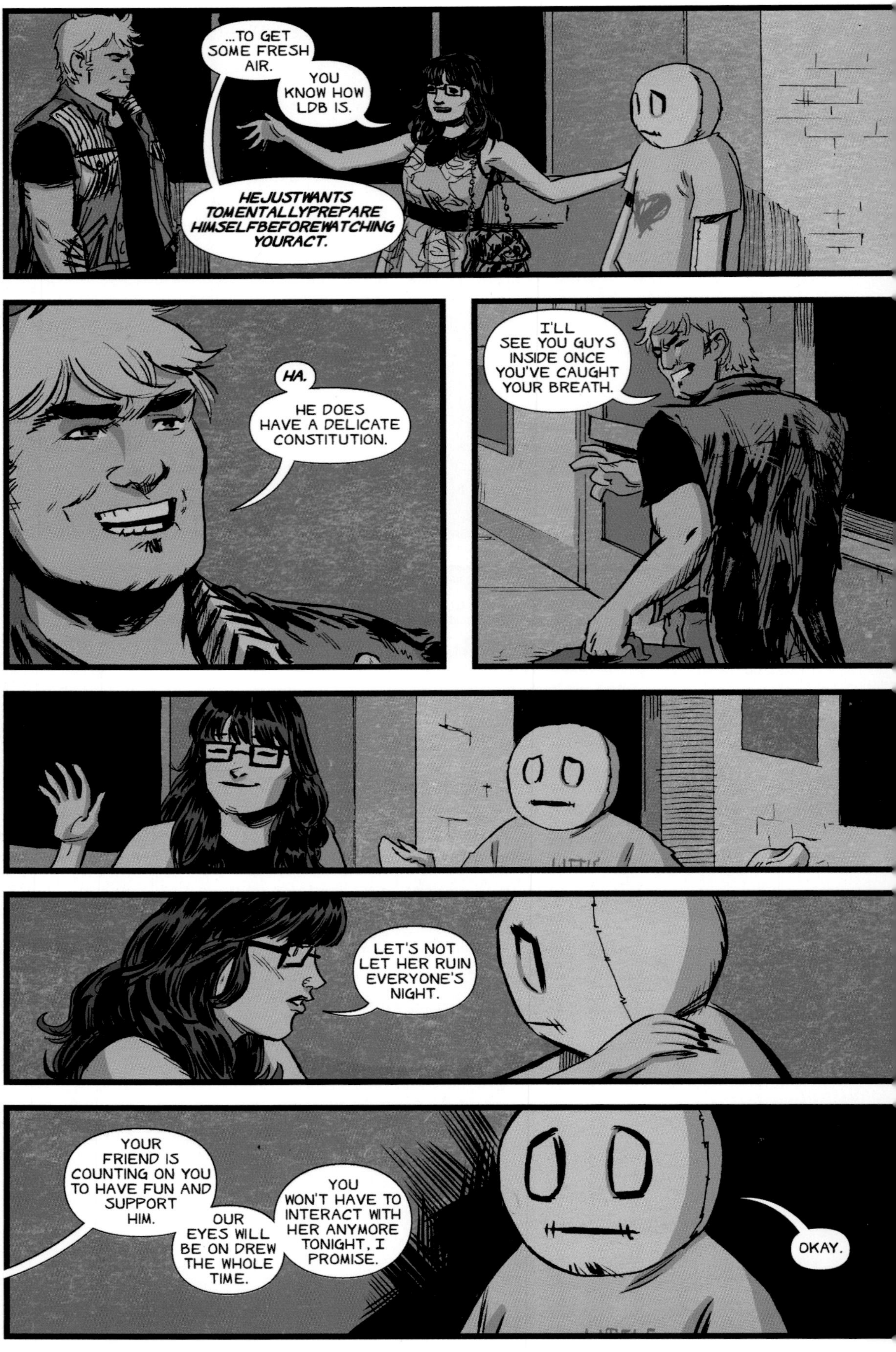
...TO GET SOME FRESH AIR.
YOU KNOW HOW LDB IS.
HEJUSTWANTS TOMENTALLYPREPARE HIMSELFBEFOREWATCHING YOURACT.
HA.
HE DOES HAVE A DELICATE CONSTITUTION.
I'LL SEE YOU GUYS INSIDE ONCE YOU'VE CAUGHT YOUR BREATH.
LET'S NOT LET HER RUIN EVERYONE'S NIGHT.
YOUR FRIEND IS COUNTING ON YOU TO HAVE FUN AND SUPPORT HIM.
OUR EYES WILL BE ON DREW THE WHOLE TIME.
YOU WON'T HAVE TO INTERACT WITH HER ANYMORE TONIGHT, I PROMISE.
OKAY.

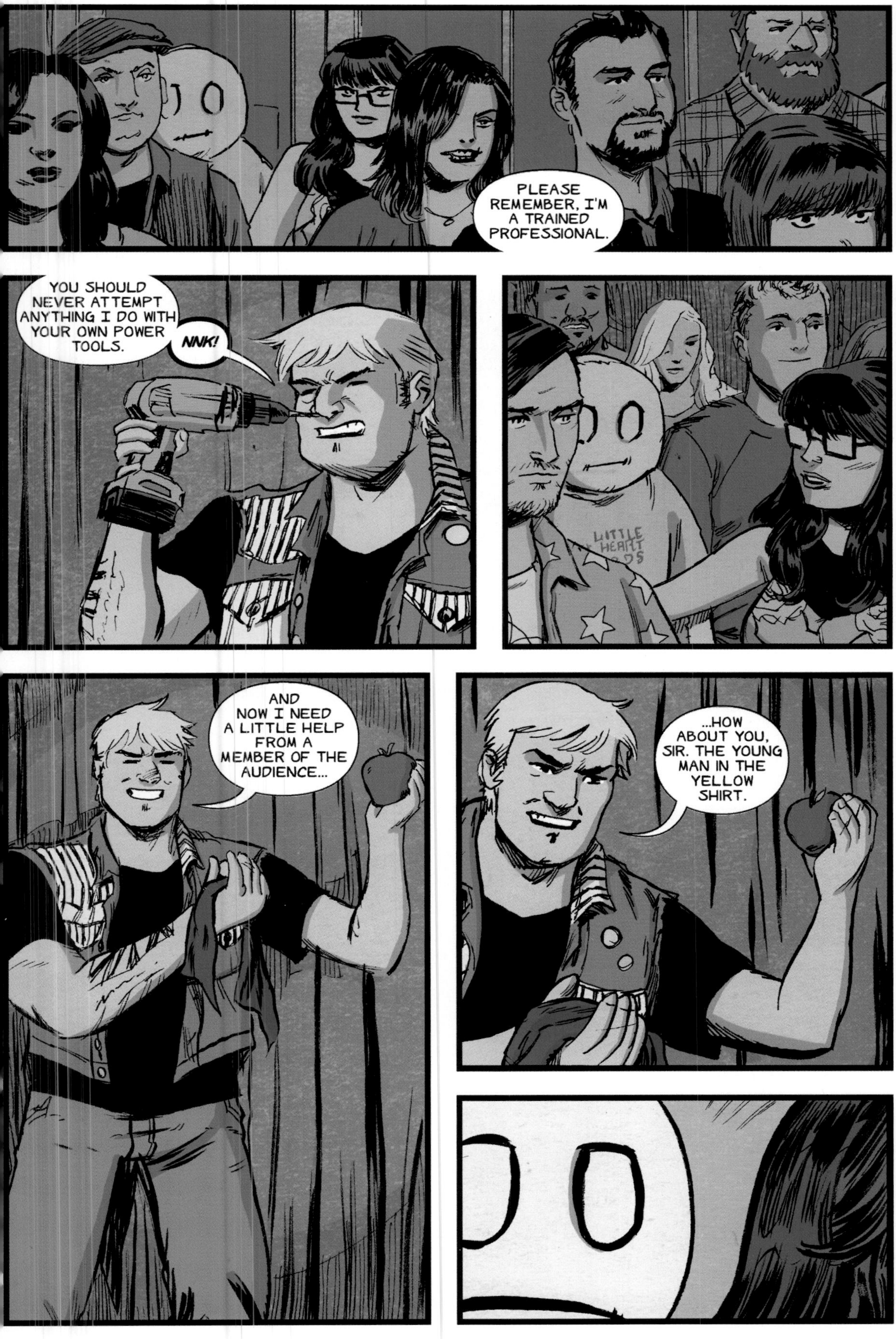
PLEASE REMEMBER, I'M A TRAINED PROFESSIONAL.
YOU SHOULD NEVER ATTEMPT ANYTHING I DO WITH YOUR OWN POWER TOOLS.
NNK!
LITTLE HEART
AND NOW I NEED A LITTLE HELP FROM A MEMBER OF THE AUDIENCE...
...HOW ABOUT YOU, SIR. THE YOUNG MAN IN THE YELLOW SHIRT.

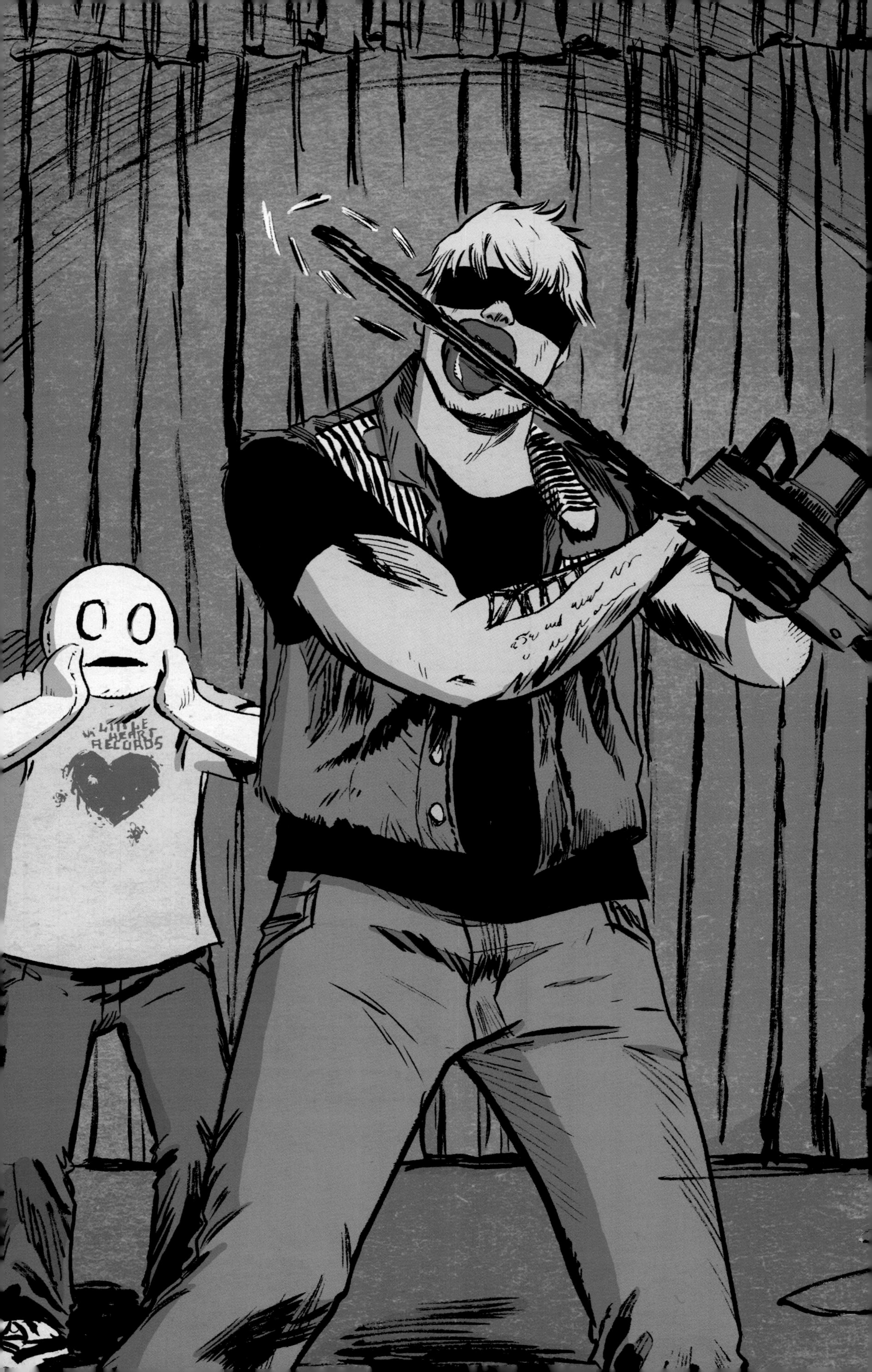
LITTLE
HEART
RECORDS

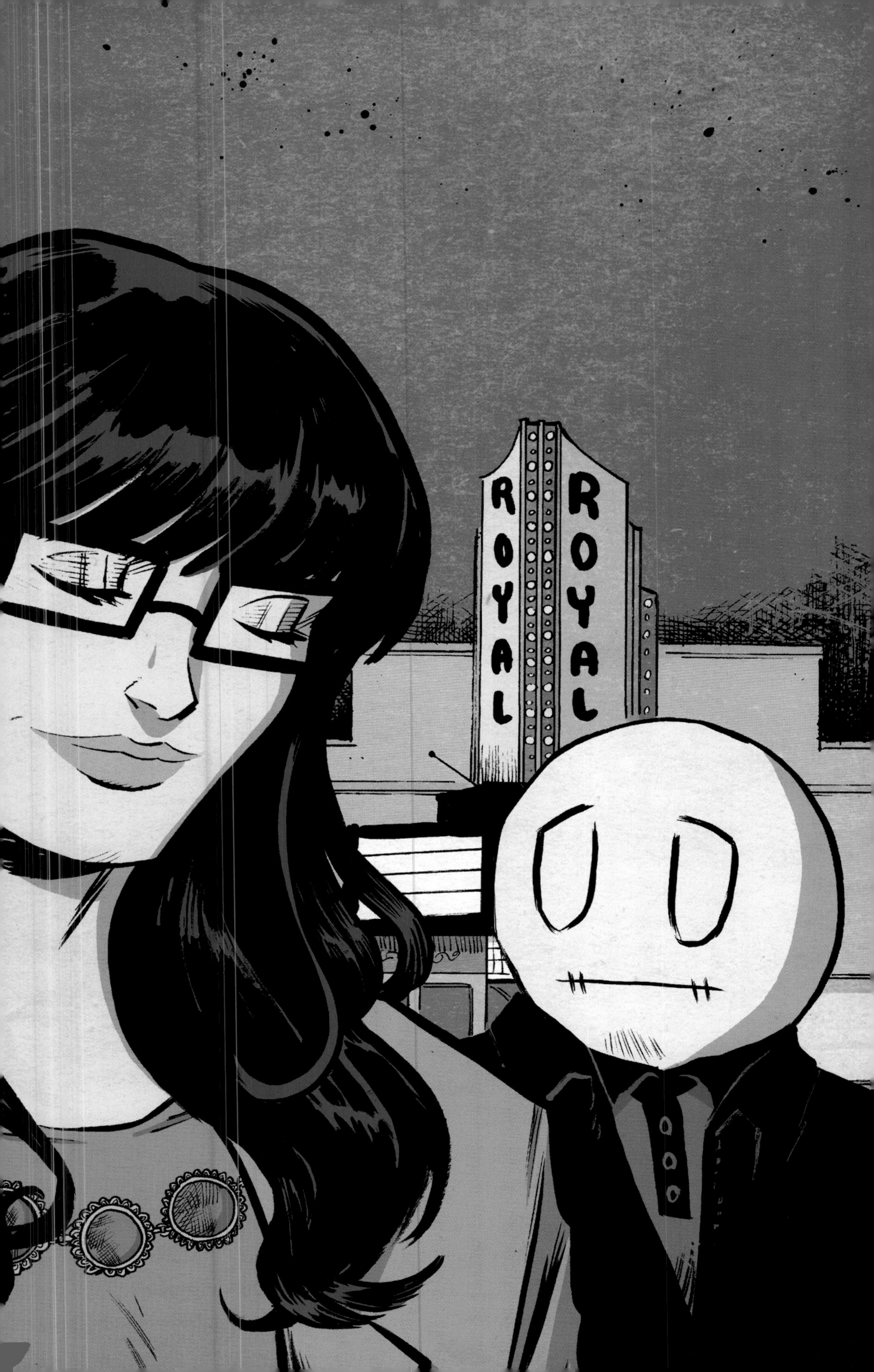
ROYAL
ROYAL

CHAPTER EIGHTEEN:
"I RAISE MY FIST"

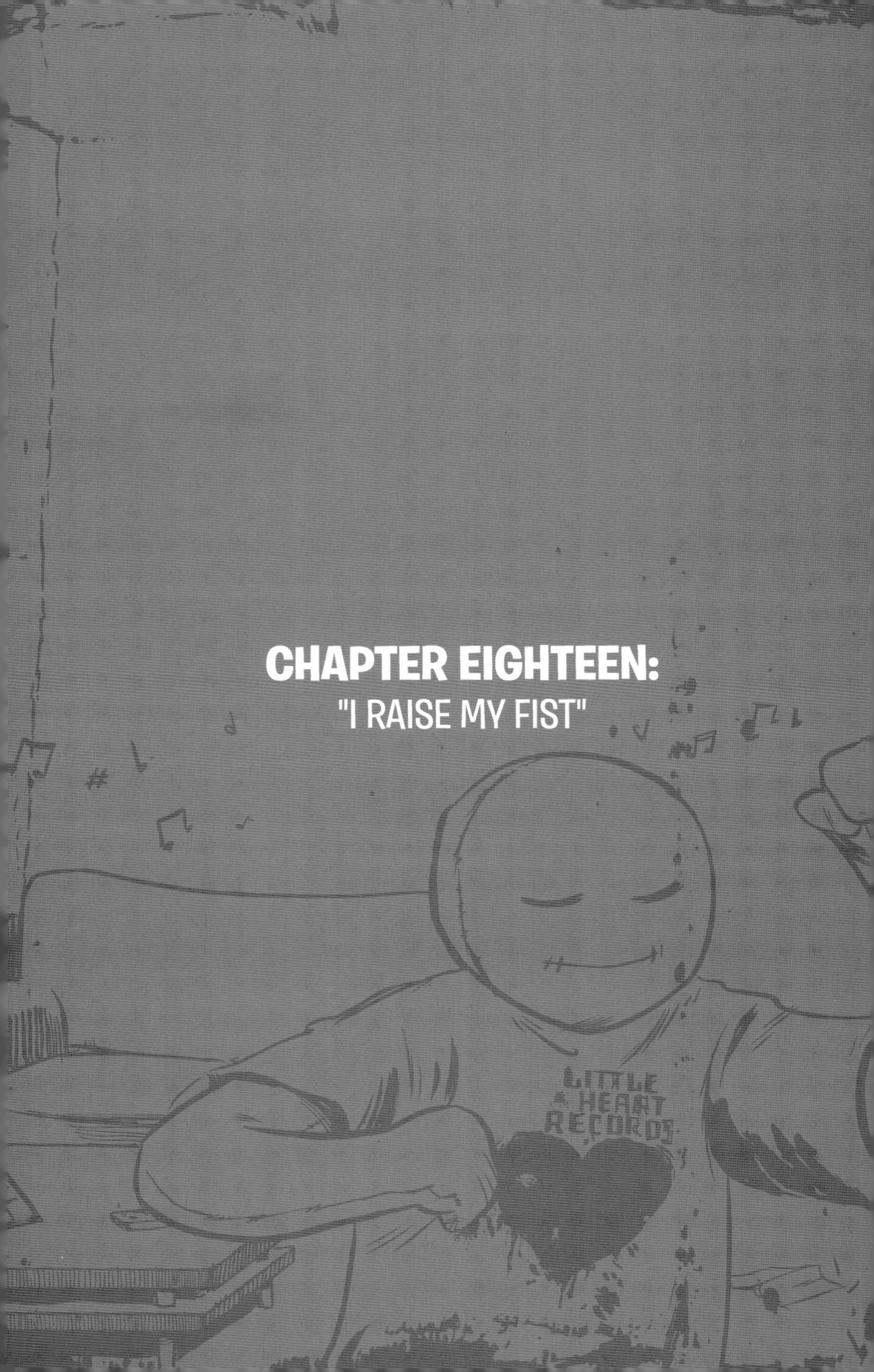
LITTLE HEART RECORDS

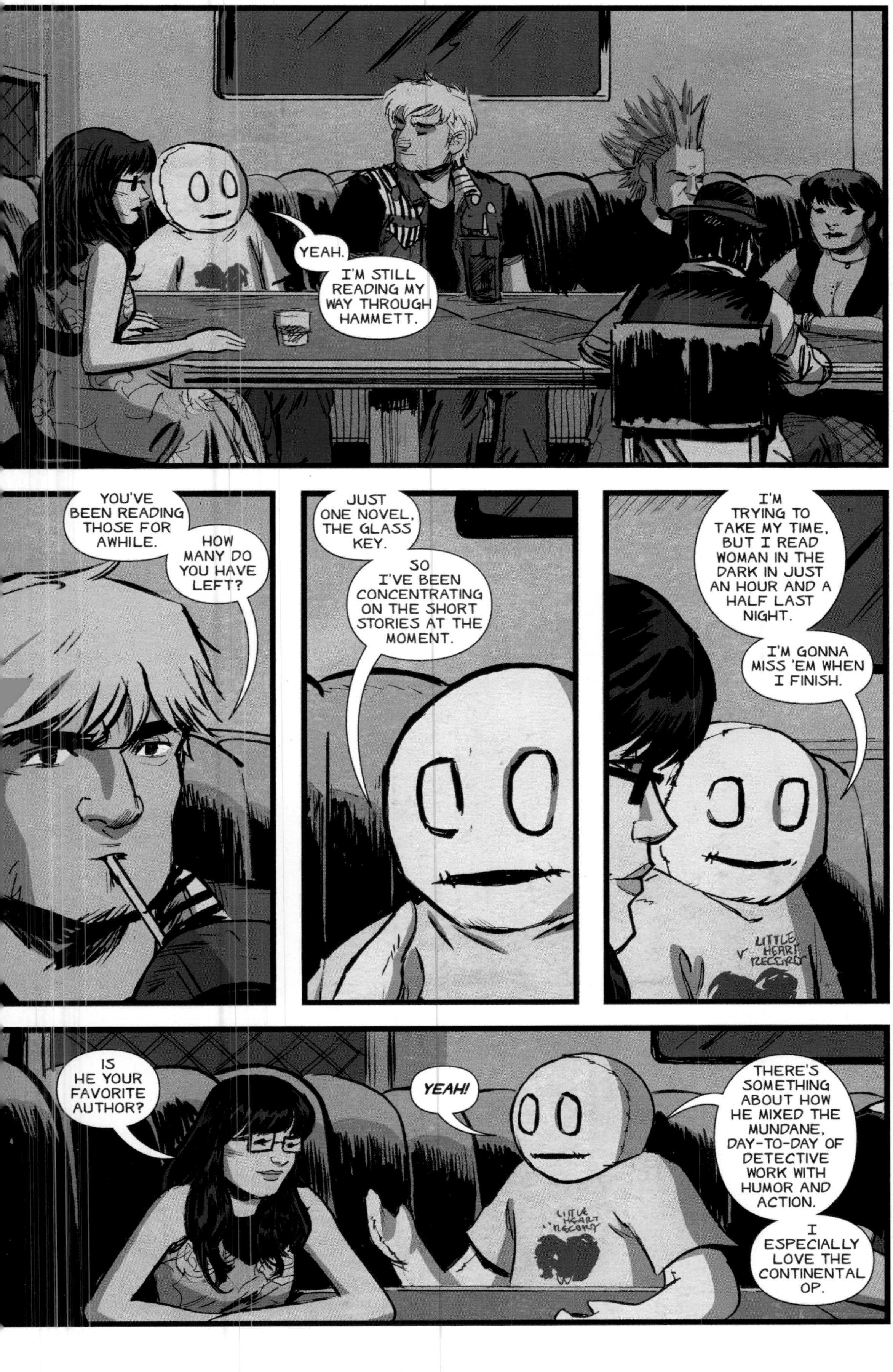
YEAH.
I'M STILL READING MY WAY THROUGH HAMMETT.
YOU'VE BEEN READING THOSE FOR AWHILE.
HOW MANY DO YOU HAVE LEFT?
JUST ONE NOVEL, THE GLASS KEY.
SO I'VE BEEN CONCENTRATING ON THE SHORT STORIES AT THE MOMENT.
I'M TRYING TO TAKE MY TIME, BUT I READ WOMAN IN THE DARK IN JUST AN HOUR AND A HALF LAST NIGHT.
I'M GONNA MISS 'EM WHEN I FINISH.
LITTLE HEART RECORDS
IS HE YOUR FAVORITE AUTHOR?
YEAH!
THERE'S SOMETHING ABOUT HOW HE MIXED THE MUNDANE, DAY-TO-DAY OF DETECTIVE WORK WITH HUMOR AND ACTION.
I ESPECIALLY LOVE THE CONTINENTAL OP.
LITTLE HEART RECORDS

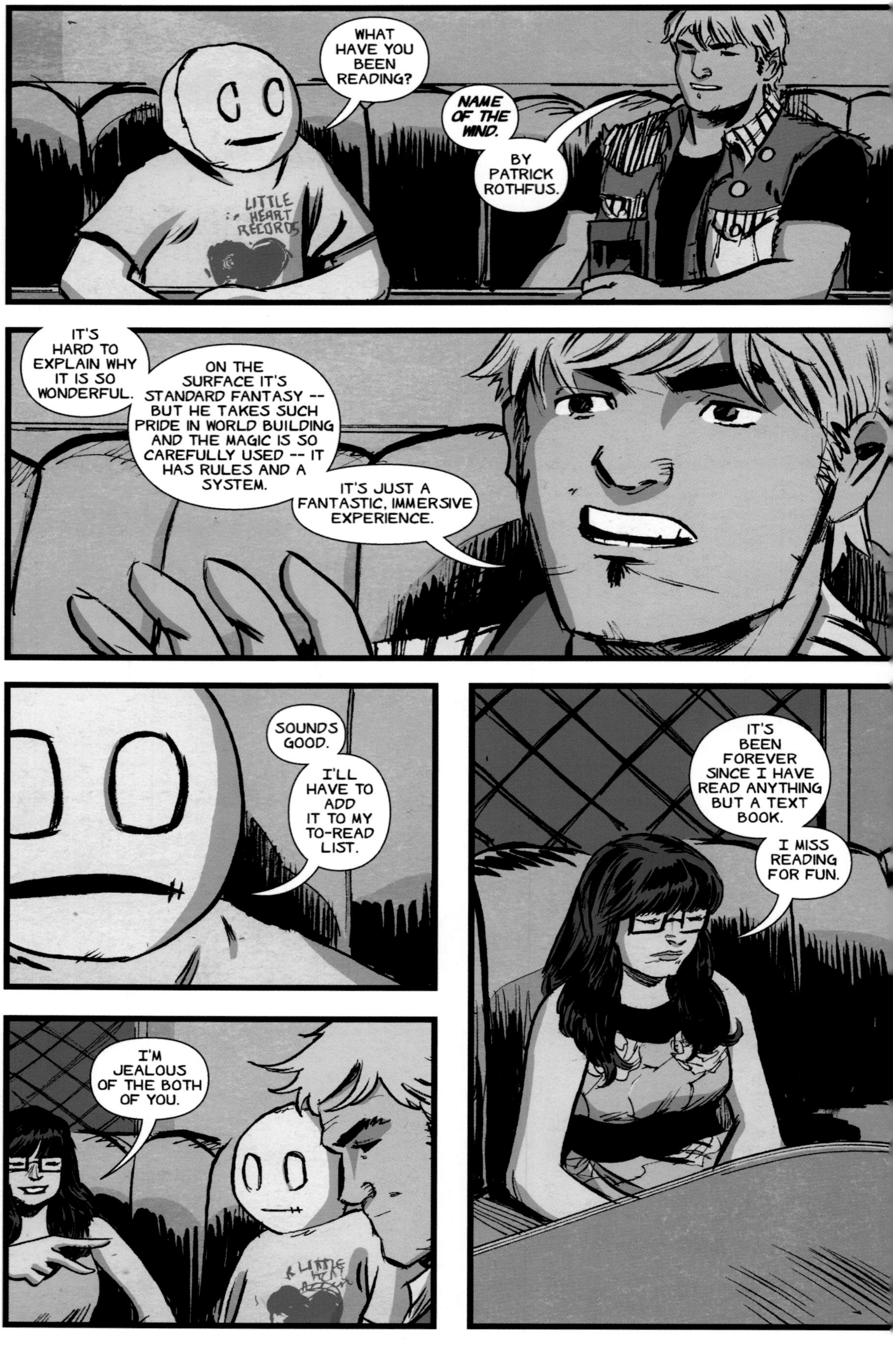

WHAT HAVE YOU BEEN READING?
NAME OF THE WIND.
BY PATRICK ROTHFUS.
LITTLE HEART RECORDS
IT'S HARD TO EXPLAIN WHY IT IS SO WONDERFUL.
ON THE SURFACE IT'S STANDARD FANTASY -- BUT HE TAKES SUCH PRIDE IN WORLD BUILDING AND THE MAGIC IS SO CAREFULLY USED -- IT HAS RULES AND A SYSTEM.
IT'S JUST A FANTASTIC, IMMERSIVE EXPERIENCE.
SOUNDS GOOD.
I'LL HAVE TO ADD IT TO MY TO-READ LIST.
IT'S BEEN FOREVER SINCE I HAVE READ ANYTHING BUT A TEXT BOOK.
I MISS READING FOR FUN.
I'M JEALOUS OF THE BOTH OF YOU.

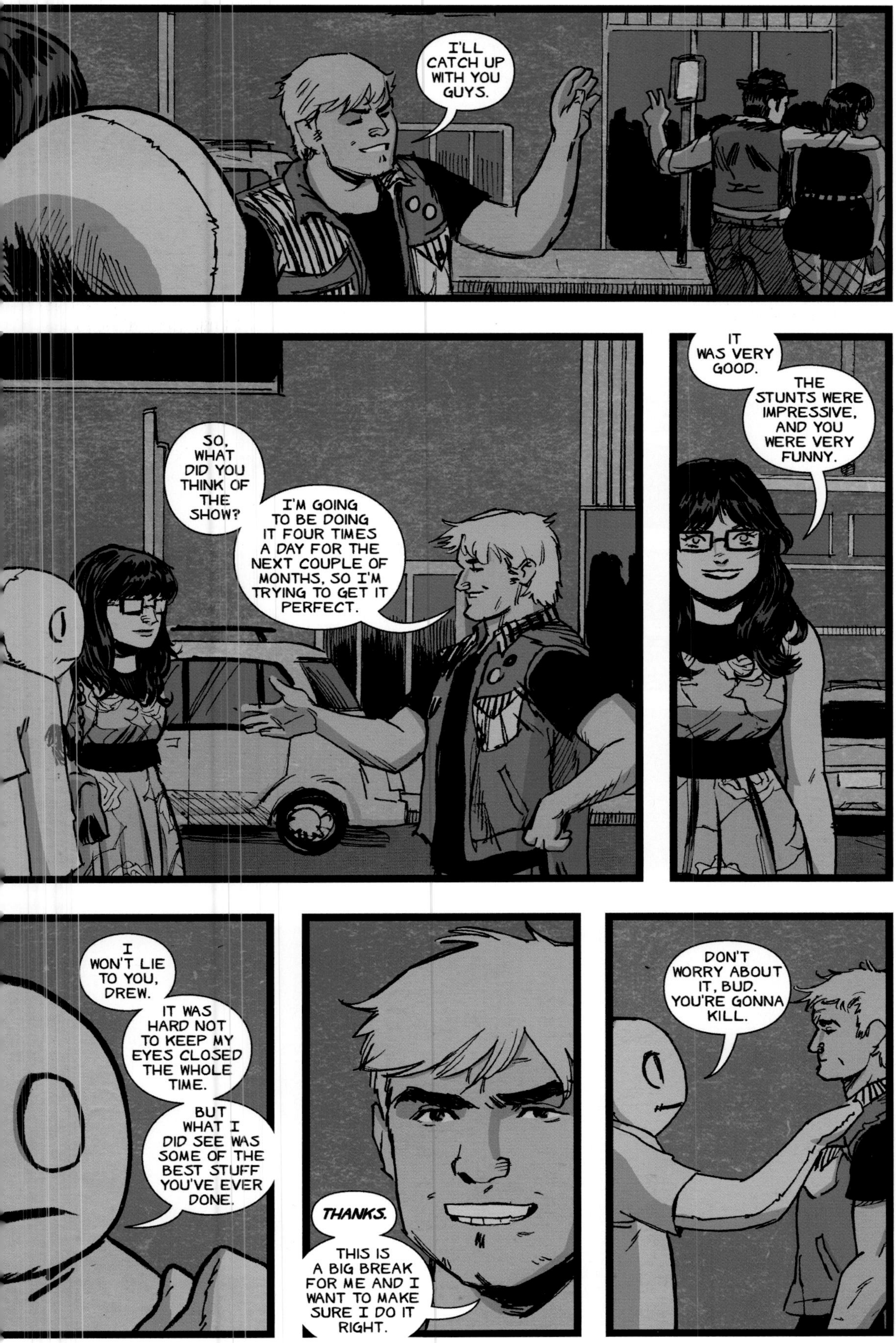
I'LL CATCH UP WITH YOU GUYS.
SO, WHAT DID YOU THINK OF THE SHOW?
I'M GOING TO BE DOING IT FOUR TIMES A DAY FOR THE NEXT COUPLE OF MONTHS, SO I'M TRYING TO GET IT PERFECT.
IT WAS VERY GOOD.
THE STUNTS WERE IMPRESSIVE, AND YOU WERE VERY FUNNY.
I WON'T LIE TO YOU, DREW.
IT WAS HARD NOT TO KEEP MY EYES CLOSED THE WHOLE TIME.
BUT WHAT I DID SEE WAS SOME OF THE BEST STUFF YOU'VE EVER DONE.
THANKS.
THIS IS A BIG BREAK FOR ME AND I WANT TO MAKE SURE I DO IT RIGHT.
DON'T WORRY ABOUT IT, BUD. YOU'RE GONNA KILL.

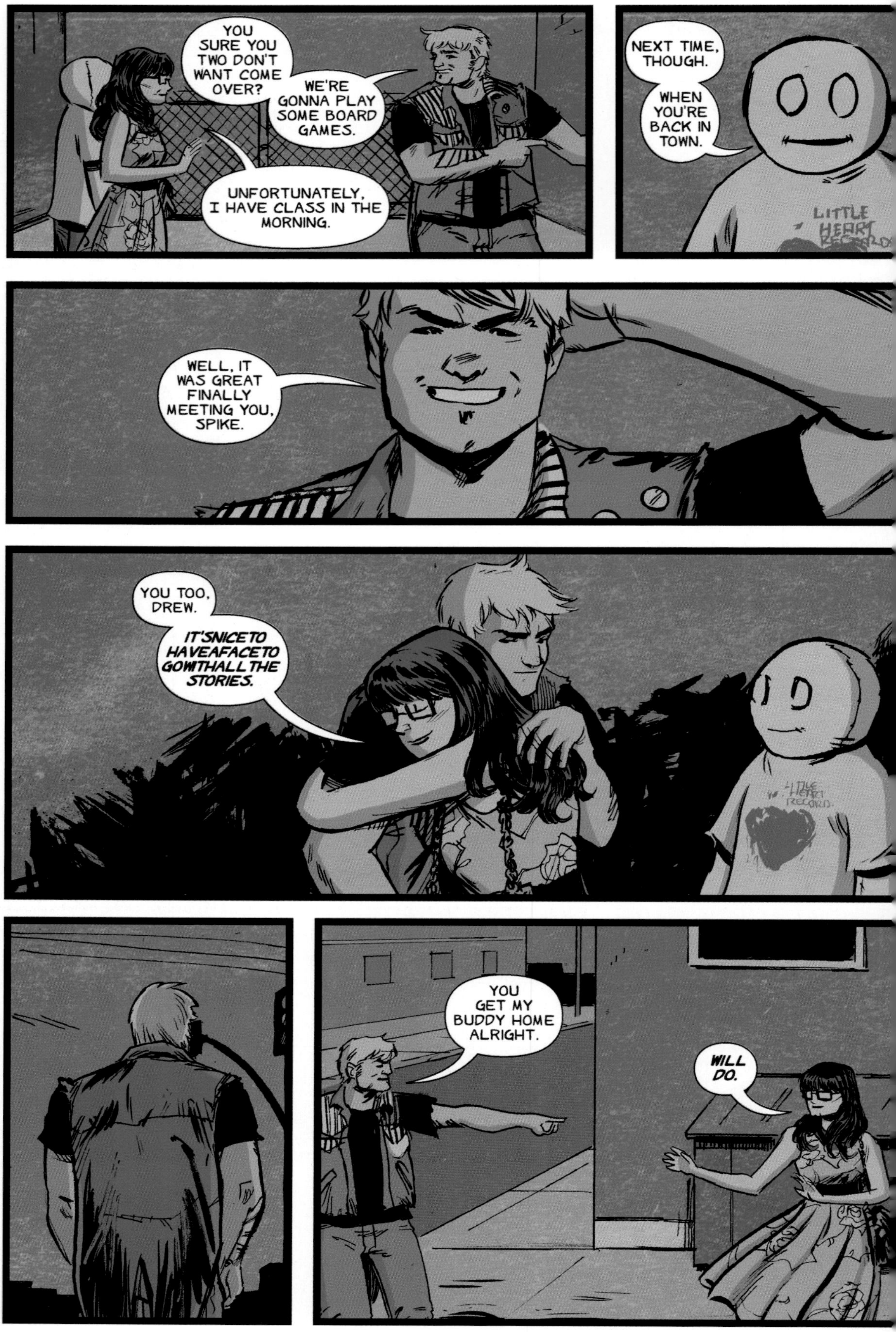
YOU SURE YOU TWO DON'T WANT COME OVER?
WE'RE GONNA PLAY SOME BOARD GAMES.
UNFORTUNATELY, I HAVE CLASS IN THE MORNING.
NEXT TIME, THOUGH.
WHEN YOU'RE BACK IN TOWN.
LITTLE HEART RECORDS
WELL, IT WAS GREAT FINALLY MEETING YOU, SPIKE.
YOU TOO, DREW.
IT'S NICE TO HAVE A FACE TO GO WITH ALL THE STORIES.
YOU GET MY BUDDY HOME ALRIGHT.
WILL DO.

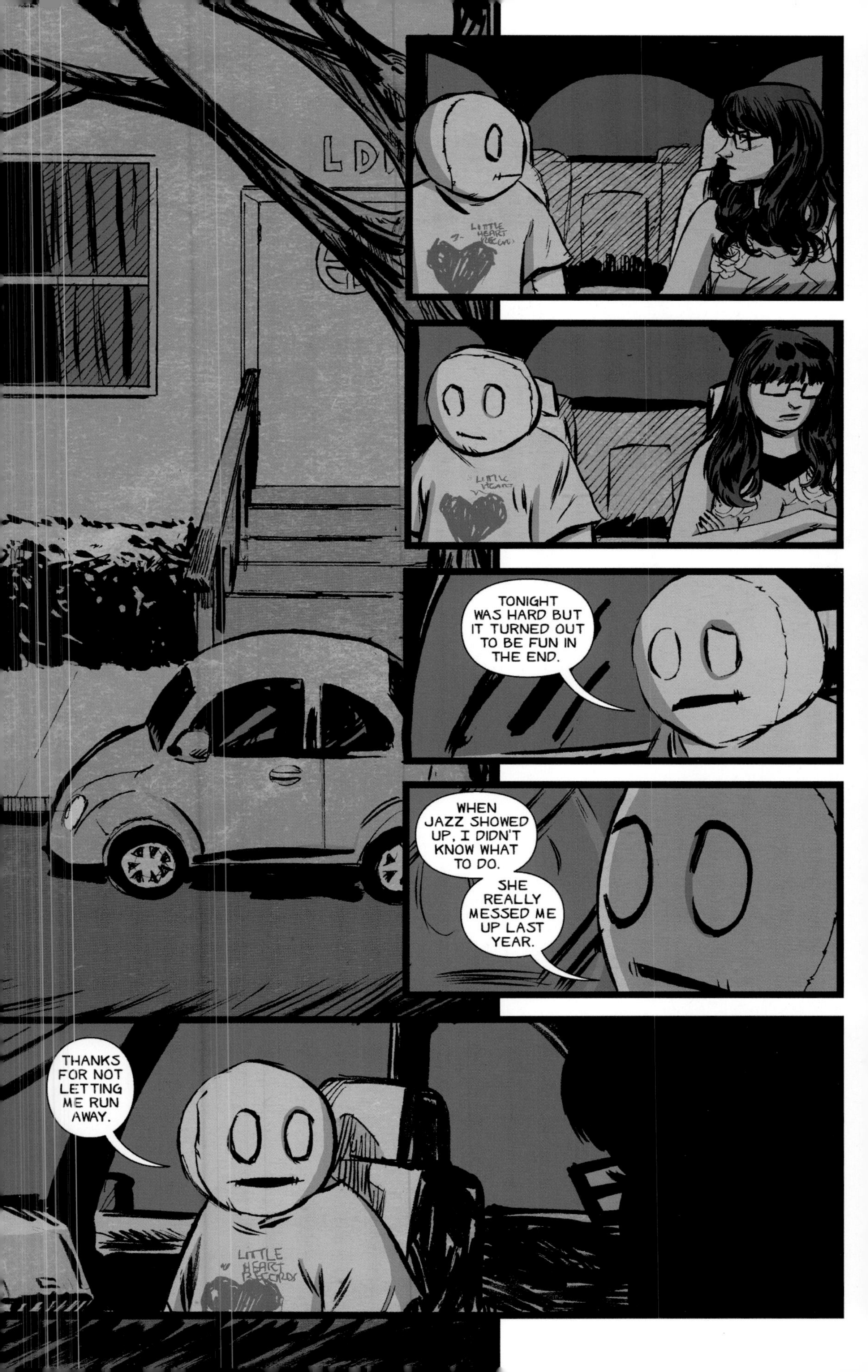

TONIGHT WAS HARD BUT IT TURNED OUT TO BE FUN IN THE END.
WHEN JAZZ SHOWED UP, I DIDN'T KNOW WHAT TO DO.
SHE REALLY MESSED ME UP LAST YEAR.
THANKS FOR NOT LETTING ME RUN AWAY.

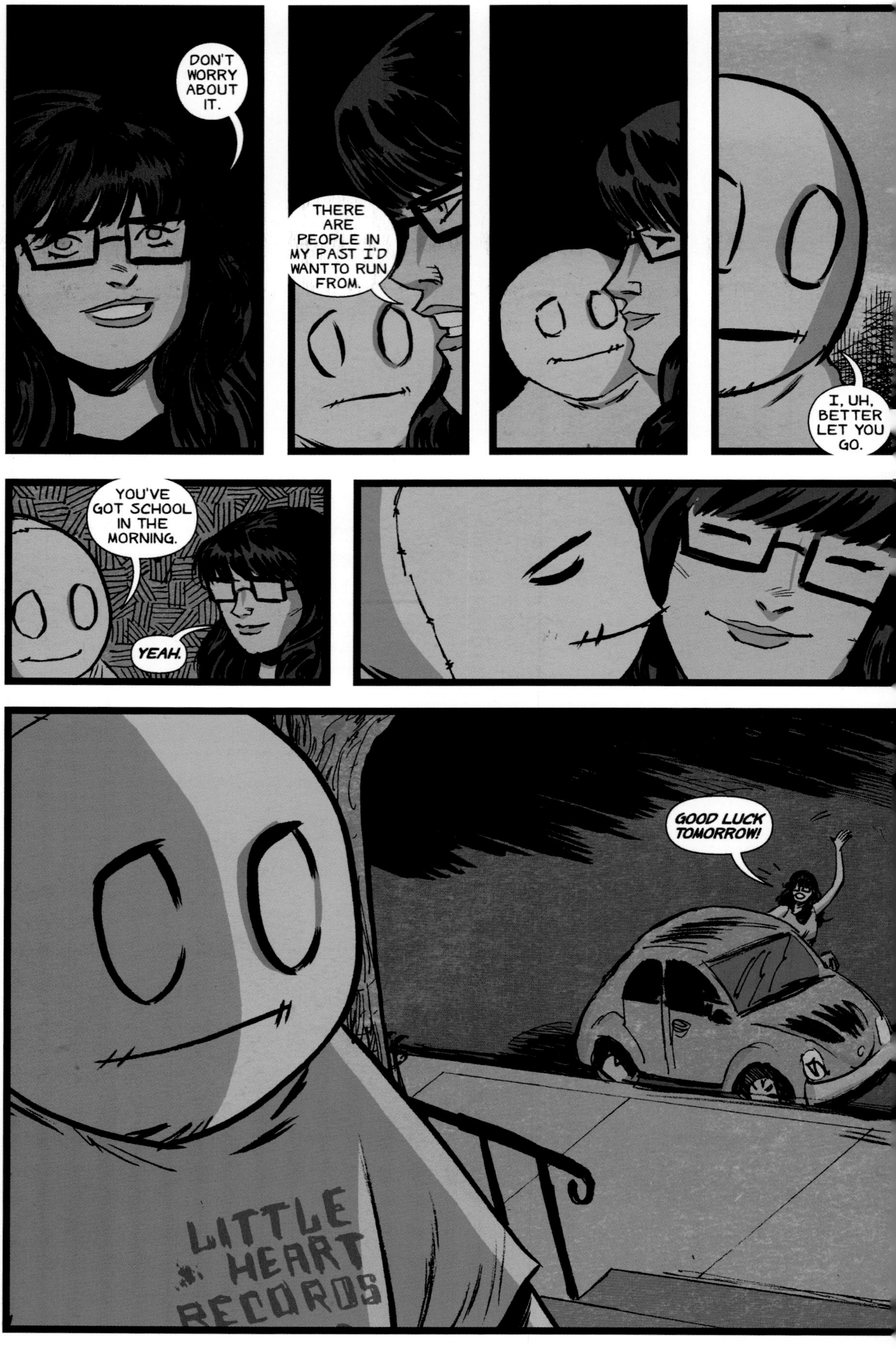
DON'T WORRY ABOUT IT.
THERE ARE PEOPLE IN MY PAST I'D WANT TO RUN FROM.
I, UH, BETTER LET YOU GO.
YOU'VE GOT SCHOOL IN THE MORNING.
YEAH.
GOOD LUCK TOMORROW!
LITTLE HEART RECORDS

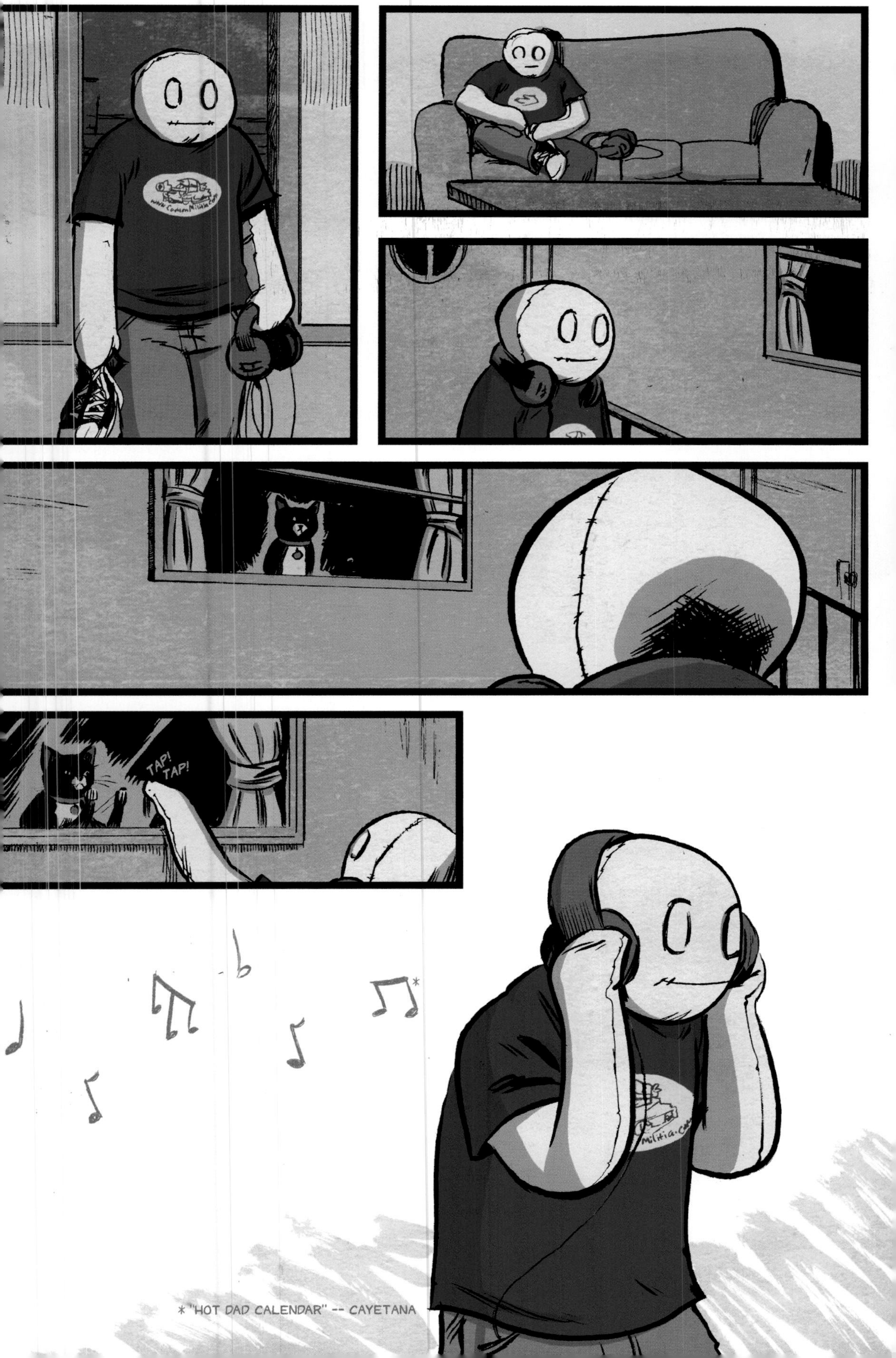
TAP!
TAP!
* "HOT DAD CALENDAR" -- CAYETANA

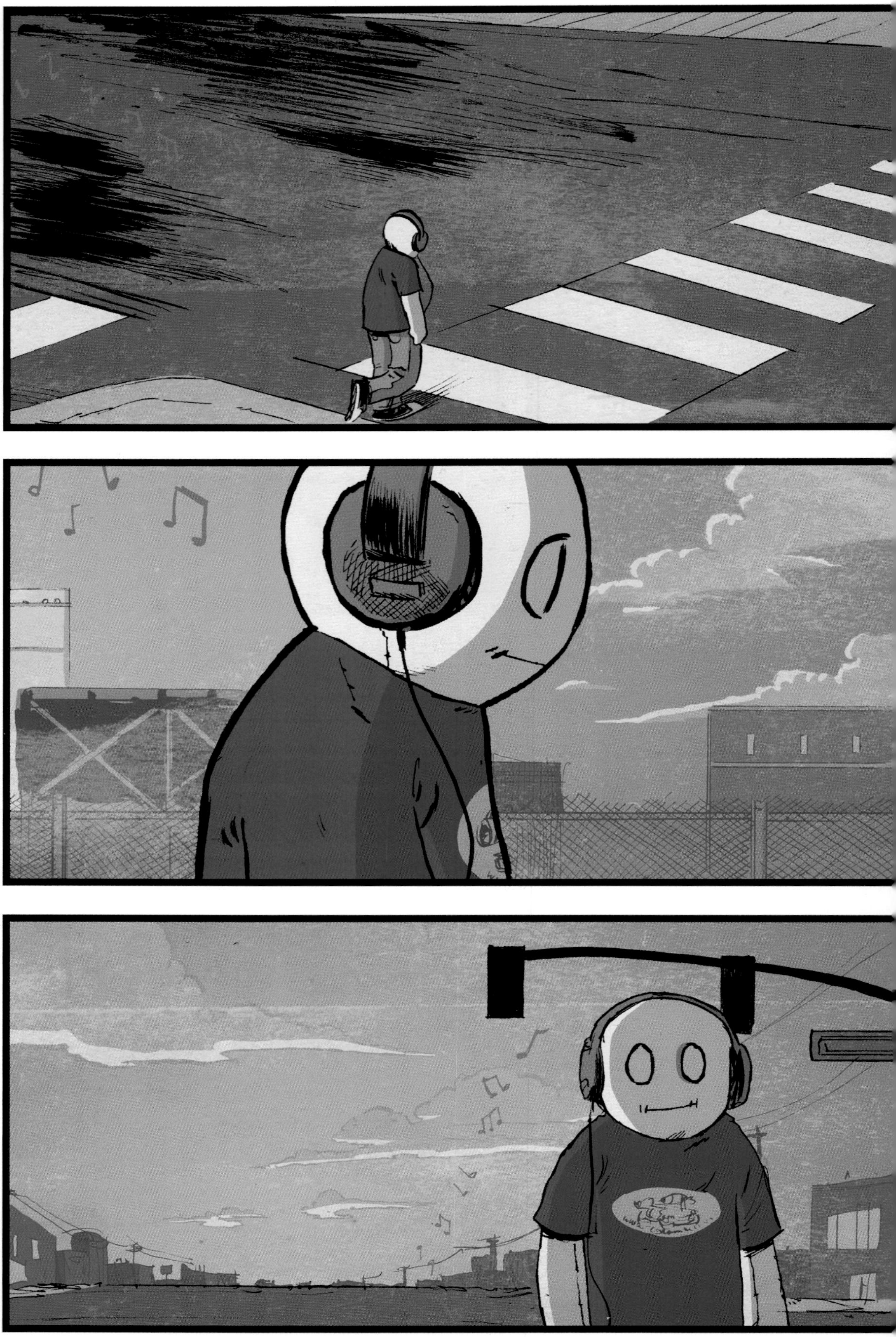

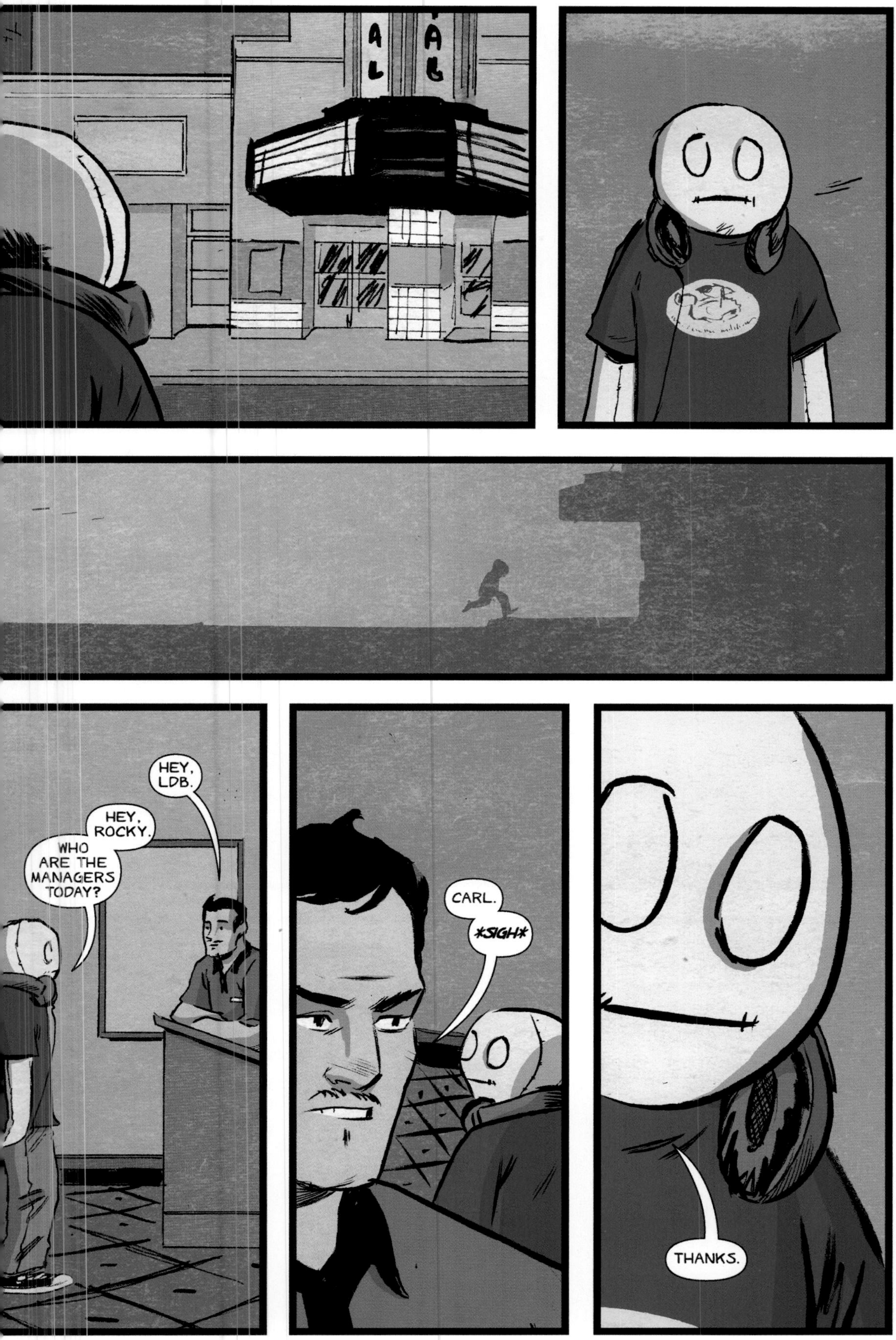
HEY, LDB.
HEY, ROCKY.
WHO ARE THE MANAGERS TODAY?
CARL.
SIGH
THANKS.

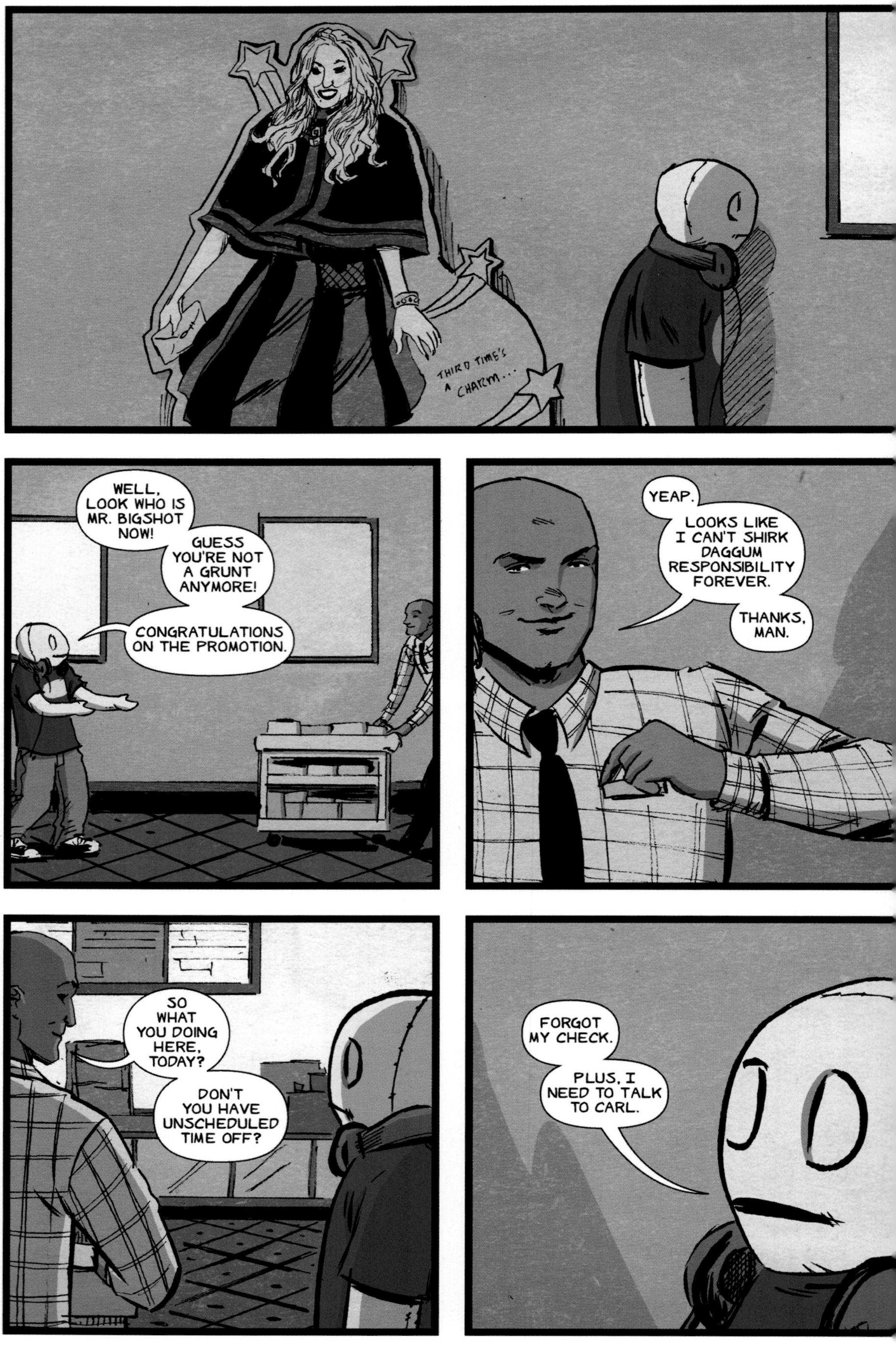
THIRD TIME'S A CHARM...
WELL, LOOK WHO IS MR. BIGSHOT NOW!
GUESS YOU'RE NOT A GRUNT ANYMORE!
CONGRATULATIONS ON THE PROMOTION.
YEAP.
LOOKS LIKE I CAN'T SHIRK DAGGUM RESPONSIBILITY FOREVER.
THANKS, MAN.
SO WHAT YOU DOING HERE, TODAY?
DON'T YOU HAVE UNSCHEDULED TIME OFF?
FORGOT MY CHECK.
PLUS, I NEED TO TALK TO CARL.

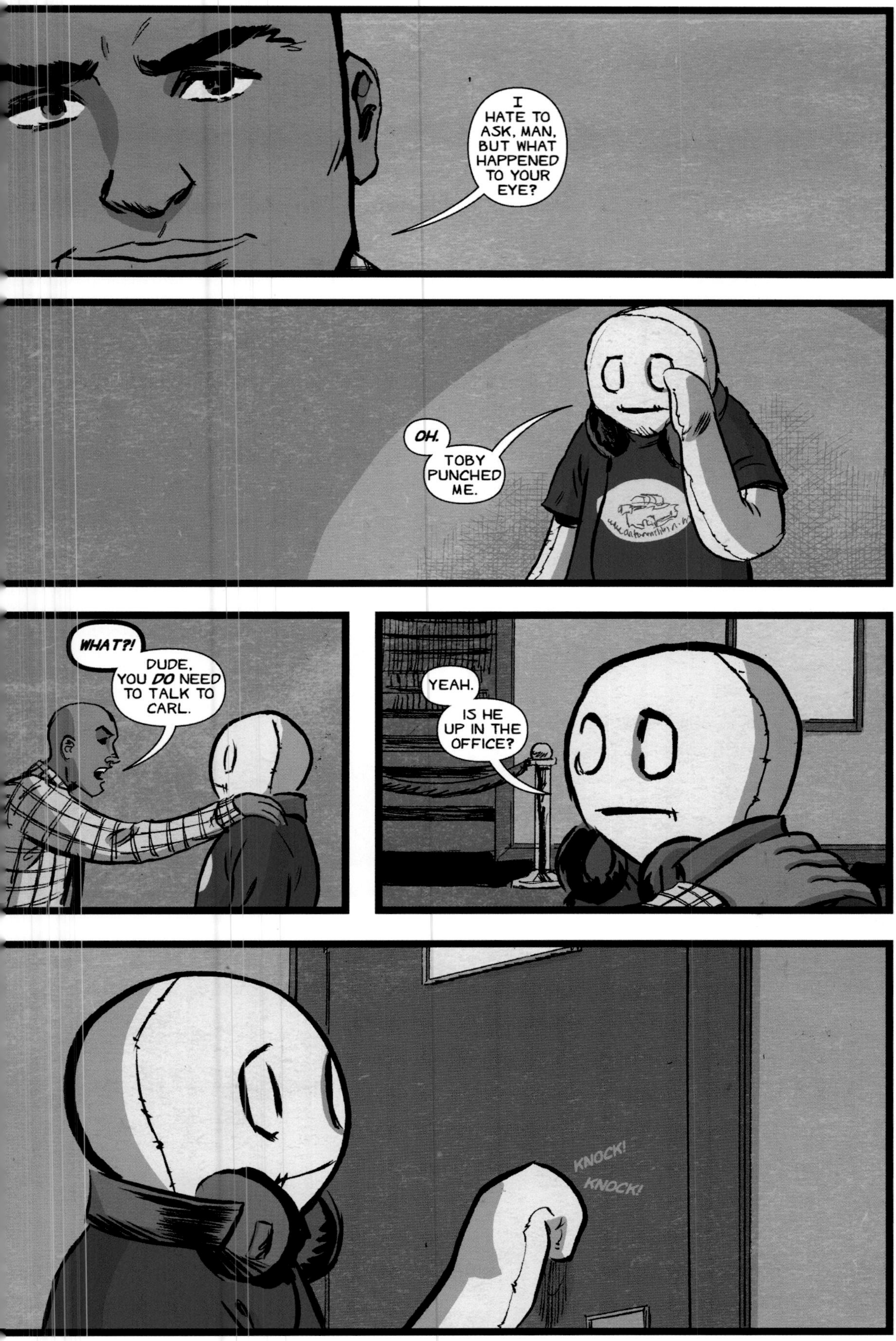
I HATE TO ASK, MAN, BUT WHAT HAPPENED TO YOUR EYE?
OH.
TOBY PUNCHED ME.
WHAT?!
DUDE, YOU DO NEED TO TALK TO CARL.
YEAH.
IS HE UP IN THE OFFICE?
KNOCK!
KNOCK!

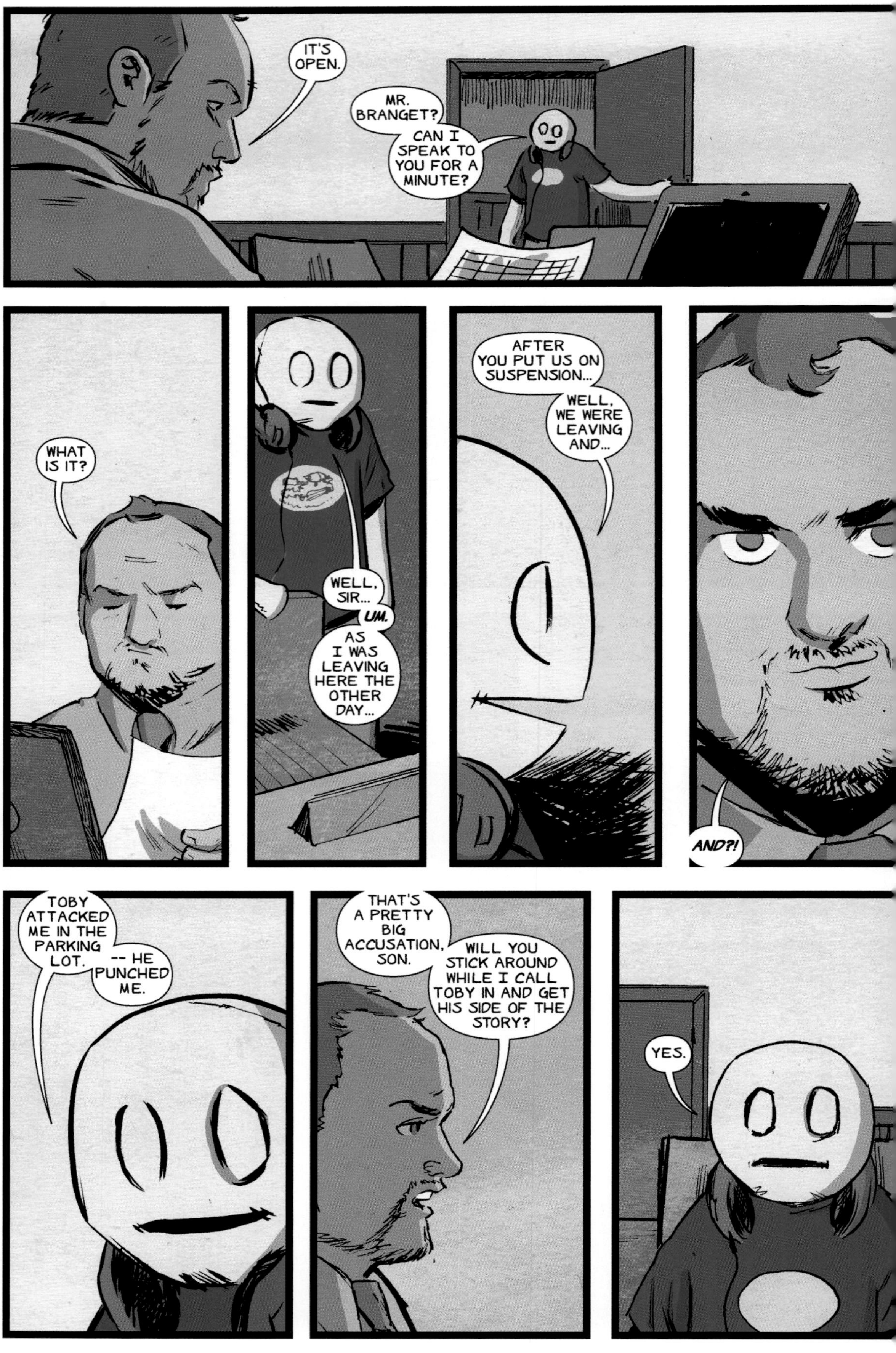
IT'S OPEN.
MR. BRANGET?
CAN I SPEAK TO YOU FOR A MINUTE?
WHAT IS IT?
WELL, SIR...
UM.
AS I WAS LEAVING HERE THE OTHER DAY...
AFTER YOU PUT US ON SUSPENSION...
WELL, WE WERE LEAVING AND...
AND?!
TOBY ATTACKED ME IN THE PARKING LOT.
-- HE PUNCHED ME.
THAT'S A PRETTY BIG ACCUSATION, SON.
WILL YOU STICK AROUND WHILE I CALL TOBY IN AND GET HIS SIDE OF THE STORY?
YES.

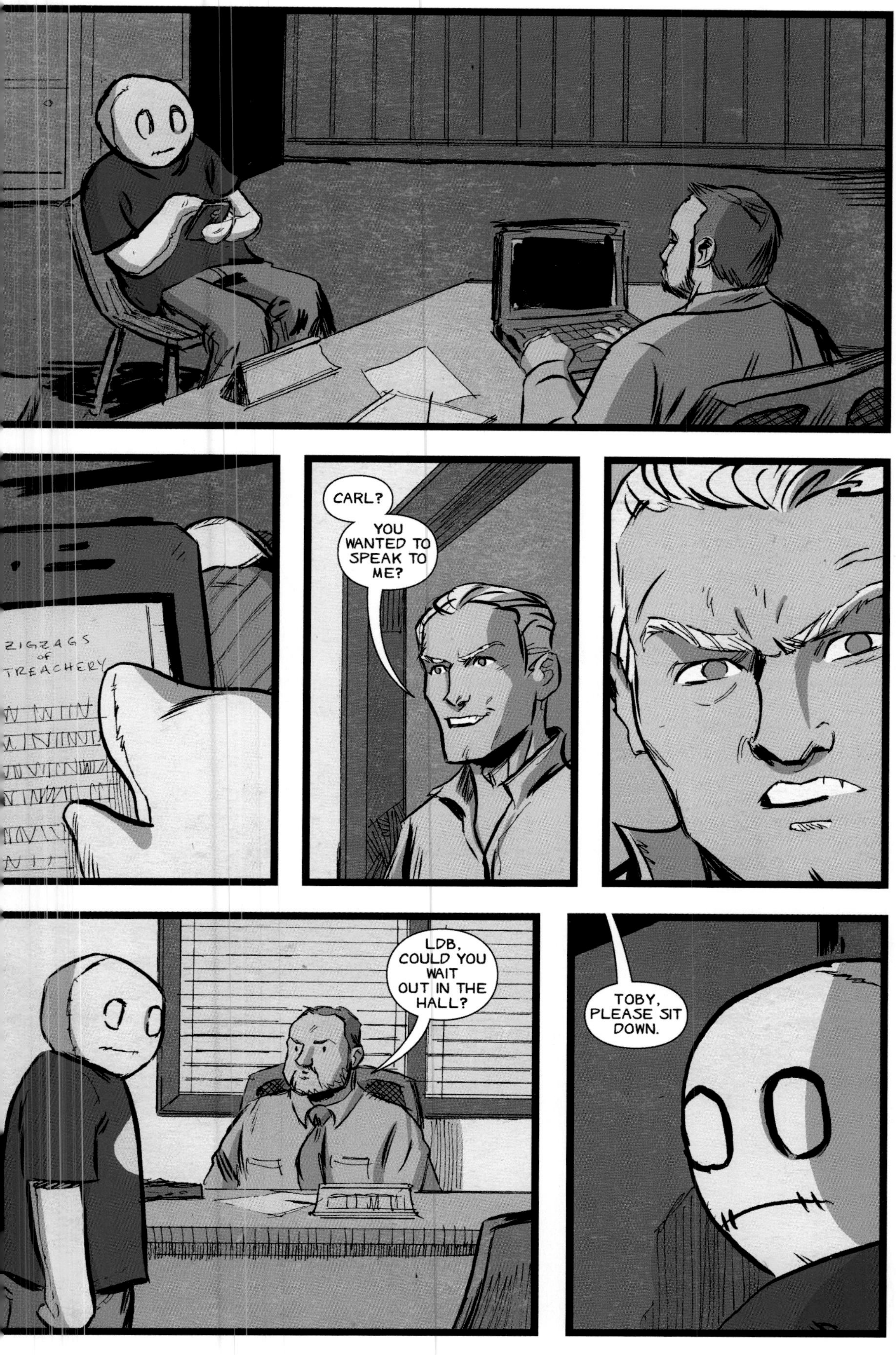
ZIGZAGS of TREACHERY
CARL?
YOU WANTED TO SPEAK TO ME?
LDB, COULD YOU WAIT OUT IN THE HALL?
TOBY, PLEASE SIT DOWN.

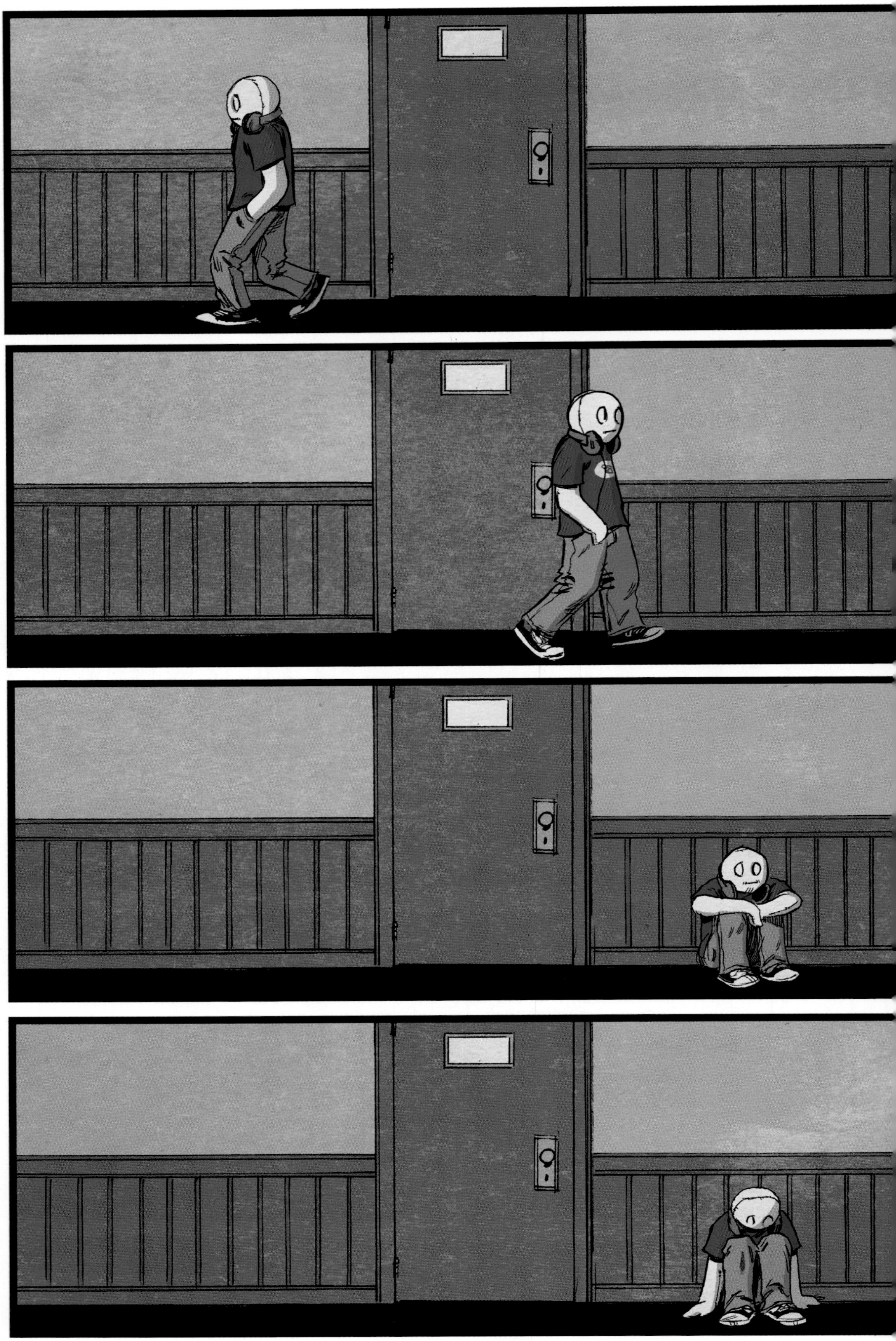

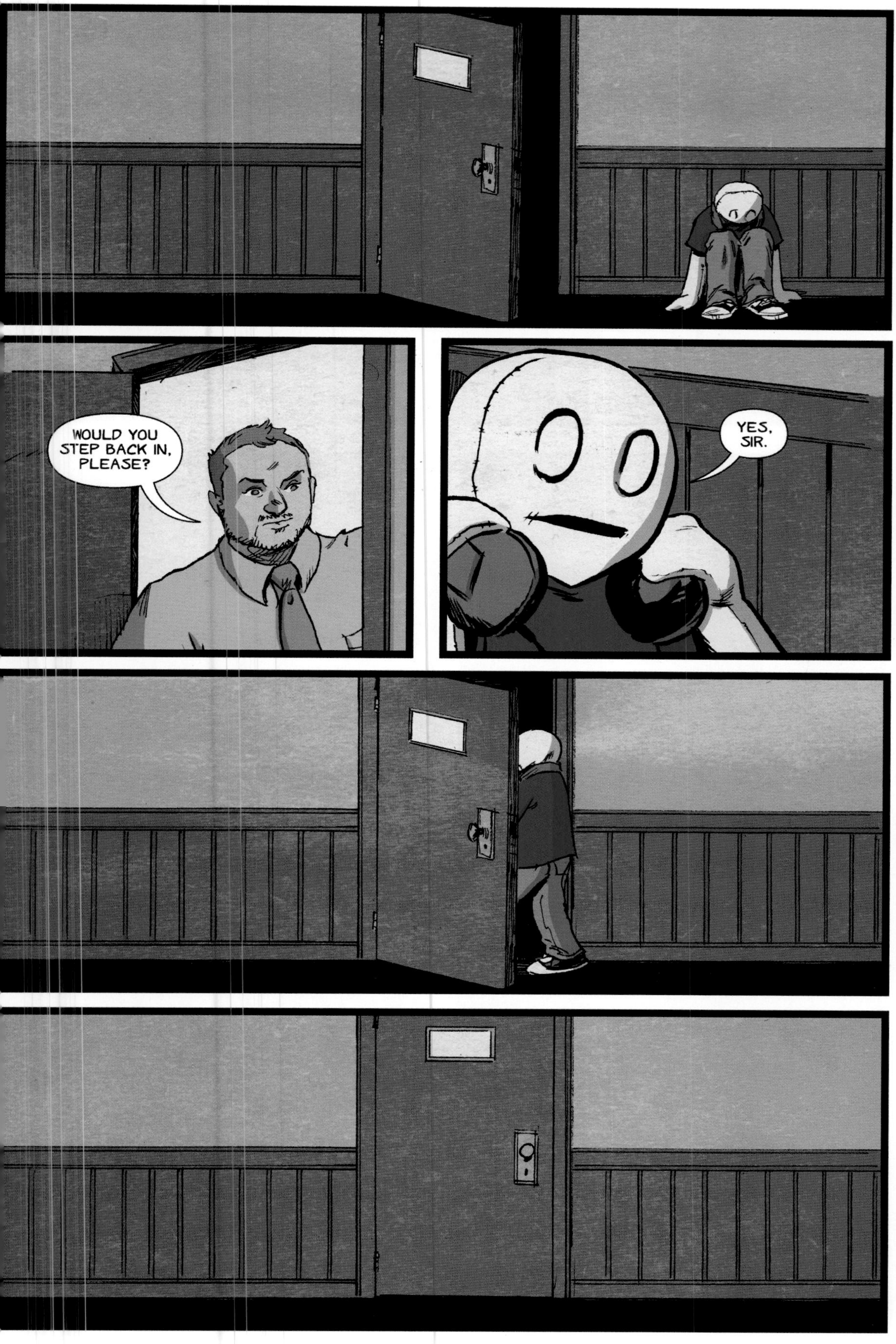
WOULD YOU STEP BACK IN, PLEASE?
YES, SIR.

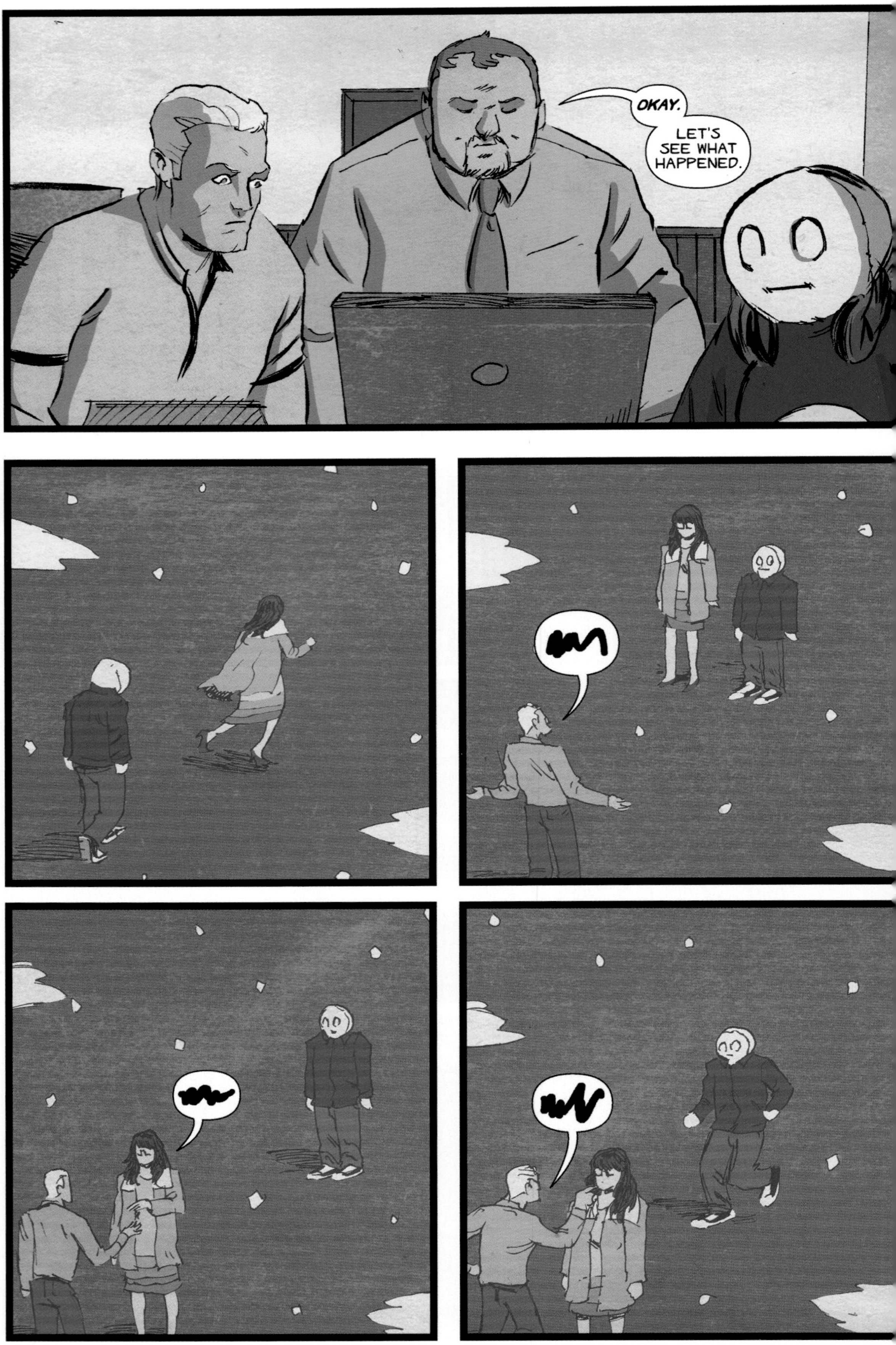
OKAY.
LET'S SEE WHAT HAPPENED.

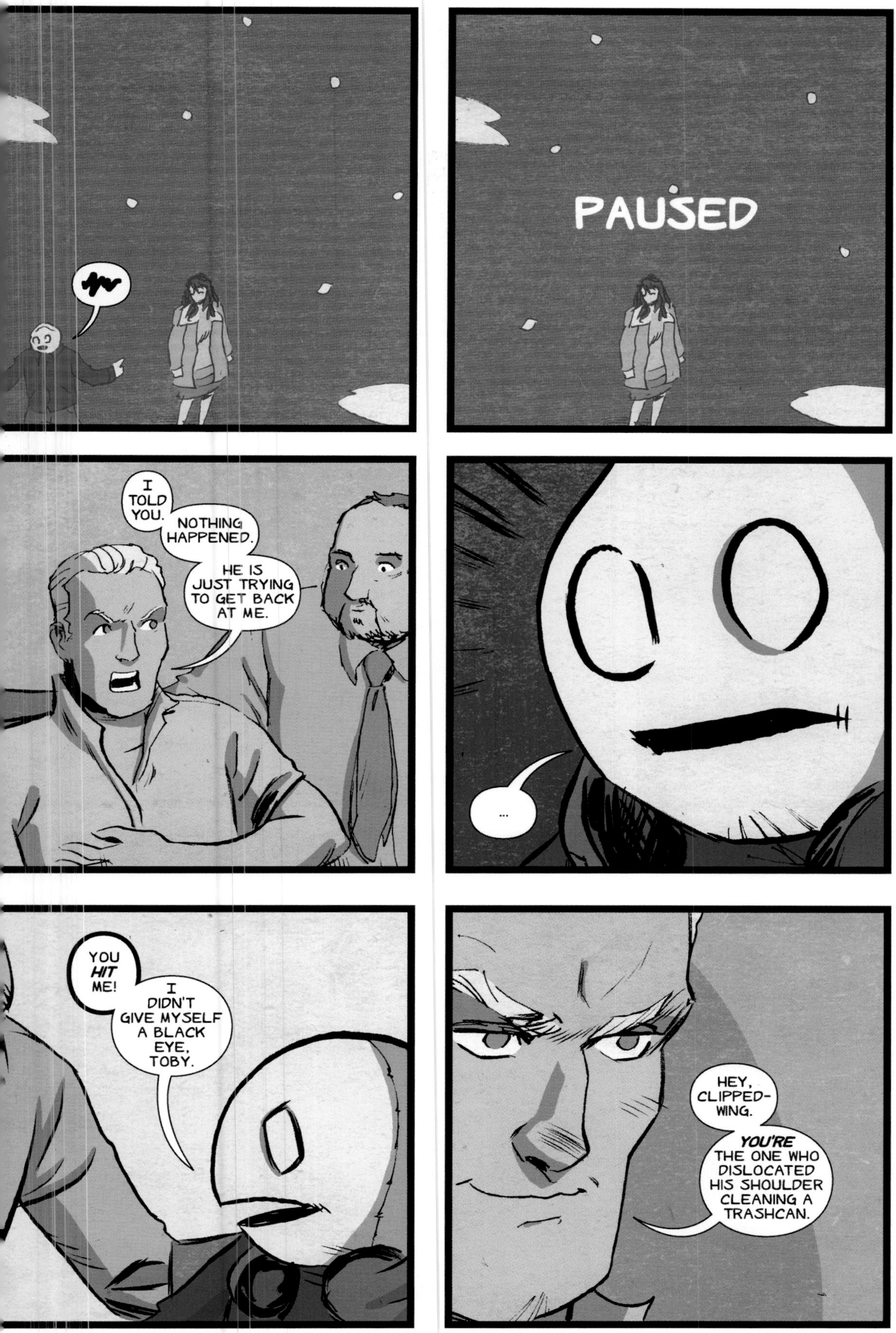
PAUSED
I TOLD YOU.
NOTHING HAPPENED.
HE IS JUST TRYING TO GET BACK AT ME.
...
YOU *HIT* ME!
I DIDN'T GIVE MYSELF A BLACK EYE, TOBY.
HEY, CLIPPED-WING.
YOU'RE THE ONE WHO DISLOCATED HIS SHOULDER CLEANING A TRASHCAN.

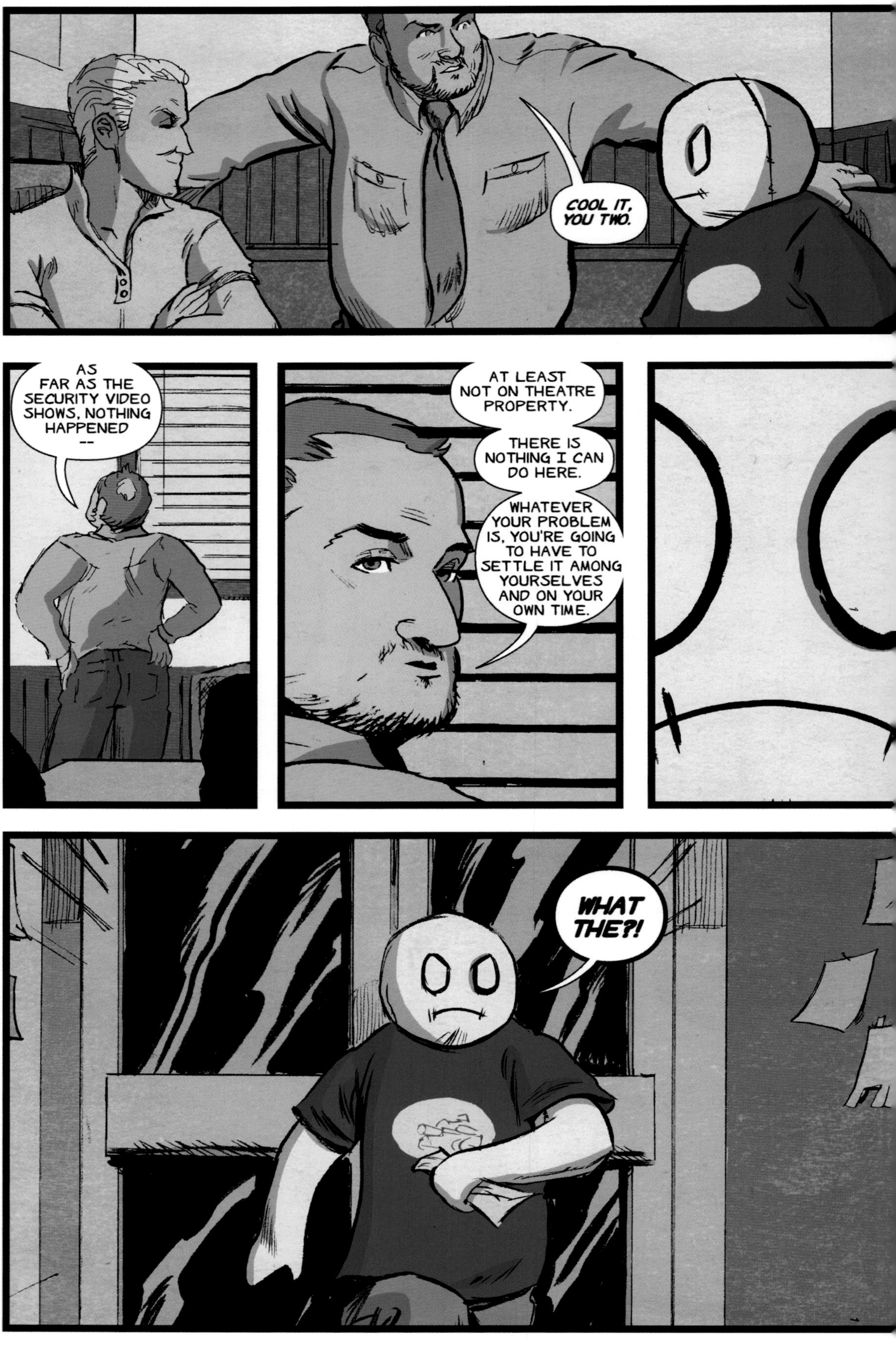
COOL IT, YOU TWO.
AS FAR AS THE SECURITY VIDEO SHOWS, NOTHING HAPPENED --
AT LEAST NOT ON THEATRE PROPERTY.
THERE IS NOTHING I CAN DO HERE.
WHATEVER YOUR PROBLEM IS, YOU'RE GOING TO HAVE TO SETTLE IT AMONG YOURSELVES AND ON YOUR OWN TIME.
WHAT THE?!

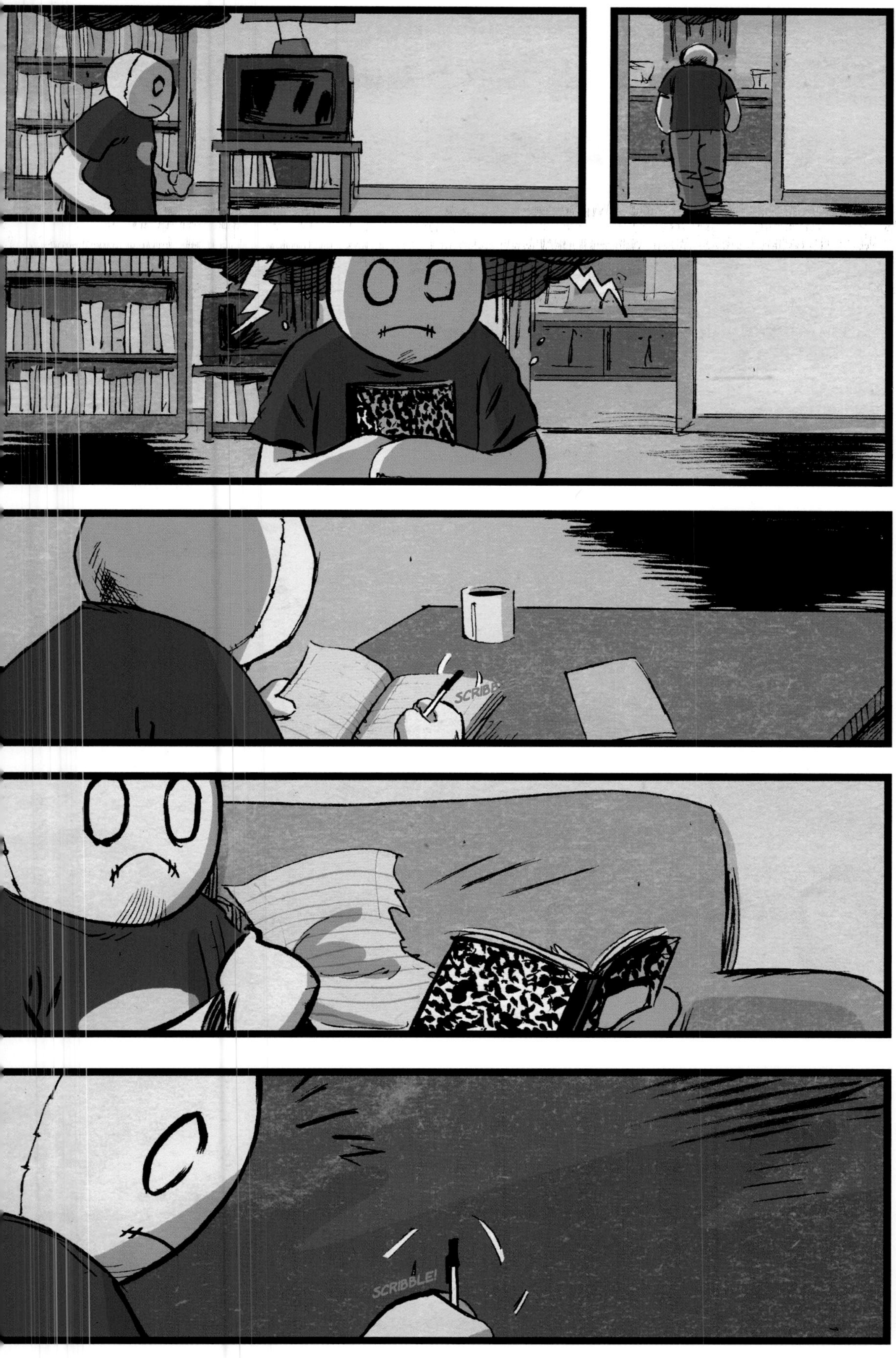
SCRIBB
SCRIBBLE!

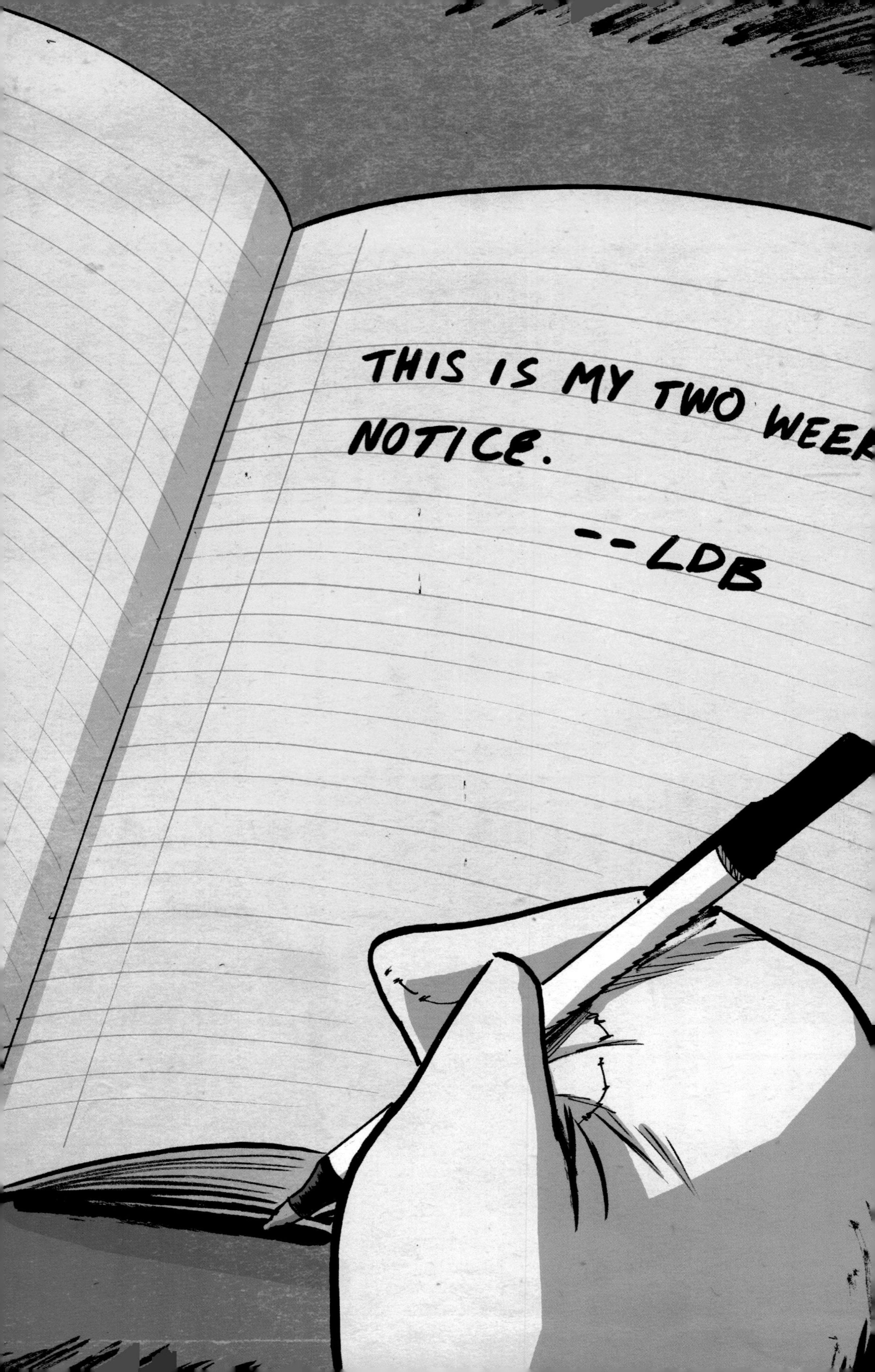
THIS IS MY TWO WEEK
NOTICE.
--LDB

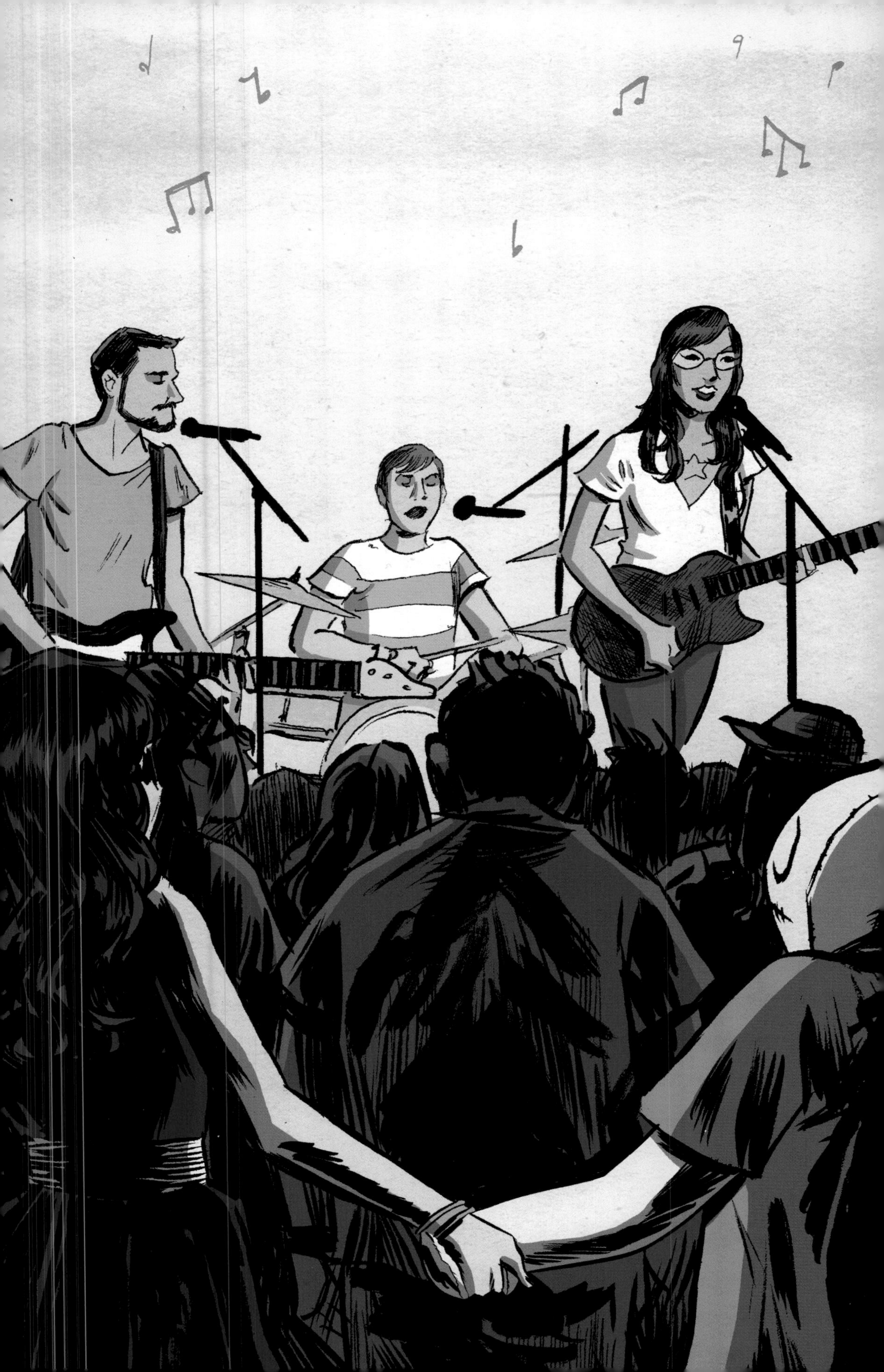

CHAPTER NINETEEN:
"BRILLIANT DANCER"

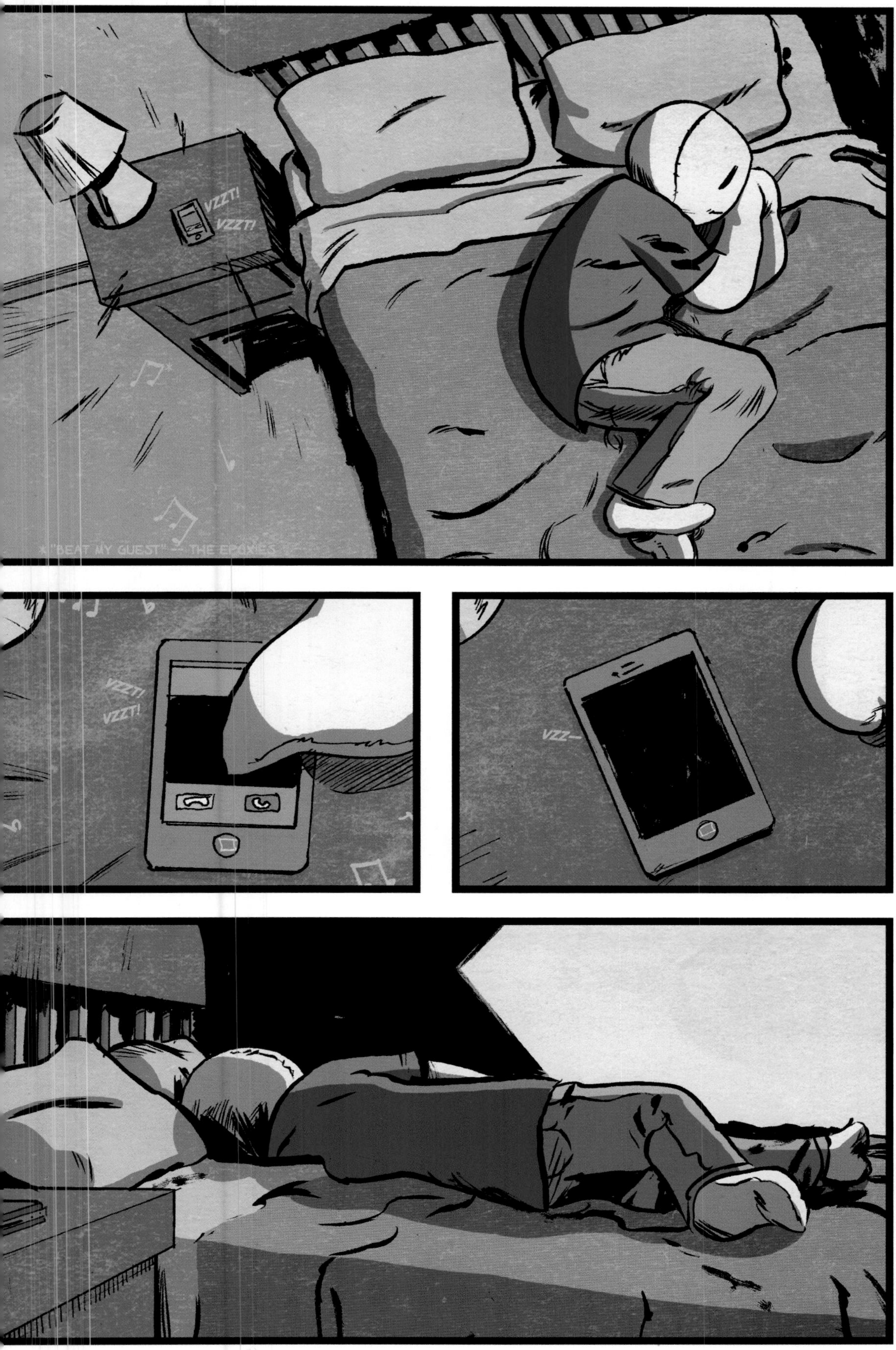
VZZT!
VZZT!
* "BEAT MY GUEST" -- THE EPOXIES
VZZT!
VZZT!
VZZ—

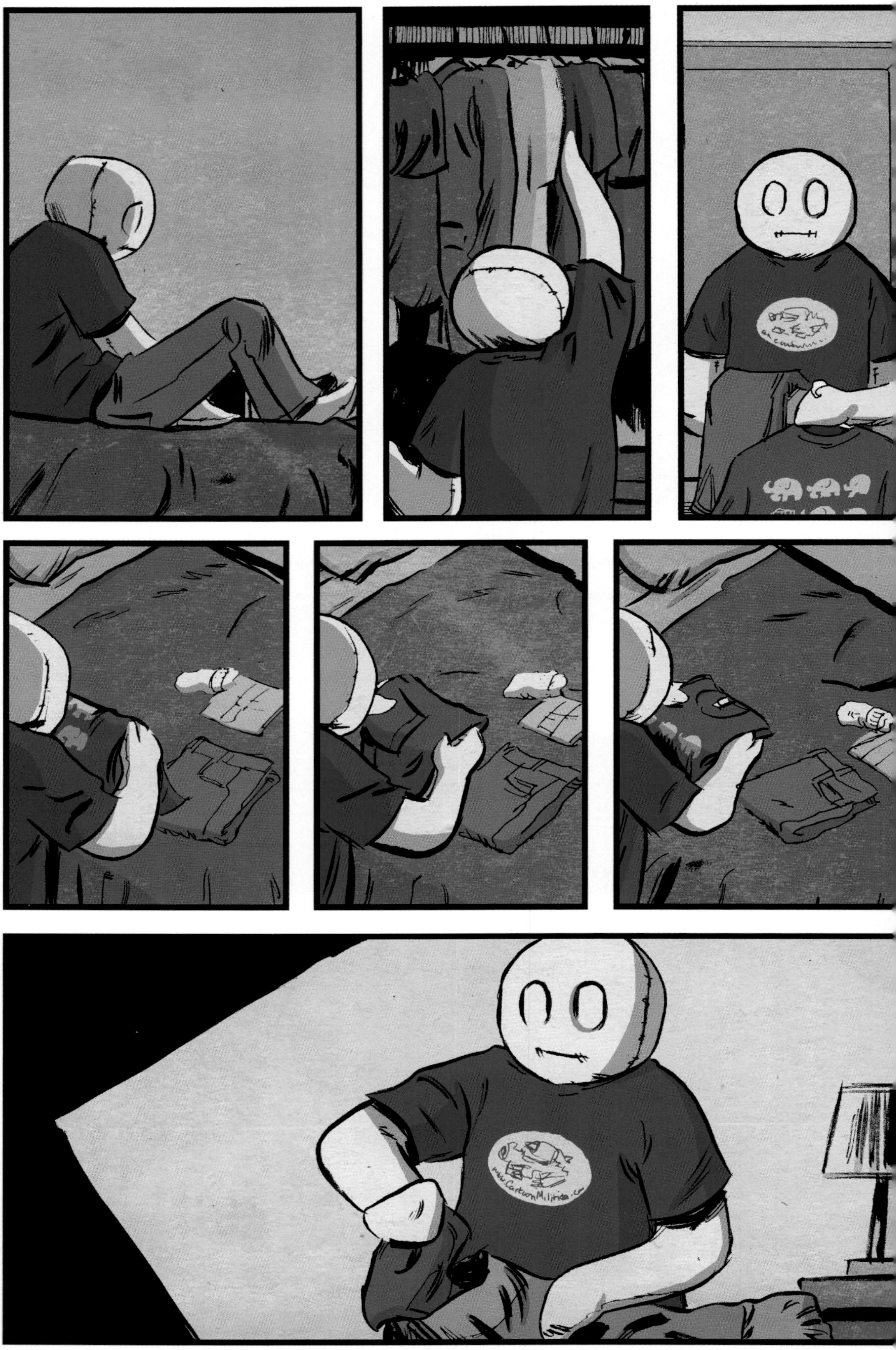
www.CartoonMilitia.c

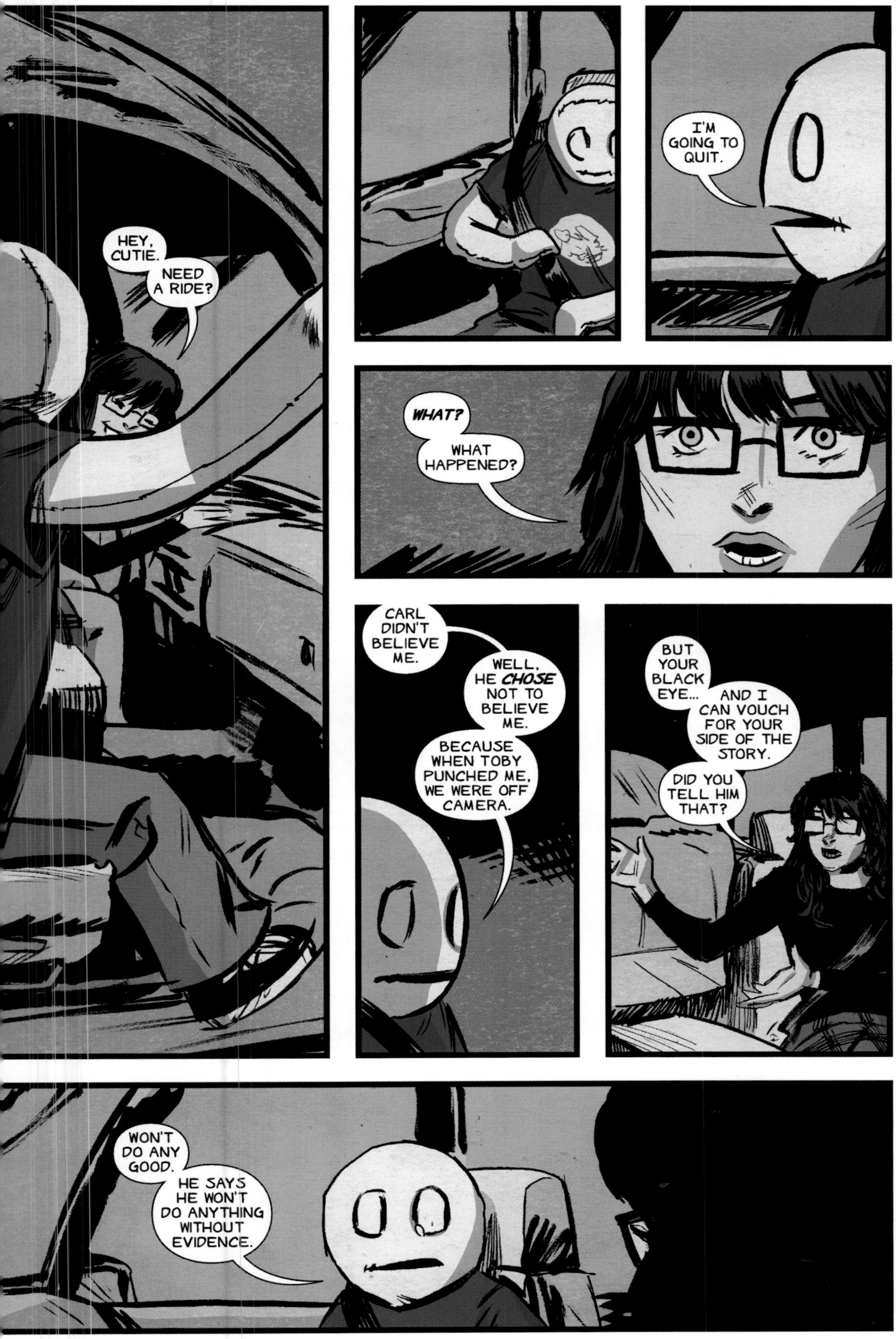
HEY, CUTIE.
NEED A RIDE?
I'M GOING TO QUIT.
WHAT?
WHAT HAPPENED?
CARL DIDN'T BELIEVE ME.
WELL, HE CHOSE NOT TO BELIEVE ME.
BECAUSE WHEN TOBY PUNCHED ME, WE WERE OFF CAMERA.
BUT YOUR BLACK EYE...
AND I CAN VOUCH FOR YOUR SIDE OF THE STORY.
DID YOU TELL HIM THAT?
WON'T DO ANY GOOD.
HE SAYS HE WON'T DO ANYTHING WITHOUT EVIDENCE.

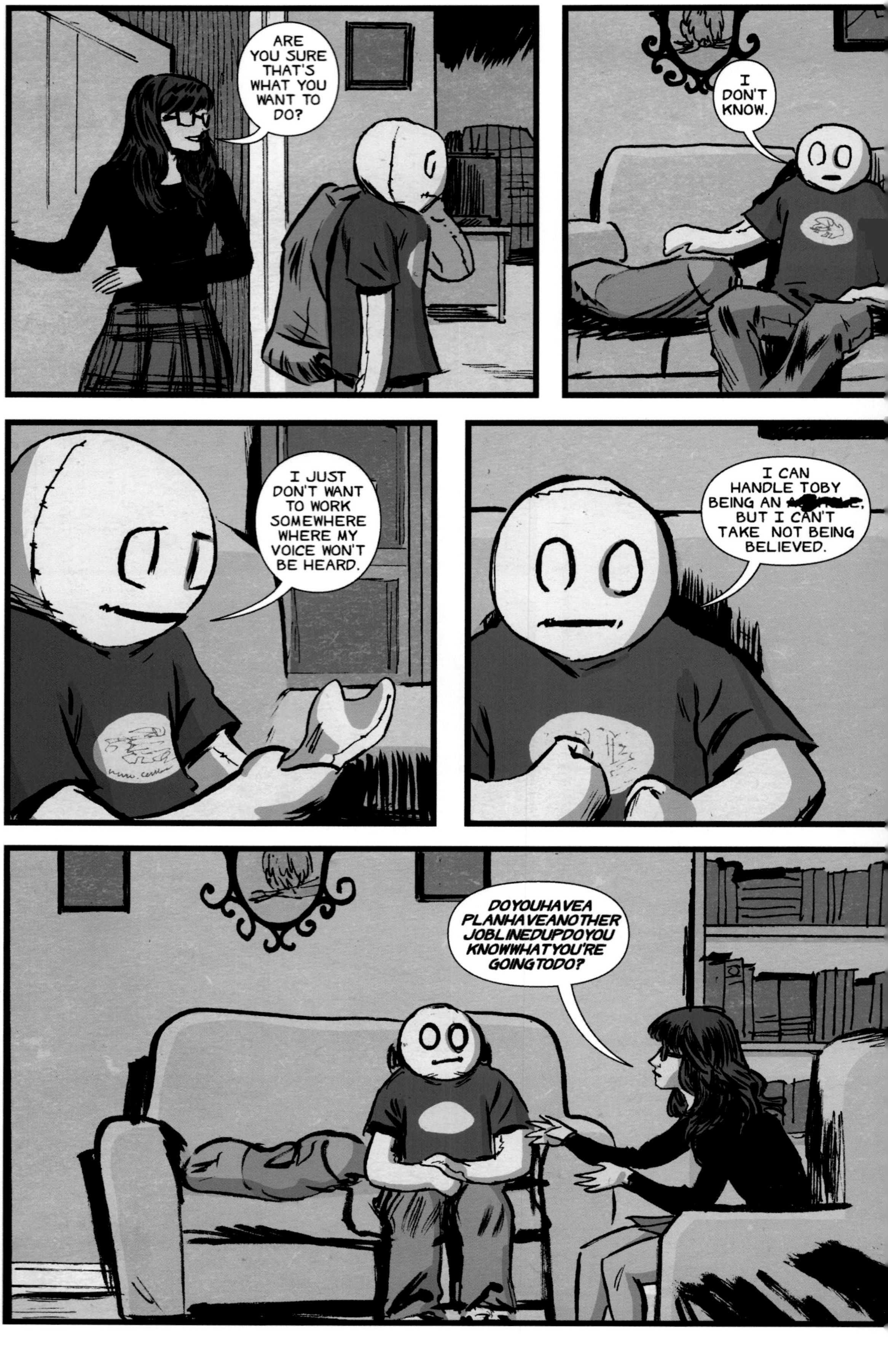
ARE YOU SURE THAT'S WHAT YOU WANT TO DO?
I DON'T KNOW.
I JUST DON'T WANT TO WORK SOMEWHERE WHERE MY VOICE WON'T BE HEARD.
I CAN HANDLE TOBY BEING AN [redacted], BUT I CAN'T TAKE NOT BEING BELIEVED.
DOYOUHAVEA PLANHAVEANOTHER JOBLINEDUPDOYOU KNOWWHATYOU'RE GOINGTODO?

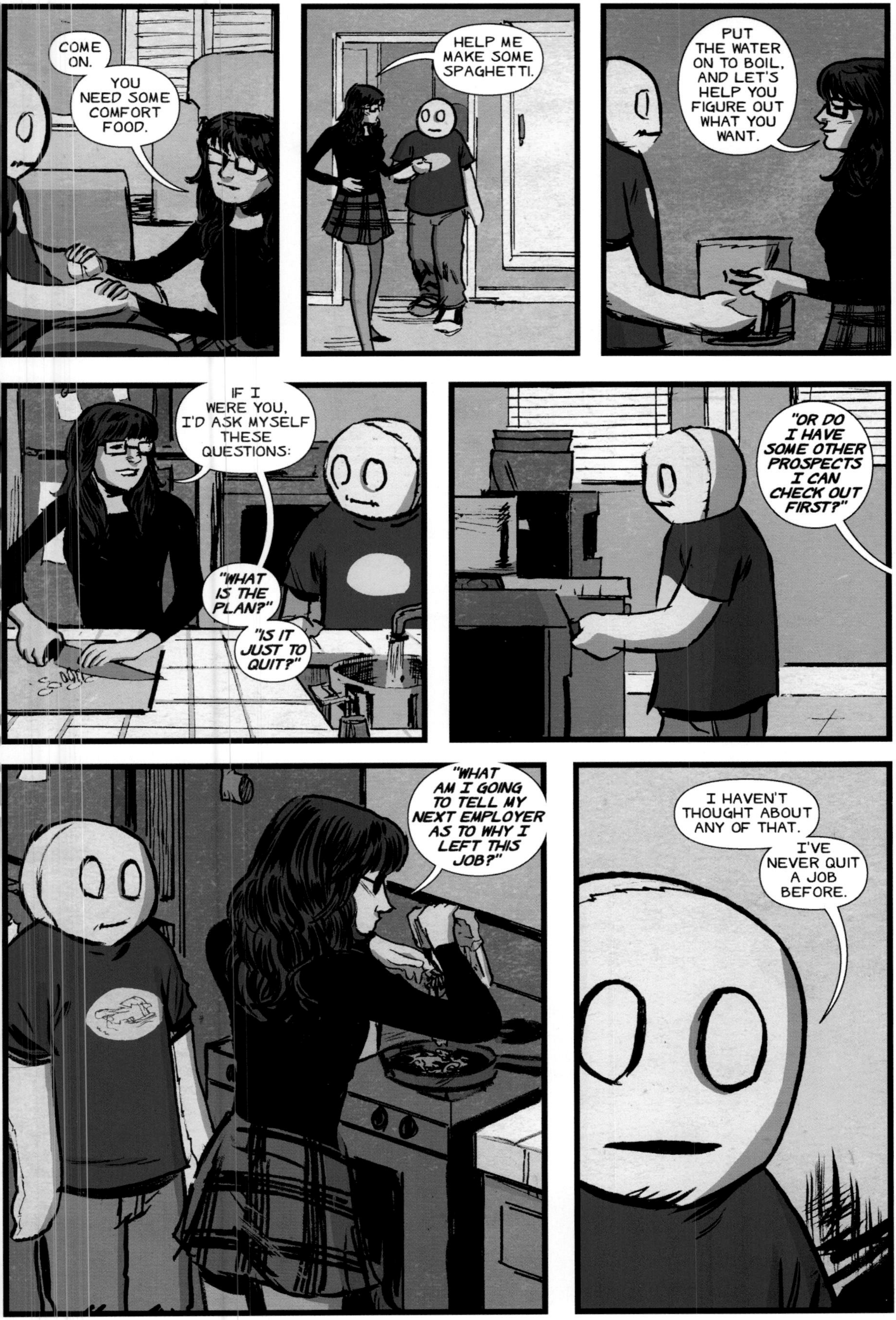
COME ON.
YOU NEED SOME COMFORT FOOD.
HELP ME MAKE SOME SPAGHETTI.
PUT THE WATER ON TO BOIL, AND LET'S HELP YOU FIGURE OUT WHAT YOU WANT.
IF I WERE YOU, I'D ASK MYSELF THESE QUESTIONS:
"WHAT IS THE PLAN?"
"IS IT JUST TO QUIT?"
"OR DO I HAVE SOME OTHER PROSPECTS I CAN CHECK OUT FIRST?"
"WHAT AM I GOING TO TELL MY NEXT EMPLOYER AS TO WHY I LEFT THIS JOB?"
I HAVEN'T THOUGHT ABOUT ANY OF THAT.
I'VE NEVER QUIT A JOB BEFORE.

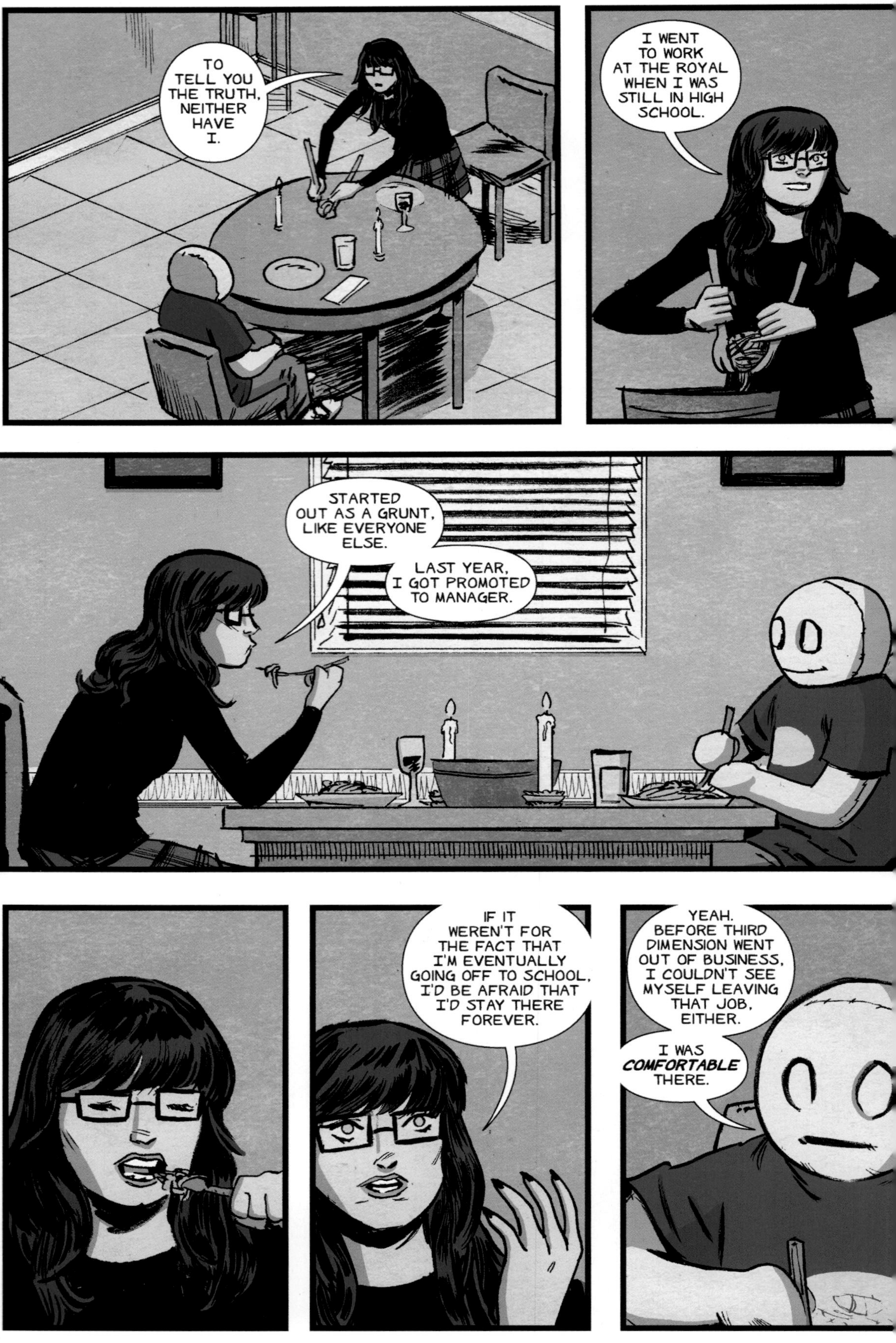
TO TELL YOU THE TRUTH, NEITHER HAVE I.
I WENT TO WORK AT THE ROYAL WHEN I WAS STILL IN HIGH SCHOOL.
STARTED OUT AS A GRUNT, LIKE EVERYONE ELSE.
LAST YEAR, I GOT PROMOTED TO MANAGER.
IF IT WEREN'T FOR THE FACT THAT I'M EVENTUALLY GOING OFF TO SCHOOL, I'D BE AFRAID THAT I'D STAY THERE FOREVER.
YEAH. BEFORE THIRD DIMENSION WENT OUT OF BUSINESS, I COULDN'T SEE MYSELF LEAVING THAT JOB, EITHER.
I WAS *COMFORTABLE* THERE.

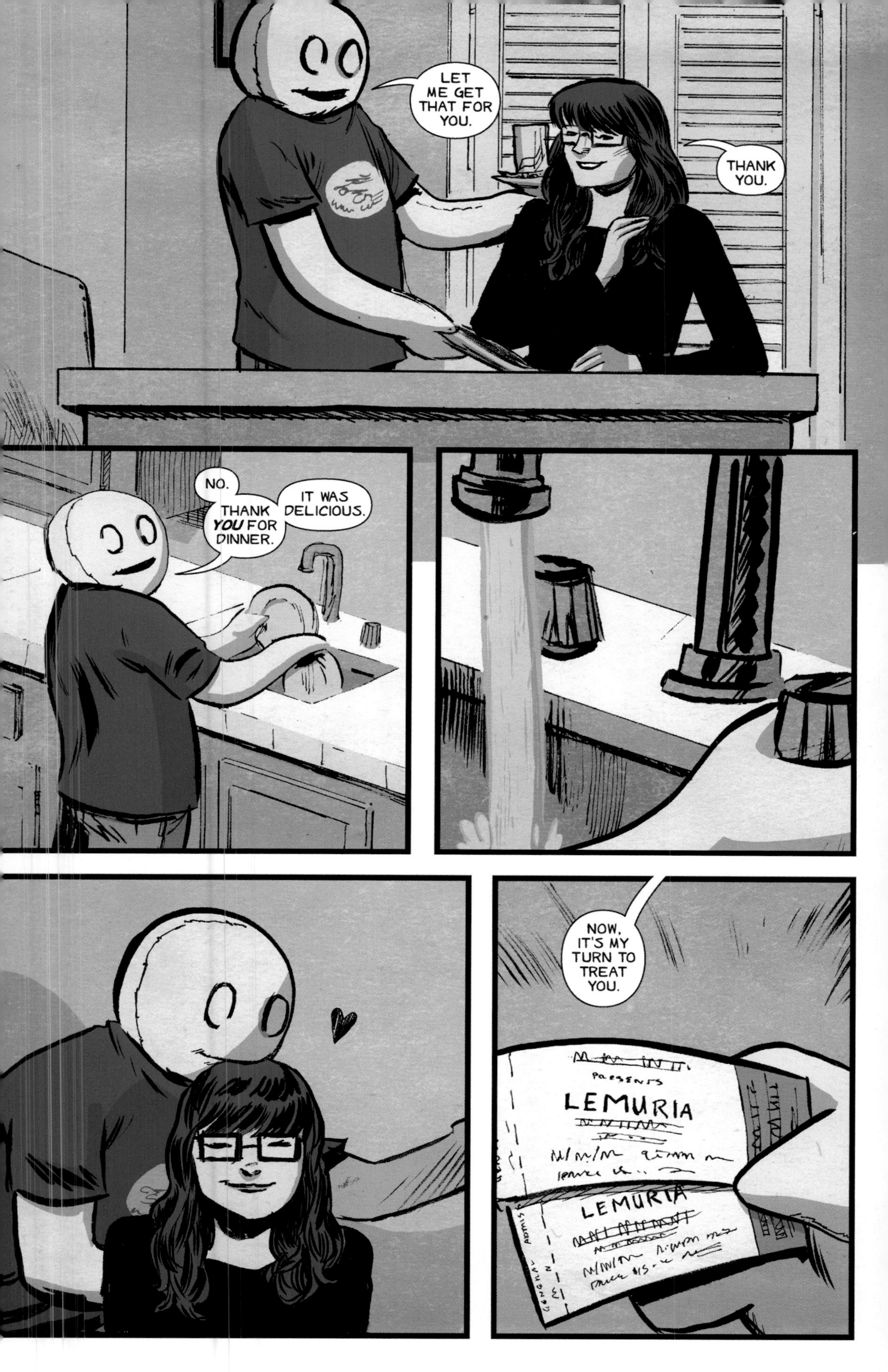
LET ME GET THAT FOR YOU.
THANK YOU.
NO. THANK *YOU* FOR DINNER.
IT WAS DELICIOUS.
NOW, IT'S MY TURN TO TREAT YOU.
PRESENTS
LEMURIA
LEMURIA

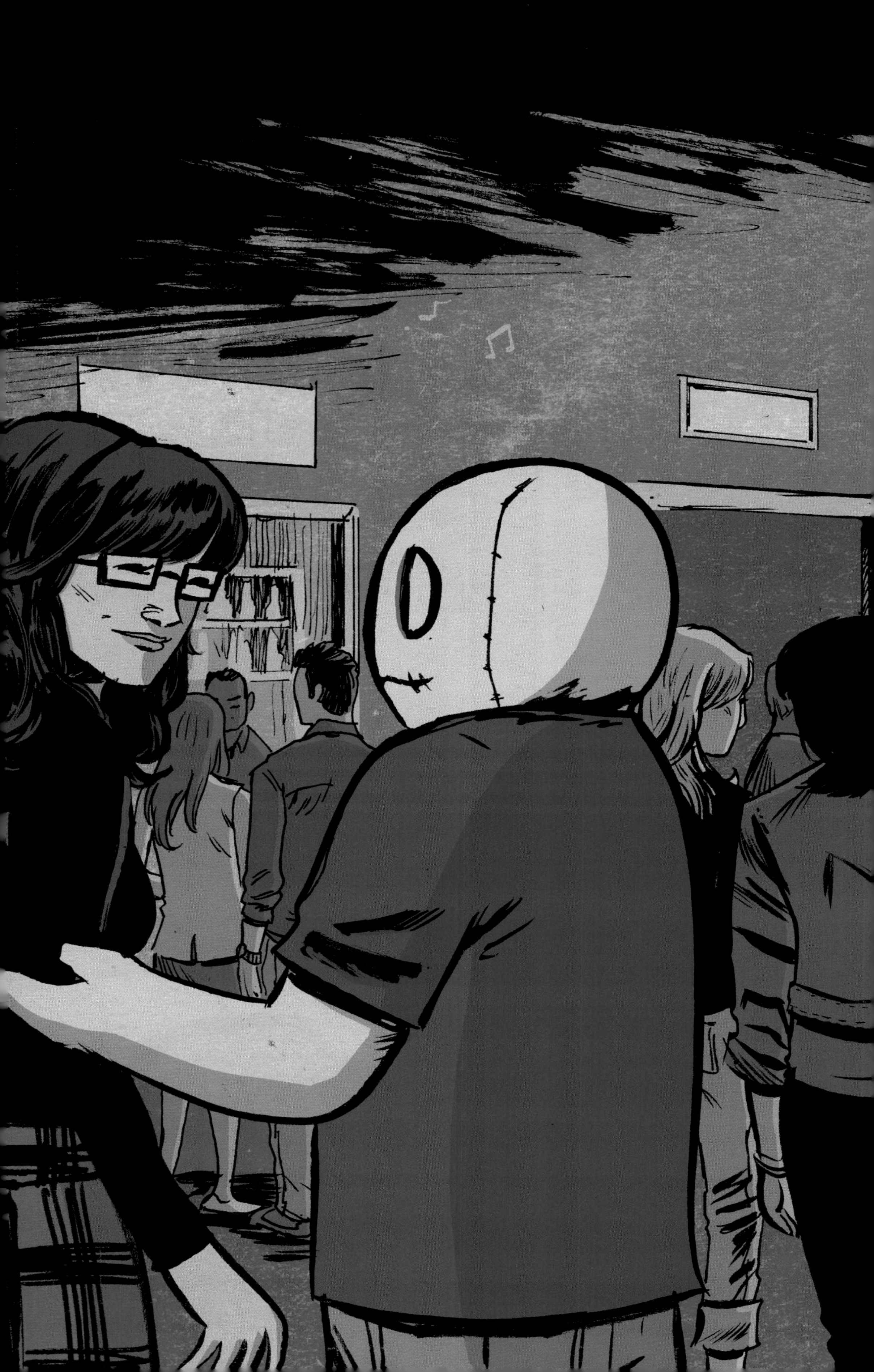

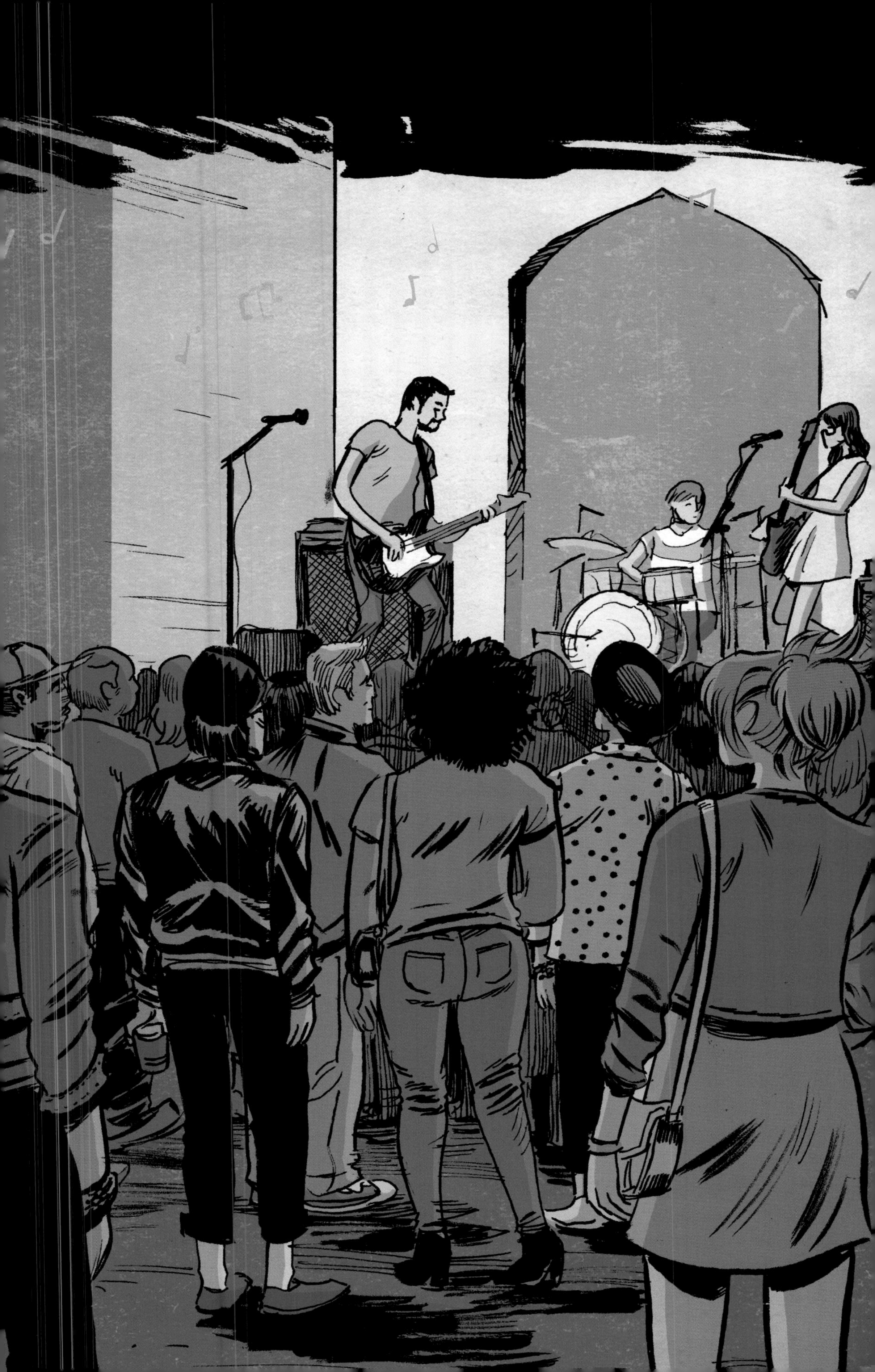

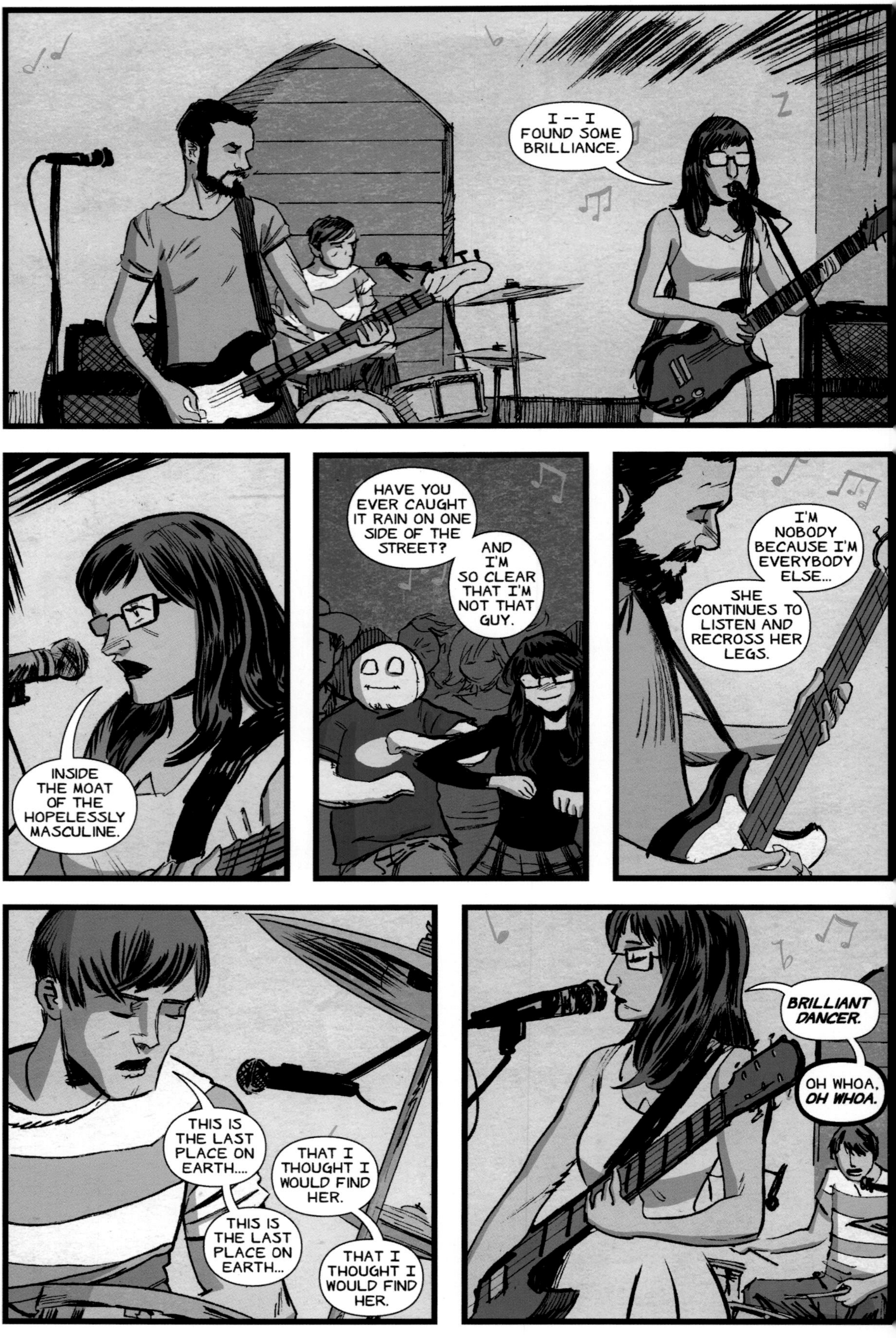
I -- I FOUND SOME BRILLIANCE.
INSIDE THE MOAT OF THE HOPELESSLY MASCULINE.
HAVE YOU EVER CAUGHT IT RAIN ON ONE SIDE OF THE STREET?
AND I'M SO CLEAR THAT I'M NOT THAT GUY.
I'M NOBODY BECAUSE I'M EVERYBODY ELSE...
SHE CONTINUES TO LISTEN AND RECROSS HER LEGS.
THIS IS THE LAST PLACE ON EARTH....
THIS IS THE LAST PLACE ON EARTH...
THAT I THOUGHT I WOULD FIND HER.
THAT I THOUGHT I WOULD FIND HER.
BRILLIANT DANCER.
OH WHOA, OH WHOA.

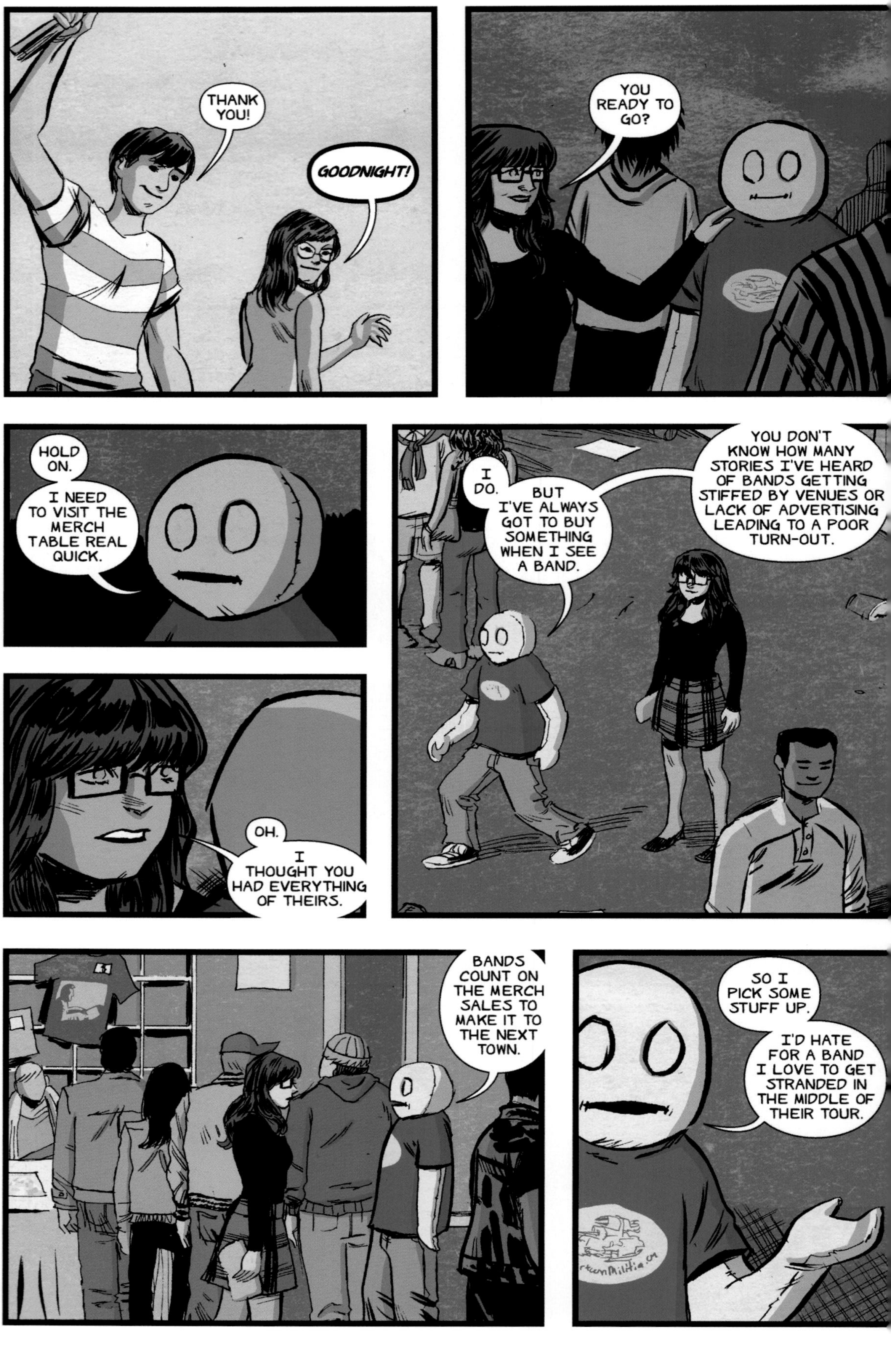
THANK YOU!
GOODNIGHT!
YOU READY TO GO?
HOLD ON.
I NEED TO VISIT THE MERCH TABLE REAL QUICK.
OH.
I THOUGHT YOU HAD EVERYTHING OF THEIRS.
I DO.
BUT I'VE ALWAYS GOT TO BUY SOMETHING WHEN I SEE A BAND.
YOU DON'T KNOW HOW MANY STORIES I'VE HEARD OF BANDS GETTING STIFFED BY VENUES OR LACK OF ADVERTISING LEADING TO A POOR TURN-OUT.
BANDS COUNT ON THE MERCH SALES TO MAKE IT TO THE NEXT TOWN.
SO I PICK SOME STUFF UP.
I'D HATE FOR A BAND I LOVE TO GET STRANDED IN THE MIDDLE OF THEIR TOUR.

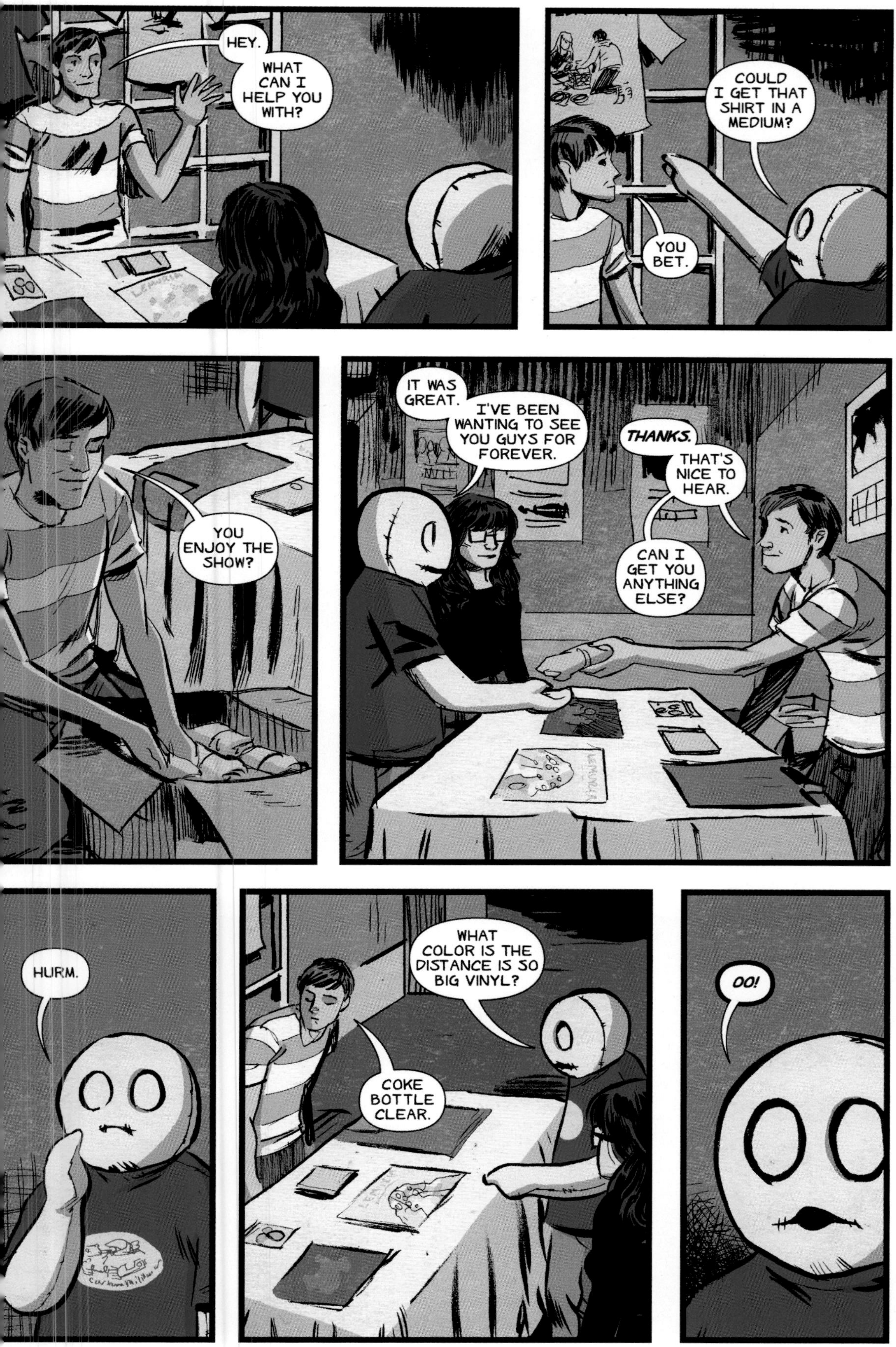
HEY.
WHAT CAN I HELP YOU WITH?
COULD I GET THAT SHIRT IN A MEDIUM?
YOU BET.
YOU ENJOY THE SHOW?
IT WAS GREAT.
I'VE BEEN WANTING TO SEE YOU GUYS FOR FOREVER.
THANKS.
THAT'S NICE TO HEAR.
CAN I GET YOU ANYTHING ELSE?
HURM.
WHAT COLOR IS THE DISTANCE IS SO BIG VINYL?
COKE BOTTLE CLEAR.
OO!

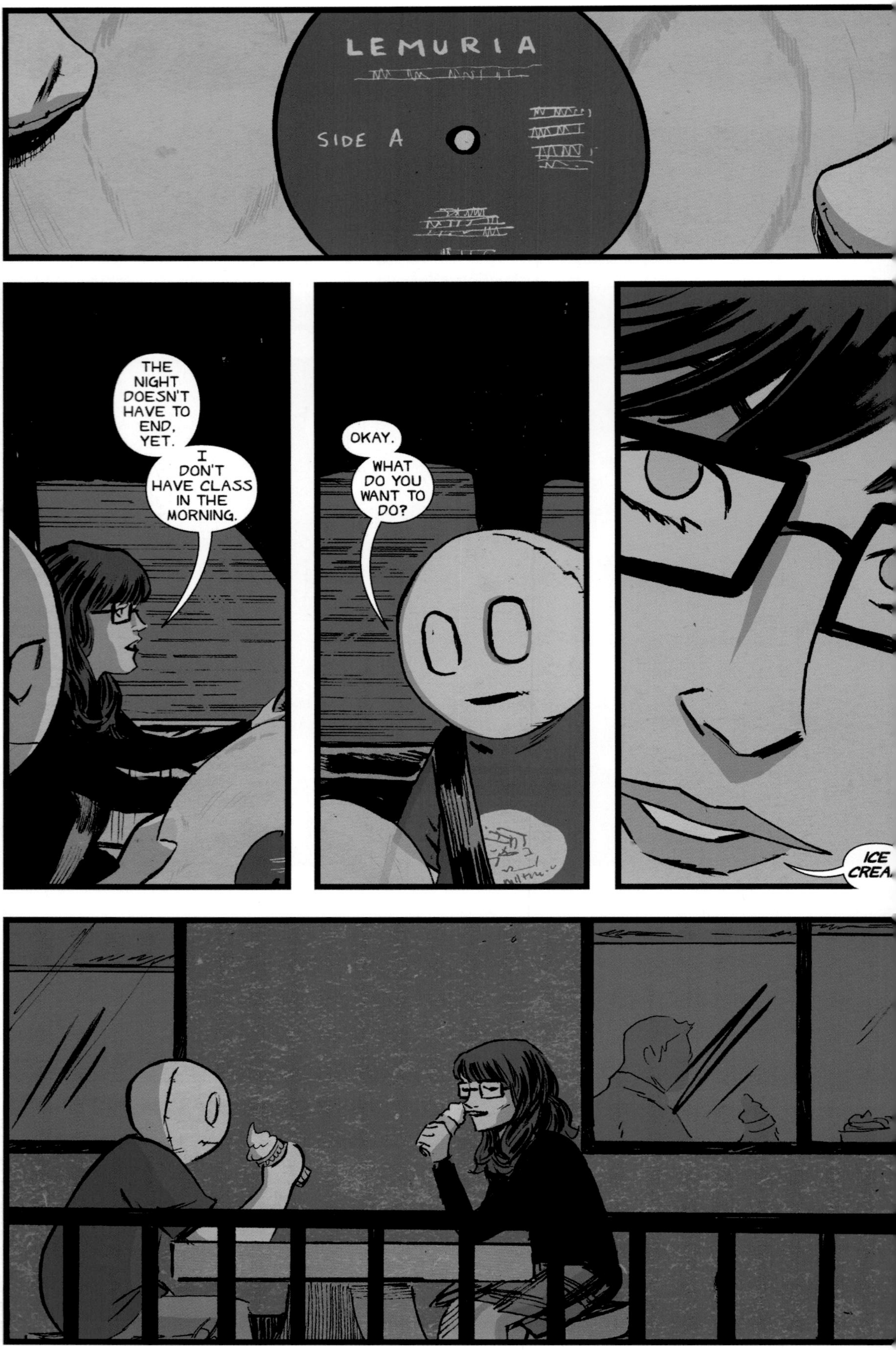
LEMURIA
SIDE A
THE NIGHT DOESN'T HAVE TO END, YET.
I DON'T HAVE CLASS IN THE MORNING.
OKAY.
WHAT DO YOU WANT TO DO?
ICE CREA

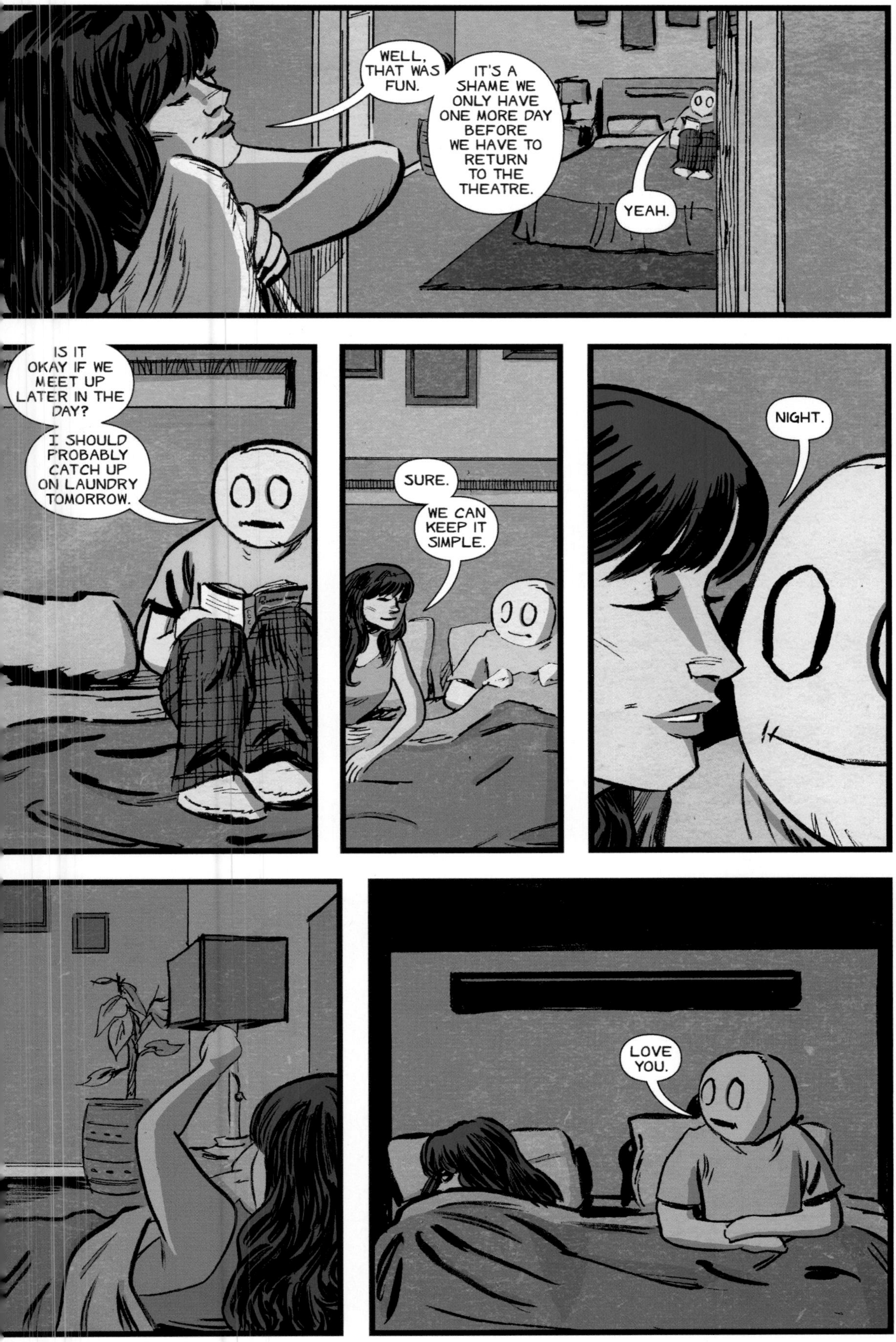

WELL, THAT WAS FUN.
IT'S A SHAME WE ONLY HAVE ONE MORE DAY BEFORE WE HAVE TO RETURN TO THE THEATRE.
YEAH.
IS IT OKAY IF WE MEET UP LATER IN THE DAY?
I SHOULD PROBABLY CATCH UP ON LAUNDRY TOMORROW.
SURE.
WE CAN KEEP IT SIMPLE.
NIGHT.
LOVE YOU.

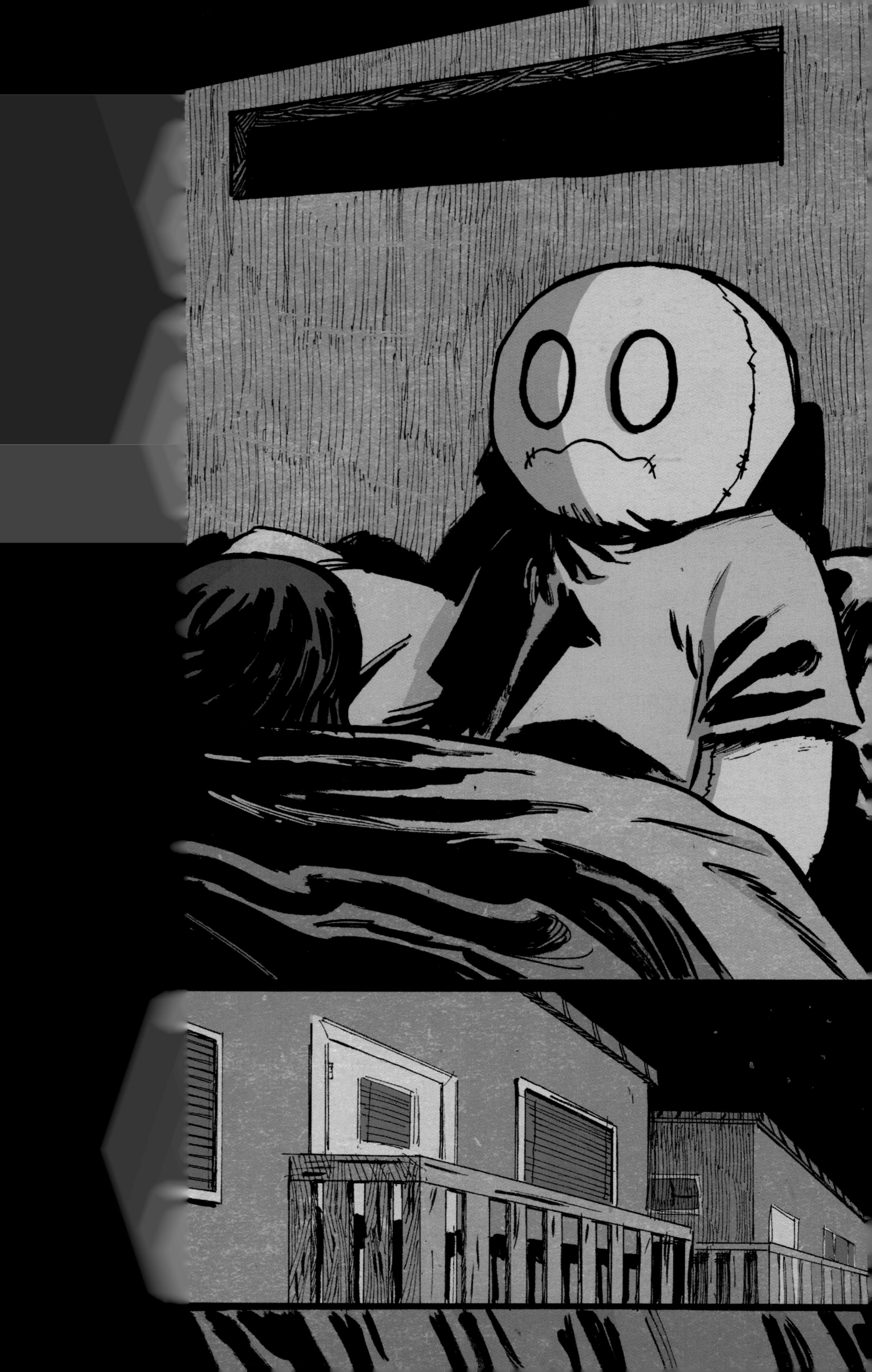

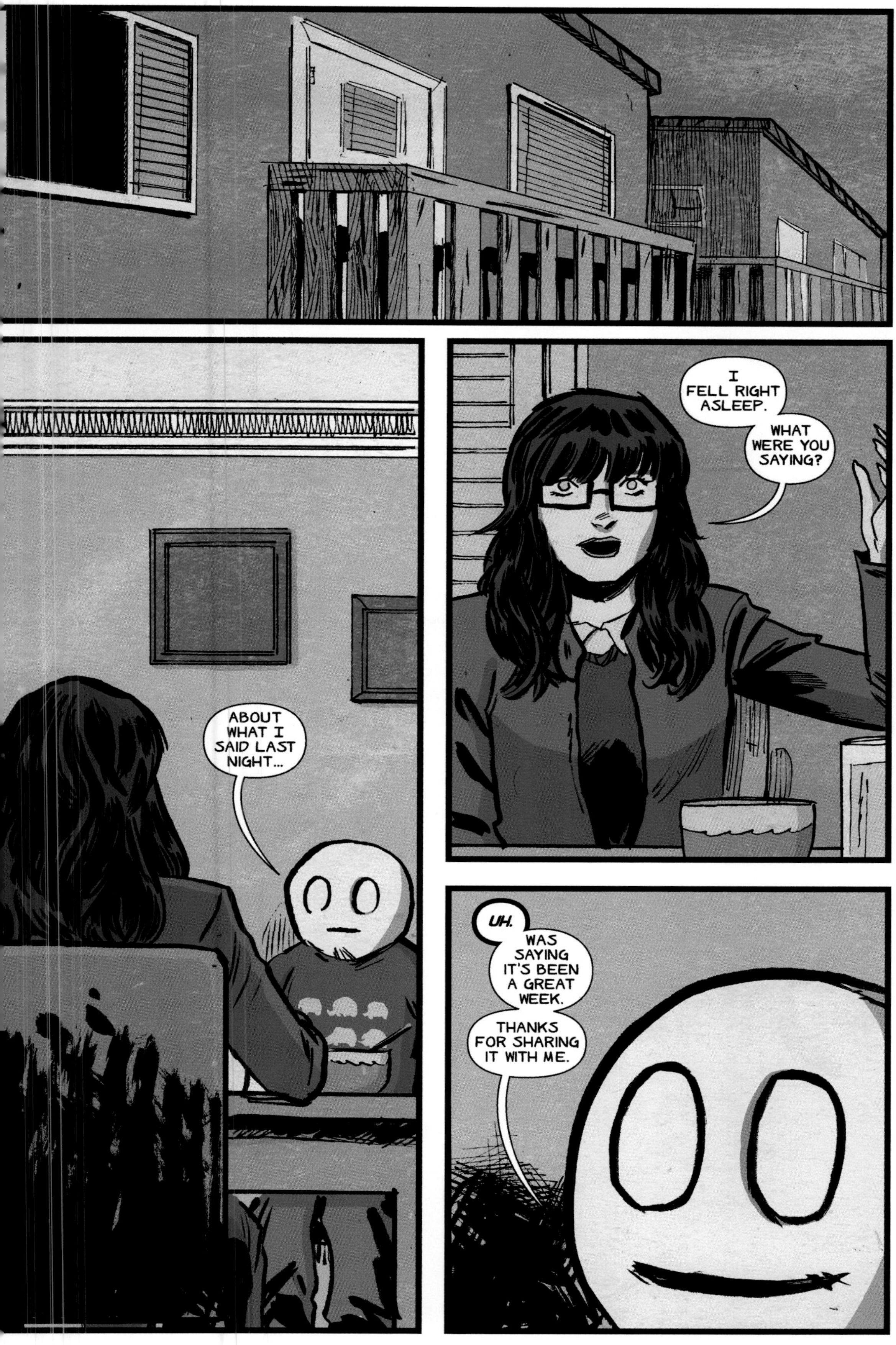
ABOUT WHAT I SAID LAST NIGHT...
I FELL RIGHT ASLEEP.
WHAT WERE YOU SAYING?
UH.
WAS SAYING IT'S BEEN A GREAT WEEK.
THANKS FOR SHARING IT WITH ME.

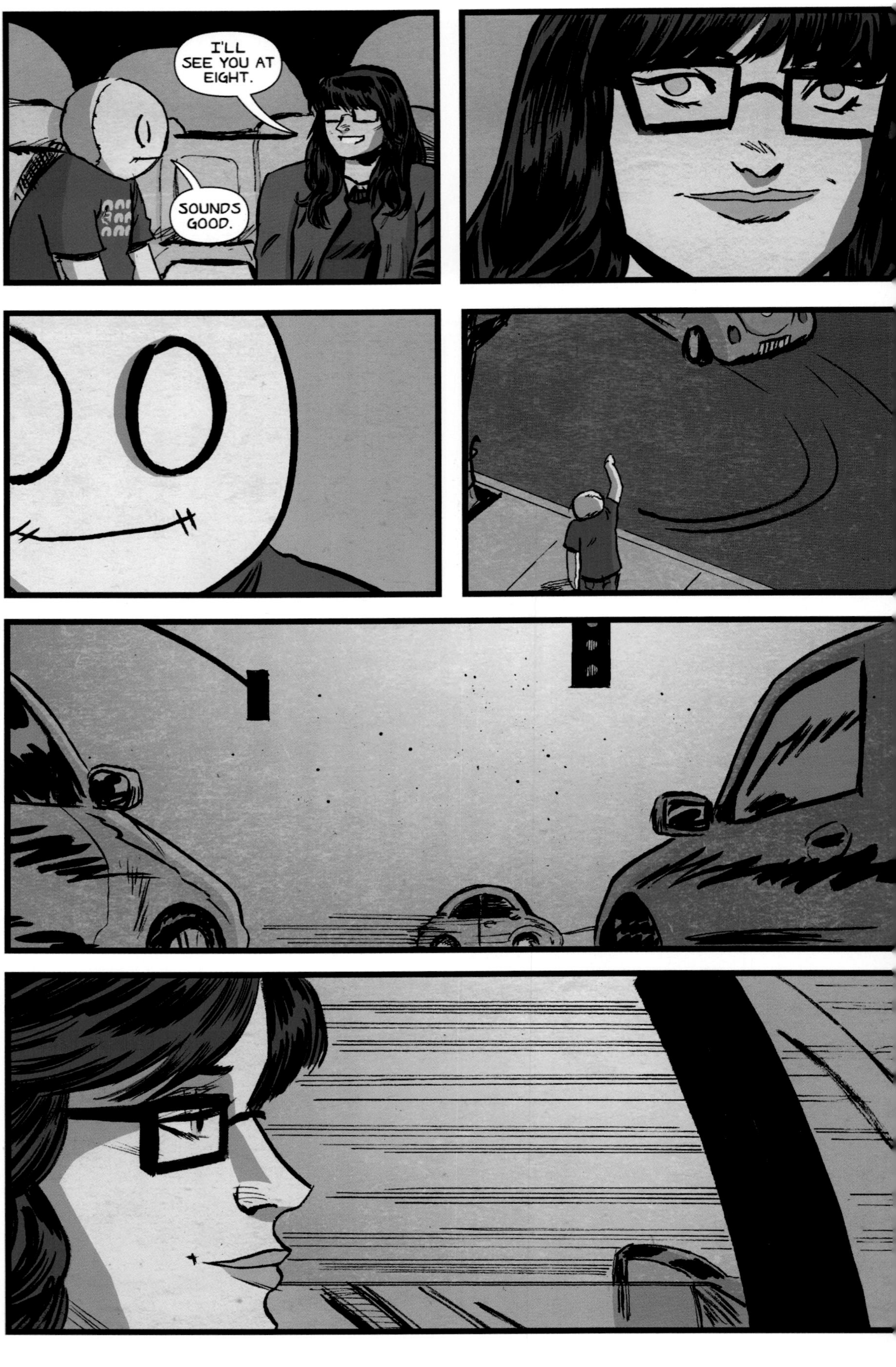
I'LL SEE YOU AT EIGHT.
SOUNDS GOOD.

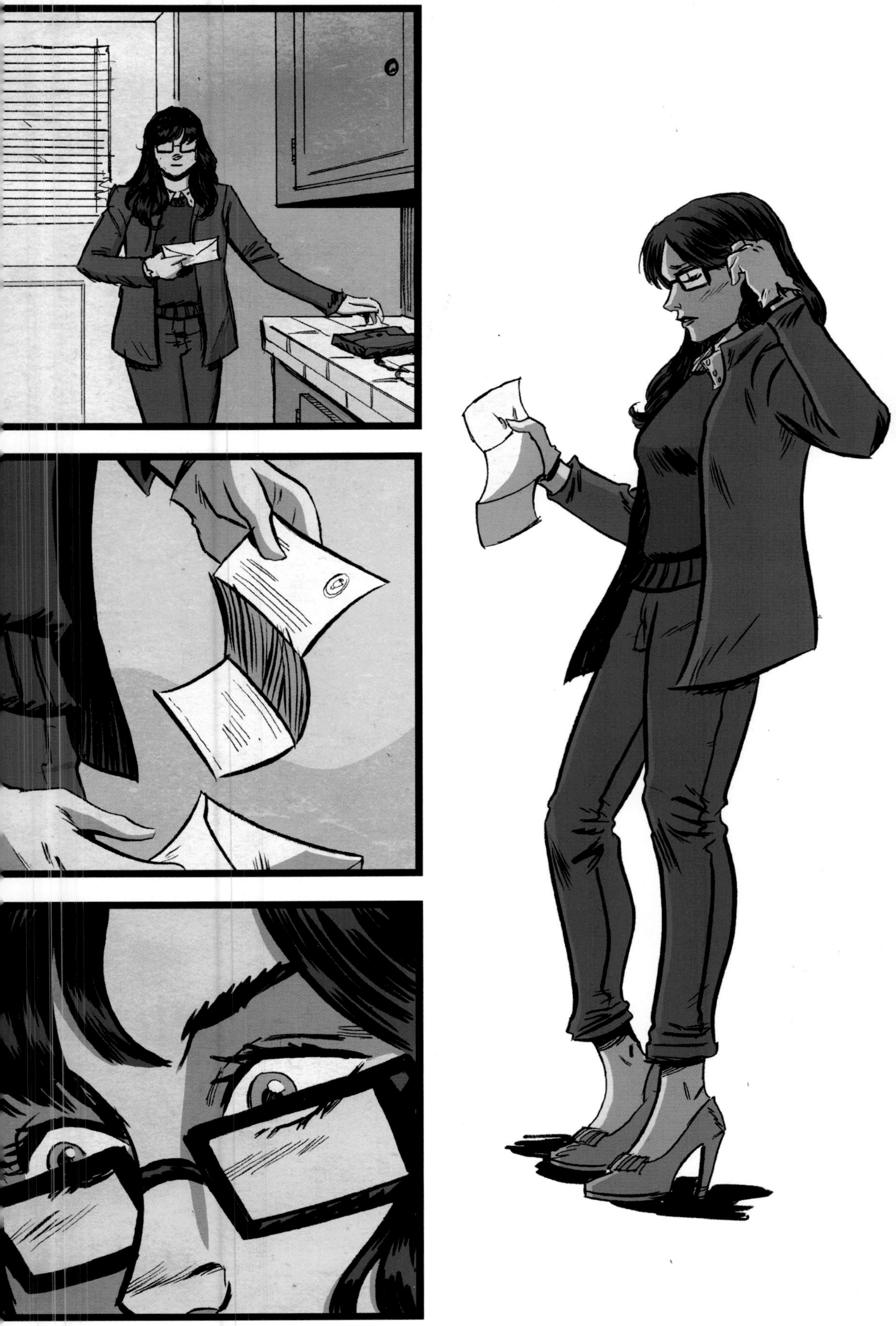

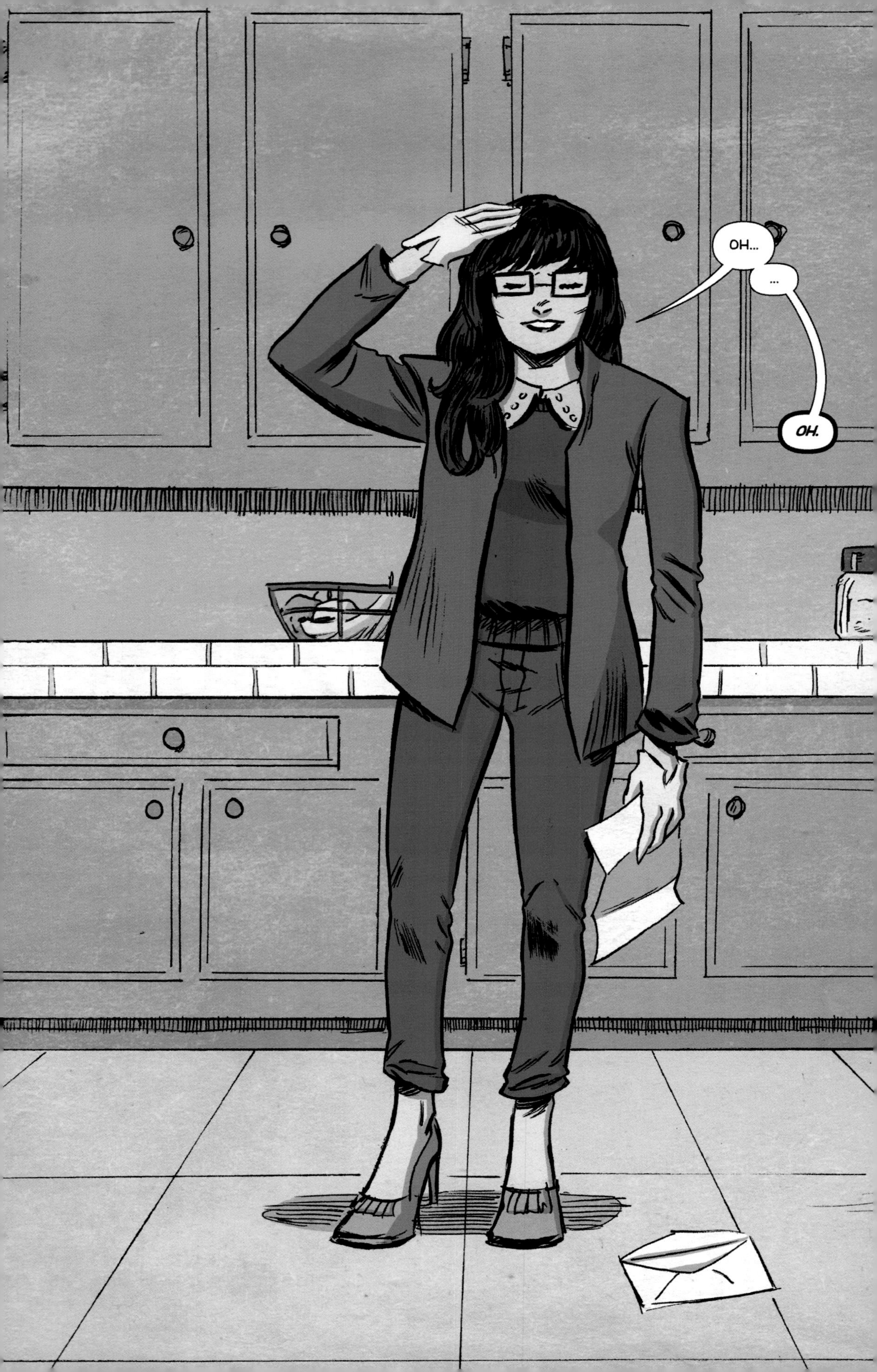
OH...
...
OH.

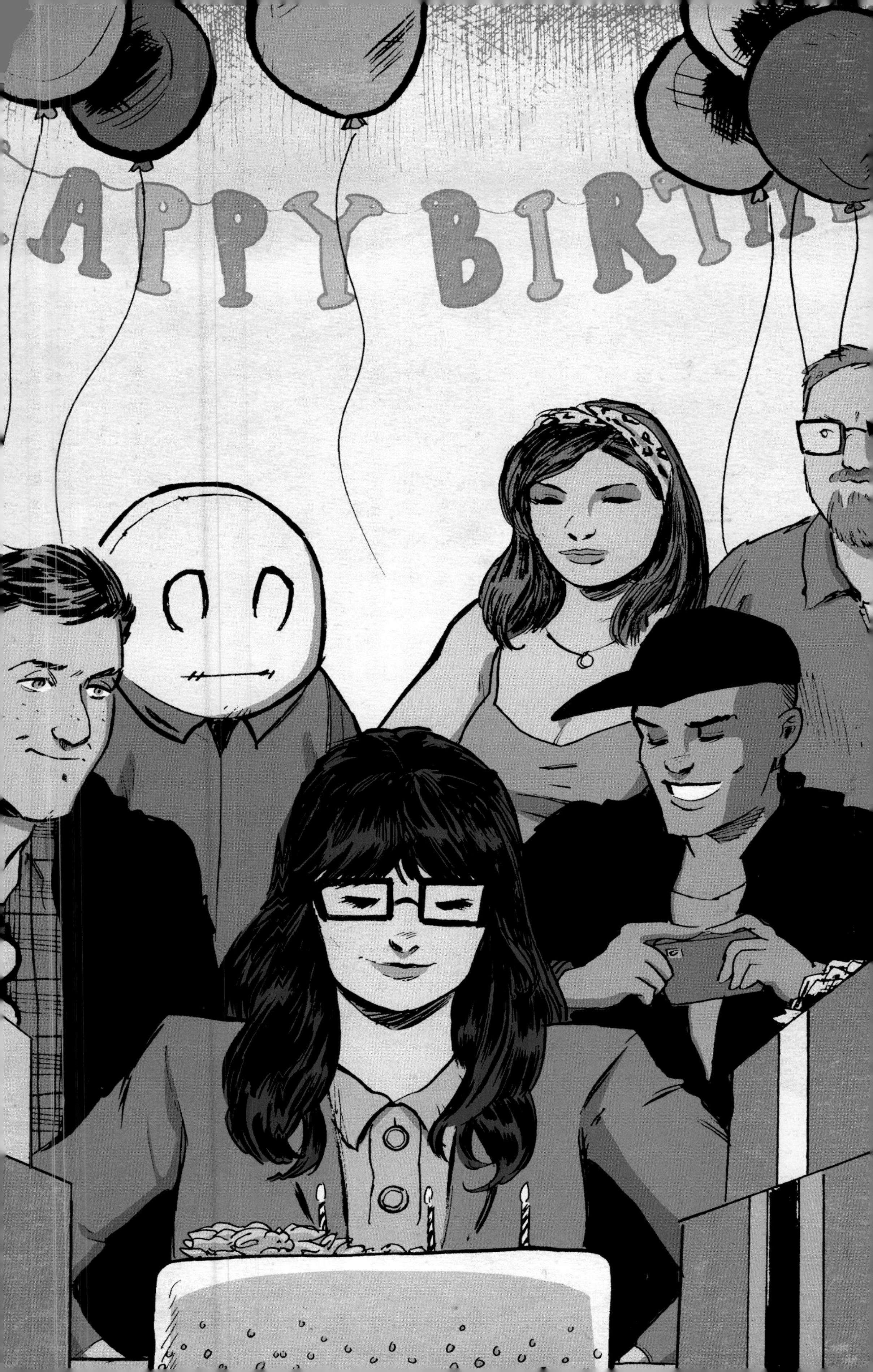
APPY BIRT

CHAPTER TWENTY:

"IT'S NOT MY BIRTHDAY"

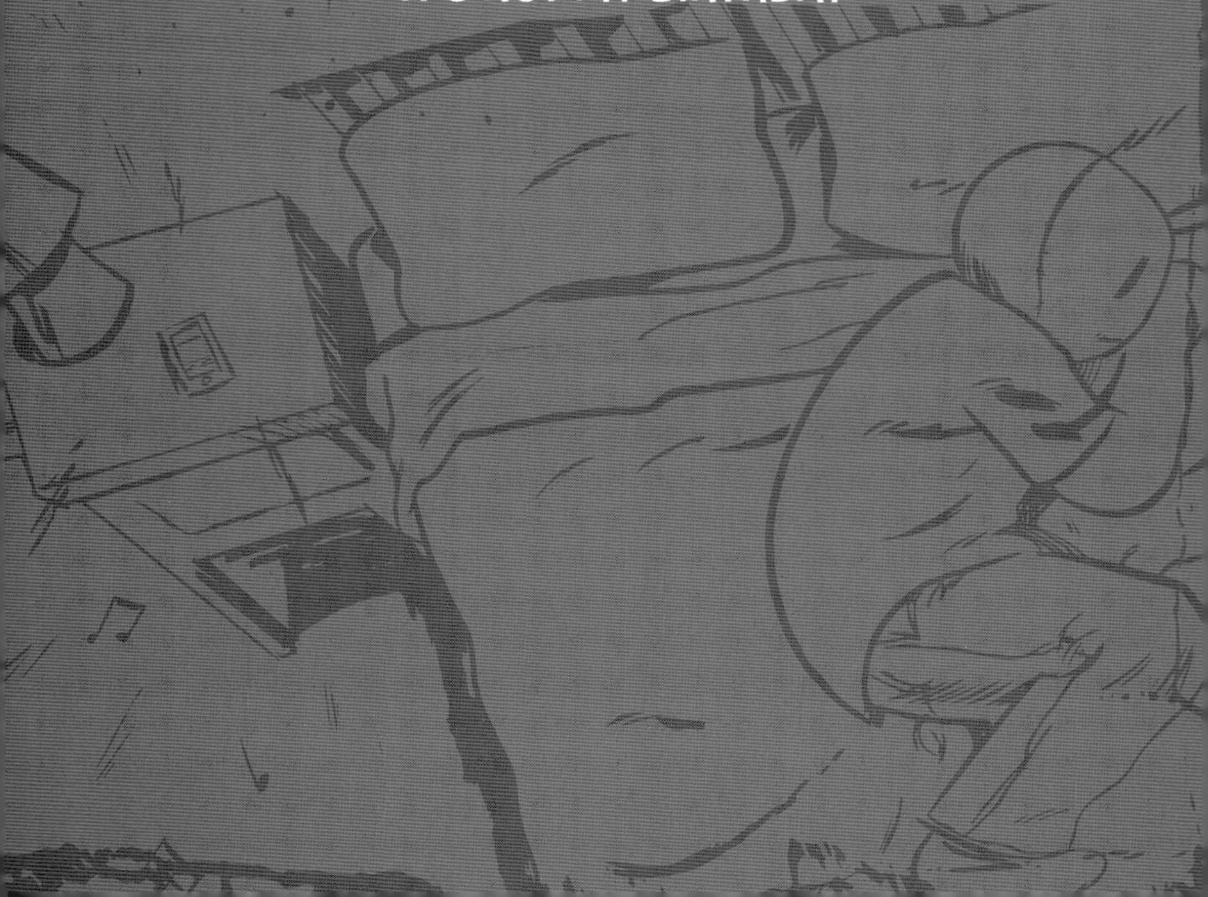

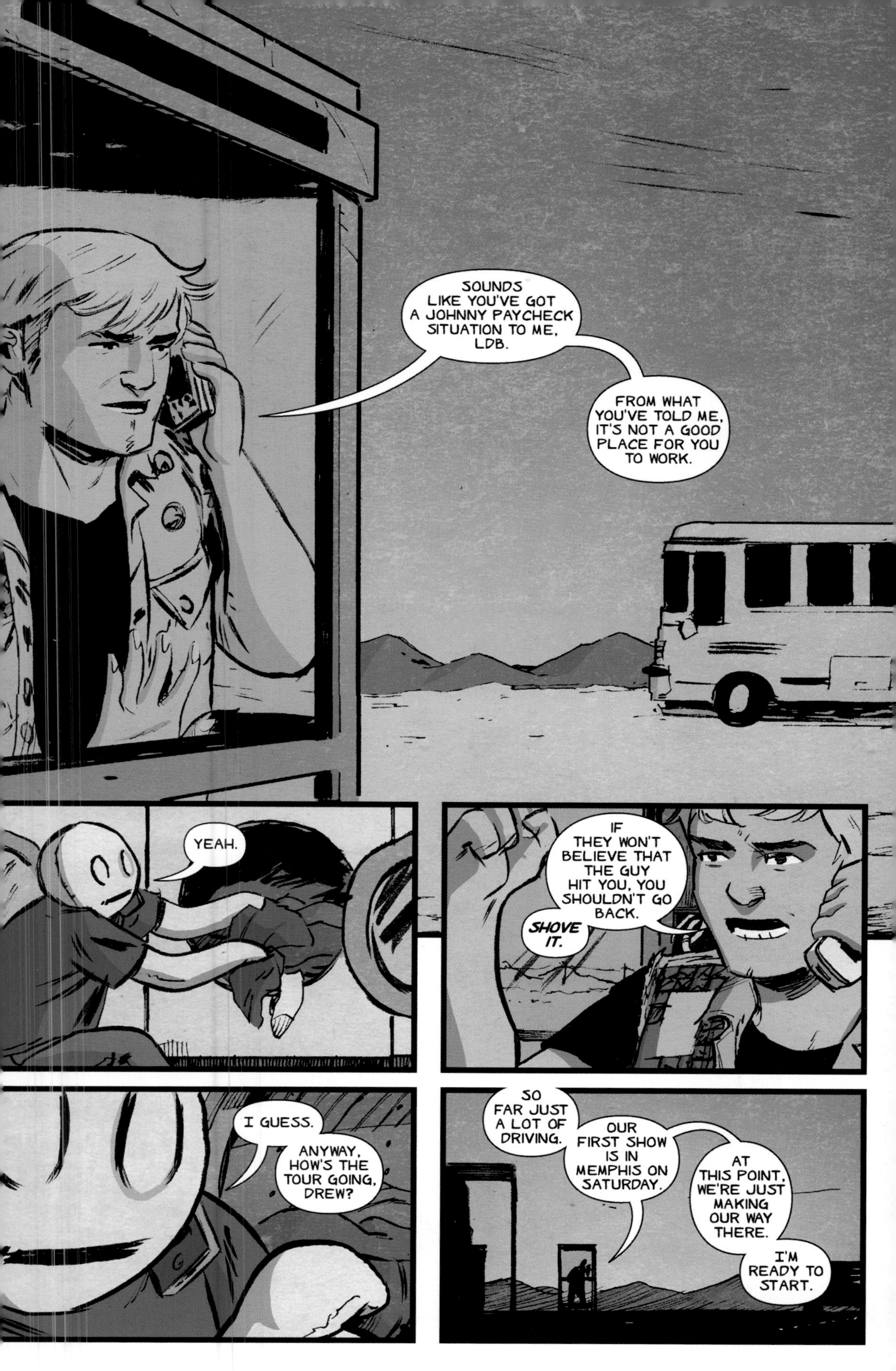
SOUNDS LIKE YOU'VE GOT A JOHNNY PAYCHECK SITUATION TO ME, LDB.
FROM WHAT YOU'VE TOLD ME, IT'S NOT A GOOD PLACE FOR YOU TO WORK.
YEAH.
IF THEY WON'T BELIEVE THAT THE GUY HIT YOU, YOU SHOULDN'T GO BACK.
SHOVE IT.
I GUESS.
ANYWAY, HOW'S THE TOUR GOING, DREW?
SO FAR JUST A LOT OF DRIVING.
OUR FIRST SHOW IS IN MEMPHIS ON SATURDAY.
AT THIS POINT, WE'RE JUST MAKING OUR WAY THERE.
I'M READY TO START.

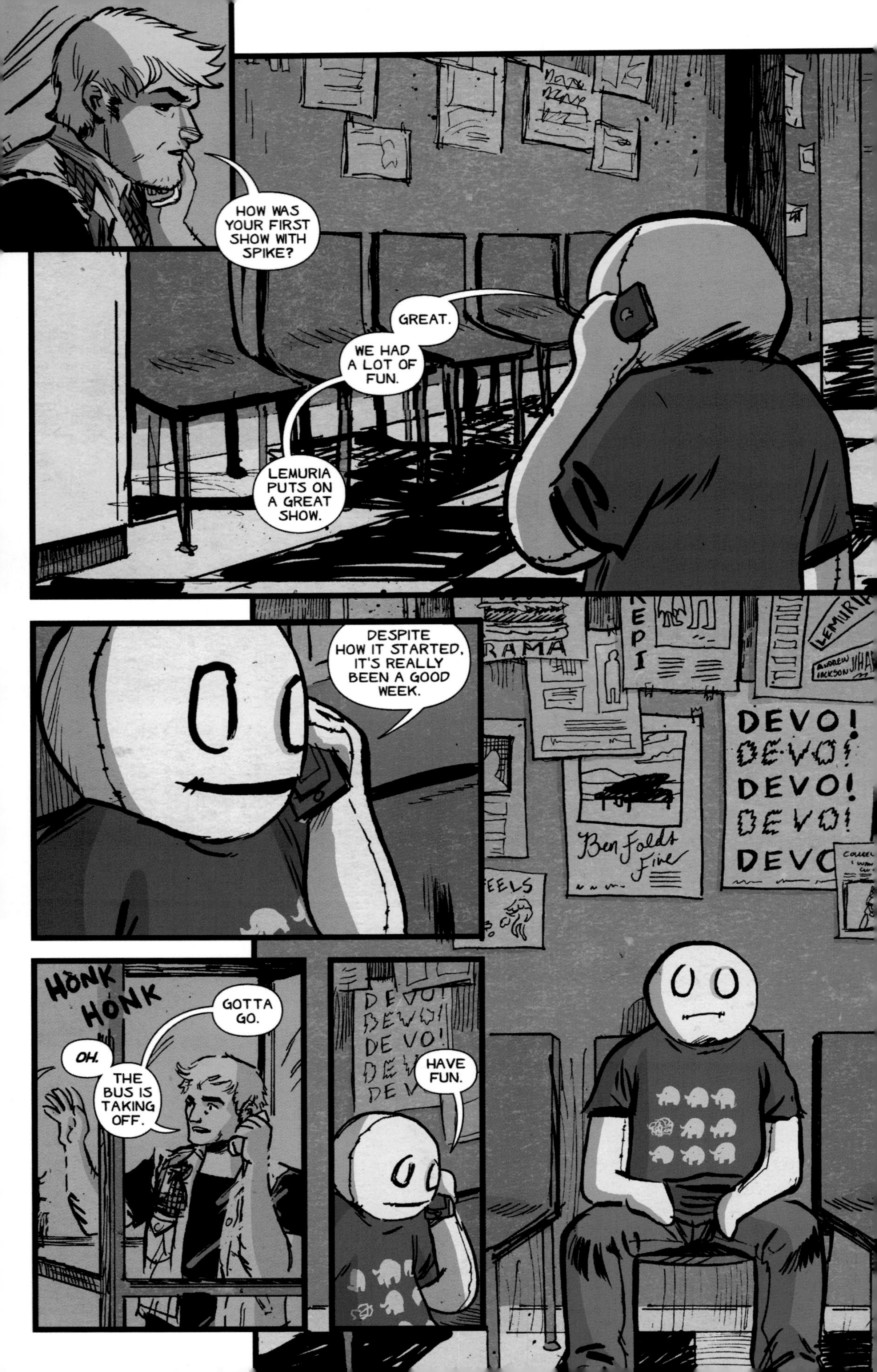

HOW WAS YOUR FIRST SHOW WITH SPIKE?
GREAT.
WE HAD A LOT OF FUN.
LEMURIA PUTS ON A GREAT SHOW.
DESPITE HOW IT STARTED, IT'S REALLY BEEN A GOOD WEEK.
DEVO! DEVO! DEVO! DEVO! DEVO
Ben Folds Five
HONK HONK
GOTTA GO.
OH.
THE BUS IS TAKING OFF.
HAVE FUN.

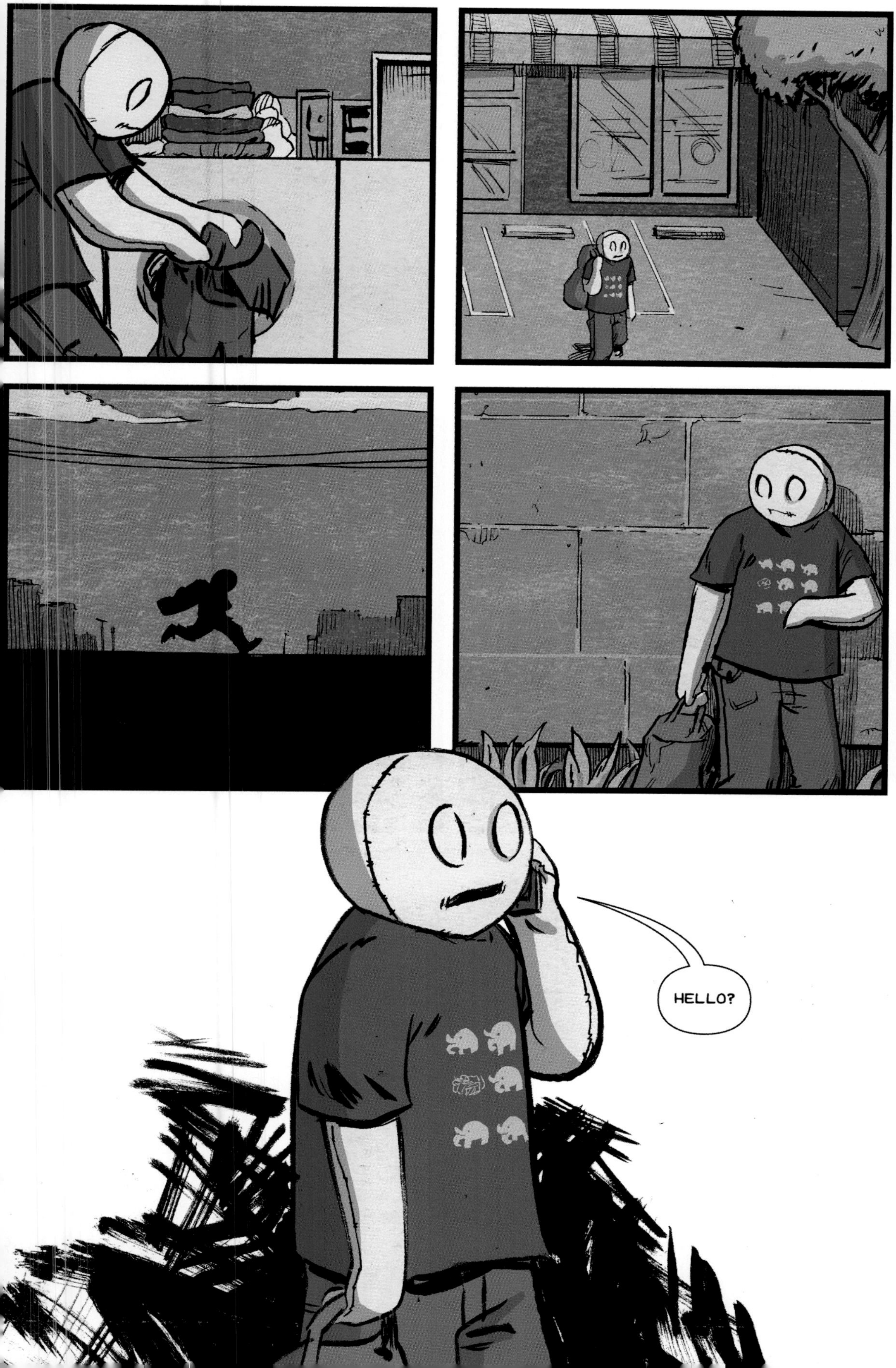
HELLO?

I'M SORRY TO SPRING THIS ON YOU AND I KNOW WE WEREN'T GOING TO MEET UP UNTIL EIGHT BUT MY BIRTHDAY IS COMING UP AND MY DAD IS IN TOWN TODAY SO MY FAMILY THOUGHT THEY'D CELEBRATE TODAY.

WOULD IT BE ALRIGHT IF YOU MEET US AT JORGE'S AT SIX?

MY FAMILY WOULD REALLY LIKE TO MEET YOU.

YEAH. I WOULD LOVE TO, SPIKE.

GREAT. I'LL SEE YOU THEN.

OH. DON'T WORRY ABOUT GETTING ME ANYTHING.

IT'S NOT MY REAL BIRTHDAY FOR ANOTHER TWO WEEKS.

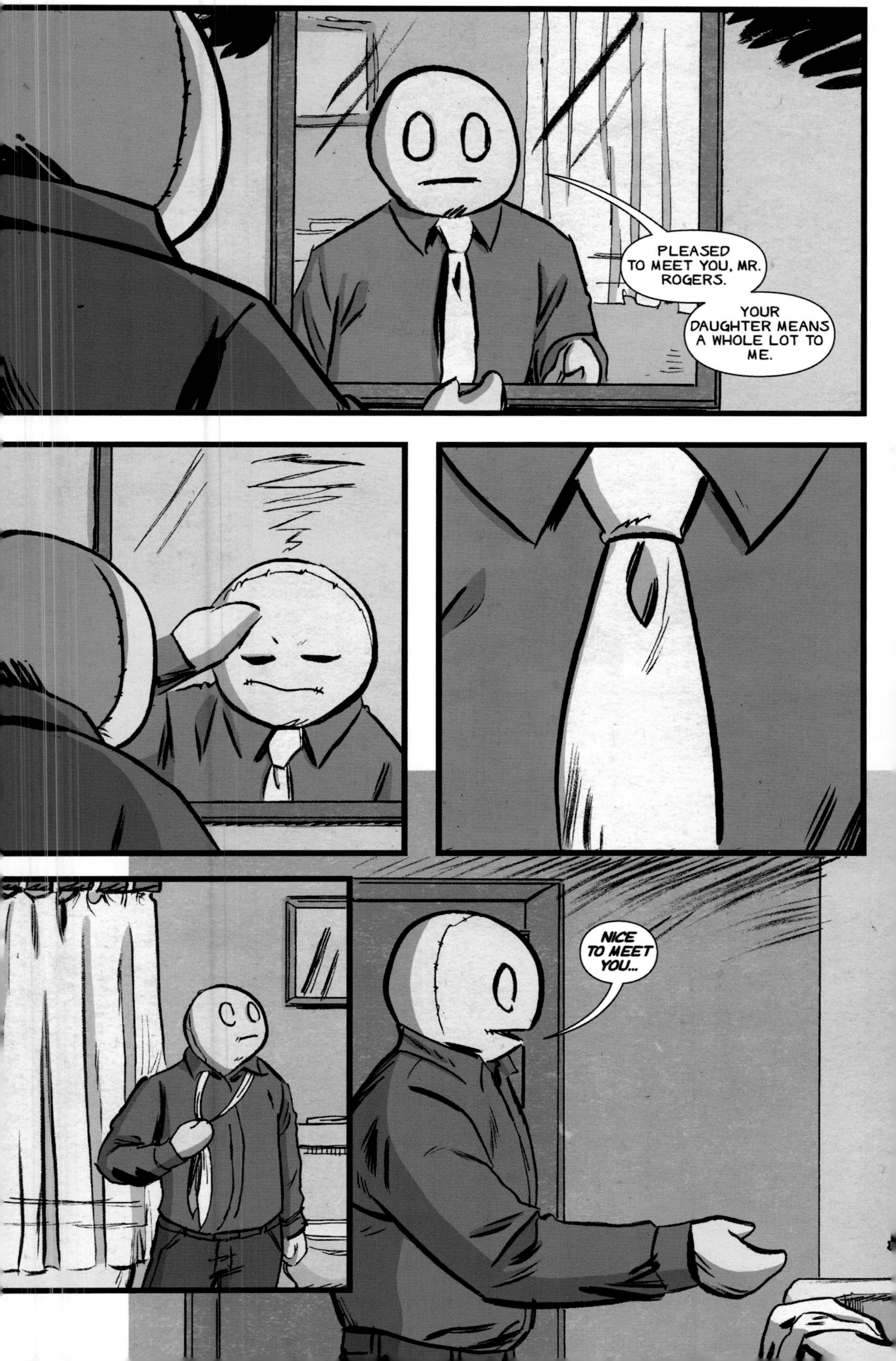
PLEASED TO MEET YOU, MR. ROGERS.
YOUR DAUGHTER MEANS A WHOLE LOT TO ME.
NICE TO MEET YOU...

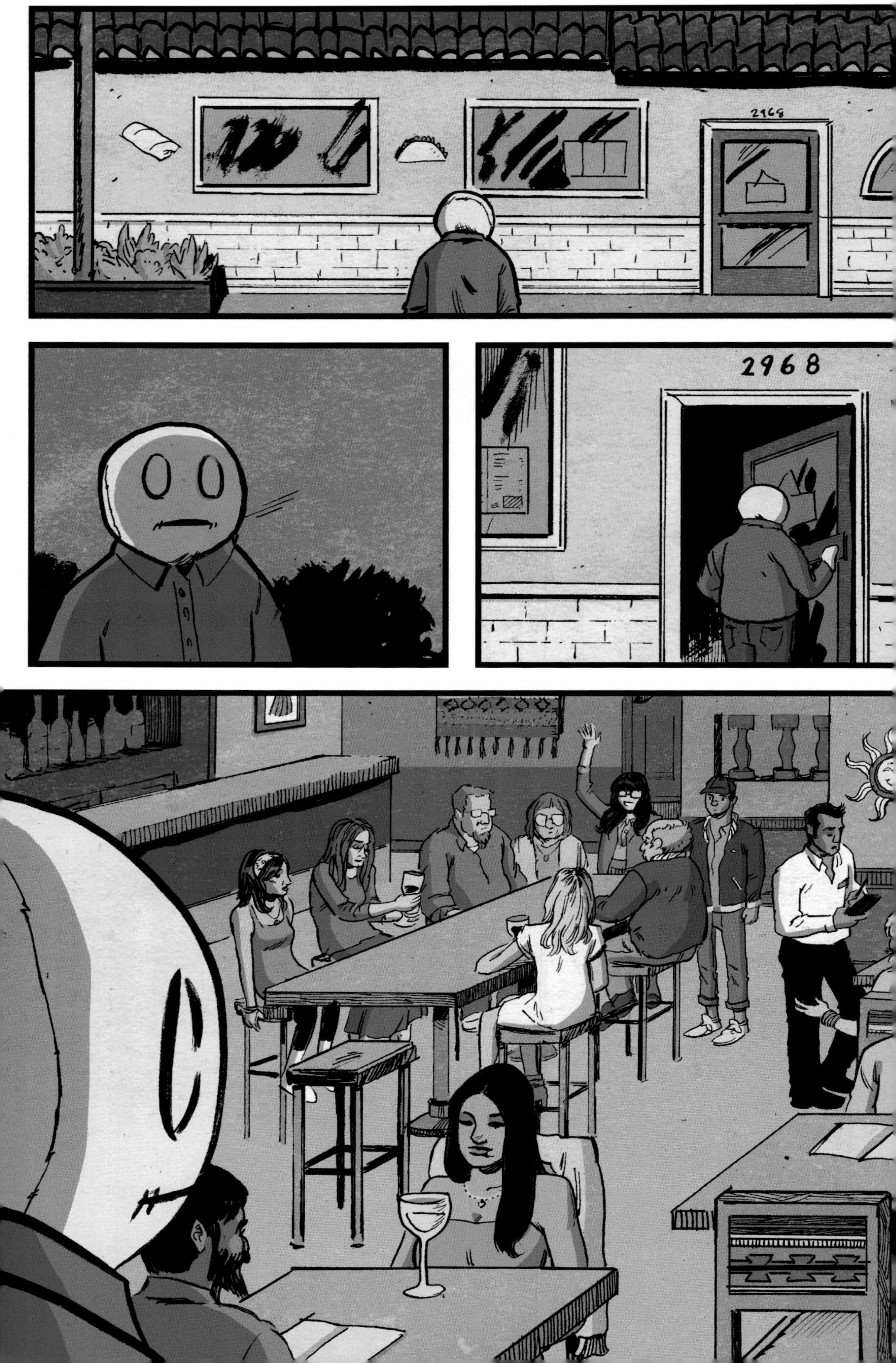
2968
2968

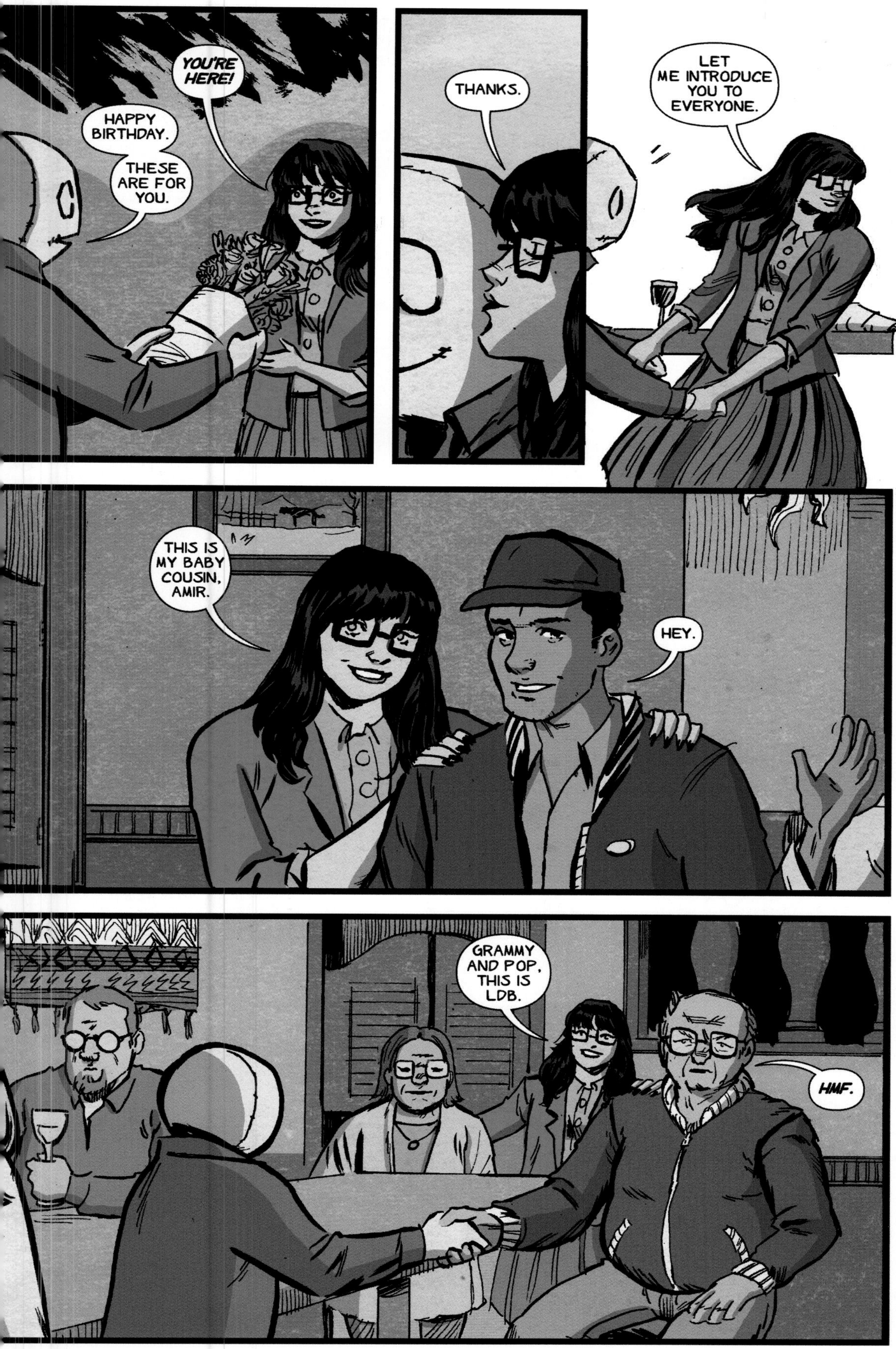
HAPPY BIRTHDAY.
THESE ARE FOR YOU.
YOU'RE HERE!
THANKS.
LET ME INTRODUCE YOU TO EVERYONE.
THIS IS MY BABY COUSIN, AMIR.
HEY.
GRAMMY AND POP, THIS IS LDB.
HMF.

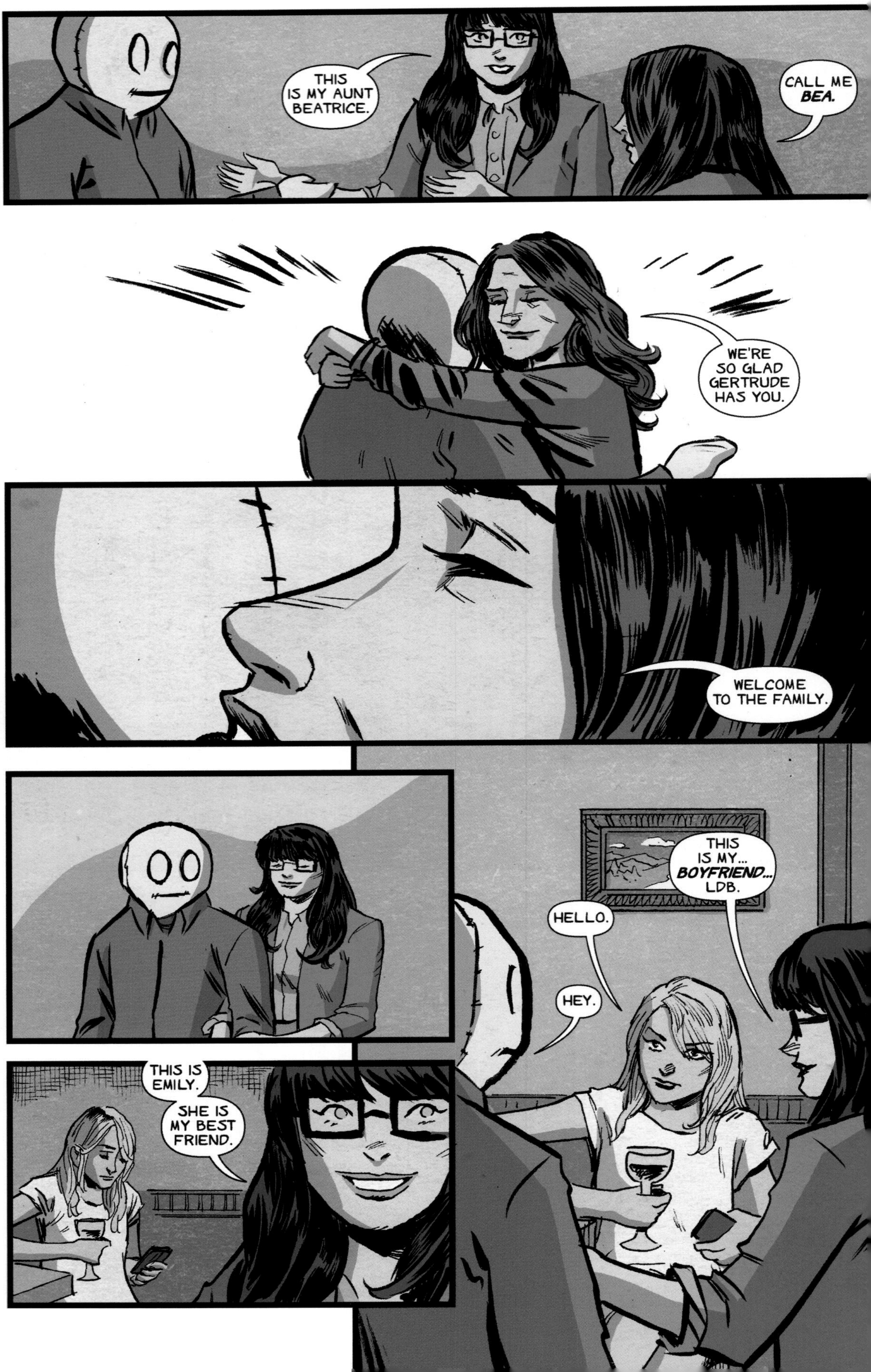
THIS IS MY AUNT BEATRICE.
CALL ME ***BEA.***
WE'RE SO GLAD GERTRUDE HAS YOU.
WELCOME TO THE FAMILY.
THIS IS MY... ***BOYFRIEND...*** LDB.
HELLO.
HEY.
THIS IS EMILY.
SHE IS MY BEST FRIEND.

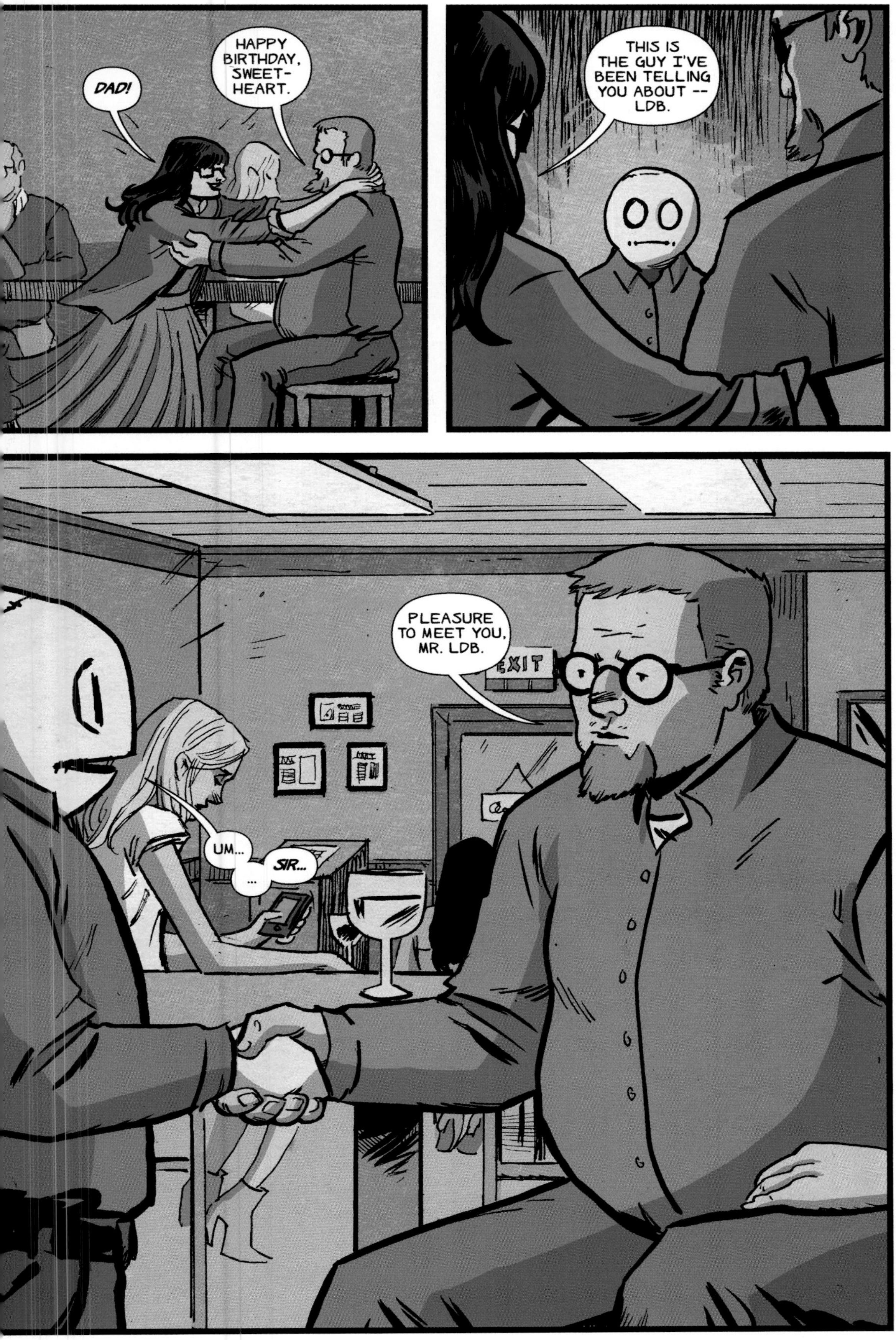
DAD!
HAPPY BIRTHDAY, SWEET-HEART.
THIS IS THE GUY I'VE BEEN TELLING YOU ABOUT -- LDB.
PLEASURE TO MEET YOU, MR. LDB.
EXIT
UM...
...
SIR...

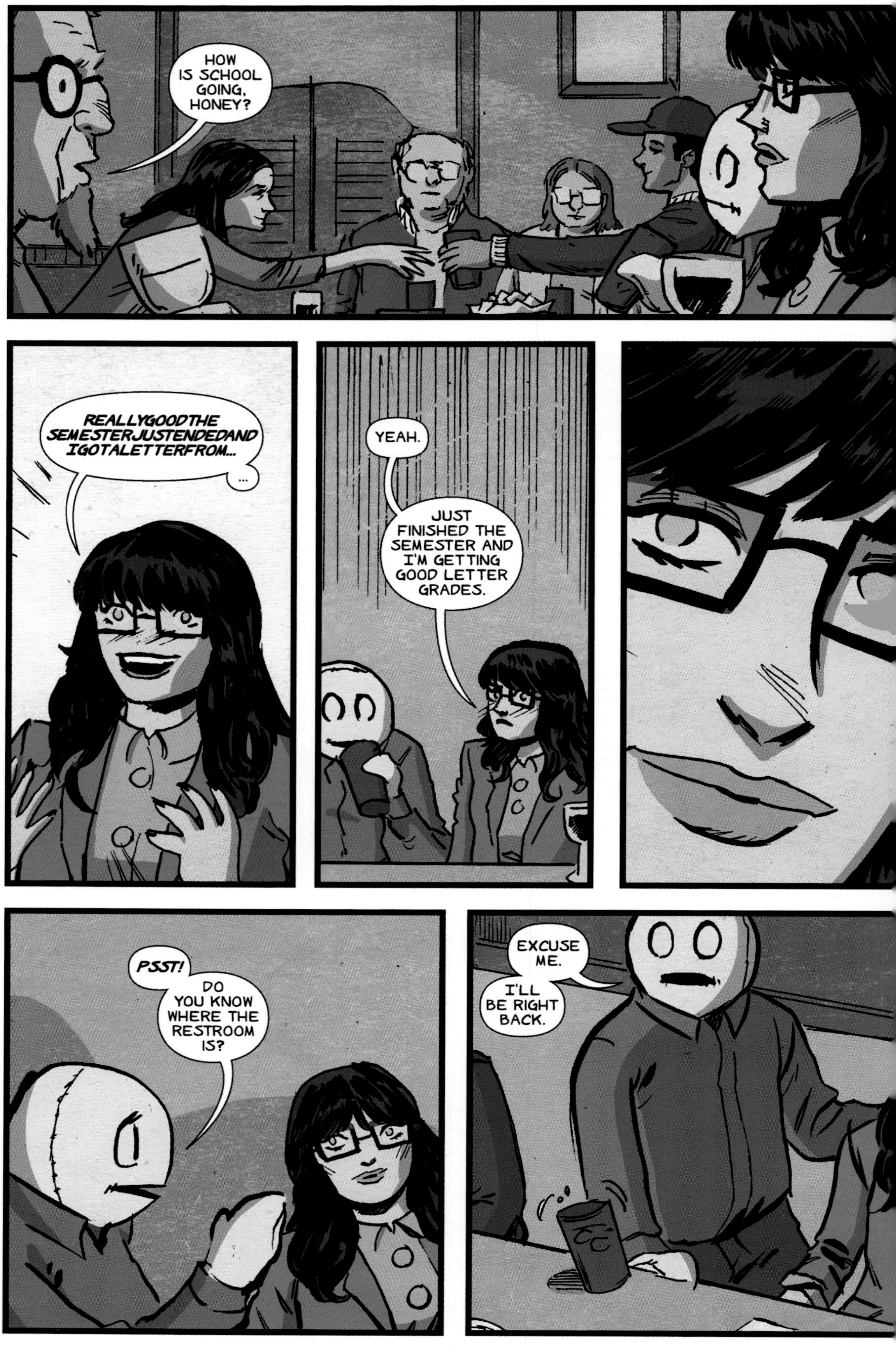
HOW IS SCHOOL GOING, HONEY?
REALLYGOODTHE SEMESTERJUSTENDEDAND IGOTALETTERFROM...
...
YEAH.
JUST FINISHED THE SEMESTER AND I'M GETTING GOOD LETTER GRADES.
PSST!
DO YOU KNOW WHERE THE RESTROOM IS?
EXCUSE ME.
I'LL BE RIGHT BACK.

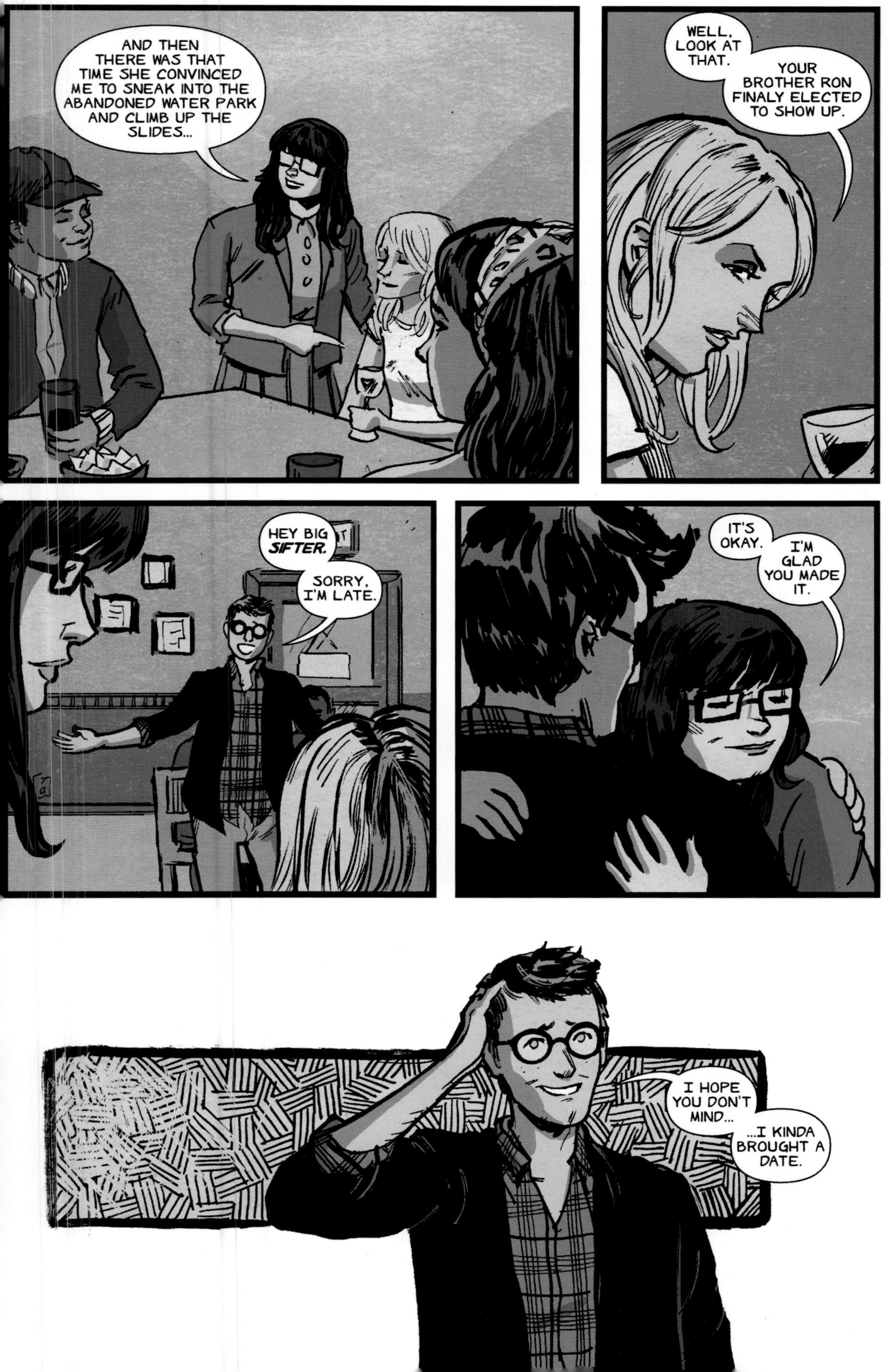
AND THEN THERE WAS THAT TIME SHE CONVINCED ME TO SNEAK INTO THE ABANDONED WATER PARK AND CLIMB UP THE SLIDES...
WELL, LOOK AT THAT.
YOUR BROTHER RON FINALY ELECTED TO SHOW UP.
HEY BIG *SIFTER.*
SORRY, I'M LATE.
IT'S OKAY.
I'M GLAD YOU MADE IT.
I HOPE YOU DON'T MIND...
...I KINDA BROUGHT A DATE.

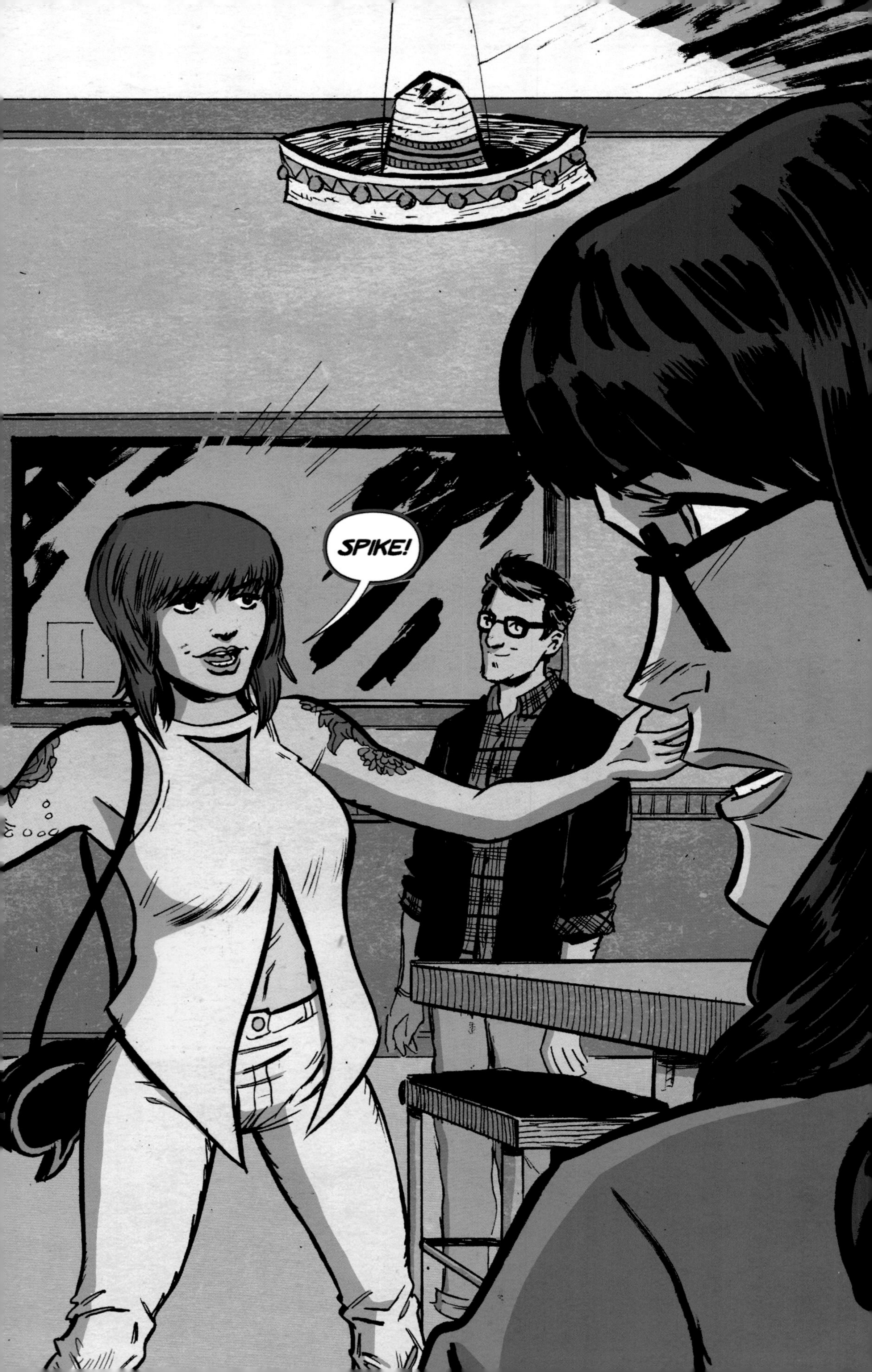
SPIKE!

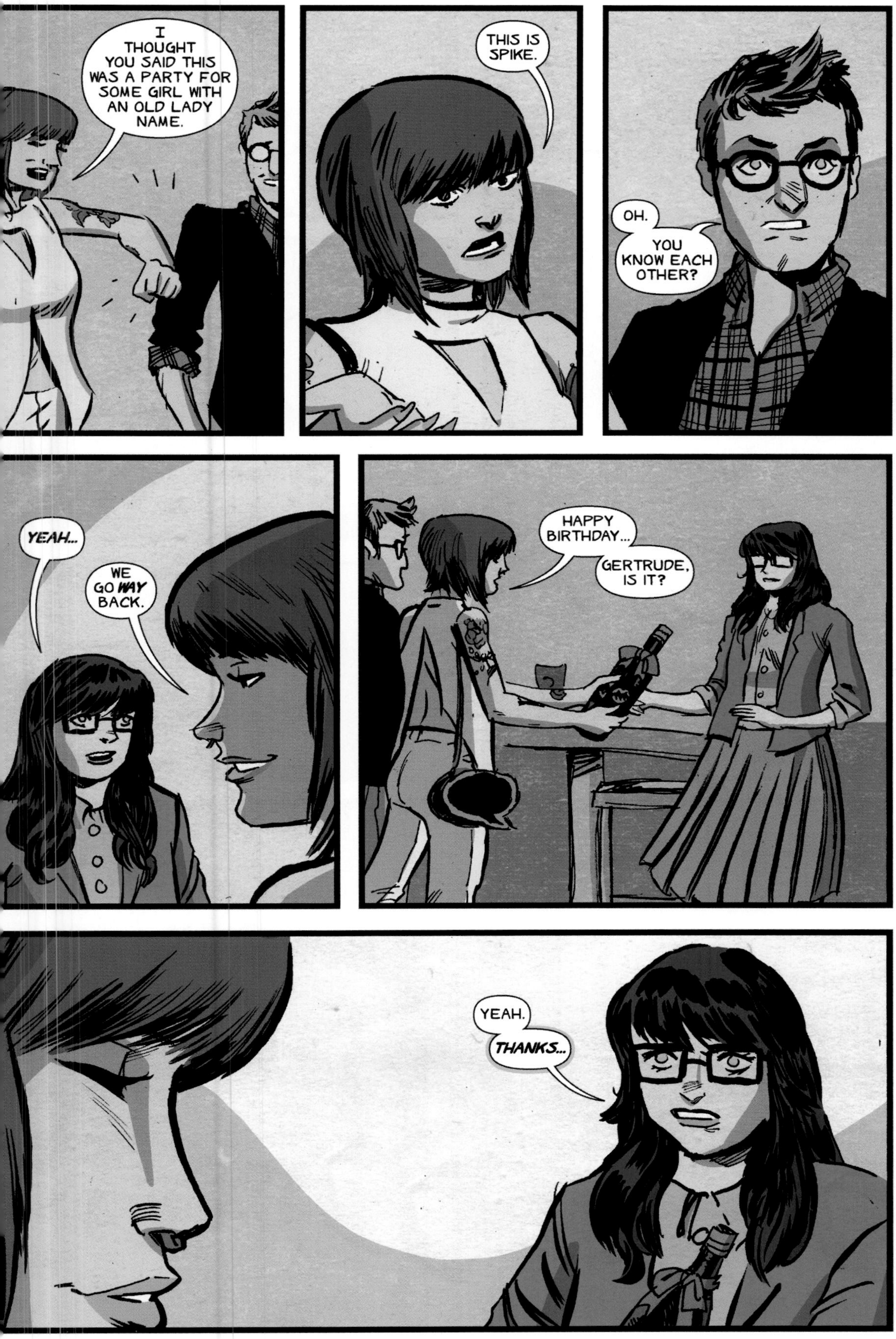
I THOUGHT YOU SAID THIS WAS A PARTY FOR SOME GIRL WITH AN OLD LADY NAME.
THIS IS SPIKE.
OH.
YOU KNOW EACH OTHER?
YEAH...
WE GO *WAY* BACK.
HAPPY BIRTHDAY...
GERTRUDE, IS IT?
YEAH.
THANKS...

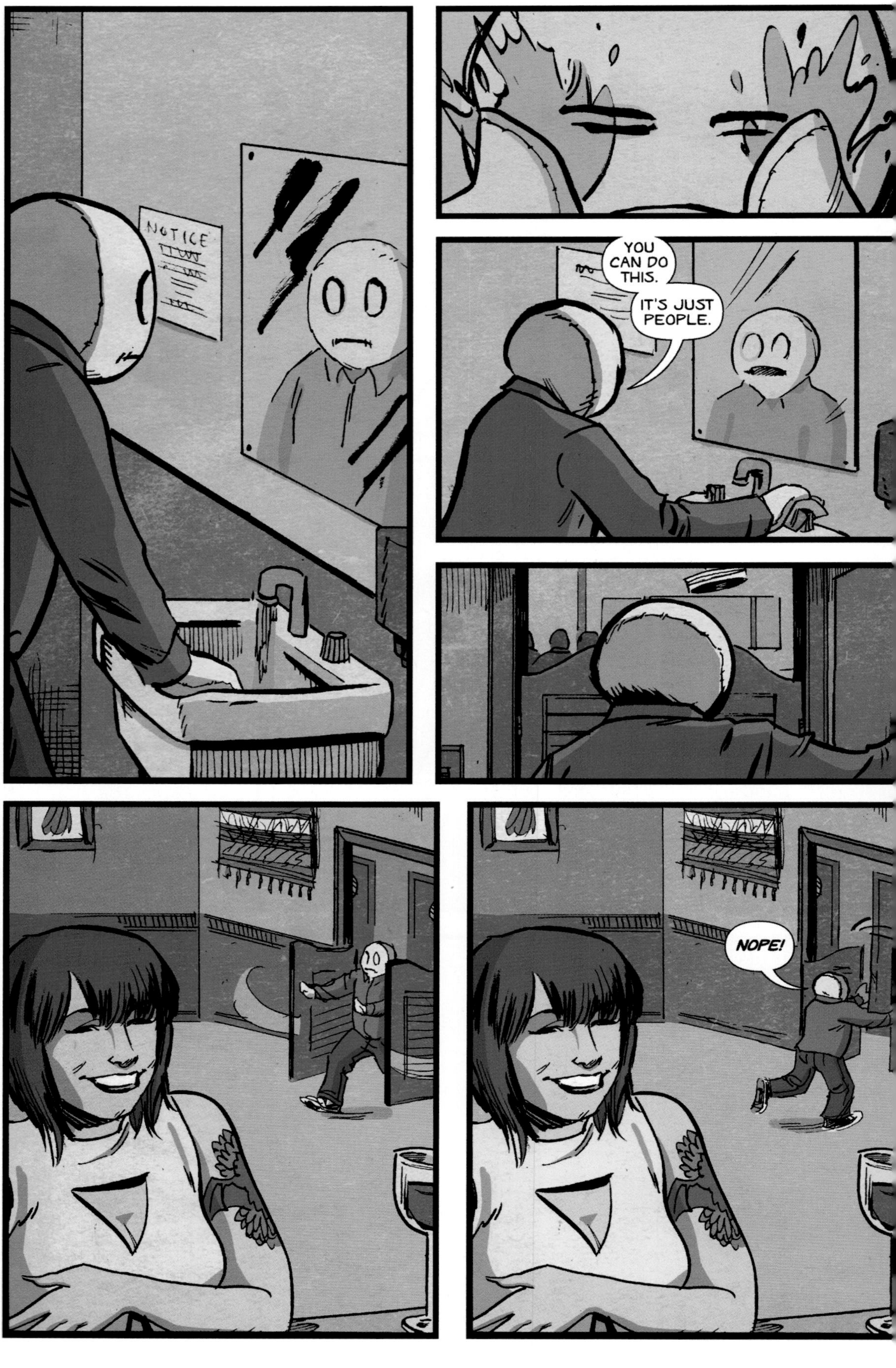
NOTICE
YOU CAN DO THIS.
IT'S JUST PEOPLE.
NOPE!

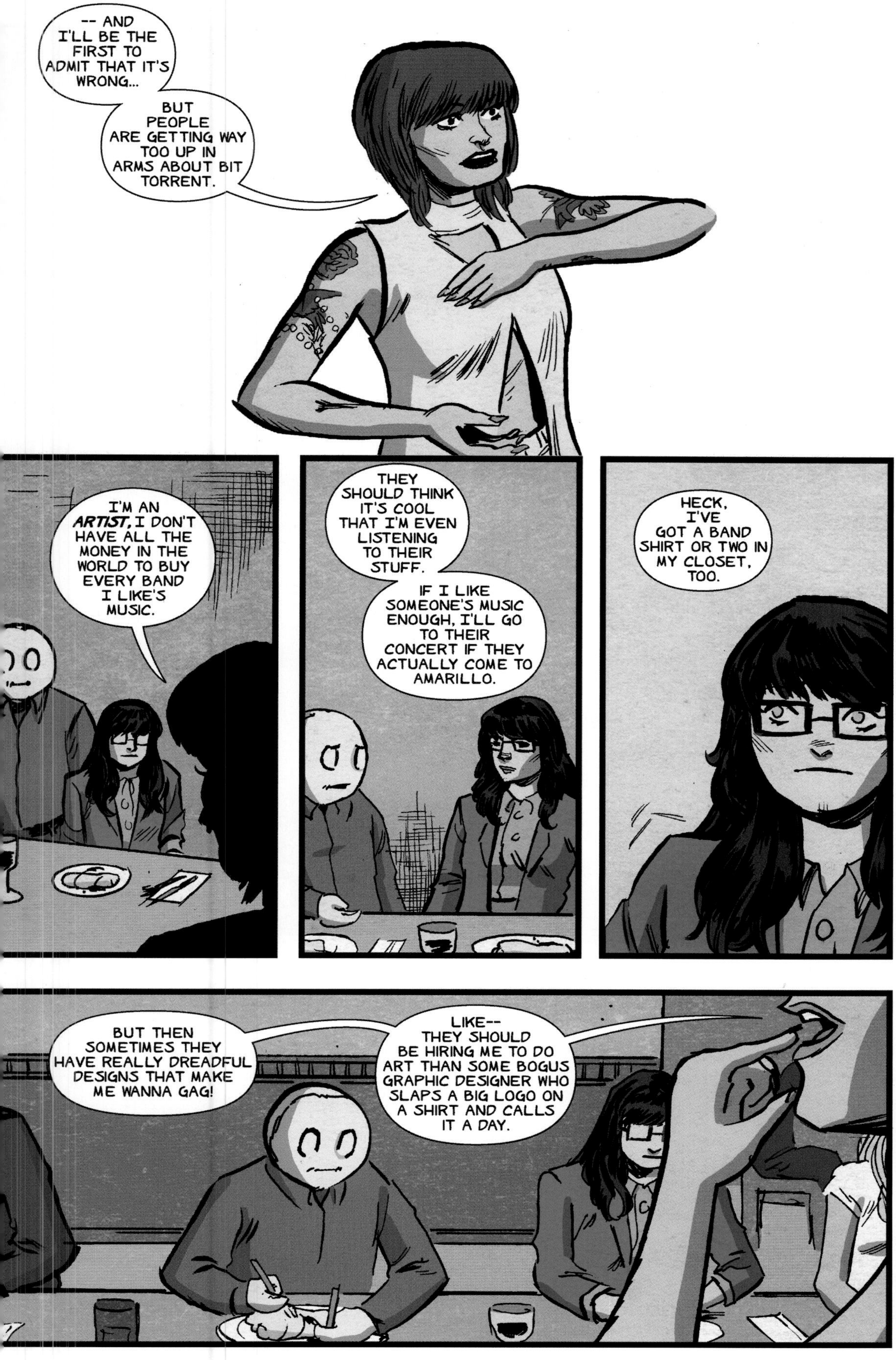
-- AND I'LL BE THE FIRST TO ADMIT THAT IT'S WRONG...
BUT PEOPLE ARE GETTING WAY TOO UP IN ARMS ABOUT BIT TORRENT.
I'M AN *ARTIST*, I DON'T HAVE ALL THE MONEY IN THE WORLD TO BUY EVERY BAND I LIKE'S MUSIC.
THEY SHOULD THINK IT'S COOL THAT I'M EVEN LISTENING TO THEIR STUFF.
IF I LIKE SOMEONE'S MUSIC ENOUGH, I'LL GO TO THEIR CONCERT IF THEY ACTUALLY COME TO AMARILLO.
HECK, I'VE GOT A BAND SHIRT OR TWO IN MY CLOSET, TOO.
BUT THEN SOMETIMES THEY HAVE REALLY DREADFUL DESIGNS THAT MAKE ME WANNA GAG!
LIKE-- THEY SHOULD BE HIRING ME TO DO ART THAN SOME BOGUS GRAPHIC DESIGNER WHO SLAPS A BIG LOGO ON A SHIRT AND CALLS IT A DAY.

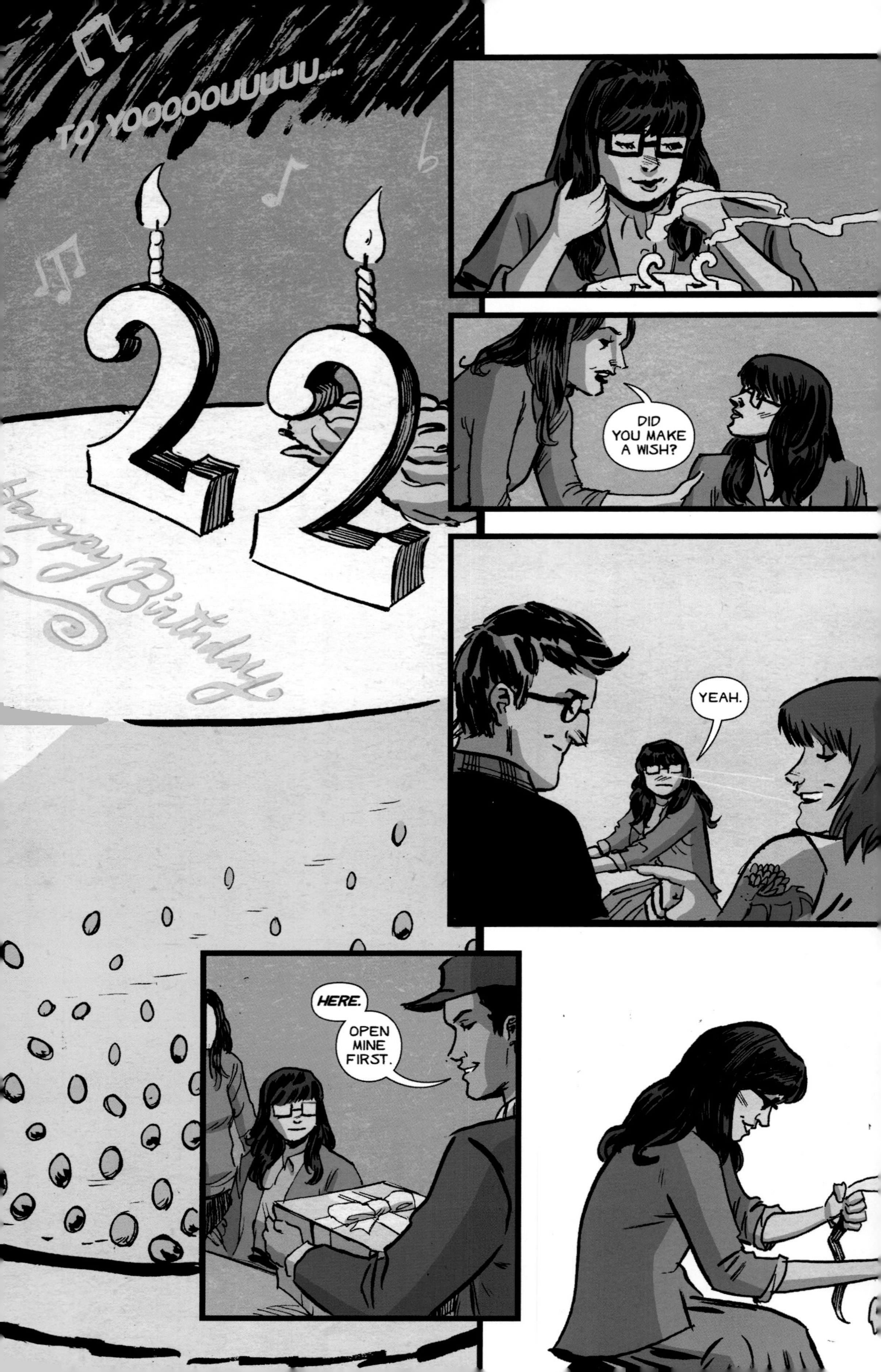
TO YOOOOOUUUUU....
Happy Birthday
DID YOU MAKE A WISH?
YEAH.
HERE.
OPEN MINE FIRST.

THAT WAS WEIRD.

I KNOW, RIGHT?

HOW DOES MY BROTHER EVEN KNOW HER?

IT'S NOT LIKE THEY RUN IN THE SAME CIRCLES.

I CAN'T EVEN PUT THEM IN THE SAME PLACE.

SHE DOESN'T SEEM LIKE THE TYPE WHO'D SPEND A LOT OF TIME AT THE LIBRARY WHERE HE WORKS.

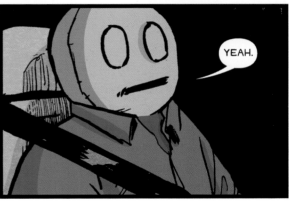

YEAH.

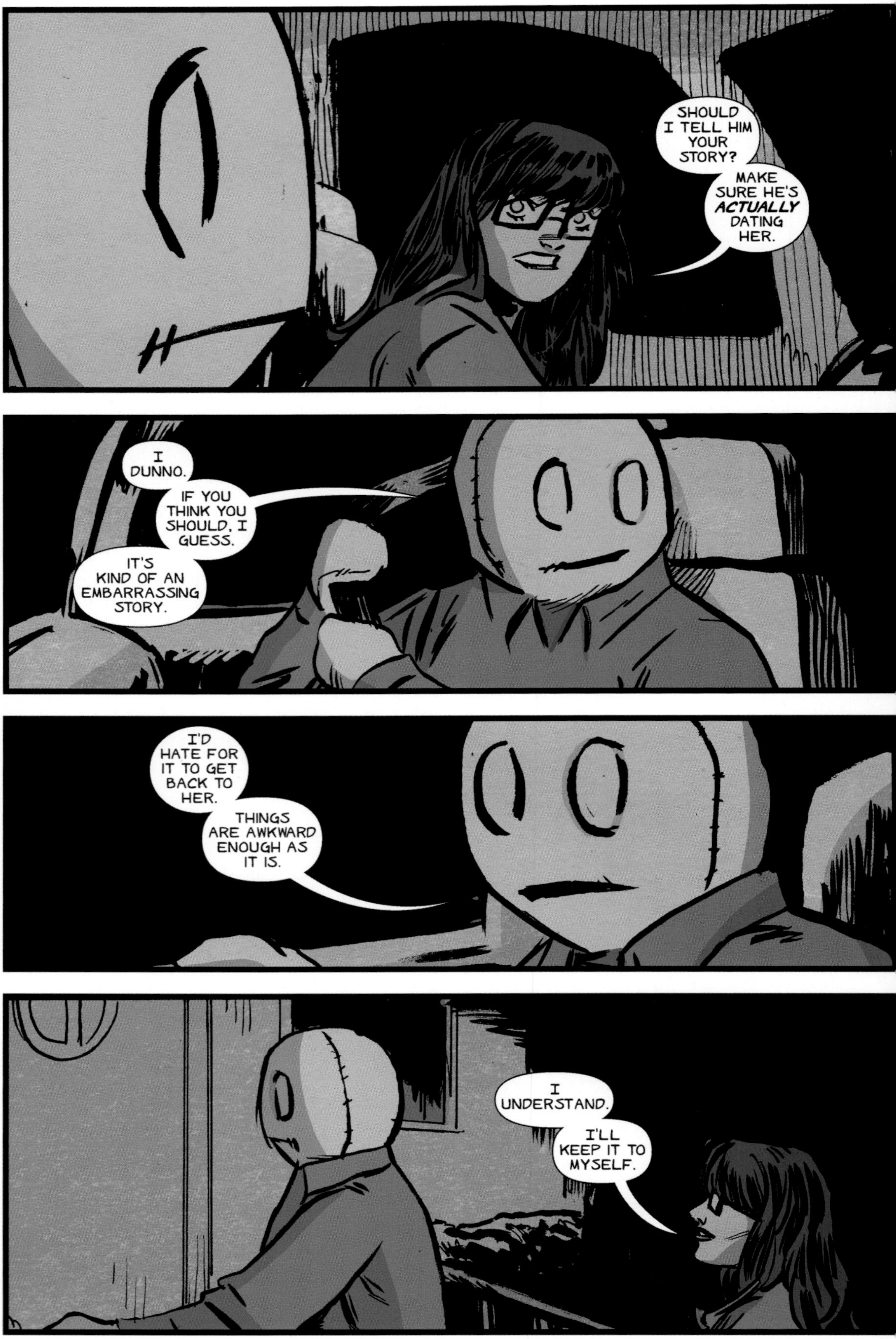
SHOULD I TELL HIM YOUR STORY?
MAKE SURE HE'S *ACTUALLY* DATING HER.
I DUNNO.
IF YOU THINK YOU SHOULD, I GUESS.
IT'S KIND OF AN EMBARRASSING STORY.
I'D HATE FOR IT TO GET BACK TO HER.
THINGS ARE AWKWARD ENOUGH AS IT IS.
I UNDERSTAND.
I'LL KEEP IT TO MYSELF.

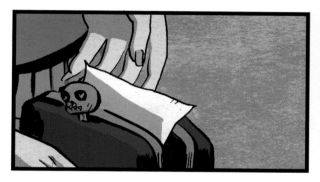

SWOO.

I WISH WE DIDN'T HAVE TO GO BACK TO WORK IN THE MORNING.

YEAH.

BEFOREIGOTHERE ISSOMETHINGINEEDTO TELLYOUA.S.A.P.

REMEMBERHOWISAID I'DHAVETOSWITCHSCHOOLSTO ACTUALLYSTUDYASTROPHYSICS WELLIJUSTGOTTHISINTHE MAILAND...

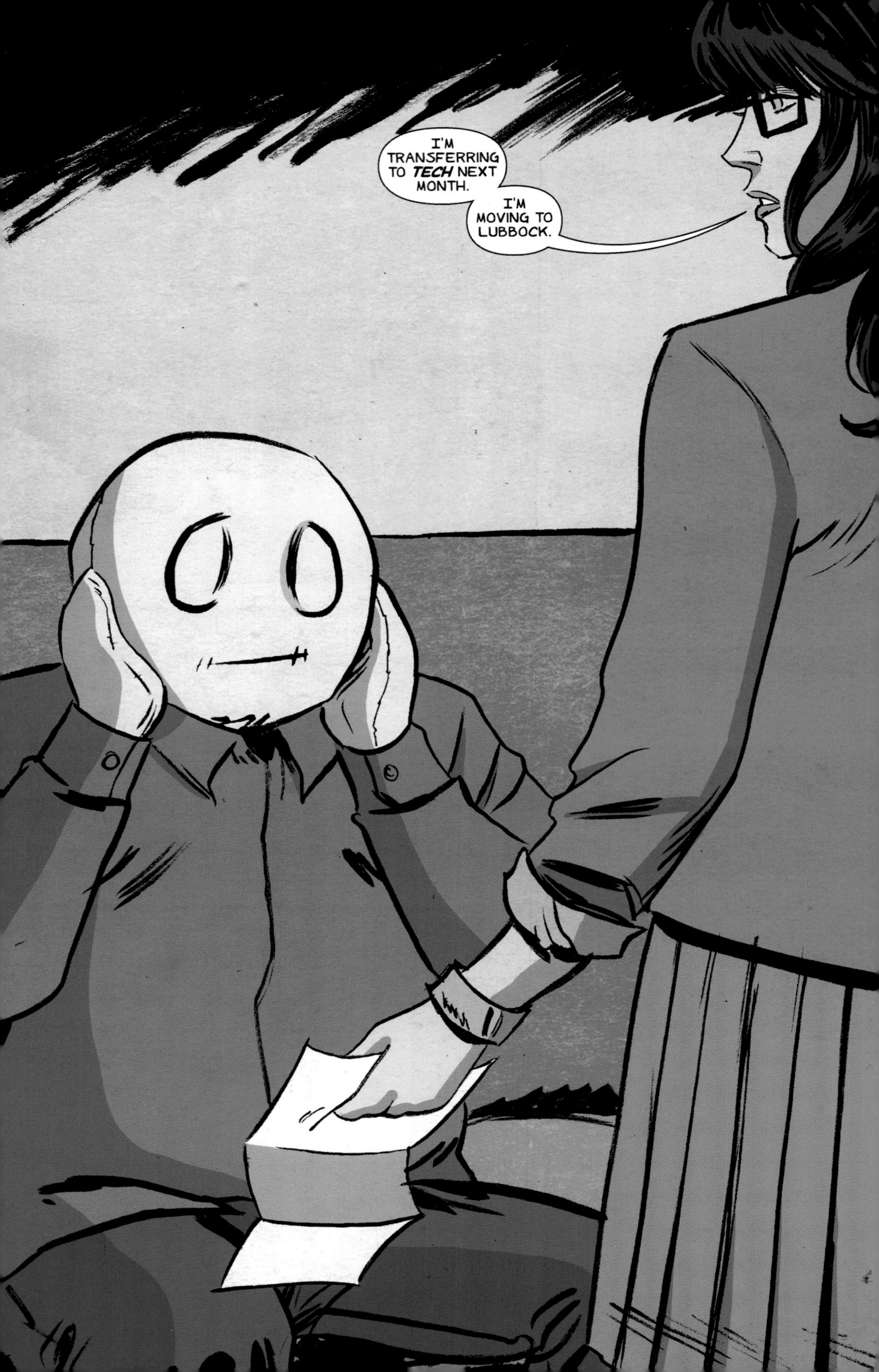
I'M TRANSFERRING TO *TECH* NEXT MONTH.
I'M MOVING TO LUBBOCK.

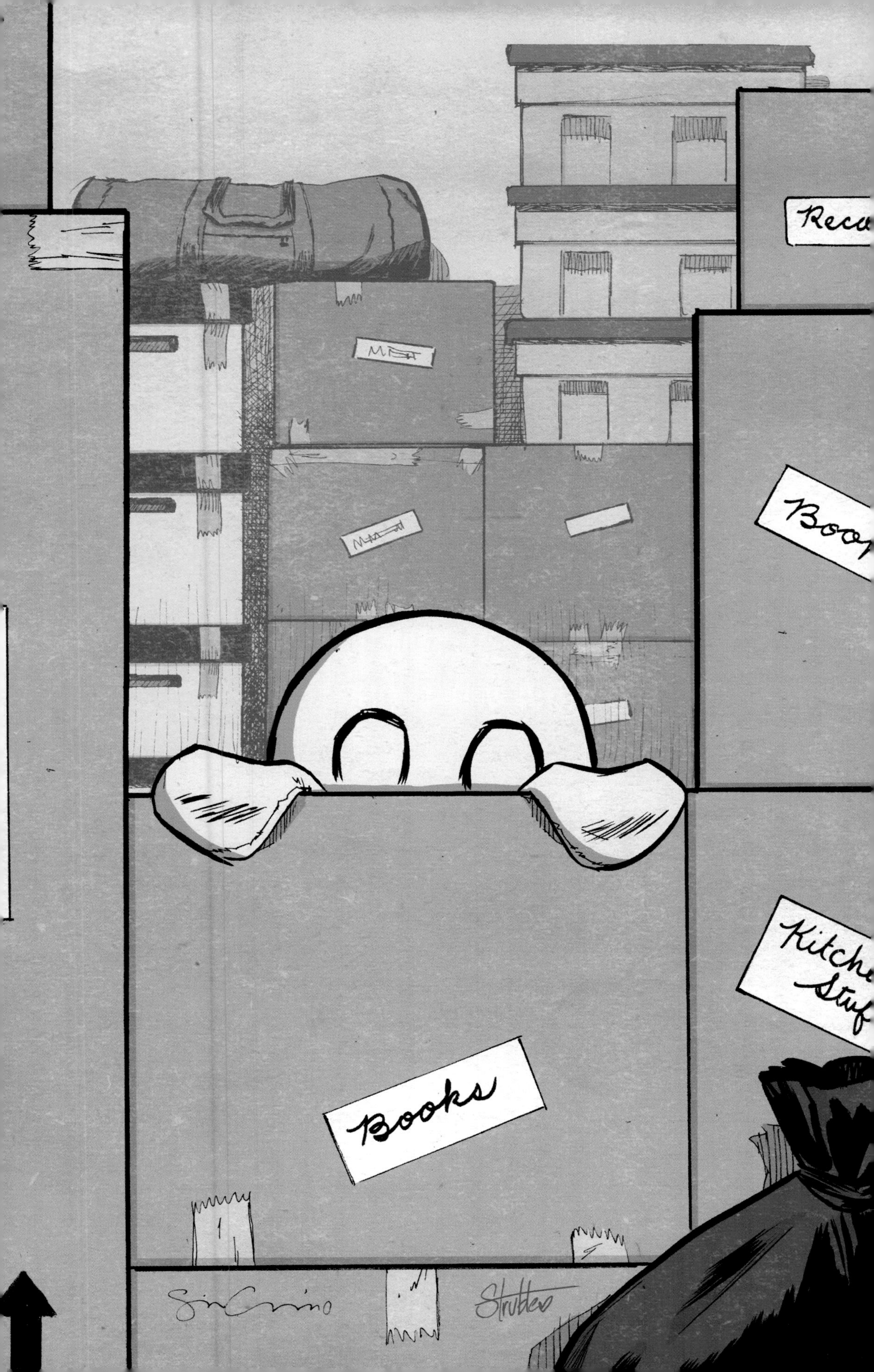
Books

CHAPTER TWENTY-ONE:

"MOVE WITH YOUR LOVER"

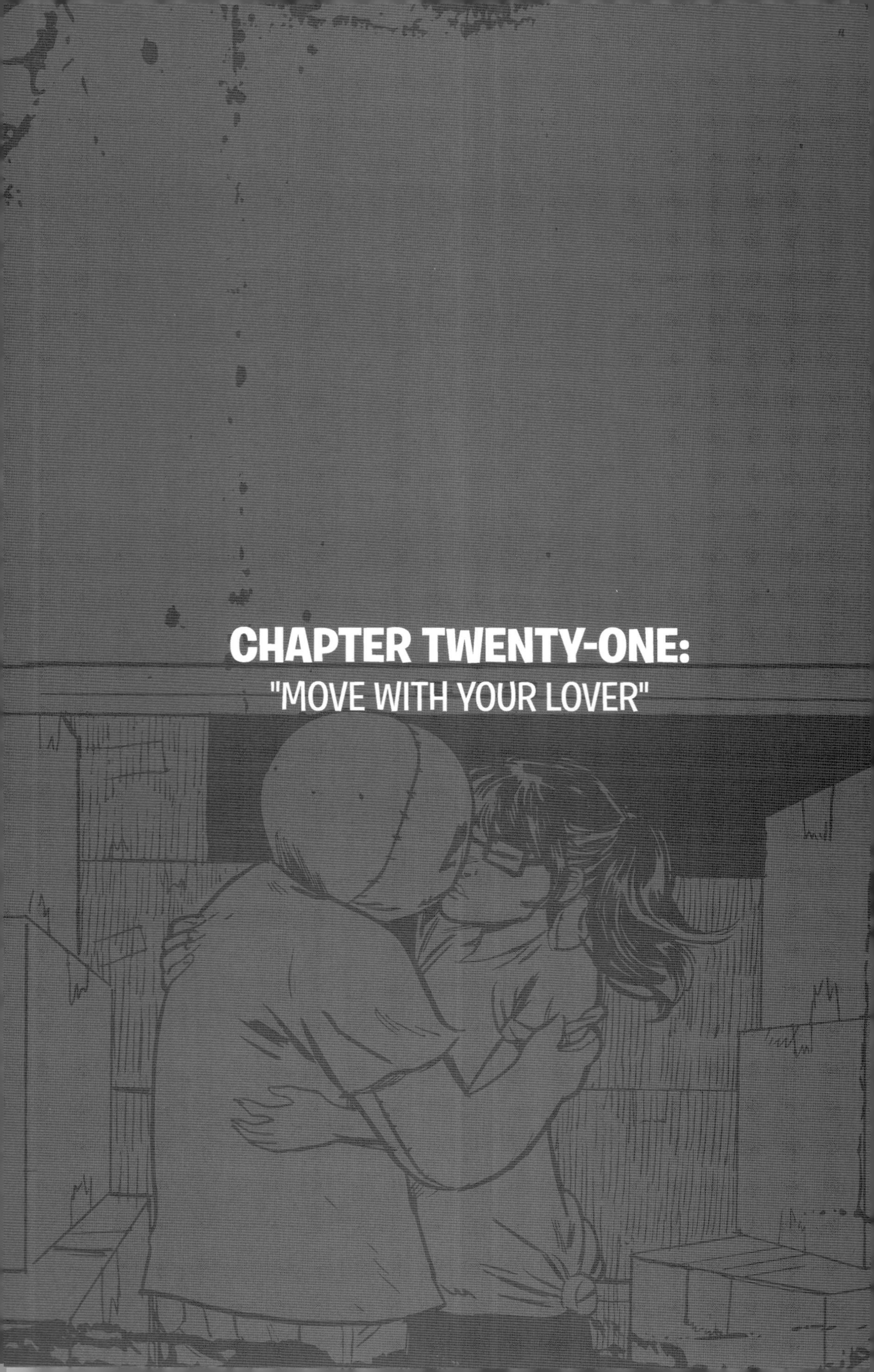

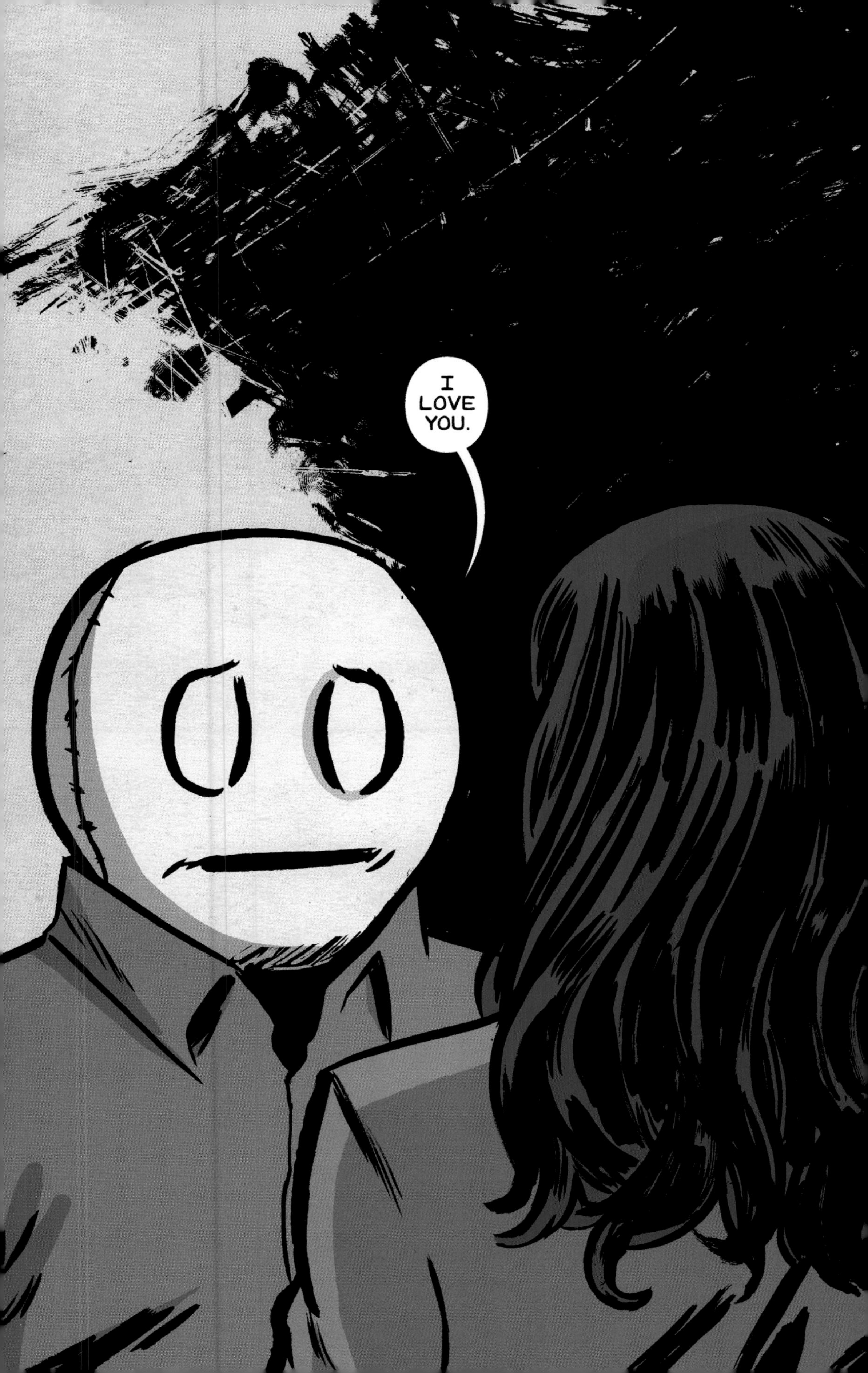
I LOVE YOU.

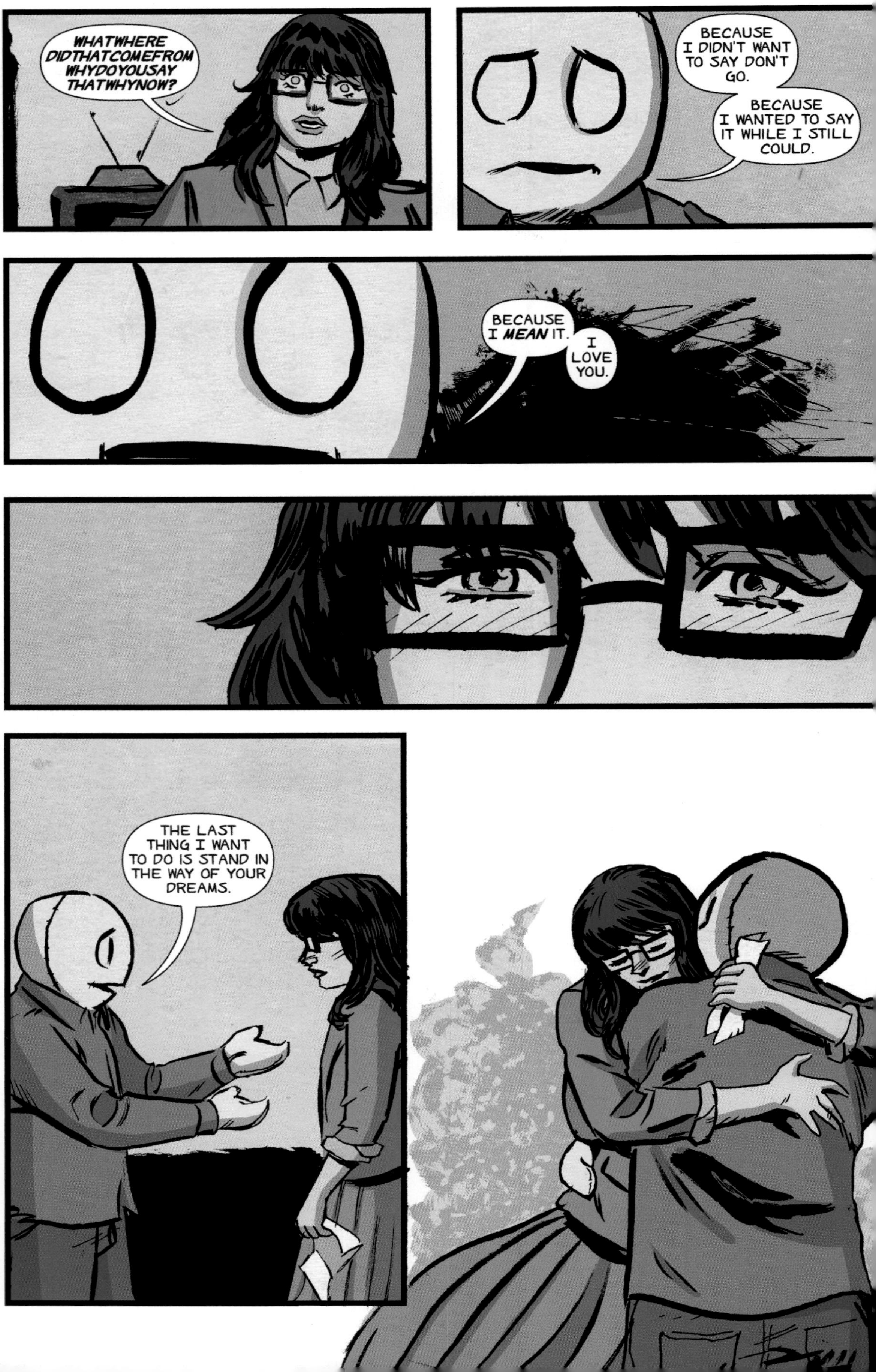

WHATWHERE DIDTHATCOMEFROM WHYDOYOUSAY THATWHYNOW?
BECAUSE I DIDN'T WANT TO SAY DON'T GO.
BECAUSE I WANTED TO SAY IT WHILE I STILL COULD.
BECAUSE I *MEAN* IT.
I LOVE YOU.
THE LAST THING I WANT TO DO IS STAND IN THE WAY OF YOUR DREAMS.

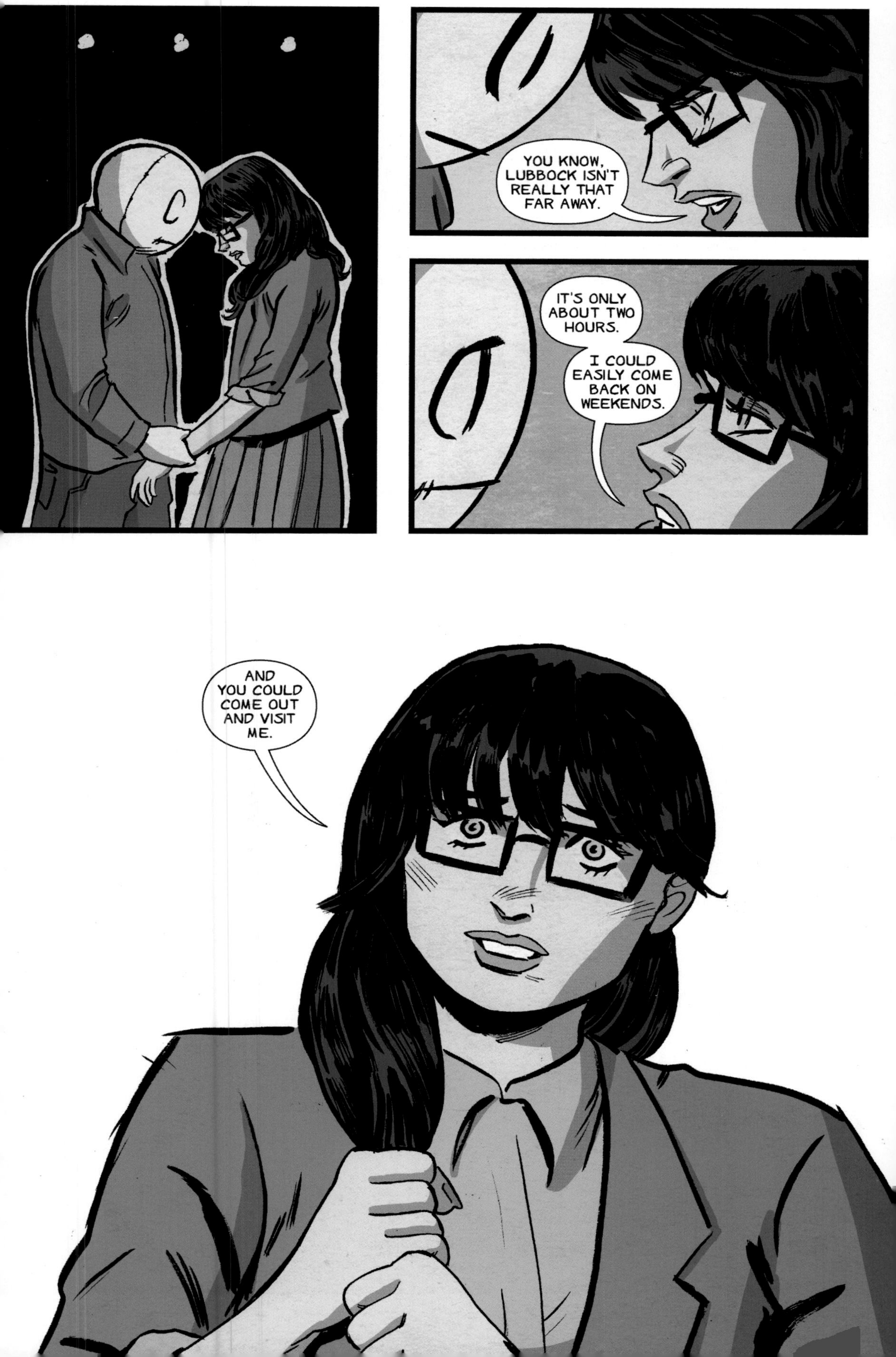
YOU KNOW, LUBBOCK ISN'T REALLY THAT FAR AWAY.
IT'S ONLY ABOUT TWO HOURS.
I COULD EASILY COME BACK ON WEEKENDS.
AND YOU COULD COME OUT AND VISIT ME.

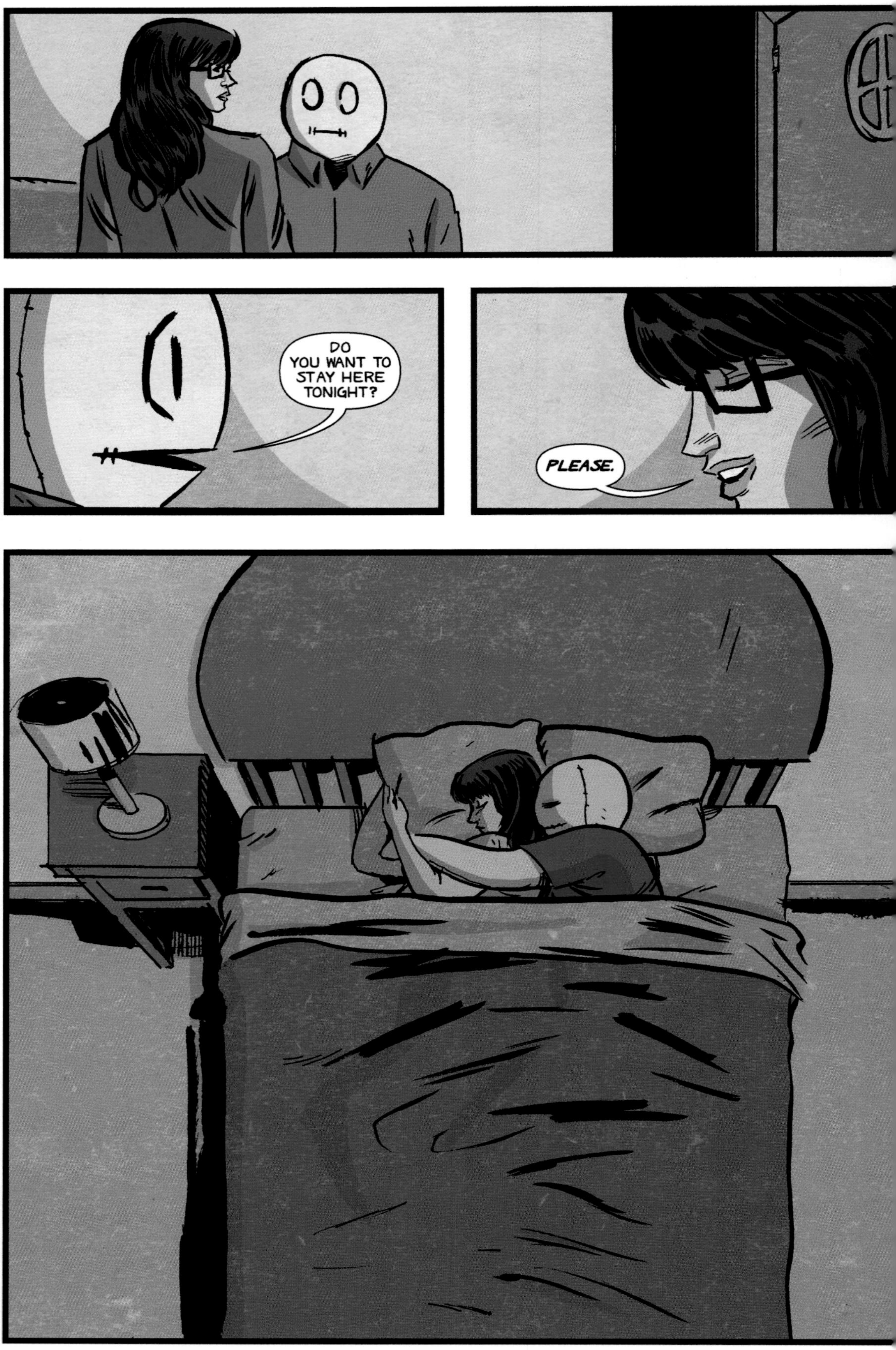
DO YOU WANT TO STAY HERE TONIGHT?
PLEASE.

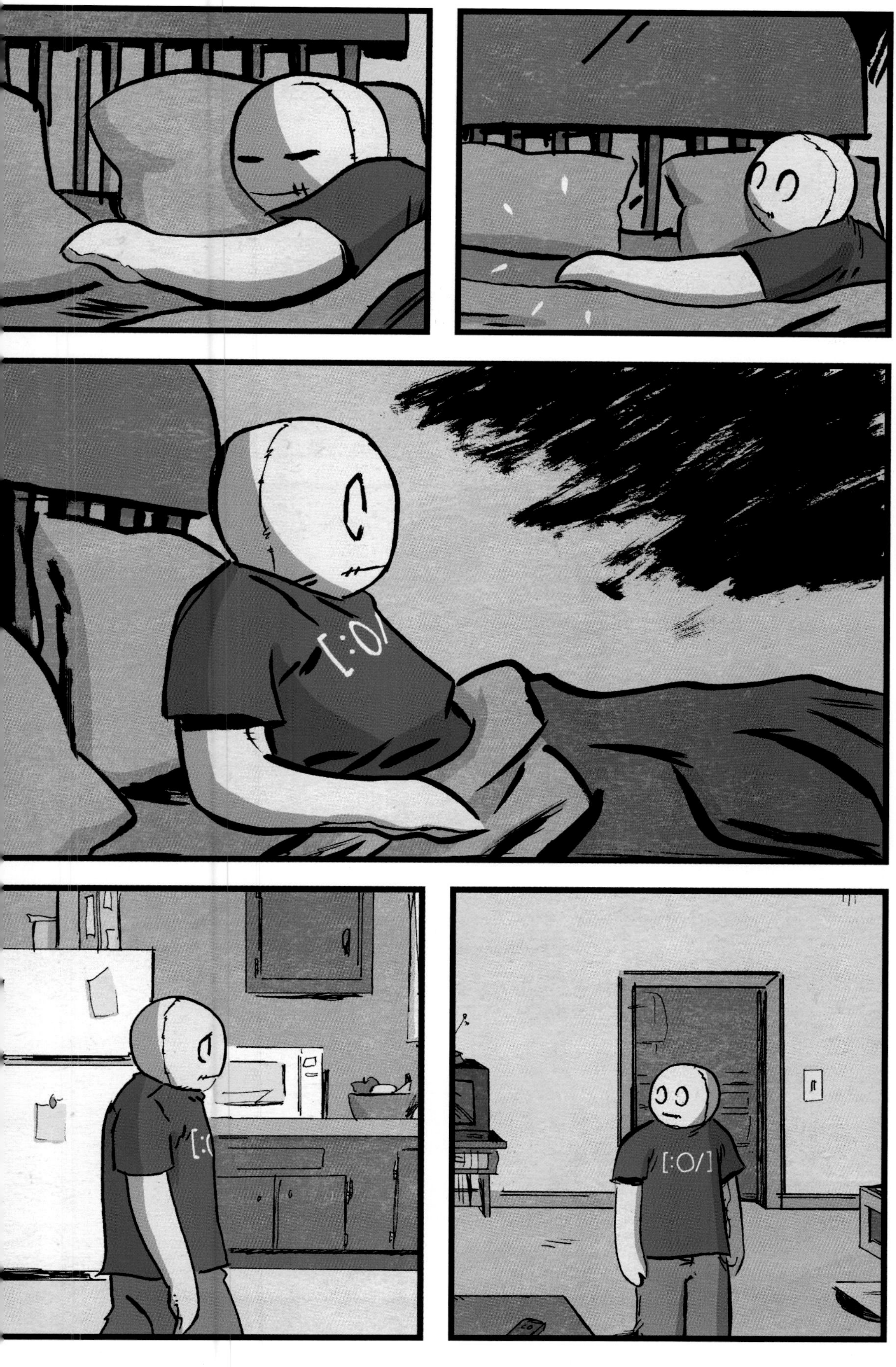
[:O/]

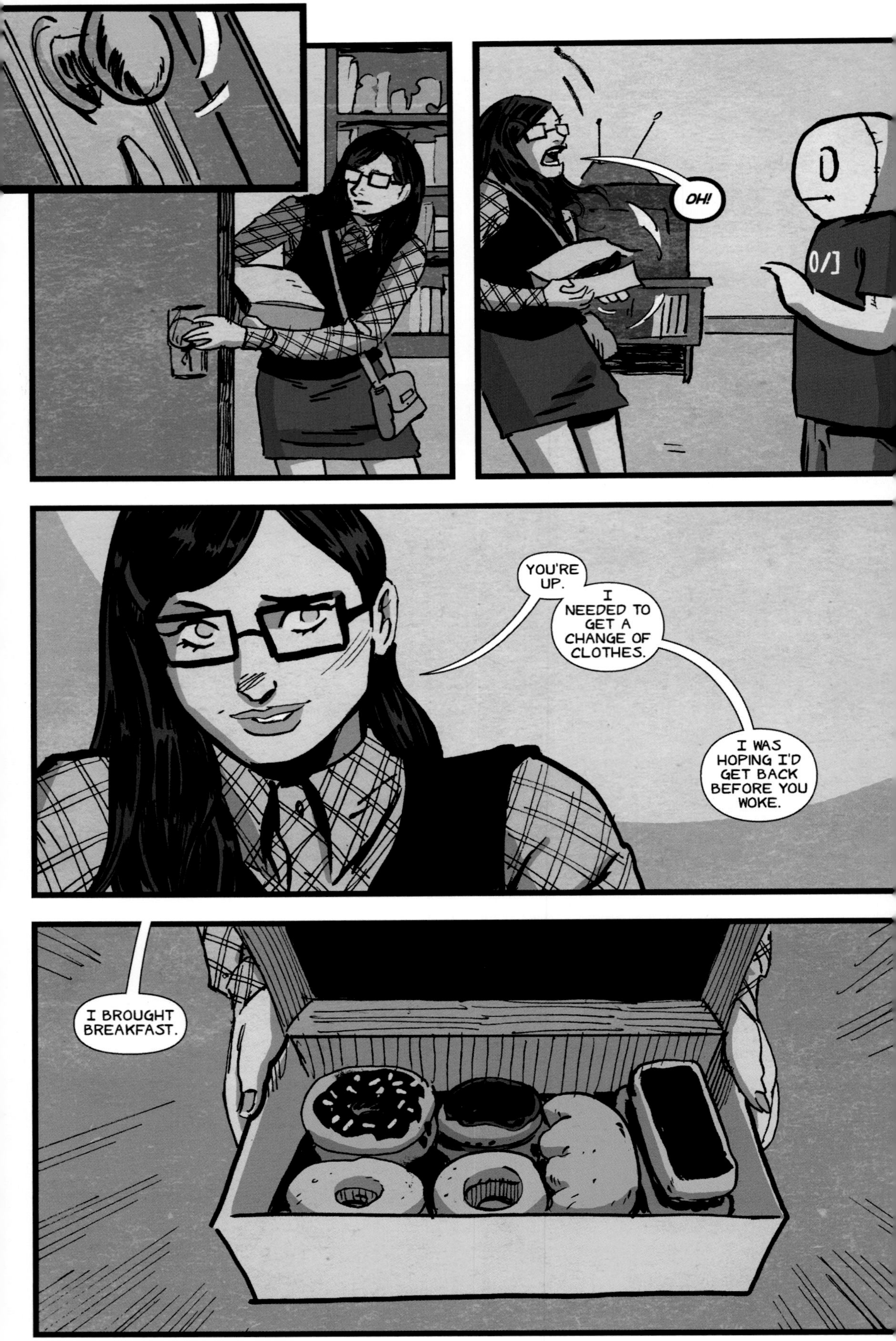
OH!
YOU'RE UP.
I NEEDED TO GET A CHANGE OF CLOTHES.
I WAS HOPING I'D GET BACK BEFORE YOU WOKE.
I BROUGHT BREAKFAST.

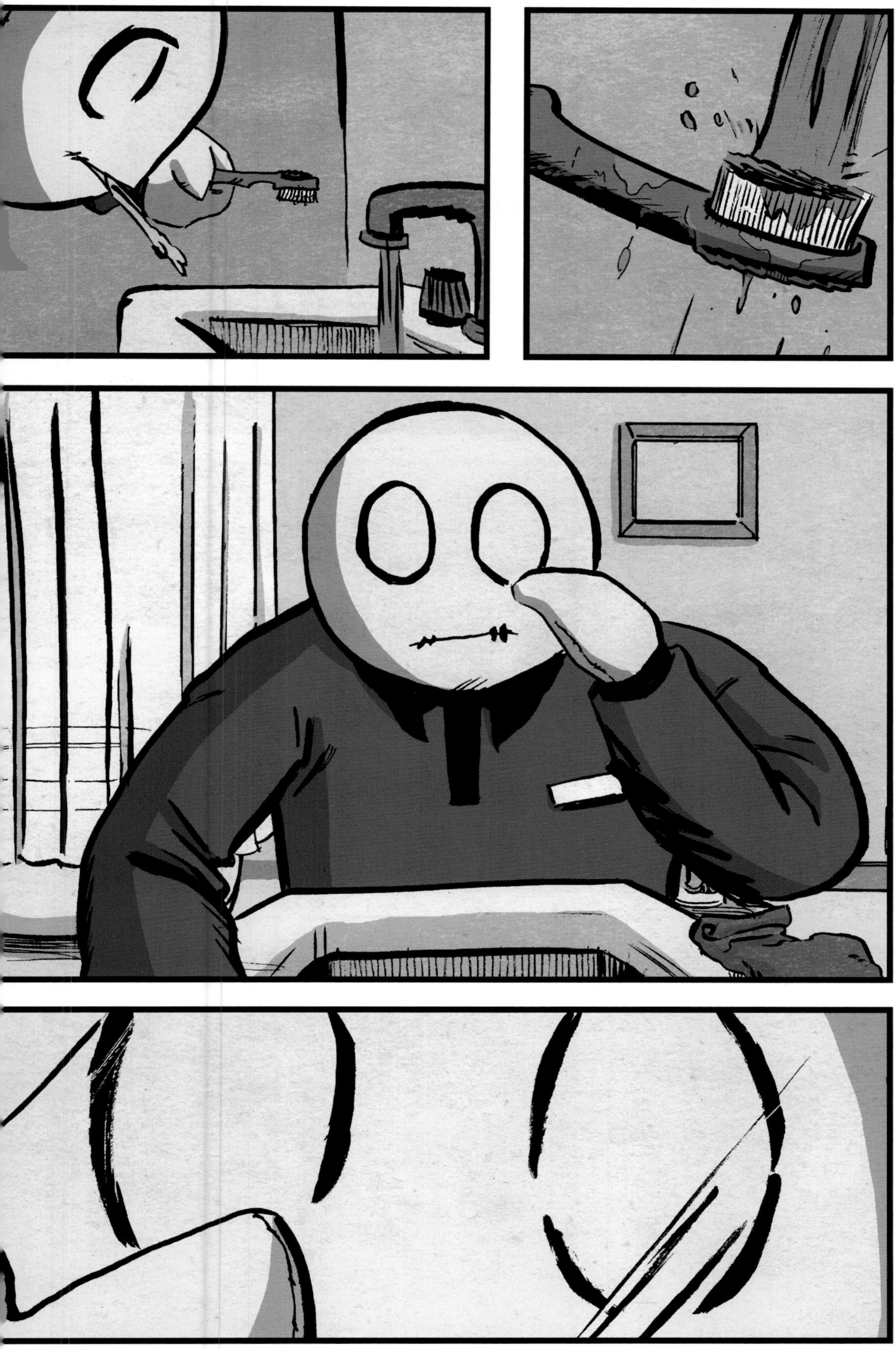

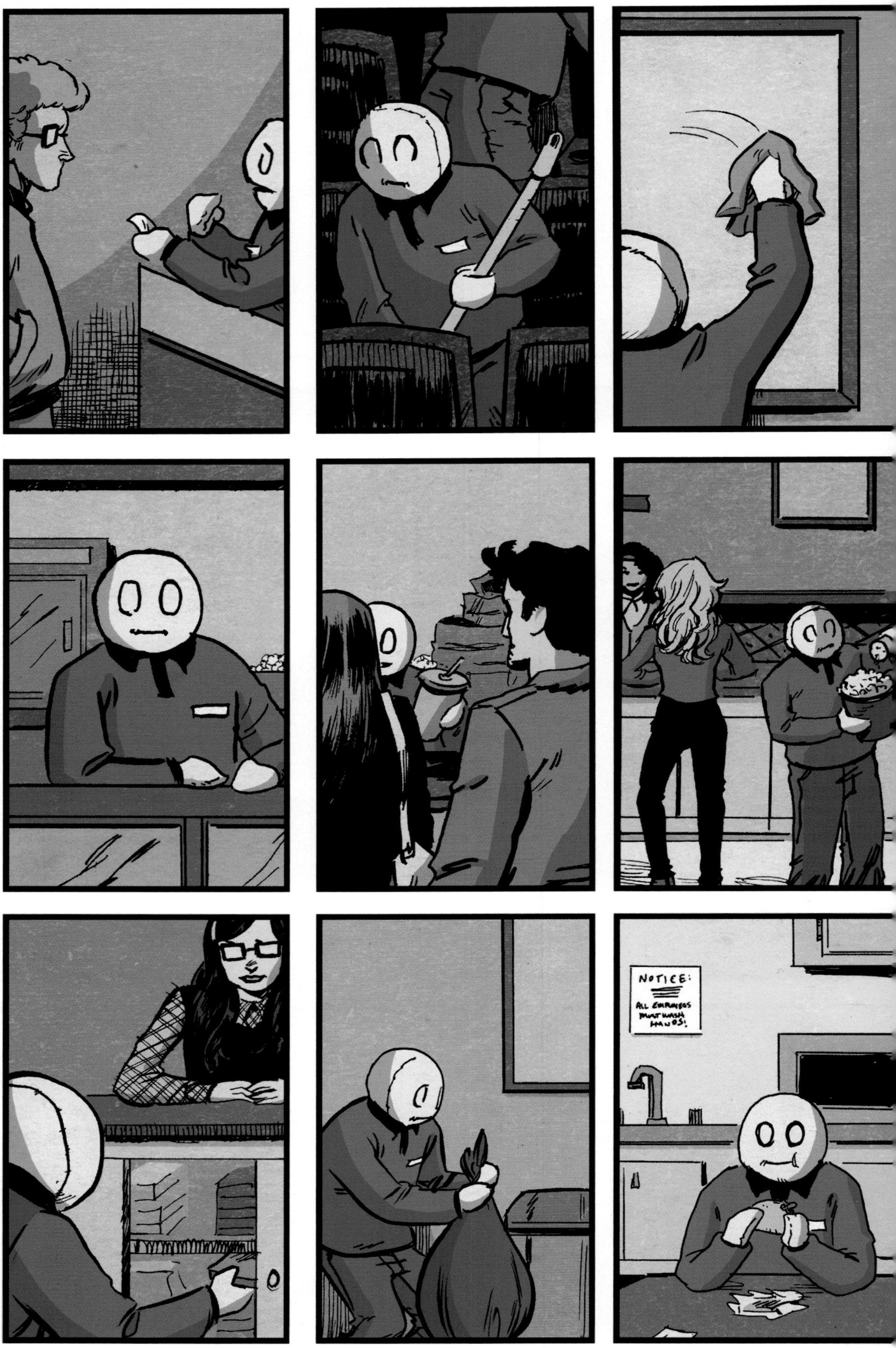
NOTICE:
ALL EMPLOYEES MUST WASH HANDS!

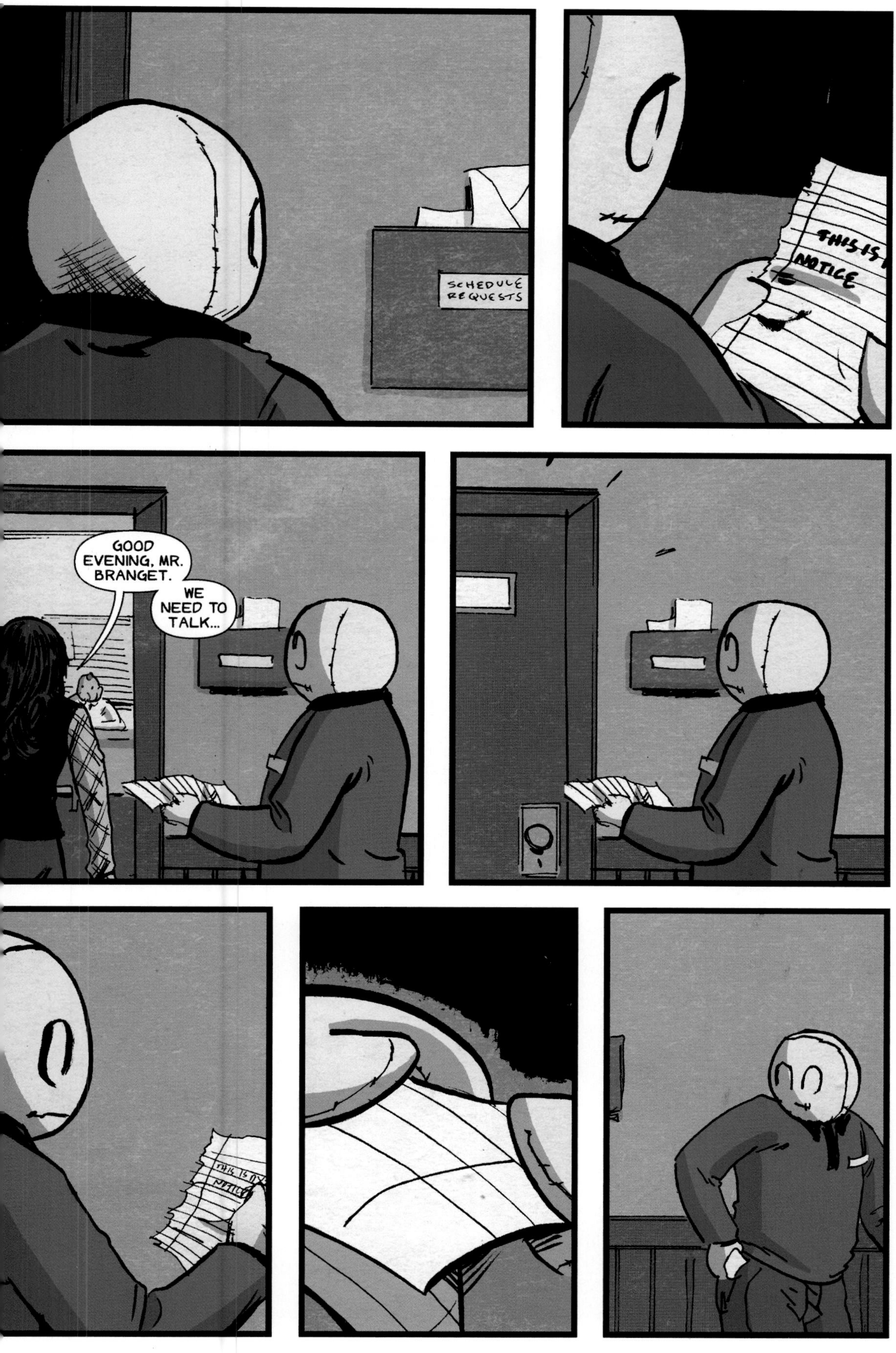
SCHEDULE REQUESTS
THIS IS
NOTICE
GOOD EVENING, MR. BRANGET.
WE NEED TO TALK...

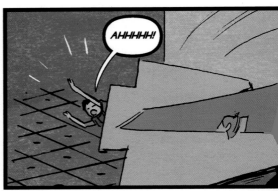

AHHHHH!

ARE YOU OKAY?

MY ARM HURTS.

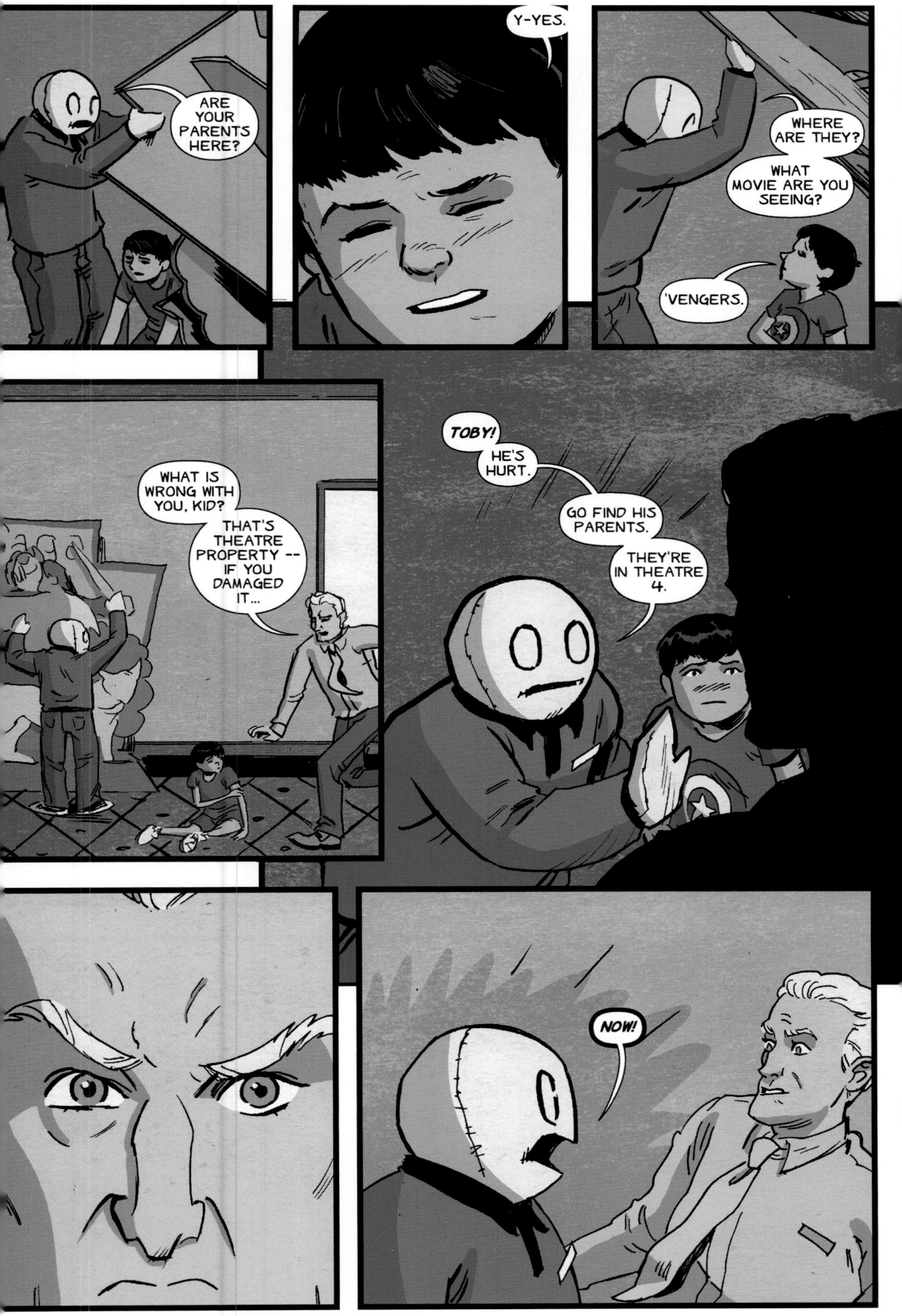

ARE YOUR PARENTS HERE?
Y-YES.
WHERE ARE THEY?
WHAT MOVIE ARE YOU SEEING?
'VENGERS.
WHAT IS WRONG WITH YOU, KID?
THAT'S THEATRE PROPERTY -- IF YOU DAMAGED IT...
TOBY!
HE'S HURT.
GO FIND HIS PARENTS.
THEY'RE IN THEATRE 4.
NOW!

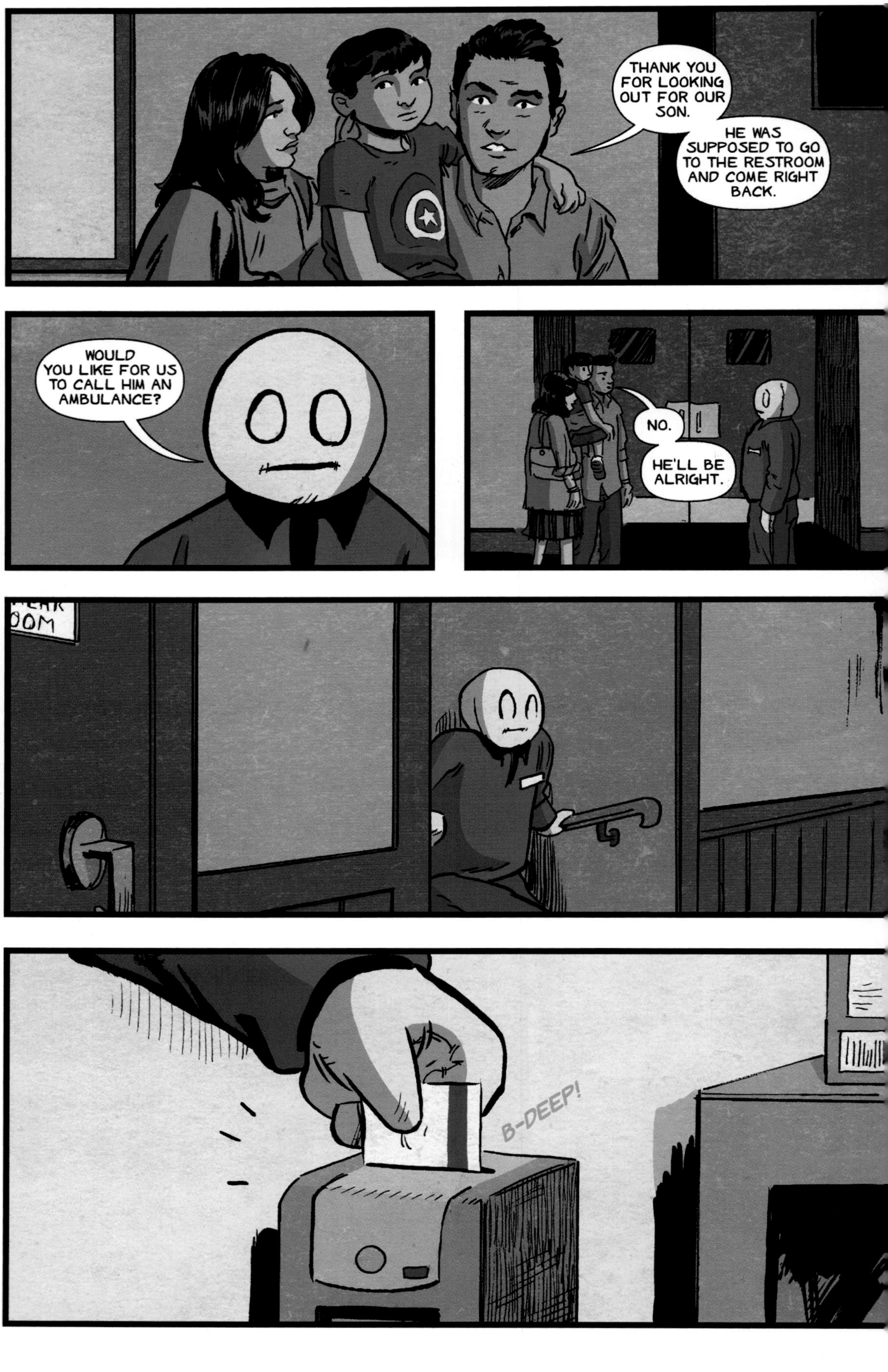
THANK YOU FOR LOOKING OUT FOR OUR SON.
HE WAS SUPPOSED TO GO TO THE RESTROOM AND COME RIGHT BACK.
WOULD YOU LIKE FOR US TO CALL HIM AN AMBULANCE?
NO.
HE'LL BE ALRIGHT.
B-DEEP!

HOW'D CARL REACT TO THE NEWS?

HE WAS SAD TO SEE ME GO, BUT HE UNDERSTOOD.

HE WISHED ME LUCK ON MY FUTURE.

HOW ABOUT YOU? DID YOU TURN IN *YOUR* TWO WEEKS NOTICE?

NAH.

YOU WERE RIGHT.

I NEED AN EXIT STRATEGY FIRST.

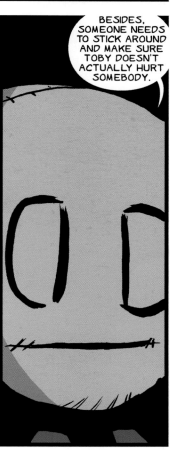

BESIDES, SOMEONE NEEDS TO STICK AROUND AND MAKE SURE TOBY DOESN'T ACTUALLY HURT SOMEBODY.

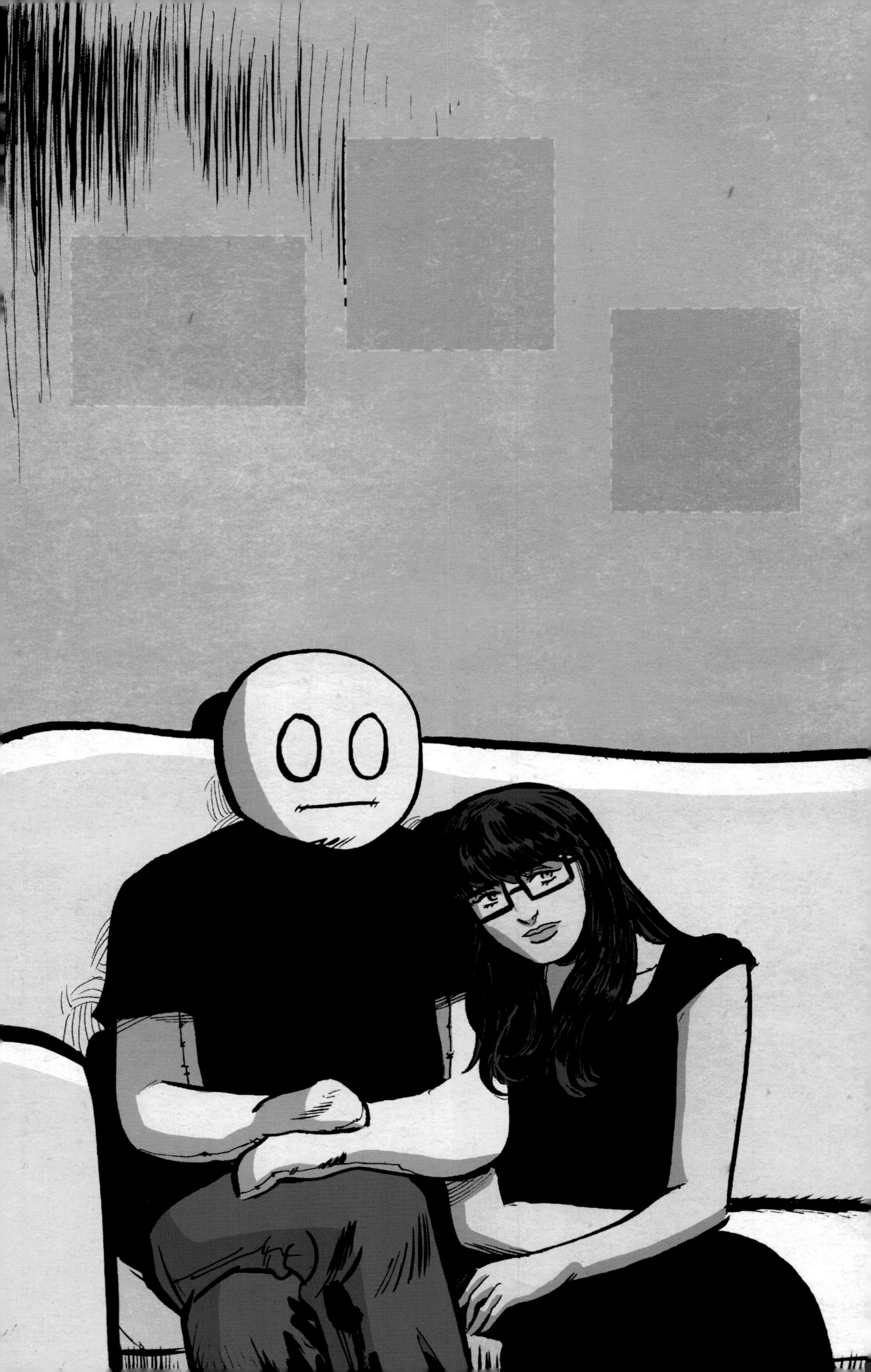

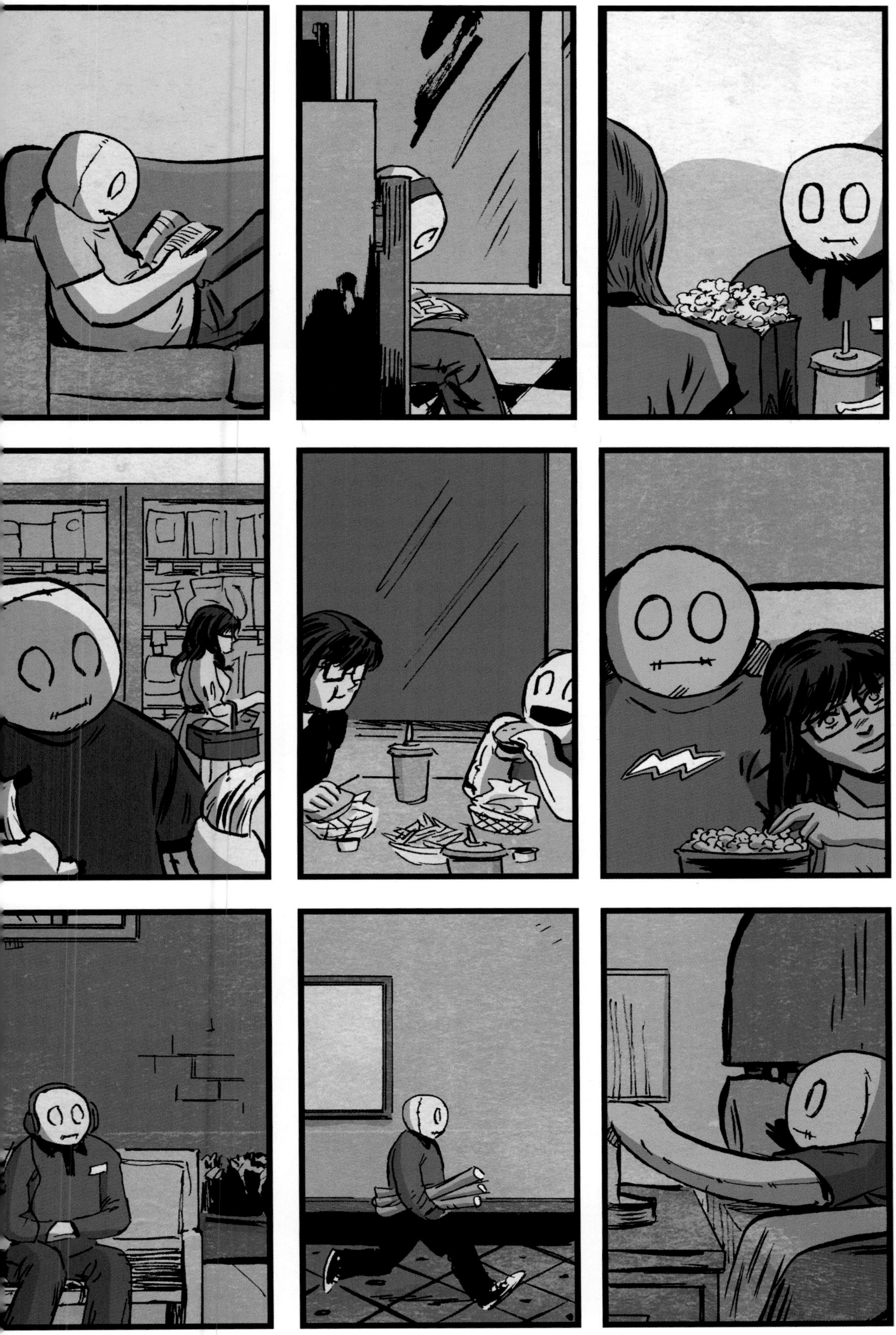

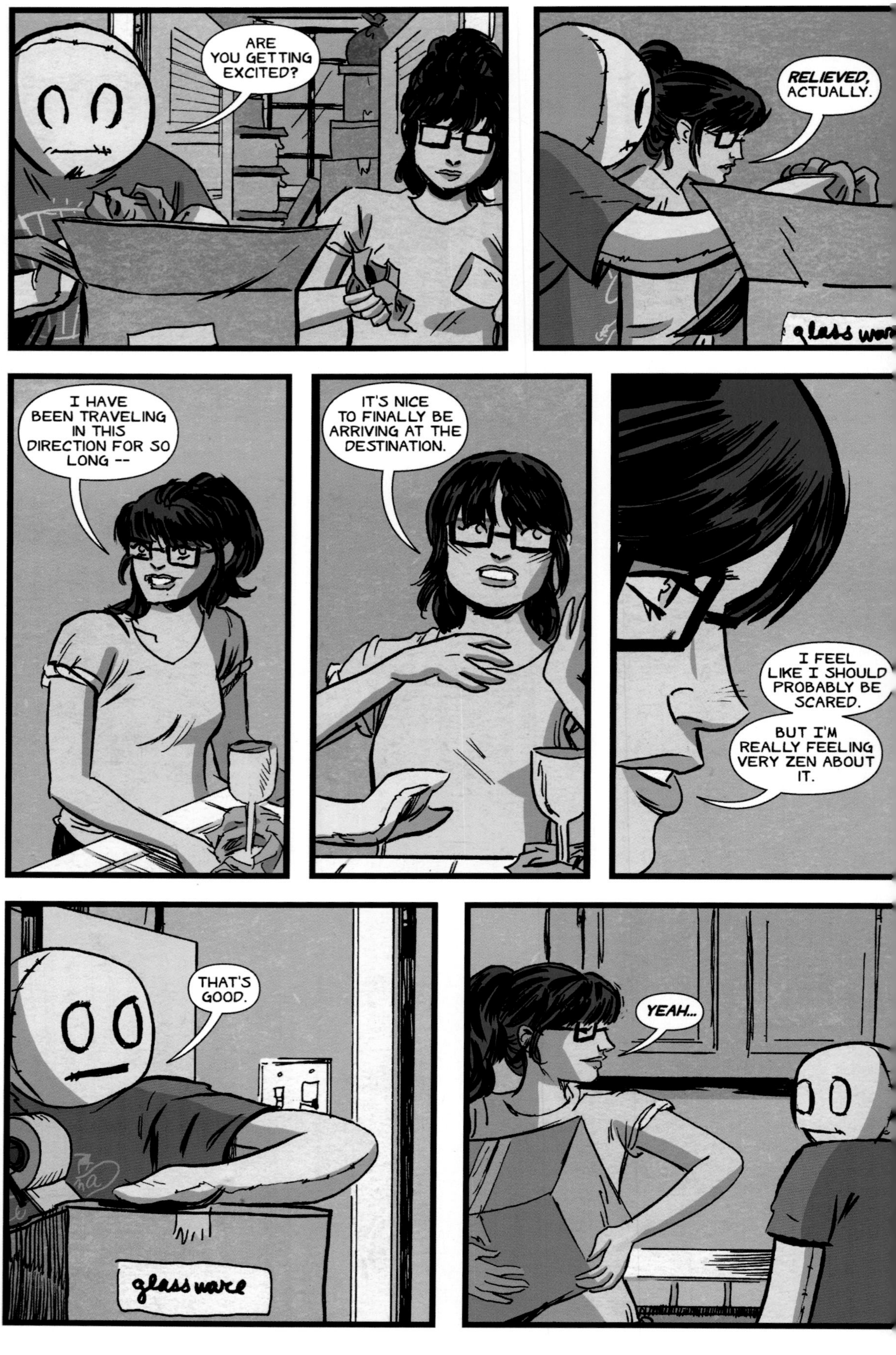
ARE YOU GETTING EXCITED?
RELIEVED, ACTUALLY.
glass ware
I HAVE BEEN TRAVELING IN THIS DIRECTION FOR SO LONG --
IT'S NICE TO FINALLY BE ARRIVING AT THE DESTINATION.
I FEEL LIKE I SHOULD PROBABLY BE SCARED.
BUT I'M REALLY FEELING VERY ZEN ABOUT IT.
THAT'S GOOD.
glassware
YEAH...

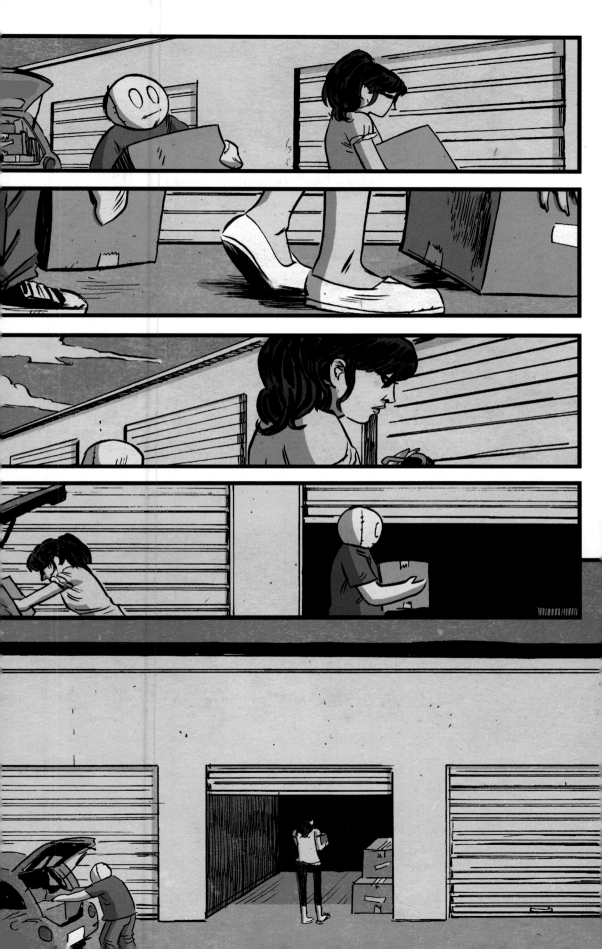

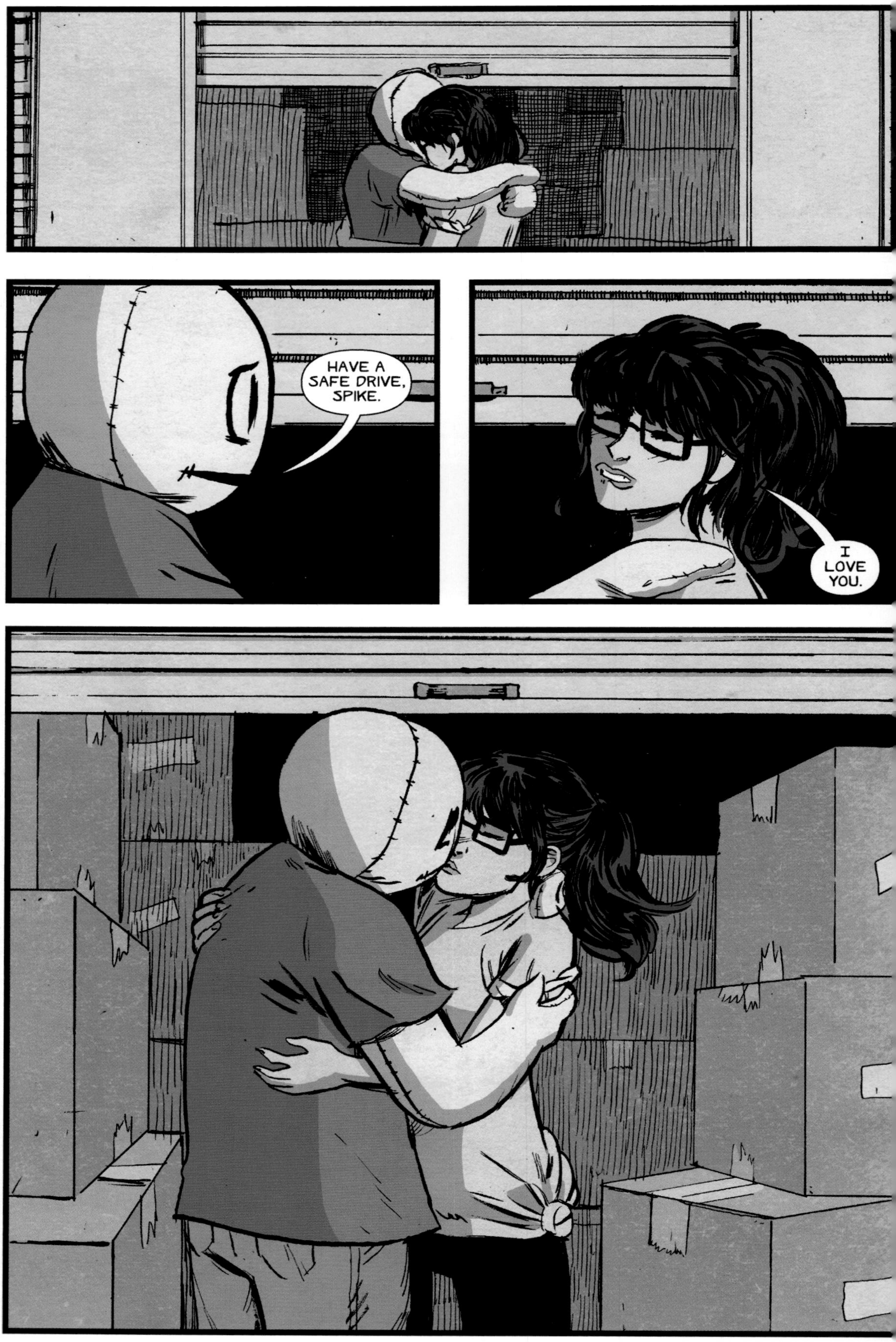
HAVE A SAFE DRIVE, SPIKE.
I LOVE YOU.

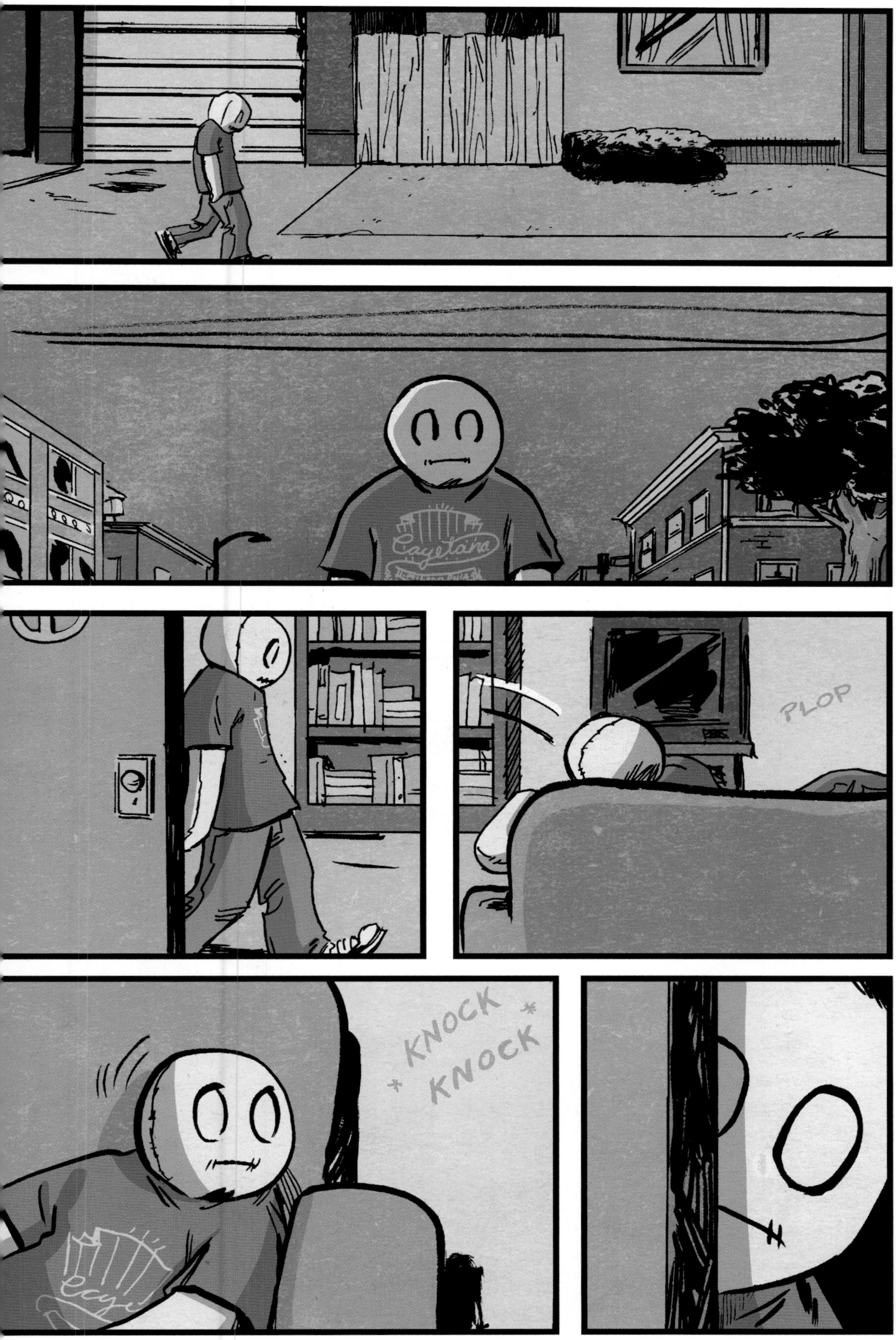
PLOP
KNOCK
KNOCK

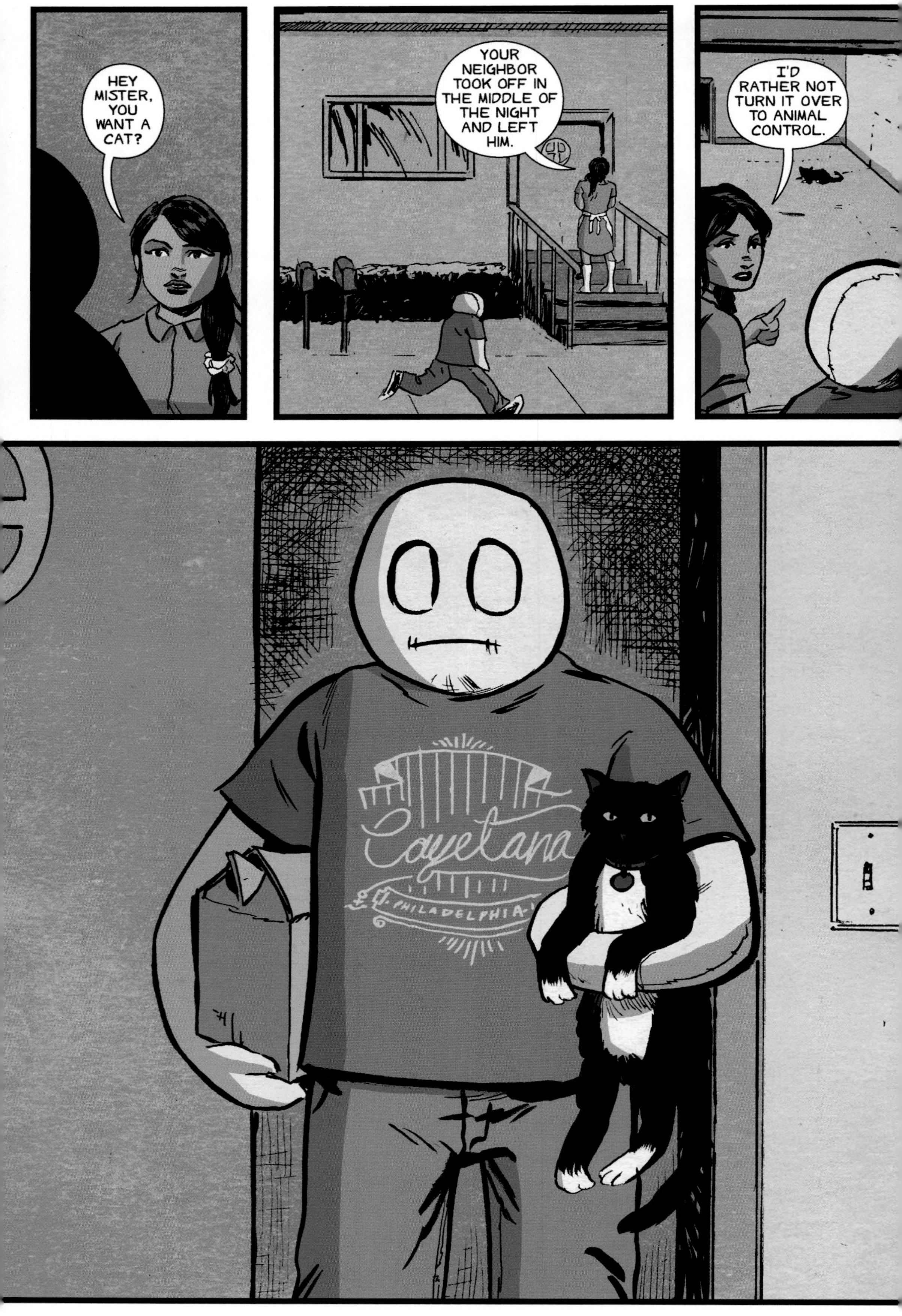
HEY MISTER, YOU WANT A CAT?
YOUR NEIGHBOR TOOK OFF IN THE MIDDLE OF THE NIGHT AND LEFT HIM.
I'D RATHER NOT TURN IT OVER TO ANIMAL CONTROL.
Cayetana
PHILADELPHIA

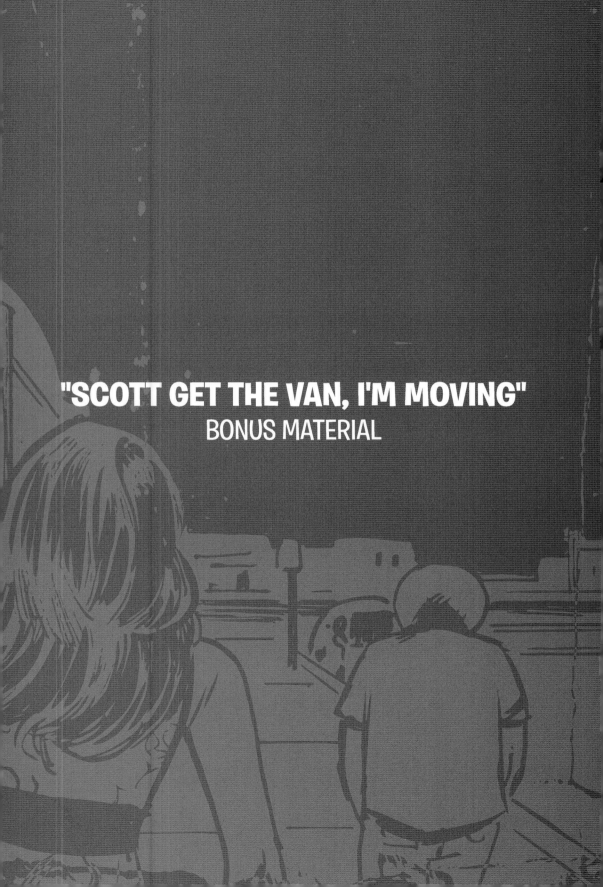

"SCOTT GET THE VAN, I'M MOVING"
BONUS MATERIAL

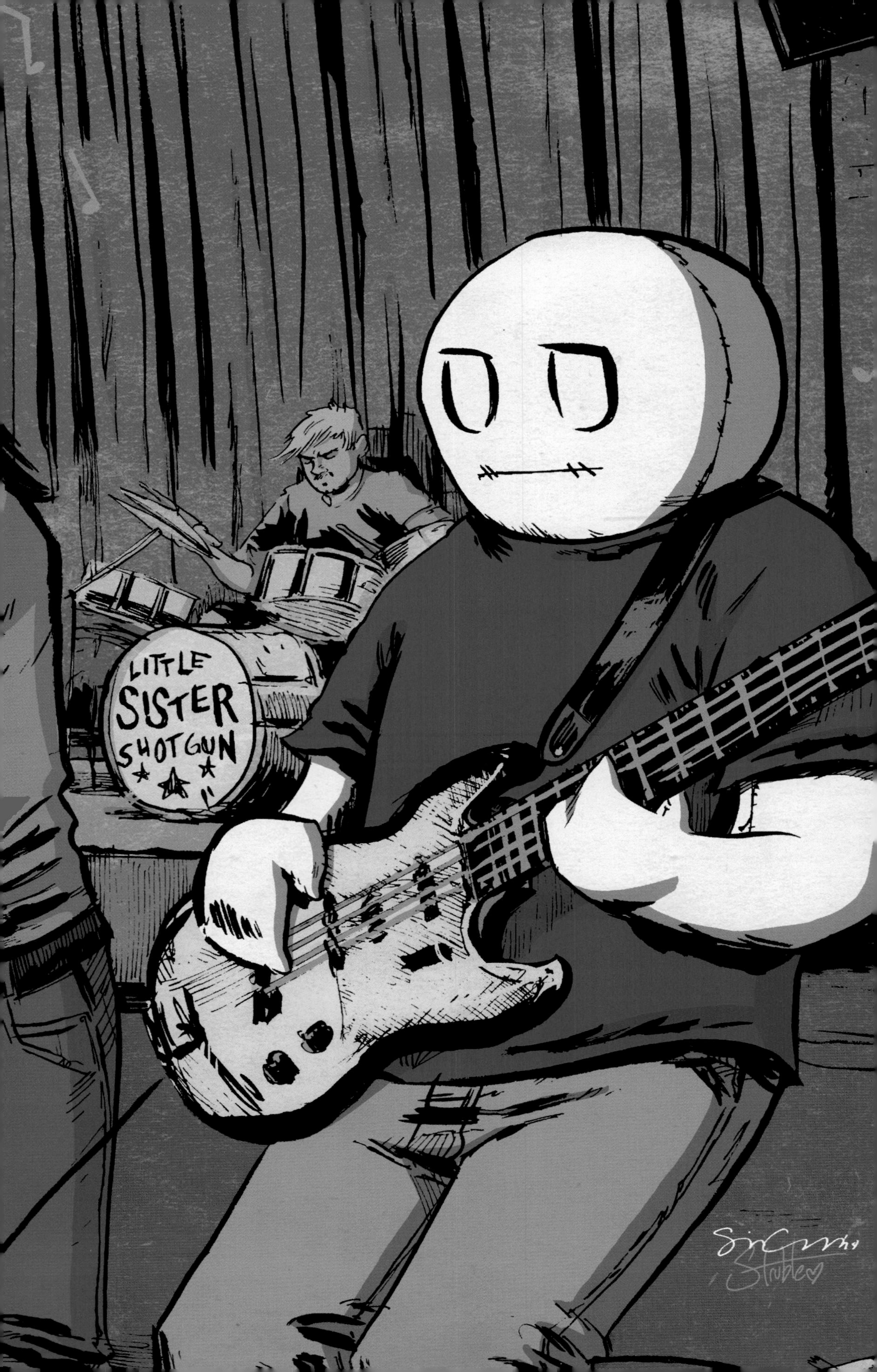
LITTLE
SISTER
SHOTGUN

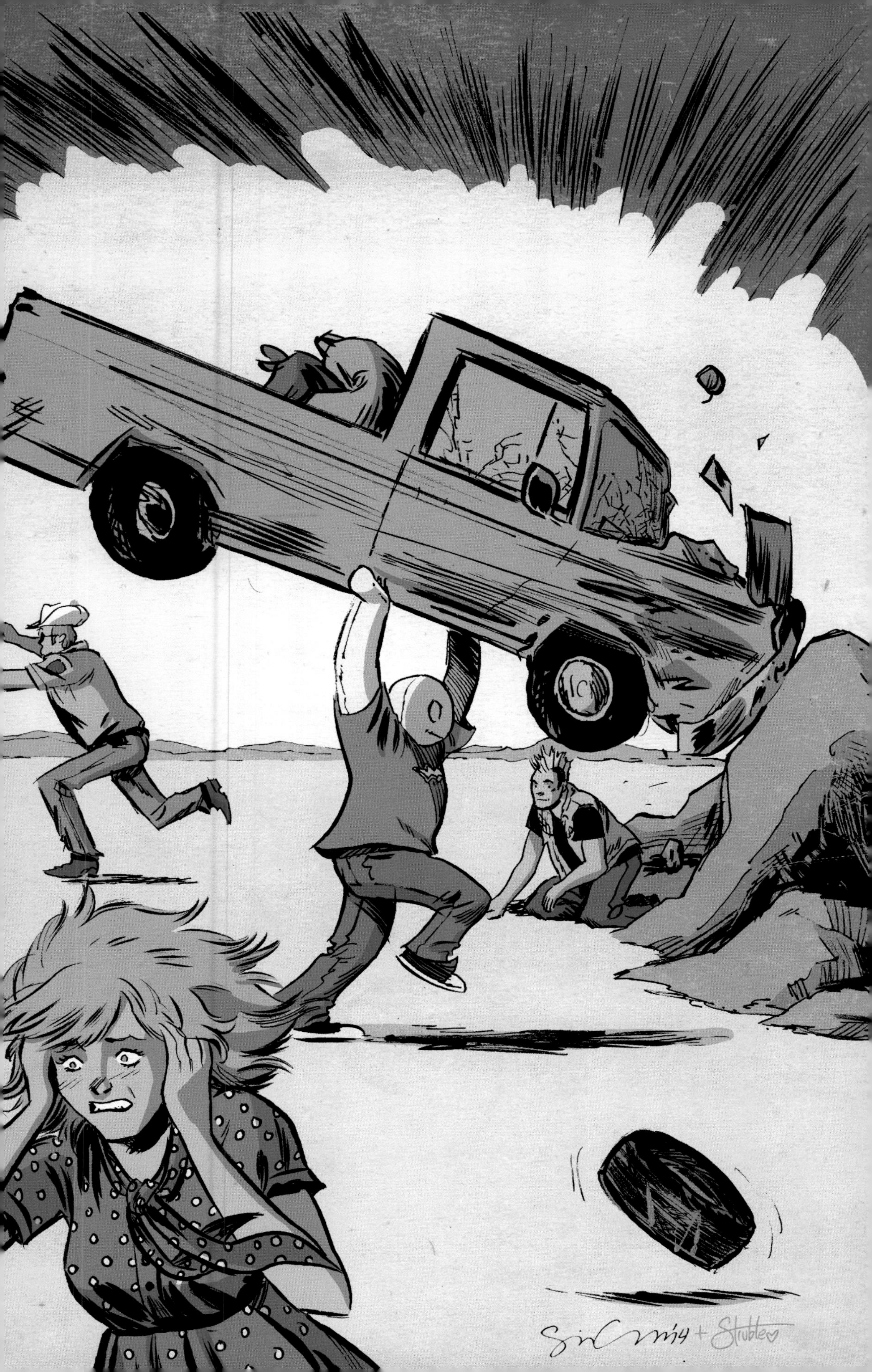

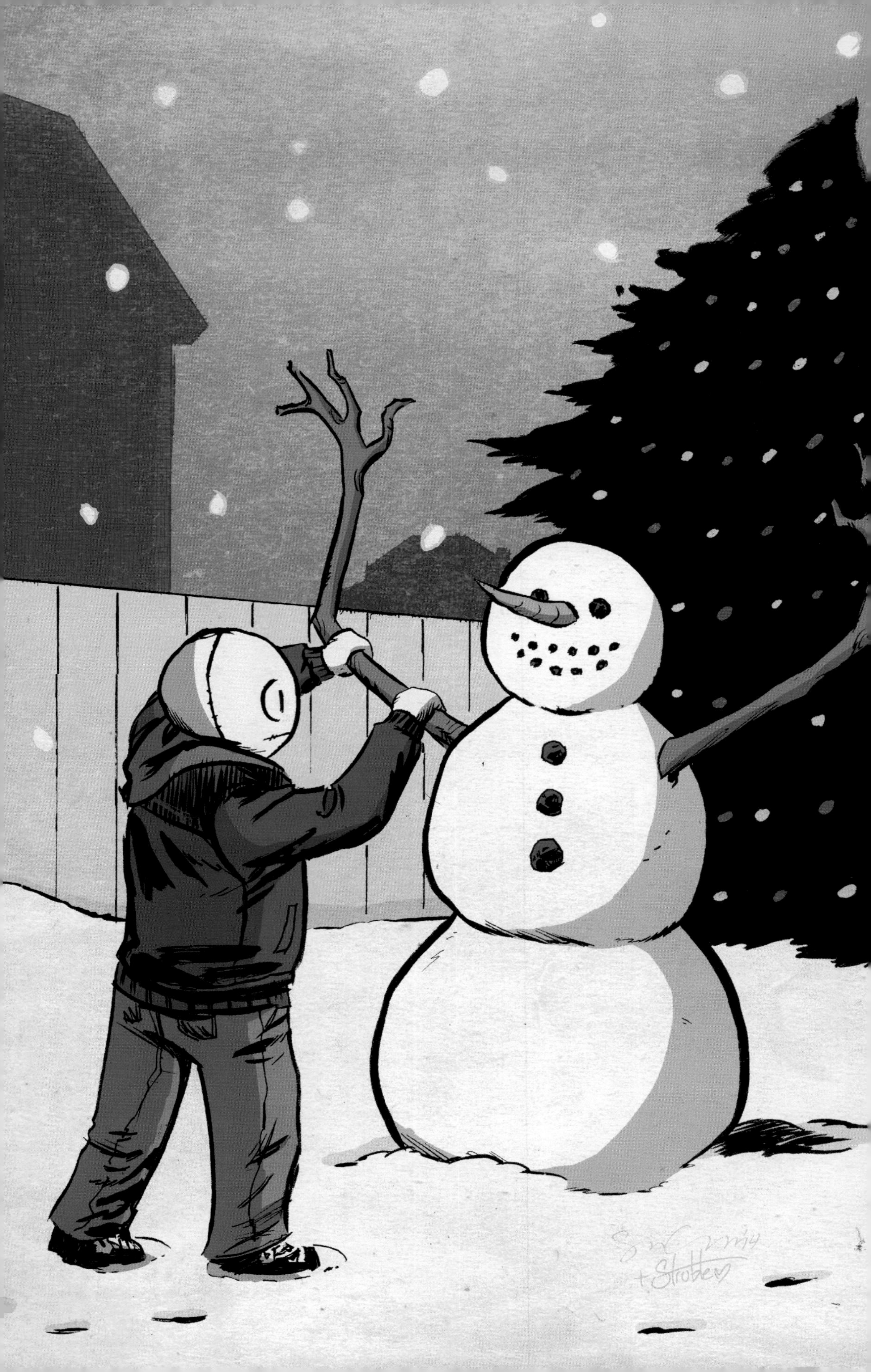

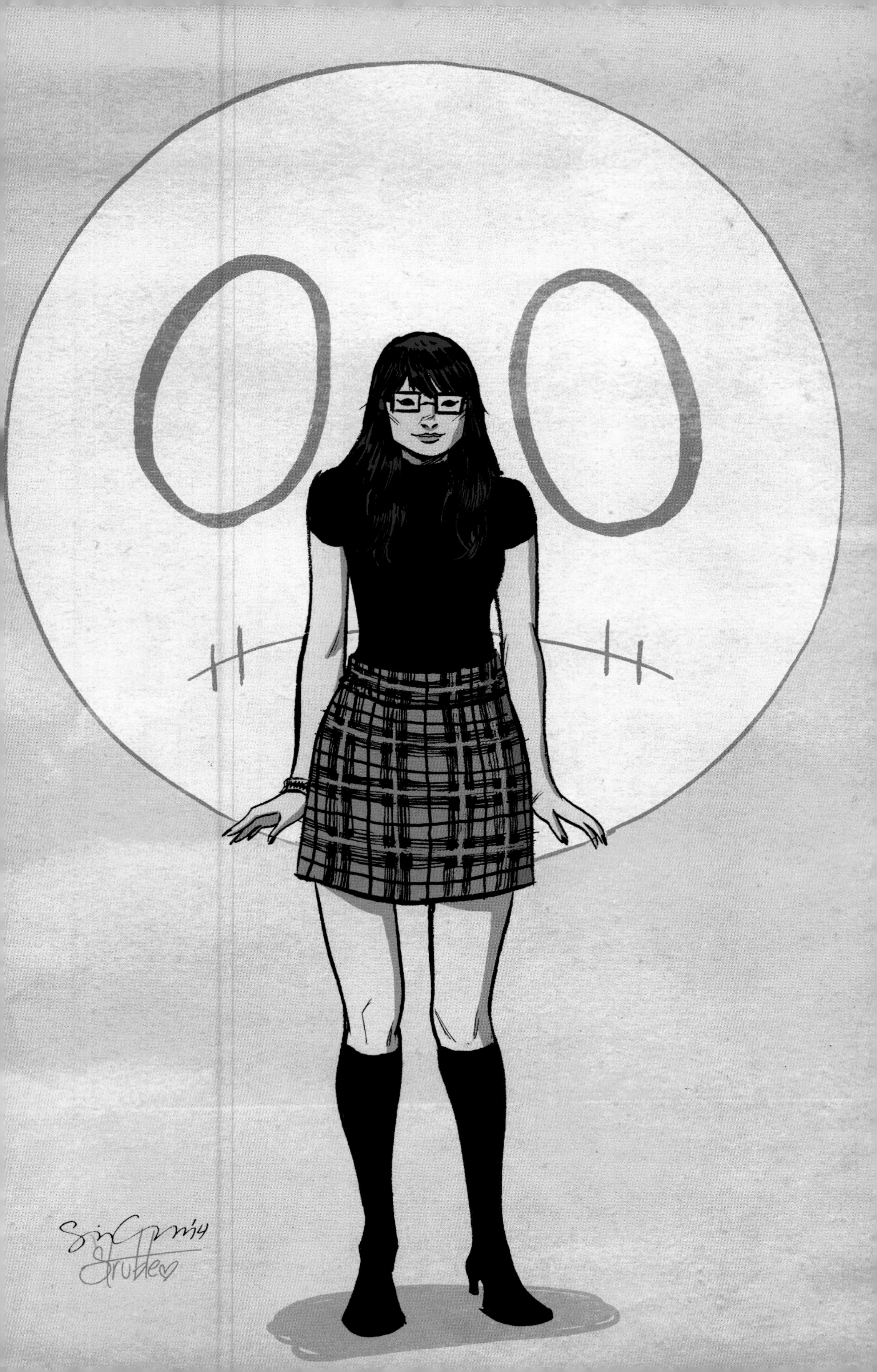

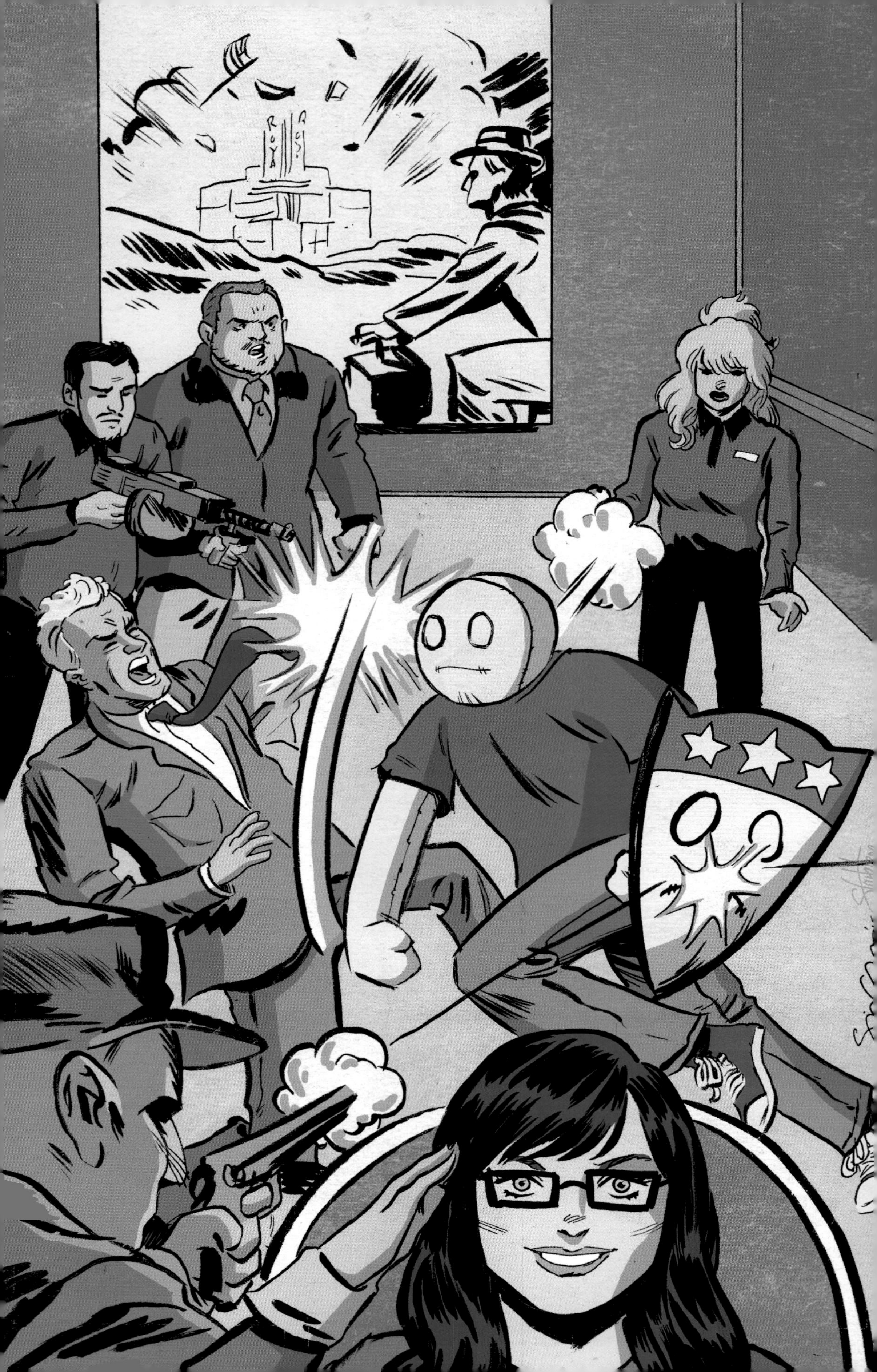

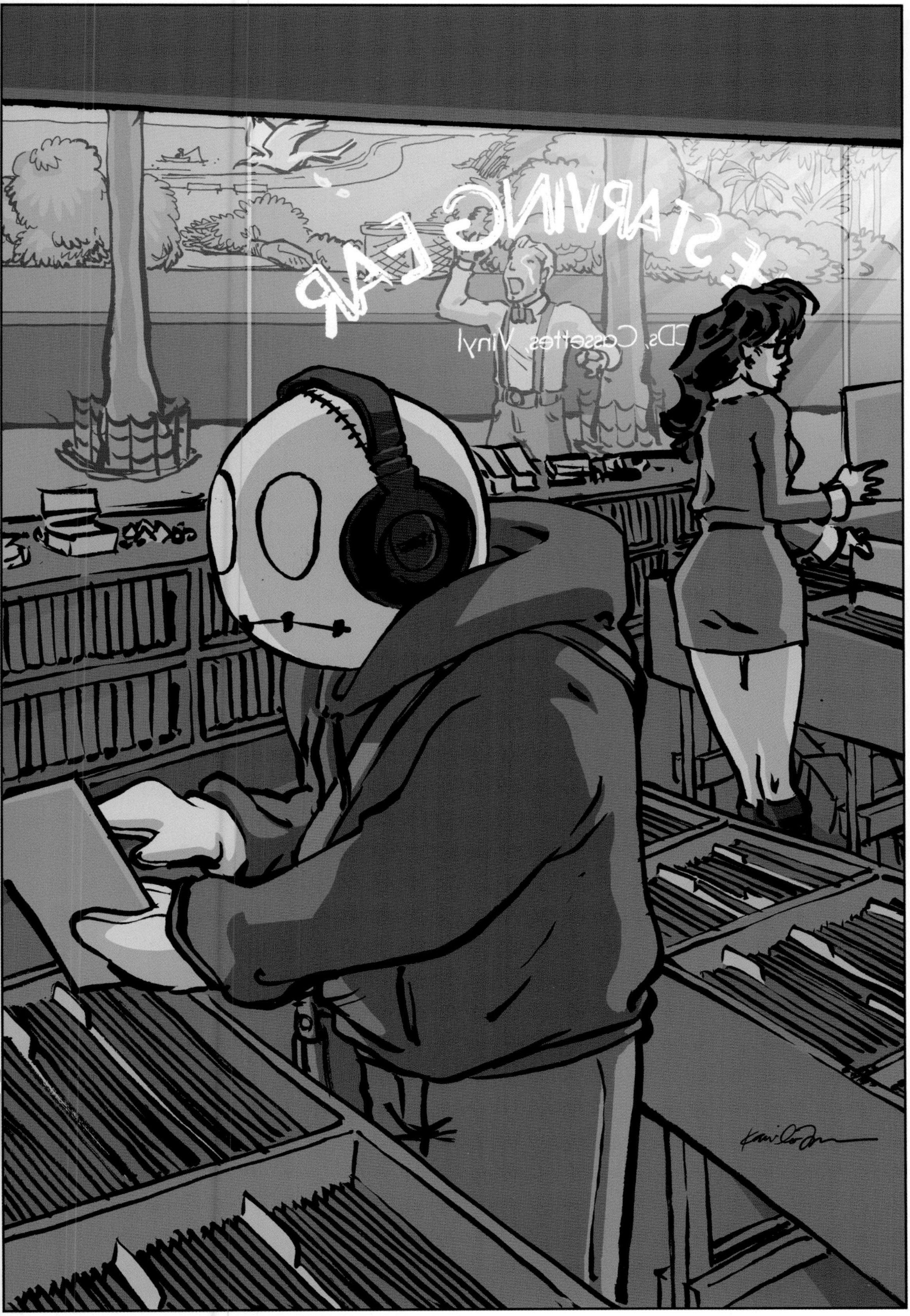
STARVING EAR
CDs, Cassettes, Vinyl

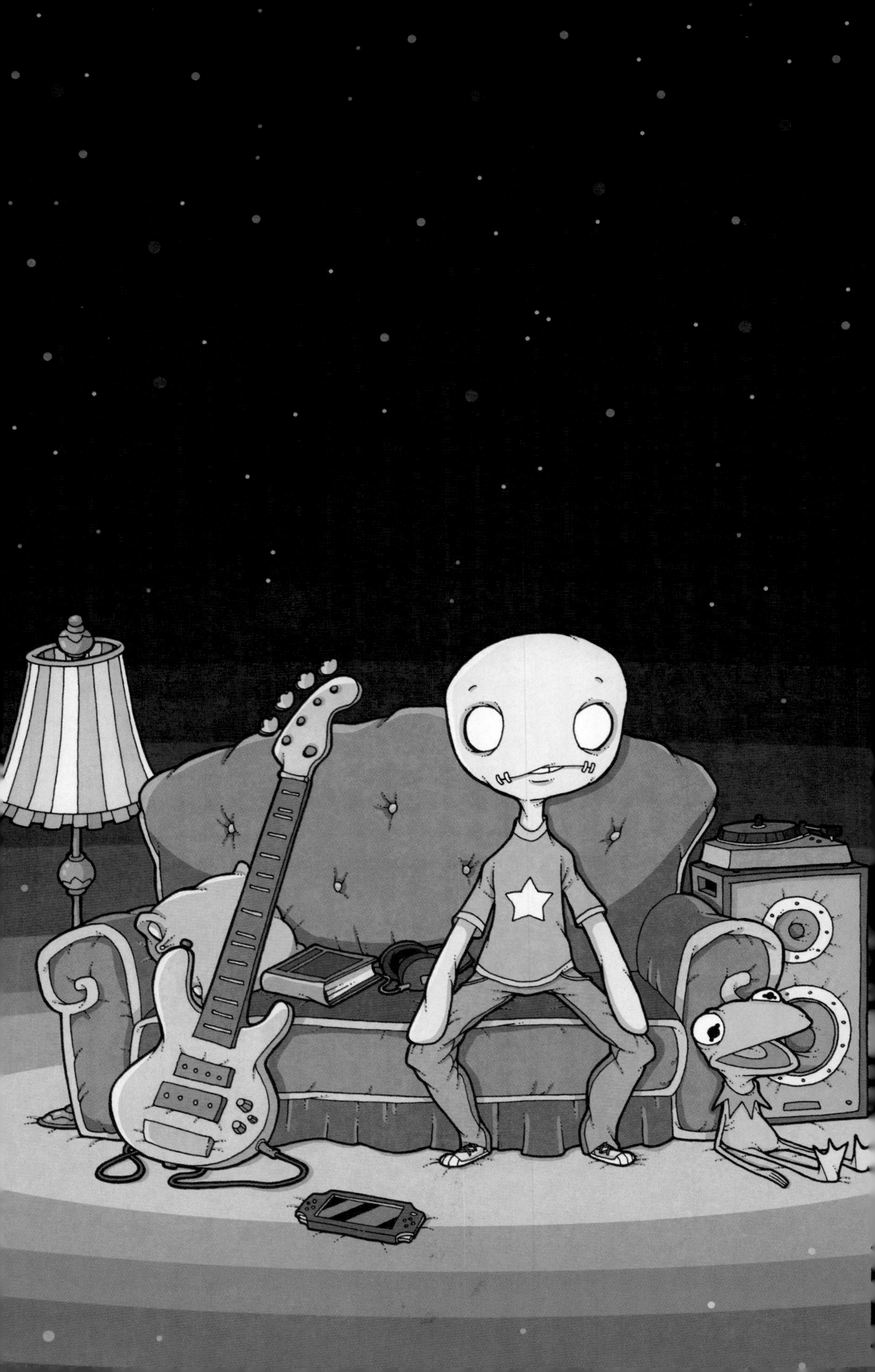

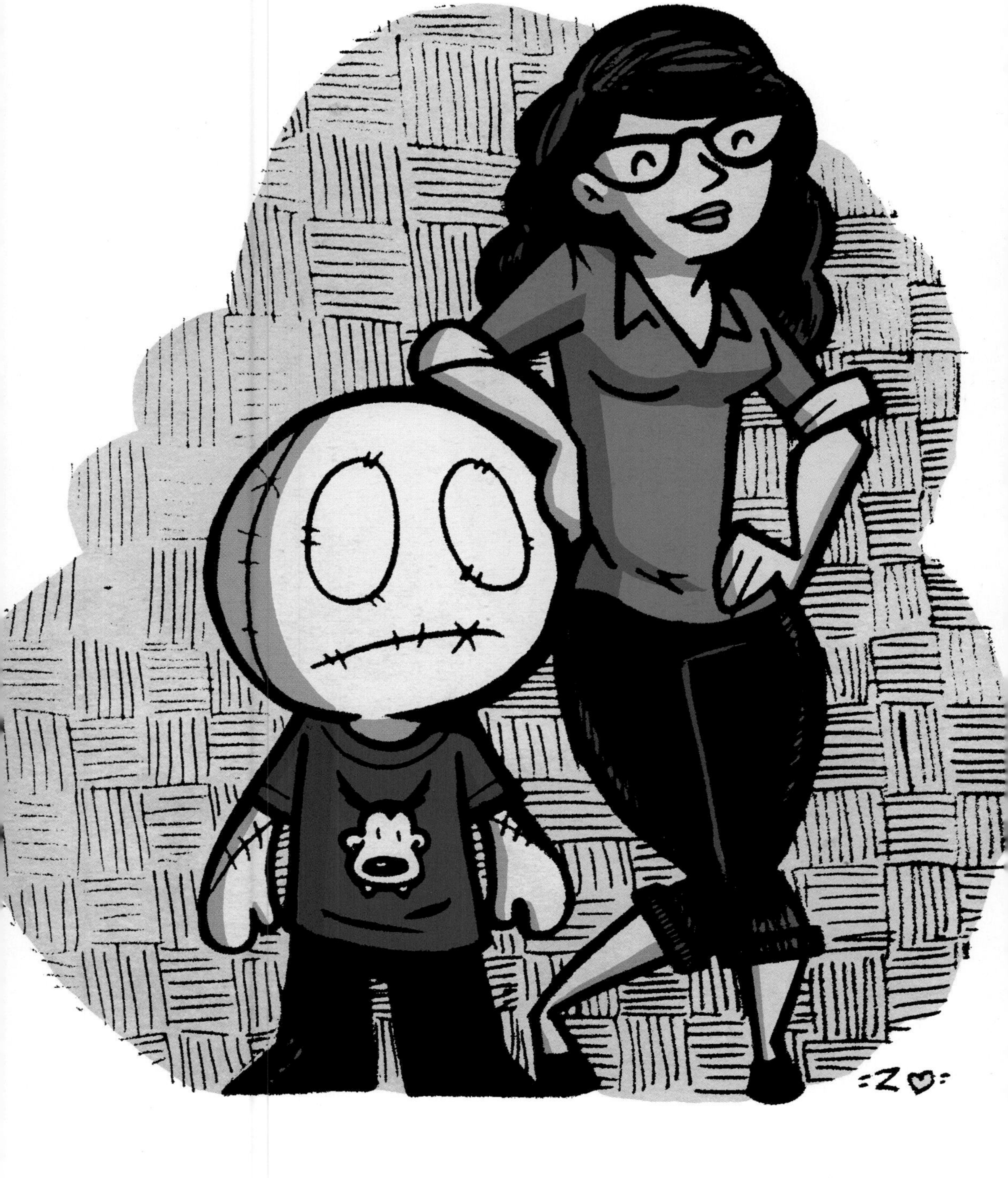

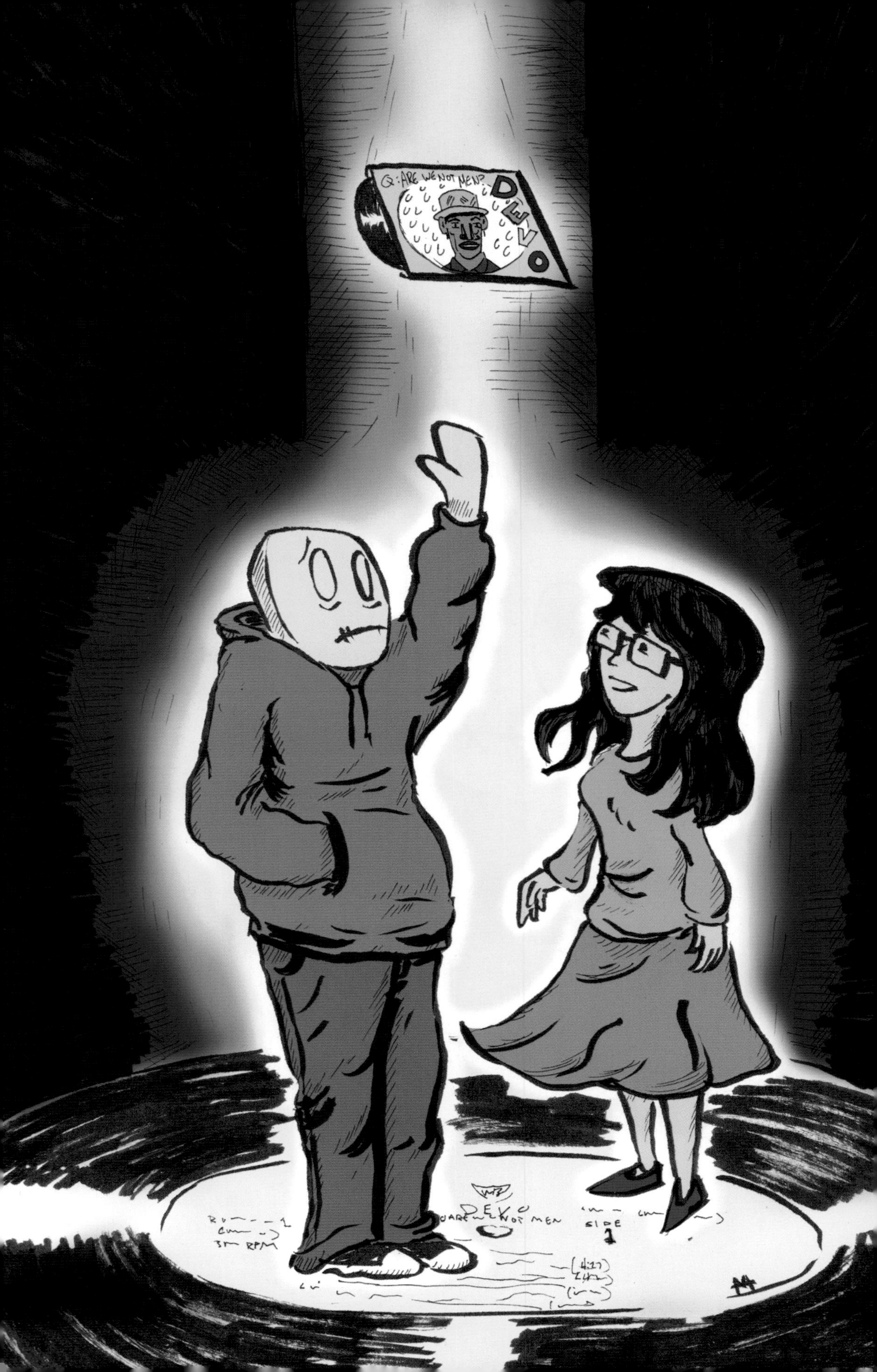
Q: ARE WE NOT MEN?
DEVO
DEVO
SIDE 1

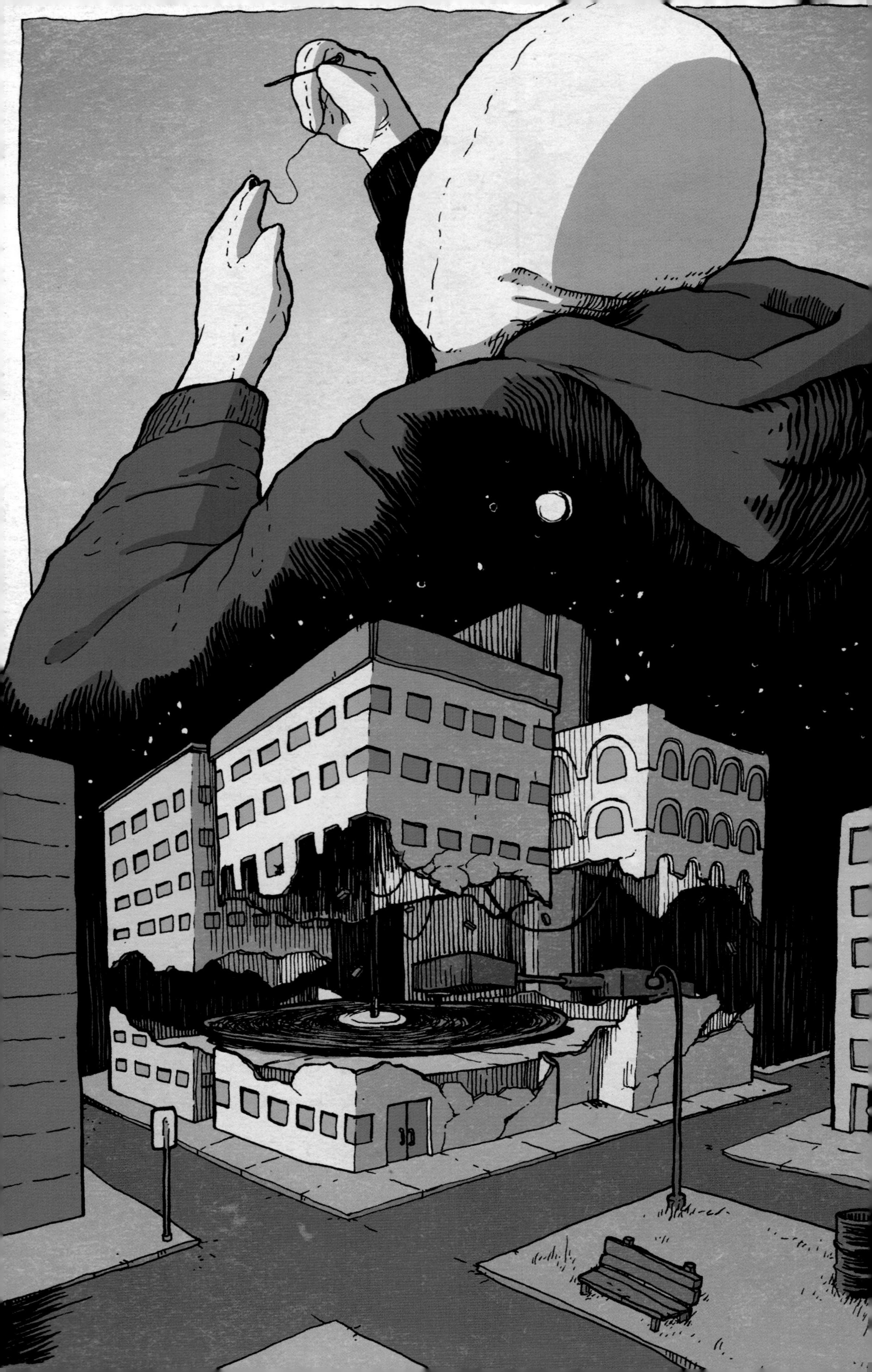

Pinups by:
Kanila Tripp -- http://xcelsiorart.com
Evgenny Yakovlev -- http://jackolevdesignart.blogspot.com
Zachary Trover -- http://instagram.com/goldsoundprint
Matt Haas -- http://riotface.com
Justin Castaneda -- http://wheniwaslittle.blogspot.com
Dave Kloc -- http://davekloc.com

Shaun Steven Struble moved to Amarillo, TX to make comic books.
Surprisingly, this plan actually worked.
He now resides in Dallas with his wife, Jenna, and cat, Buddy.
More at www.illiteraterainbow.com

Sina Grace can be found in coffee shops around Los Angeles working on various Image Comics titles, including the graphic memoirs Self-Obsessed and Not My Bag, Burn the Orphanage, as well as Penny Dora & the Wishing Box.
More at www.sinagrace.com